DATE			

TURNING DARKNESS
INTO LIGHT

BY MARIE BRENNAN

A Natural History of Dragons
The Tropic of Serpents
Voyage of the Basilisk
In the Labyrinth of Drakes
Within the Sanctuary of Wings
Turning Darkness Into Light

Midnight Never Come
In Ashes Lie
A Star Shall Fall
With Fate Conspire

Warrior
Witch

TURNING DARKNESS INTO LIGHT

Marie Brennan

TOR

A TOM DOHERTY ASSOCIATES BOOK

NEW YORK

TURNING DARKNESS INTO LIGHT

Copyright © 2019 by Bryn Neuenschwander

Edited by Miriam Weinberg

A Tor Book
Published by Tom Doherty Associates
120 Broadway
New York, NY 10271

www.tor-forge.com

Tor® is a registered trademark of Macmillan Publishing Group, LLC.

The Library of Congress Cataloging-in-Publication Data is available upon request.

ISBN 978-0-7653-7761-6 (hardcover)
ISBN 978-1-4668-5694-3 (ebook)

Our books may be purchased in bulk for promotional, educational, or business use. Please contact your local bookseller or the Macmillan Corporate and Premium Sales Department at 1-800-221-7945, extension 5442, or by email at MacmillanSpecialMarkets@macmillan.com.

First Edition: August 2019

Printed in the United States of America

0 9 8 7 6 5 4 3 2 1

TURNING DARKNESS
INTO LIGHT

STUPENDOUS FIND IN AKHIA
Newly Discovered Cache of Draconean Inscriptions
Lord Gleinleigh's Triumph
"True history will be revealed at last"

Though nearly barren of water, the deserts of Akhia are a wellspring of secrets. Year by year, their sands disclose the remains of the ancient Draconean civilization, which has fascinated the public for hundreds—nay, thousands—of years.

Today they have given into the hands of mankind a priceless treasure, nearly the equal of the Watchers' Heart itself: a tremendous cache of inscriptions, hidden by unknown hands in the deepest recesses of a cave, lost to memory until now. An expedition led by Marcus Fitzarthur, the Earl of Gleinleigh, ventured into the barren region known as the Qajr, where archaeologists had little hope of significant discovery. While sheltering from the midday heat, the earl himself found the cache, containing hundreds of tablets never before seen by modern scholars.

What hands buried them in the sheltering earth of that cave, so far from any settlement yet discovered? Was this the act of some ancient hermit or miser, protecting his library against the eyes of others? Was it an attempt to safeguard these texts against the violence of the Downfall that ended Draconean rule? We may never know, unless the words themselves give some hint to their value or origin. But the content of the tablets is as yet unknown; Lord Gleinleigh insisted on their prompt removal, before looters could flock to the site and steal away this priceless treasure. He is already making plans to bring them to his estate at Stokesley, where he has amassed one of the most extensive private collections of Draconean antiquities in the world.

When approached for comment, Simeon Cavall of the

Tomphries Museum offered the following statement: "We congratulate Lord Gleinleigh on his stroke of good fortune, and hope that the world shall not find him behindhand in sharing the details of this cache with the public."

From: The Office of the Curator of Draconean Antiquities
To: Alan Preston

14 Nivis
Tomphries Museum
#12 Chisholm Street, Falchester

Dear Alan,

All right, you win. Lord Gleinleigh is every bit as insufferable as you warned me. I drove through the dark just to stay at an inn, rather than accept that man's hospitality for the night.

His private collections are every bit as stupendous as rumour claims, but it's hard for me to admire anything when I know he must have acquired half of it in shady overseas markets, and the other half from our own shady markets here in Scirland. He is exactly the kind of customer Joseph Dorak and his ilk like to cultivate: he clearly cares nothing for the artifacts in their own right, only for the prestige they bring him, especially the Draconean materials. When I think of the bas-reliefs alone—treasures chiseled off their original homes to decorate the walls of that hulk he calls an ancestral estate, and probably smuggled onto our shores—I tell you, I could weep. The Akhian government would never have given him permission to search the Qajr if they'd had the slightest clue he would find anything of value there. Now he is in possession of what the papers insist on calling "the greatest archaeological find since the Watchers' Heart" (bah—I'll lay odds he bought that coverage himself), and there is nothing anyone can do about it.

I cannot decide whether it would be better or worse if he had any facility at all for languages. Such knowledge would give him a greater appreciation for what he has found; on the other hand, he would probably undertake to study the inscriptions himself, and undoubtedly make a botch of it, for he has not the dedication to do it well. As it stands, Lord Gleinleigh is so jealous of his find that I had to argue with him for hours before he would even let me see the whole of it, rather than a few scattered tablets—never mind that I cannot possibly be expected to deliver a well-informed judgment on the material if I have no information to judge from.

But I finally convinced him, and so here is the long and short of it.

The cache consists of two hundred seventy-one tablets or fragments thereof. Some of those fragments likely belong together; there are at least three pairs I'm certain of, but a great many more that would require further examination. If I had to guess, the final count will be closer to two hundred thirty.

Their condition is highly variable, though it's unclear how much of that is due to botched conservation. Credit where it is due; Gleinleigh did have the sense to attend to that right away, so we hopefully shouldn't see any more salt damage. But some of the tablets are fairly weathered (from before their burial, I imagine), and a few have suffered extensive surface crumbling, which I fear will make decipherment of those sections difficult, if not impossible.

In terms of subject matter, they're an assortment, and I didn't have enough time to do more than make a quick assessment. Some queen lists; a few carved into limestone that look to be royal decrees; quite a lot that appear to be completely prosaic tax records. (I sometimes think the literary production of Draconean civilization was fifty percent tax records, if not more.)

But as for the rest . . . yes, the rumours are true, or at least

I think they are. Fourteen of the tablets are shaped to a uniform size and thickness, with what looks like the hand of the same scribe at work on them. They seem to form a continuous text, judging by the notably archaic nature of the language— it's riddled with obsolete signs, which made assessing anything quite a challenge. What little I was able to parse at a glance seems to be a narrative. Whether Lord Gleinleigh is right to call it the "lost history of Draconean civilization" I cannot say without further examination, but it is unquestionably a breathtaking find.

And completely wasted on such a man.

However, there is hope! Given how reluctant Gleinleigh was to let me see the tablets, I thought I would have to spend months persuading him to have them translated and published. But apparently he recognizes that no one will care about what he has found five years from now unless they know what it says, because he suggested translation before I could even bring it up. What's more, I have persuaded him that the dignity of his ancient name requires the greatest care and attention be given to these tablets. Your mind has already leapt in a certain direction, I'm sure, but I shall surprise you by steering you two generations down: I think we should recruit Audrey Camherst.

In my opinion she is easily her grandfather's equal, where knowledge of the Draconean language is concerned. Furthermore, she has the advantage of her sex. You yourself said that Lord Gleinleigh treats every man who comes near him as either an inferior or a threat to his own prestige, neither of which would serve us well in this instance. Miss Camherst, being a woman, will not provoke him to such displays of superiority. And if he does try to throw his weight around—well, Audrey has her grandmother's name to use as weapon and shield alike. Given that her family's attentions are currently focused on preparing for the Falchester Congress next winter, I doubt her grandfather could spare the time and care this task would require, but Audrey would leap at the chance.

I have not yet recommended her to Lord Gleinleigh's attention, as I think the lady deserves some amount of warning before I drop him on her doorstep. But unless you have a strong argument to the contrary, I intend to write to her as soon as possible. The world is panting to see what those tablets have to say, and we should not make them wait.

Your friend,
Simeon

From the diary of Audrey Camherst

4 PLUVIS

Arrived at Lord Gleinleigh's estate today, in a torrential downpour that transformed me into a drowned rat in the brief interval between motorcar and door. Wouldn't have happened if his footman had the common sense to keep an umbrella in the car. Bad service? Or calculation on Lord Gleinleigh's part? I know Simeon doesn't think the earl will feel the need to posture at me, since I'm not a man, but I am unconvinced. My impression, based on an admittedly short acquaintance thus far, is that he's utterly delighted that the granddaughter of *Lady Trent herself* has come all this way to look at his tablets—but from what Simeon said Alan said, I can't help but wonder if he fears the stories will start being all about me, instead of him. Letting me get soaked might be his way of putting me in my place.

If being put in my place is the entry fee for seeing the tablets, I will pay it. From what I hear of him, Lord Gleinleigh's usual habit is to huddle over his find like a mother dragon brooding over her eggs. (Why is it that we still use that simile, even though Grandmama has made it clear that most of them don't brood?) It is nothing short of a miracle that he is eager to see his new find published, and I can't quite trust that he won't change his mind. If he does . . . well, I am not above smuggling out copies of my papers, and the consequences be damned. Father will bail me out, I'm sure. Then I can look all tragic and determined for the press, who will eat it up with a spoon.

Lord Gleinleigh was taken aback when he saw me, and I don't think it was because of my soaking. People have a tendency to forget who my mother is, even though anything our family does becomes headline news. They expect me to look Scirling, and are always surprised when I don't.

But he recovered quickly, I will give him that much. "Miss Camherst," he said, offering the appropriate courtesies. "Welcome to Stokesley. I am sorry your journey was so fatiguing."

"It's like the monsoon out there," I said, dripping steadily onto his marble floor. "But that's all right. I would have swum all the way here if that's what it took. When can I get started?"

That took him aback again. "With the— My dear girl, you only just got here! I would not dream of putting you to work so soon."

It always sticks in my craw when someone calls me "girl." I am twenty-three, and a grown woman. But I'm likely to be a girl in everyone's eyes until I'm grey or married. "You're not putting me to work," I said. "I'm putting myself. Really, I can't wait to see the tablets. Just let me towel myself dry—"

Of course I was wasting my breath. First I had to be shown to my room. Then Lord Gleinleigh's maid tried to insist on drawing a bath, saying I must be chilled to the bone. Which I was, a little, but I didn't care. I did dry myself off, and then happened to glance in a mirror and discovered my hair was going every which way, as it does when the weather is damp. The maid wanted to fix that for me, but it was obvious she didn't have the first notion how to subdue my mane. I pinned it up myself, put on dry clothes, and sallied out again in search of my host and my purpose for being there.

Only of course he had to take me on a tour of the family pile, entirely so he could show off his collection. The man has *no taste*! Nor any sense of order whatsoever. He has crammed Nichaean friezes around Coyahuac frescos with a monstrous great Yelangese vase in front of them so you can hardly see what's behind. And the Draconean antiquities ... I don't think he knows or cares that he has hatching murals looming over mortuary stele in a way that would have appalled the ancients. But Simeon warned me, so I oohed and aahed as expected, and only made faces when his back was turned.

Eventually we got down to business. Lord Gleinleigh said, "I should tell you, Miss Camherst, that I have some requirements for this undertaking. If they are agreeable to you, then you may begin work tomorrow."

No wonder he hadn't shown me the tablets yet. Mind you, he could have had the decency to inform me about these "requirements" before I came all the way out here ... but Lord Gleinleigh isn't a complete fool. He knew it would be that much harder for me to refuse when I was in the same building as the tablets, separated from them only by a few thin walls. "I should be glad to hear your requirements," I told him, as politely as I could.

"They are not onerous," he promised me. "The first is that I will need you to work here, rather than removing the tablets elsewhere. I shall of course provide room and board as part of your compensation for as long as you require, and make arrangements for your belongings to be brought here."

Live at Stokesley! I shouldn't be surprised; it's entirely reasonable for studying materials in someone's private collection. But from what Simeon said, this won't be a quick job. I'll be here for months.

I could hardly argue, though. "Quite right. I don't think I'll need much; I'm used to living on ships, with all my belongings crammed into a single trunk, and most of that filled with books."

He nodded in a way that made it clear he was entirely un-interested in my personal life. "The second is that I do not want word of the tablets' contents leaking out until I am ready to present them in their entirety. Given bits and pieces, people will speculate and form all kinds of theories. I would rather they have the whole text at once."

Diary, I almost squawked in frustration! Of course he wants to make a grand reveal of the whole text—and to be honest, I don't entirely blame him. It will be much more exciting if people can read it all at once, even if the more usual thing would be to publish portions as I go along. But given the length of the main text, that means I will have to wait for *ages* before I can share it with the world!

Then I thought through what he had said. "When you say 'leaking' . . ."

"I mean that you will not be permitted to share information about it with anyone. Not until you are done. I'm afraid I must insist on security, Miss Camherst—I'm sure you understand."

Oh, I understand. He is a greedy old worm, that much is clear, and he doesn't have the first idea how such things work. "But what if I run into difficulty? It's common practice to con-sult with other scholars along the way."

He affected surprise. "I was given to understand, Miss Cam-herst, that you are one of the brightest minds in your field. Your grandfather was a pioneer in deciphering the language, and your grandmother—well, her reputation is known around the world. Dr. Cavall at the Tomphries told me that you began studying Draconean writing when you were six. But if you need to consult with others, perhaps I should approach one of them instead."

I went hot all over. "What I mean is—ancient texts are often very unclear. I might need to compare what you have against different tablets, things at the Tomphries or in private hands." That's only one of the reasons, but it was the only one I could think of that he wouldn't hear as a confession of incompetence.

He said, "Surely you can do that without needing to divulge what you yourself have learned."

I *can*; it will only be a tremendous annoyance. And yet . . . the alternative is to not work on these tablets at all. He knew very well how much they tempted me, and how much he had needled my pride.

So I agreed. Of course I agreed. How could I do otherwise?

"Excellent!" he said, with such heartiness that I think he may have been genuinely worried that I would refuse. "You can start work first thing tomorrow, then. I've even lined up an assistant for you."

The hypocrisy of that man! First I must keep everything secret; then he drops some stranger on me, saying nothing except that I will meet her tomorrow. And before I could tell him what I thought of that, he asked me how soon I thought I could be done.

My first instinct was to laugh in his face. How can I predict such a thing without first studying the text? But I have better self-control than that, whatever Simeon says. And I have Simeon's report on the size of the tablets, the density of the script, and its archaic cast, which is enough to make at least a rough estimate. "A great deal will depend on how obscure the text is, you understand. But I would guess perhaps two tablets per month."

"Splendid," Lord Gleinleigh said, slapping his knee. "That will do very well, Miss Camherst."

He was so satisfied, in fact, that I gave him a suspicious look. "I should be clear. Two tablets a month if it goes well, which it may not. And that is only for a first draft—something that gives a clear sense of the text's meaning. Polishing it, making sure my translation is as accurate as I can achieve, will take a good deal longer."

Lord Gleinleigh waved away my comment. "Of course— I'm sure it will need more study going forward—but the important thing is to know what it says, yes? The finer points can wait. You might be ready for publication by, say, next Gelis?"

Ten months from now. If he were only doing the simple arithmetic of seven months for fourteen tablets, he would have said Fructis; if he were speaking generally, he would have said a year or so. Gelis is both random and specific.

And I could guess why.

Maybe it would have been better for me not to have said. But I was calculating in my head, and when I got to my conclusion, it just popped right out of my mouth. "You mean, before the Falchester Congress."

Really, I should have seen it coming. Why else would he be so eager to have someone translate these tablets, when up until now he's hidden his collections away for the enjoyment of himself and his friends? Because the congress will be taking place next winter. Everyone will be thinking about the Draconeans then, with their delegation coming here and the future of the Sanctuary up for international debate; the translation will positively fly off the shelves.

He coughed delicately. "It would be convenient, yes."

Not to mention profitable. With the way he spends money on antiquities, you'd assume he must be rolling in dough, but

I hear that lots of peers these days are having difficulty keeping up their estates. Maybe he's gotten himself into debt. Or maybe he just wants more money to buy even more antiquities with. Either way, he'll be able to do it, if this translation comes out on time—not to mention that he'll be famous.

And so will I.

That shouldn't be the first thing on my mind. I should take my time with this text, and make certain it isn't published until I'm absolutely convinced it's the best I'm capable of delivering—even if that means it doesn't come out until I'm forty. Fame means nothing if later people say, "Oh, Audrey Camherst? You mean the one who wrote that sad little attempt at translation a few years ago?"

But it's so hard when I can *feel* everyone looking at me, waiting to see what I'll do. Not my family, of course; if I decided I wanted to retire to a country cottage and spend my life growing roses—not even award-winning roses; mediocre, aphid-chewed ones—they would hug me and wish me well. It's the *rest* of the world that expects me to do something spectacular, because Papa did, and Mama, and Grandpapa, and above all Grandmama. When am I going to prove my right to stand with them?

I don't have to prove anything.

Except to myself.

And I *know* I can do this. If it means working long hours to get it done in time . . . well, that's what coffee is for.

From the notebook of Cora Fitzarthur

A new woman has come to Stokesley. I knew someone was
going to visit, but Uncle didn't tell me ahead of time that she will
be living here for months, which is very inconvenient of him.
The good news is that she doesn't have a little yappy dog that will
shed all over everything like our last houseguest. (The dog was
the one shedding, of course, not the houseguest.) I told Mrs.
Hilleck to put her in the lilac room and to find out what she likes
to eat.

Her name is Audrey Isabella Mahira Adiaratou Camherst.
She is twenty-three years old, and Uncle has hired her to translate the tablets. I saw her going into dinner, though she did not
see me.

Uncle says it is very important to know who someone's
people are, so last night I looked hers up in *Webber's Almanac of
the Peerage and Other Illustrious Persons of Scirland*. It says she is
the granddaughter of Isabella Trent, née Hendemore, formerly
Camherst, 1st Baroness Trent, who is a dragon naturalist, and
both very famous and very scandalous. (The almanac does not
say she is scandalous, but I know that much myself.) Audrey's
paternal grandfather was Jacob Camherst, second son of a bar-
onet. Her step-grandfather, if that is a proper word, is Suhail,
Lord Trent, who is Akhian, and an archaeologist and linguist.
He is also famous, though less so, and not very scandalous. Her

father is The Honourable Jacob Camherst, an oceanographer. Her mother is Kwenta Adiaratou Shamade, of the Talu Union, an astronomer. That explains why Audrey is a dark brown colour, except her hair, which is black and looks like a cloud when she lets it free. Her maternal grandparents are not in the almanac, probably because they are neither peers nor Scirling.

I don't know why it is important to look these things up. The almanac has no entry to tell me whether they are the Right Sort of People. I don't think Uncle believes they are, though.

My instructions are to help Audrey in any way she tells me to (even if all she tells me to do is fetch her tea) and to read all of her letters before they go to the post, and to tell Uncle if she tells anyone anything about the tablets, or if she says anything unkind or suspicious about him. The letter Audrey has written to the Tomphries Museum only says that she has arrived here and that Lord Gleinleigh is exactly as she expected, which might be rude depending on what she expected, but I don't think that's the kind of thing Uncle had in mind. Still, I suppose I should tell him, just to be sure.

From the diary of Audrey Camherst

5 PLUVIS

Lord Gleinleigh is not at breakfast. How inconvenient of him! The footman says he does not often take breakfast. I wonder if he is even awake yet? He spends a great deal of his time on the Continent; perhaps he has acquired the Continental habit of keeping late hours. I did my best to sleep in until what most people would consider a civilized time, but after so much of my life on ships with Papa and Mama, the habit of waking at daybreak is difficult to shed.

Someone must be up, though, or else the servants pinched bits of the food on the assumption that no one would be eating it. Who else is here, I wonder?

LATER

Well, that's several questions answered at once. But what I think of the answer, I am not yet sure.

When I was done with breakfast I went straightaway to the library, where Lord Gleinleigh had promised the tablets would be laid out for me. I was half convinced he would have failed to do so—or possibly "failed"—because surely he could not let me see them without him present to gloat over his trophy. But there they were, set in an organized row on a sheet to protect the long table that dominates the center of the room. (Why does a man who cares so little for actual learning have such an enormous and well-stocked library? Prestige, I suppose.)

I pinned my hair up and began to examine the array. That room needs better lighting; I have already pestered the footman to bring me a lamp with a long enough cord that I may drag it around as I require. To begin with, though, I had to carry one of the tablets to the window, so I could see it clearly.

And then I found myself grinning like a monkey, because there I was, with a priceless treasure in my hands! Of course it is not the first time that I have handled a Draconean text. I will never forget the day Grandpapa first put a clay tablet into my hands, explaining to me that I was holding history itself. I was five, I think, which always horrifies people when they hear— what if I had dropped it? The tablet was only a tax record. Still a loss if I had shattered it, mind you, but not one that would haunt me until the end of my life.

It would haunt me until the end of my life and *beyond* if I dropped one of these. Our modern Draconeans do not know everything about their ancestors, the Anevrai, any more than I know what ancient Scirlings or Utalu did or thought. We have only these fragments, the texts that happen to have survived the Downfall of their ancient civilization. I am sure the people who rebelled against Anevrai rule had very sound reasons for it—but if I could, I would go back in time and ask them not to destroy so much in the process. No matter how tyrannical their rulers were, what gain was there in burning down palaces and cities? Who benefited, when they smashed the texts that held all the learning of their world? They plunged themselves into a darkness so deep that we are only beginning to shine lights into the nearest corners of it.

The lump of clay I held in my hands today might prove to be a very bright light indeed. I tilted it back and forth, letting the light bring out the faint impressions where the scribe's fingers had once gripped the edges, before it was fired. I would be the first to read his words!

. . . or so I believed at the time.

I had just sat down at the center of the table to write some preliminary notes when someone behind me said, "That's my chair."

If I tell this story later I shall describe myself as turning around with flawless poise and composure, but the truth is that I squeaked. The speaker was a girl—well, I call her a girl; I think she is only a few years younger than I am. But she was dressed very plainly, in a dove-grey frock I would have said was ill-fitting; only later did I realize the tailoring was not at fault. She held herself so awkwardly that it made the dress look like a sack. And since I am a terrible judge of fashion, I can only think that she will have an appalling time of it when she comes out—if indeed she ever does.

"That's my chair," she repeated, clutching a notebook to her chest.

She clearly was not a servant. I rose and said, "Are you . . . Lord Gleinleigh's daughter?" He is not married, but she might have been his natural-born child. Only there is no polite way to ask whether someone is a bastard.

"I'm his ward," she said. "I sit there every day while I work on the translation."

"On the—" It turned into another squeak, only this one was decidedly angrier.

I thought—Simeon was *very clear*—this job was supposed to be mine! It is one thing for Lord Gleinleigh to foist this girl on me as an assistant, without so much as a by-your-leave. But it is a slap in the face for him to have her start on the work before I even arrive! And why did he say nothing of this to me last night? Likely because he knew how I would react and, coward that he is, dodged the problem by letting me stumble across this interloper while he was still warm in his bed.

She held a stack of books and notepaper clutched to her chest. Now I saw the room in a new light: the table, with its protective sheet and row of tablets. Lord Gleinleigh had not set them out. This girl had. And she sat in the very chair I had chosen and began unlocking the secrets of this cache, which was supposed to be *my* responsibility and privilege.

I know it is dreadful of me to write it like that. If Grandmama heard me being such a greedy little drake, she would lock me in my room without books for a week. Except she also knows how infuriating it is to be denied the proper respect—and if it hadn't been this awkward girl who upstaged me, I think I might have lost my temper completely. (If it had been *Lord Gleinleigh* . . . well, I might have laughed him out of the room, because I know he hasn't a scrap of skill for the job. But some other man like him? I would have been apoplectic.)

As it is, I can't say I was very polite. "Let me see it, then," I said, holding out one hand.

"See what?" But from the way she clutched her stack more tightly, I knew she understood what I meant.

"The translation," I said. "I presume you are the assistant Lord Gleinleigh mentioned to me"—laying stress on the word "assistant." Under no circumstances was I going to let myself be pushed into a subordinate position. "Since you have been so kind as to start on the work already, I shall look it over."

Her jaw set in a mulish line, but she put down her stack and retrieved some pages from a folder. I was relieved to see they were so few: I was half afraid she had gone through everything already, even though I know that isn't possible. Sitting down very pointedly in the chair she had claimed as her own, I began to read.

The pages were an utter mess, filled with crossed-out lines where she kept changing her mind, so it took me a few moments to even thread my way through the tangle and figure out what she had written—and then a few moments longer to digest the absurdity of what I had just read. It was such an incredible disaster that a part of me wanted to burst out laughing. But coming so close on the heels of my snit, it was hard for that impulse to win out, and the result is that I just sat and stared at the pages long after I had stopped reading, trying to think what to say.

Of course I could not sit there forever. I finally looked up—still without the slightest notion what I would say—and found her waiting, body rigid in that plain grey dress.

No one intelligent enough to produce even that muddle out of a Draconean text could possibly be stupid enough not to realize how bad it was. I saw in the set of her jaw a kind of challenge, as if she were waiting to see what I would say. Would I make polite noises, as if her work did not read like it had been written by a five-year-old? Or would I tear into her for having done such a dreadful job?

I found I could do neither. The gentleness of my own voice surprised me when I said, "Have you ever translated ancient Draconean before? Or the modern tongue?"

The answer came in a tight little shake of her head. Then, while I searched for more words, she spoke. "Uncle said, you like reading, and you like puzzles. You should try this one."

As if liking puzzles qualifies one to deal with a dead language! But it sounded exactly like the kind of thing Lord Gleinleigh would say. "Have you done much translation of any kind?"

"I speak Thiessois and Eiversch," she said.

If she's anything like other young ladies, she only speaks them well enough to sing a few songs. "But no translation? I mean long passages." When she shook her head again, I said, "It is quite a challenge, and although it is a bit like a puzzle sometimes, it is also very different. You . . . have made a good start here."

Her jaw tightened again. Then she said bluntly, "It's dreadful."

In the face of a statement like that, tact could no longer win out over my natural candour. "It's dreadful," I agreed. "But even making it that far is an achievement."

She stared at her shoes. A smile began tugging at the corner of my mouth—I could not suppress it. Then she started laughing, and that set me off, and the little knot inside me began to relax.

When we finally stopped laughing I stood up to get a chair for her. Only by the time I turned around, she'd taken my chair—her chair, I mean, as I have a feeling I'm sailing into the wind where that's concerned. It didn't seem worth arguing about any more, so I sat down in the one I'd pulled close.

"I'm Cora," she said.

"And I'm Audrey Camherst."

"I know," she said. "I mean, figured it out. Uncle said you would be coming. But you don't look Scirling."

Most people don't say it to my face like that, though I know they're thinking it. "I'm half," I said. "My mother is Utalu. From Eriga."

I said that last bit because most Scirlings tend to think of Eriga as an undifferentiated mass, a whole continent lumped under one label, and couldn't point out the Talu Union on a map if you threatened to keelhaul them for failure. But Cora nodded before I was even done clarifying. "You're Lady Trent's granddaughter. And your grandfather, your step-grandfather I mean, is the one who deciphered Draconean."

"Well, him and a lot of other people. It isn't like he just looked at it one day and said, by gum! I have it! But yes, he's the one who translated the Cataract Stone, and theorized that the language is related to Lashon and Akhian. And then Grandmama proved him right."

"Have you met any Draconeans?"

"Oh, yes, lots. I've even been to the Sanctuary." I shuddered at the memory. "The people are lovely, but what they call 'summer' there would barely pass muster as a brisk spring day here."

Cora said, "I've never been outside of Scirland. I don't think I would like it very much, but Uncle travels all the time. Mostly to Thiessin and Chiavora—he didn't like Akhia."

All manner of uncharitable responses rose to mind at that, but I bit down on them.

"If you don't want me to help you," Cora went on, "then tell me. Uncle said I should do whatever you say."

Like she's some kind of servant! Or worse, a slave. "I do want your help," I said. "But only if *you* want to help."

She shrugged. "I don't know how I can. You saw what happened when I tried. And it made you angry, didn't it? That I had tried to translate something."

The polite thing to do would have been to lie. But Cora is so straightforward that I found myself responding in kind. "Well, yes, a little. But I shouldn't have been angry. As for translating, it usually takes years of study before anyone is ready. There are other things you can do, though—and to be honest, I'd be grateful for them. Your uncle wants this done very fast, so having someone helping out with all the side tasks would make my life a lot easier."

She nodded, unsurprised. "When the tablets arrived, he said they'd change everything."

Diary, I tell you: Lord Gleinleigh has a very high opinion of the import of his find, and I'm beginning to wonder why. He's discovered a long narrative text, and that's very exciting if you care much about ancient Draconean civilization; we've found a few poems before now, a few brief mythical tales or bits of history, but nothing approaching this scale. I'm sure it will teach us all manner of things we didn't know about their society. But to say it will change everything? That seems unwarranted, when we don't even know yet what it says.

Which makes me wonder if he somehow *does* know. Only I can't think how he possibly could! It's easy enough to get the gist of a tax record at a glance, but narrative is much more difficult, and even a few minutes of study tells me this one's a real corker. The language is so archaic, I can't think of many people who would even know what to do with it, and the best of them couldn't just skim it and tell you what it says, not in any detail. I told Lord Gleinleigh I could get through two tablets a month; I only hope I can keep my word. So how could he—a man who probably doesn't even know what a determinative is—begin to predict what effect this is going to have?

Pfah. I am putting the tail ahead of the dragon. Lord Gleinleigh just has an inflated opinion of himself, so naturally anything he finds must be stupendously important.

I didn't say any of this to Cora, of course. I'm not *that* birdwitted. I just said, "Well, we'll see. It's going to take long hours of work before we have any real sense of what this says."

I said the same thing again at supper tonight, to see if Lord

Gleinleigh reacted, but he didn't. We dined alone, without Cora; when I asked why, he replied only that "she doesn't care to dine in company." Then, oozing disapproval out every pore, he said, "I heard you were in the garden all afternoon."

He thought I was shirking! I said, "Yes, because I began copying today. I don't know why, but I find that natural light is best for letting me see the inscription clearly—lamps just aren't the same."

"Copying?" he echoed.

He didn't even attempt not to sound suspicious. I sighed and said, in my best diplomatic voice, "The tablets may be in good condition for the most part, but they won't remain that way for long if I'm constantly handling them. Much better to work from a copy—an exact drawing of the signs as the scribe wrote them—and only consult the original when I think there may be an error. Once that's done, I will transcribe the text—" I saw that I had lost him. "Write out the sounds in our alphabet," I said. "These are necessary steps, my lord, I assure you. Ask any translator and they will tell you the same."

Lord Gleinleigh dismissed this with a flick of his hand. "No, no, quite right. I am not questioning your methods, Miss Camherst." (He was . . . but I did not point that out.)

The footman brought out the soup course. One thing I'll say for Lord Gleinleigh; he lays on a good feast. Though with soup I'm always afraid I'll slurp and embarrass myself. The earl addressed his own bowl very quietly, and then unbent enough to ask, "How are you getting on?"

"Well so far. I made it a good way into copying the first tablet today." I laughed. "Though I would have gotten further if your gardeners and footmen hadn't constantly been interrupting to offer me a parasol. I *told* them that I need the direct light for my work, but they kept trying!"

"They are only concerned for your health," he said.

And my complexion, I'm sure—as if that weren't already a lost cause, by Scirling standards. But for pity's sake, this isn't Eriga or the Akhian desert. I don't think the sun here could burn me if it tried all summer—much less in the middle of winter.

Then Lord Gleinleigh cleared his throat and said, "And what of the text itself? I know you said these other steps come first, the copying and so forth, but . . . ?"

If I let him, he will press me to do this all rumble-jumble, instead of following proper standards. Well, I shan't let him—and I have good reason why not. "It's difficult to say. You know" (I doubt he knows anything of the sort) "that there's a mark in the Draconean script used to separate words, in the way we use a blank space? That's a later innovation in their writing; earlier texts don't have it, and this is definitely an earlier text. So while I can pick out a word here and there, a great many more all blur together, so that I'm not sure whether it says *zašu kīberra* or *zašukī berra*. I'm afraid it will be quite some time before I have anything clear enough to share with you."

"Can Cora not help? She has been working on the tablets since they arrived."

Obviously he hasn't looked at any of her work, or he would know the answer to that. Well, I was not going to tell him that her efforts had made us both laugh. I merely said, "We'll see," and left it at that.

(Looking back over what I have written, I can hear Grandmama tsking at me. "You young people and your given names! You've hardly known one another three minutes before you're addressing each other like the closest of friends." Well, I'm not going to write "Miss Fitzarthur" every time I refer to Cora, and I don't think she minds. That's her surname—she must be the daughter of Lord Gleinleigh's brother, since she calls him "Uncle." I didn't realize he had a brother, though. It's shocking really, how little I know about the Scirling peerage, when I'm going to inherit Grandmama's barony someday.)

From the diary of Audrey Camherst

6 PLUVIS

Blasted Scirling winters! It's been drizzling rain all day, and while I don't mind a wetting, the light is no good for looking at the tablets. I wonder if I could persuade Lord Gleinleigh to re-locate me to Trinque-Liranz or Qurrat or someplace sunnier while I work on the text? No, I promised Lotte I would be nearby if she needs me—though what I could do to improve her Season I don't know, given the utter disaster I made of mine.

No, I shall just have to work with the lamps, or find some-thing else to do with myself in foul weather. I suppose I can begin my transcription of what I've already copied.

LATER

Transcription went slower than it might have, but that's because I was teaching Cora. It's clear that some of the errors in her translation were because she confuses the characters for *ša* and *ma*, and also *gil* for *suk*—very common beginner's mistakes, and they explain the random tree branches and such she'd come up with.

Oh, I should not have written that. Grandpapa is always going on about how one should take each step in order: copying, *then* transcription, and only when that is complete, translation.

(And every time he does, Grandmama makes a tart remark about his "damnable patience," and then she tells the story of that disintegrating door in the Watchers' Heart and how he made her draw it before he'd let anyone through to see what it had guarded.) But I am not made of such patient stuff, and I have the first part of the transcription already . . .

Everyone else is abed. It will be our little secret, diary.

Tablet I, invocation
translated by Cora Fitzarthur

Listen with your wings in the ditches and the rocks in all corners.

Through me I say how clay was made, dirt and water and ceiling and wind and grains and animals of the ground and flounders and sky, the three heart reeds and the four that were three later. Stone my words for the coming year, because mind records are the one real forever. When this clutch is recorded, we live with them, and the goodness of their treasure will keep the going generations doing things.

One was red from the sun and was shaped like many iron hands.

Two were green water and grew from being slept tall.

Three were sky blue and came smartly with their tree branches.

Four, which were male, covered black and were written down for the first time.

Four broke a single egg together, which was a thing nobody had done before.

Together they went down and up, and became darkness through light.

Tablet I, colophon
translated by Audrey Camherst

Hark, spread your wings to hear, from the canyons to the heights of stone, in every corner of the world.

Through me this clay will speak of how everything was made, the earth and the waters, the heavens and the wind, the plants and the beasts of the land and the rivers and the sky, the three peoples and the four who afterward were three. Preserve my words for the ages to come, for memory is the only true immortality. So long as these four are remembered, they will live in us, and the blessings of their deeds will remain.

The first was golden like the sun, and her hands were fitted for weapons.

The second was green as water, and planted the earth so that crops grew tall.

The third was blue like the sky, and was clever in the crafting of things.

The fourth was a brother, black of scale, and he was the first to record speech in clay.

These four were hatched from a single shell, which had never been seen before.

Together they descended and rose again, turning darkness into light.

From the diary of Audrey Camherst

7 PLUVIS

Oh, Cora is *clever.* She may be abysmal at translation, but she has a very tidy mind, and has discovered something I hadn't yet noticed.

I mentioned before that when I first came into the library, the tablets were laid out in a row. I'm so accustomed to working with texts someone else has already been at, it never occurred to me to think anything was odd when I asked for the first tablet and she handed it to me without hesitation. But of course I should have wondered: how did she know that was the first one?

The answer, of course, is in the bit I've already translated. She might not have been able to read it very well, but she could see it was different. "That part was marked off with a horizontal line," she said when I asked her. "None of the others have a marked-off bit, not like that. It didn't seem logical that they would do that at the end of the series, or somewhere in the middle—not when it was in the top corner like that."

"It's almost like a colophon," I said, bending over the tablet in question. "Except not at all, really. Normally a Draconean colophon will tell you all kinds of things, from a summary of the text or some key phrases to which scribe wrote it out to who commissioned it and why. This gives a bit of a summary, but the rest of that information isn't there. Is it on the final tablet? Sometimes they put it at the end instead."

Cora shook her head. "If it is, they didn't mark it off."

A quick glance at the last tablet in the sequence was enough to tell me that the final text wasn't a colophon, either. Then I frowned, gazing down the length of the table. "Are you sure this is the last one?"

"As sure as I can be," Cora said. "I put them in order first thing, before I tried to start translating."

I had stumbled from one mystery into another. "How do you know they're in order?"

Though I hadn't gotten very far in my copying yet, I *had* looked each tablet over, and noted the absence of marginal notation. Which makes sense; this text is obviously a very early one, and seems to predate the idea of putting a numeral and the text's incipit on the edge of the tablet, the better to keep documents together and in order. But without that, and without the ability to read the text, how on earth did Cora have any sense of their sequence?

She brightened when I asked her that. I think she knew she had been clever, and was justifiably proud. "Look," she said, rushing back to the start of the row. "You see here, at the end of this tablet? And then the beginning of the next one."

I did indeed see. The final glyph on the first tablet was the sign for "two," and the first character on the second tablet was the sign for "one." The second tablet ended with "three" while the third began with "two," and so forth down the line.

Which is obvious when you know what to look for—but for someone like Cora, whose knowledge of the language is as rudimentary as an Anevrai schoolboy's, spotting that is a tremendous achievement! Especially with two of them so badly damaged (may the sun burn whoever is responsible for that!). And all of them of course have text on both sides, but only mark the numerals at the beginning of the obverse and end of the reverse, with no other feature to tell you which side is which. A quick look even showed me two places where the reverse side begins with a numeral or the obverse ends with one, but simply as a normal part of the text, not as a sequencing aid. "Yes," Cora said when I pointed those out. "They gave me a lot of difficulty for a while."

"I have never seen this before," I marveled, scribbling down some hasty notes. (Never mind the translation; I suspect I could spend the rest of my life writing journal articles and monographs about other aspects of these tablets.) "None of the Draconean texts I've examined have used this method of ordering. And it's so odd that there's no colophon—they used those on just about everything that wasn't a throwaway document, because it was the only way to sort their libraries. I mean, this is clearly a very old text, so perhaps they hadn't developed those techniques yet. But still."

"How can you tell it's old?" Cora reclaimed her notes and put them away in a leather folder. "All Draconean texts are old. But you mean it's older still, don't you?"

Hunching over the row of tablets had made my back stiff; I stretched it, blessing my Utalu mother for never seeing the point of Anthiopean corsets, even before they started going out of fashion. "Because of the orthography—the way it's written. Early texts tend to have defective double consonants, meaning that the scribe didn't write them both; you just have to work out whether it ought to be double or single. That's why you had 'slept' instead of 'planted' in your translation, by the way; you didn't know that the scribe had meant a geminated M in the verb. And these tablets are so archaic that they use triconsonantal root signs, which might stand in for any one of a dozen nouns or verbs built from that root."

Cora looked puzzled. "How are you supposed to know which one it is?"

I shrugged. "You guess."

Puzzlement turned to outright offense. My hand to the sun: I have never in my life seen someone so outraged by *orthography*. "Draconean is like that," I said, as if further explanation would mollify her. "Sometimes you're supposed to read a given character as its word meaning, like *galbu* for 'heart.' Sometimes you're supposed to read it for its syllabic value instead, *lal*. And sometimes it's a determinative—meaning you don't pronounce it at all; it's just there to tell you something about the next bit. The heart determinative means that whatever follows is a person or people, even if it doesn't look like it. 'Three heart reeds' is actually 'three peoples,' in the sense of races or nationalities."

Cora's mouth opened and shut a few times as she sputtered. Finally she said, "How does anybody *read* this language?"

"With great difficulty," I said, shrugging. "Now you know why I can't just pick the tablets up and read them off like a menu in a Thiessois restaurant."

"Yes, but how did *they* read it? The ancient Draconeans?"

I laughed. "The same way we do. One of the first texts Grandpapa translated in full turned out to be a letter from a young Anevrai scribe to the priest of his home village, complaining about how much he hates learning determinatives and how mercilessly his teacher beats him when he misses a geminated consonant in his reading."

"It's completely irrational," Cora said, fuming. "There must be so many ways to get the meaning wrong."

"Yes, but generally you realize after a while that you *have* got it wrong. We'd make fewer errors if we spoke the language fluently, like the ancients did, but of course we're also having to work out the vocabulary at the same time. We've come a long way since the Cataract Stone, mind you—we can read quite a bit now. But it's still slow going."

I don't think I convinced her of anything, though to be honest, I'm not sure there's anything *to* convince her of. Draconean writing is really quite irrational, when you get down to it. But it was the first time anyone had invented writing, anywhere in the world, and we can't really fault them for not doing a very good job on the first try.

And when you think about it, they did a good enough job that their texts have survived for millennia and we can still read them today—albeit with a lot of effort. I'll be lucky if anything I do lasts a thousandth as long!

The opening invocation said something about a male Draconean who was "the first to record speech in clay." If this is a mythic narrative, it may describe how writing and other things were created. I wonder how much the stories will be like the ones remembered today?

Tablet I: "The Creation Tablet"
translated by Audrey Camherst

Before cities, before fields, before iron, before time, the three came together, the three called Ever-Moving, Ever-Standing, and Light of the World, the three called Source of Wind, Foundation of All, and Maker of Above and Below.

Together they crafted the world; together they made the sky and the earth, the rains and the rivers, and all that flies or crawls or digs in the ground. They made these things, but they were still lonely. They said to each other, "Who is there that is capable of knowing us? Who shall sing our names and give us praise? Who looks upon what we have made and recognizes its beauty?"

So they came together at the highest point, at the place where Ever-Standing meets Ever-Moving and the Light of the World smiles down, at the place where the mountain breathes smoke to the sky,[1] the place named the Censer of Heaven. The Source of Wind spoke first, saying, "I will make a creature that knows the glories of the sky. From on high it will see everything; it will look upon what we have made and recognize its beauty."

It took the wind and braided it, many strands of breeze and gale, with rain to give it substance, and set its cre-

---

1 I wonder if this is a specific mountain? A volcano, one presumes. One we might be able to identify?—AC

ation free. The first *issur*[2] soared through the sky, and the Ever-Moving was glad. From on high its creation saw everything, looking upon what the three had made.

But the creation of the Ever-Moving was flawed. It looked, but did not recognize. It did not know the three. It did not sing their names and give them praise. Though it was a thing of beauty, it lacked the capacity to recognize beauty. It lacked a mind.

And so the Foundation of All said, "I will make something better. I will sculpt a creature that knows the bounty of the earth. From the ground it will experience everything; it will explore what we have made and appreciate its beauty."

It took the soil and shaped it, dirt and stone, with the roots of growing things binding it together, and set its creation free. The first *āmu*[3] walked the earth, and the Ever-Standing was glad. From the ground it experienced everything, exploring what the three had made.

But the creation of the Ever-Standing was flawed. It experienced, but it did not appreciate. It knew the three, but in its arrogance it did not sing their names, it did not give them praise. Though it was a thing of understanding, it lacked the humility to acknowledge the three.

And so the Light of the World said, "We must make something better. It must have the beauty of the *issur*, the understanding of the *āmu*. It must combine what is good

---

2 The context makes me think this must refer to dragons, but normally they'd use *umharra* for that. So maybe not? Maybe something mythical? Or this is just an older term.—AC

3 If the first word is indeed "dragon," then this would presumably indicate humans. But again, it isn't the usual word (that would be *lansin*), so I'm not sure.—AC

in both, and it must have what each of them lacks. I know the shape it will have, but to make it as it should be, all three of us must join in the work."

They took the wind; they took the soil. They made a creature with the wings of the *issur*, the eyes of the *āmu*. Of breezes and stone was it made, of rain and the roots of growing things. The *issur* came and breathed upon it as a blessing. The *āmu* came and shed its blood upon it as a gift. And last of all the Maker of Above and Below placed its light within their creation, the divine spark, so that it would know the three and do them honour.

It came to life. It looked around. It walked the earth and flew through the air; it saw the world from above and below. It sang the names of the three and gave them praise.

All this came to pass in the time before the world was changed.

LOOTED TEMPLE FOUND
Seghayan Site Stripped to the Stone
Rouhani Mourns Destruction
"So much history has been lost"

Archaeologists exploring near the city of Djedad in Seghaye have found another ancient Draconean temple, hewn out of the living rock of the Ghurib hills—but alas, they were not the first to discover it. Hormizd Rouhani, leader of the expedition, says that looters had already ransacked the site, carrying away unknown riches.

"We will never know what used to be here," Rouhani wrote in a letter to the Seghayan Antiquities Commission. "Undoubtedly many of the artifacts have already made their way to the black market, but without their context, they lose much of their power to tell us about the past."

The temple is of a type seen elsewhere, with an inner chamber whose ceiling contains an oculus, an opening to the sky that scholars believe would have been covered in ancient times. During ceremonies, the priests would have removed the covering at the key moment, allowing the light of the sun to enter the chamber. An earthquake in the area caused the blockage over the oculus to collapse, which Rouhani believes is how looters found the site.

When asked whether the temple could have been picked over in past centuries, he replied, "I cannot say what condition it was in when the looters entered it. But we have found cigarette butts, candy wrappers, and the rubble where they attempted to chisel a mural off the wall, destroying it in the process. There is no question that they were here recently—I would say within the last five years."

What remains hints at the temple's previous glory. There are painted murals, their colours still visible, depicting an as-yet unidentified Draconean queen engaging in rituals for the preservation of her empire. In the back of the chamber stands an empty tablet chest of the "foundation" type, left free-standing when the surrounding stone was quarried away. Shards found next to the chest show its sides were once decorated with winged sun discs of painted ceramic, one of which was badly broken during removal and abandoned by the looters.

Discoveries of ransacked sites are increasingly common in recent years, as excitement over the upcoming Falchester Congress drives public interest in Draconean artifacts to levels not seen since Lady Trent's heyday. According to Joseph Dorak, one of Scirland's most prominent antiquities dealers, "Even ordinary artifacts are being sold for two or three times the price they would have fetched five years ago." The fervor is only expected to mount as the congress draws nearer.

From: Alan Preston
To: Simeon Cavall

14 Pluvis
#17 Rue des joncs
Ecraie, Thiessin

Dear Simeon,

Here's a peculiarity for you to chew on.

I received a letter the other day from Rafaat ibn Hazir in Sarmizi. The usual sort of thing, difficulties of funding and his endless personality conflicts with ibn Fulaih—and by the way, he's hoping I can interest you in financing a joint expedition, the Tomphries and the al-Bahatulaam, to go do some proper excavations on the breeding pens at Ribaysah, not (and I quote) "that hack job Viadro did at Shahtri"—but you and I can discuss that when I'm back in Scirland next week.

Anyway, of course he brought up this whole business with Gleinleigh's tablets. You know how things are in Akhia these days—constant push and pull between those who want to learn more about the Draconean past, and those who worry that digging up even one more cylinder seal means that the modern Draconean population will come swooping in and reclaim the entirety of southern Anthiope for their new empire. Right now the latter are on top, which means there's been essentially no patrolling of the Qajr to keep out looters.

When I read that, I had to put down the letter and pace outside for a while until my head cooled off. Every time the anti-Draconean nationalists get the upper hand, we lose countless historical treasures to the underground antiquities market—not that it's possible to stop that anyway; there are just too many sites, and the only way to protect them all would be to put the entire able-bodied male population of Akhia to work as watchmen. But it's one thing to fall short, and another to not try at all, the way the nationalists do. I presume you saw the news about that temple near Djedad? At least the Seghayan government is doing what they can, even if things still slip through.

My one solace is that the western Qajr is so barren and remote—not to mention lacking in obviously attractive targets like the Labyrinth of Drakes has—that the looters may find it as daunting to raid as the army does to patrol.

Back I went to Rafaat's letter. Only to find him lamenting that the Akhians cannot even mount their own expedition to the region! They would like to search around and see whether that cache was the only thing there . . . but it turns out the permit sold to Lord Gleinleigh was for the exclusive right of excavation and collection in that part of the Qajr. For the next three years.

Before you can crack a tooth with grinding, though, let me tell you the rest of it.

Naturally I was incensed. The nationalists got one of their own appointed to handle permits last year; I think he must have been banking on Gleinleigh's dilettante nature to give up before his people found anything, or perhaps he just assumed there was nothing to find. At any rate, until that time is up, the only other people who can explore that area are looters.

Yes, the thought crossed my mind. But before I convinced myself to break the law and hire people to conduct clandestine excavations on our behalf, I thought I might at least try the straightforward approach. So this morning, hearing that he was in town, I went to talk to Gleinleigh.

I didn't expect anything to come of it. The meeting was just a way of persuading myself not to add fuel to the fire that is the illegal market. (For starters, you would disown me as a friend, after how I bludgeoned the Tomphries into making that pledge not to buy from Dorak and the rest of the black market.) I can hardly fault Lady Trent for discovering a living population of Draconeans and announcing their presence to the world ... but the appetite for antiquities has been ferocious ever since, and there are all too many poverty-stricken locals willing to smash their way through sites in search of items they can sell for a few dinars. The last thing I should be doing is encouraging that sort of thing.

As it turns out, I won't have to.

Lord Gleinleigh's permit is exclusive, yes—but that means he can grant permission to anybody he likes. The Akhians asked right after he found the cache, and he turned them down ... but when I spoke to him this morning, I pointed out that if anything else significant is found there later on, everyone will think he's a fool for not having searched further. Whereas if he let me go have a look around, he'd be the rich patron getting credit for further discoveries.

I honestly didn't expect it to work. I've spent years trying to shut Dorak down, and I'm sure at least half of Gleinleigh's collection came through that bastard's warehouses. But his ego is as big as his collection, and I think the prospect of other people mocking him was too much to bear.

He didn't agree right away, mind you. At first he said vague things about future plans, only right now he's wholly occupied with the tablets and not really able to devote as much attention as he would like to hunting for more finds—as if he's doing any work at all, entertaining himself in Ecraie while Audrey chips away at the translation one glyph at a time. I'm not surprised he isn't eager to decamp to Akhia again. In fact, I think this Qajr expedition was the first time he's gone into the field himself (unless you count Continental resorts as "the field").

But then he got down to business and gouged me for a hefty license—making back some of what he paid for his own permit, I'm sure—and, well, I was so surprised to find him willing at all, I agreed.

I don't think he expects me to find anything. In fact, I wonder if he's already searched the area so thoroughly, he knows there's nothing left to find, and therefore doesn't care if I poke my nose around. But his people can't possibly have been there long enough to be certain of that, not when that part of the Qajr is pocked with so many little caves. And if nothing else, I can at least tell myself I did my best to get to anything useful before the looters did.

So apparently I'm going to Akhia, and soon. Buying that license means I can't finance more than a brief trip out of my own pocket, but I have a hunch Lord Trent might be persuaded to assist with funding, what with his granddaughter working on the original cache and all. (Your own budget is safe, never fear. At least until I come around next week and talk to you about Rafaat's proposal.)

How is Audrey getting on, anyway? I know it's only been a week or so, but I would have expected to get six letters already with updates on her progress. Lord Gleinleigh isn't censoring her mail, is he?

Your friend,
Alan

From the notebook of Cora Fitzarthur

Audrey wrote a letter to her father today. I'm not sure if I should tell Uncle or not. It says that the work is surprisingly difficult; that she's excited to do it anyway; that it will probably take her a long time, though she doesn't say how long; and that she's read enough so far that she doesn't think it's right for her to work on something this important by herself. Then she asks her father if he thinks someone named Kudshayn would be available, assuming she can make the arrangements with Uncle for another person to assist her.

She's right that I'm not enough of an assistant, though she doesn't say it outright. The language is much more complicated than I realized, and besides which, it annoys me. It doesn't make any sense, even more than Scirling doesn't make sense.

None of that says anything about the tablets, not really, nor about Uncle, which is what he wanted me to look for. But she wants to work with this Kudshayn, and that would mean telling him all about what she's doing. Even if she decides not to talk to Uncle about the idea, I think he should know she was considering it, because he wants this all to be kept secret until it's ready.

I will write to him tomorrow.

From the diary of Audrey Camherst

19 PLUVIS

I am writing it down here, so that I can't funk out and pretend I didn't make this decision: today I'm going to talk to Lord Gleinleigh about Kudshayn.

He's finally back at Stokesley. He was in Thiessin on a matter of business, and came back with crates of new acquisitions—sun knows where he'll put them, as this place is already stuffed to the ceilings. Mostly Erigan, if you can believe it; he says that's because of me. I think he means it to be flattering? He wanted my opinion on them, and it was all I could do not to say "I hope they aren't looted." They aren't antiquities for the most part, but I cannot look around Stokesley without hearing Alan, Simeon, and Grandpapa in my mind, all gnashing their teeth in chorus. Not just the Draconean materials, though of course those are the most galling; I'm sure Gleinleigh got half these things on the black market.

Maybe if this translation makes him piles of money, he'll be happy enough with me that I can persuade him to stop doing that.

Honestly, it's been a bit of a relief to have him gone. I'm glad he wants to assist me in any way he can, but it's rapidly become clear that Lord Gleinleigh is the kind of man who cannot see an idea without needing to put his own "improvements" on it. (He installed *mirrors* in the greenhouse, after I realized I could use it to work on transcription during rainy spells. They don't do much good when it's gloomy out, and on sunny days I feel like an ant being fried by a sadistic schoolboy.)

And every time I see him, he asks how things are going. Which is understandable enough—except I can *see* the gears in his mind turning like a calculating machine, checking my current progress against the timeline I gave him. I'm doing reasonably well, but having him peering over my shoulder with a pocket watch in his hand (metaphorically speaking) doesn't make the work any easier.

Though I have to admit that in some ways, his requirement of secrecy *is* making this easier. If I were writing to all my friends and family as usual, I'd have *them* peering over my shoulder (metaphorically speaking), and I care much more for their opinions than I do for Lord Gleinleigh's. Secrecy at least means Grandpapa never has to know that I've been doing this all out of order, translating as I go rather than copying and transcribing the whole thing first.

He's probably right that I'll wind up regretting it eventually. Later on I'll realize the scribe had a certain quirk I've been overlooking by doing things piecemeal or something else foolish like that. But I certainly don't regret it so far! With most texts, copying and transcribing is enough to give you a good sense of what they say, with only bits here and there that feel like running headfirst into a brick wall. This one is long stretches of brick wall punctuated by just enough easy reading to lure you into a false sense of optimism. If I didn't translate as I went, I'd have to wait ages to find out what it says! I'm not made of stone. (Though I suppose the Anevrai would say I am, being human and all. Assuming *āmu* really does mean "human.")

Now I've lost the thread of my thought. Lord Gleinleigh—

that's right. We're having luncheon together today (Cora still doesn't eat with me); I intend to ask then. I'm a little worried he'll think I'm breaking my promise of secrecy, but I won't breathe a word, even to Kudshayn, unless Gleinleigh gives me permission.

I am very determined to make *sure* he gives me permission, though. Because from what I've seen of the text so far, this isn't just a history; it's a sacred story. And it simply isn't right for a human like me to be the first one to read it.

LATER

I've spent *days* imagining ways that conversation might go, and none of them looked anything like what actually happened.

It started off like I expected, because of course he asked how the translation was progressing. I am shameless: I pretended my scattered approach was actually for his sake. "I know you must be very keen to learn what it says," I told him, "and so I have been translating as I go along, rather than doing all the copying and transcription first. Just yesterday I completed the first tablet—though it's hardly as polished as the finished draft will be."

Lord Gleinleigh barely looked up from his plate. He only said, "Excellent; I am pleased to hear it."

That man! I said, "Do you not want to know what it says?"

This is the thing that frustrates me the most about him. He is all in a rush to make certain these tablets are translated, but I swear he doesn't care a toss what they're about. He only wants to be famous as the man who found them. I simply *cannot* understand it. They're lumps of fired clay, for pity's sake! They have no value at all in their own right; I could go make my own if I wanted, like I did when I was nine and Mama and I got stranded on that island in Trayarupti Bay. Their only worth is in what they can tell us. And yet that is the part he cares about the least.

So my tone may have been a bit on the sharp side. Enough so that Lord Gleinleigh put his knife and fork down and said, "Yes, of course. I will read it tonight, if you like. But give me the general sense of it now."

"It is a creation story," I said eagerly. (I may have played up my enthusiasm a bit beyond what it naturally was, in the hopes of getting him to be enthusiastic, too—but it was mostly genuine.) "But not the one the modern Draconeans tell! Of course that's only to be expected; after all, thousands of years have gone by, not to mention a great deal of change in their society. You wouldn't expect people living in villages in the frozen mountains to tell the same stories as the masters of a worldwide empire. But there are some intriguing similarities. Are you familiar with how the modern Draconeans say they came into being?"

He returned to his beef, but gestured for me to go on. Warming to my subject, I said, "According to their story, the sun's heat made wind, the wind became four Draconean sisters, and the scales they shed became mountains. And I suppose the mountains created gravity or some such—they don't say it that way, but the weight of the mountains dragged the sisters down to earth, which sounds like gravity to me.

"The sisters were heartbroken because they could no longer fly, only glide a little. They wept, and that created the waters of the world, all the rivers and lakes and so forth. Then they bathed themselves, and that created new creatures. Because male Draconeans are associated with writing and language, they say the water the sisters used to rinse their mouths made the first brother. Then the waters they used to wash their fronts made the first humans—the front of a Draconean being more human-like—and the waters they used to wash their backs and their wings made the first dragons."

"And this is not the story in my tablets."

I bridled a bit to hear him call them "*my* tablets." Never mind my own proprietary feelings toward them; they are a treasure for the world, not just one earl. But I made myself smile. "No, the tablet story puts the creation in a different order. But it speaks of a trinity—three gods, though it doesn't use the word 'god'; I imagine the ancients didn't need that spelled out—who echo the modern story a little bit, because it sounds like they're the sun, the wind, and the earth. The order of creation is different, though. They make the world, then dragons, then humans, and finally Draconeans, instead of the Draconeans coming first." I did *not* tell him that the tablet makes both dragons and humans out to be failed prototypes on the way to creating the best people. That might get up his nose, right when I wanted him to be in a good mood. And it isn't as if our own Scripture is all that flattering about some things.

"Fascinating," Lord Gleinleigh said. "Do send it along to my study, and as I said, I will read it tonight."

Up to this point, everything was going just as I'd anticipated. My plan then was to put on a look of artful disappointment and tell him how sorry I was that I couldn't tell him more yet, that Cora was very helpful but not well-versed in the finer points of Draconean orthography and poetics, and the work would go so much faster if I had someone to puzzle it out with . . .

Then Lord Gleinleigh said, "You know, Miss Camherst, it has occurred to me that in my rush to secrecy, I have overlooked something very important."

I tell you, diary, I nearly choked on my beef. After I got it to go down the right pipe, I said, "Oh?" with very little art at all.

He said, "We've agreed that it would be best to have the translation published before the Draconean congress in Falchester next year. And it seems to me that it would give a great insult to the Draconeans if they were not at all involved in the process of translating this epic. Your family is renowned for your friendships among them; is there a scholar you would recommend to me? Not to replace you, of course—your work so far has been quite satisfactory. But you said before that it was sometimes necessary to consult with an outside scholar, so perhaps someone you could work in partnership with."

Words utterly failed me. I have spent so many nights trying to plan the best way to ask this of him, but not one of those scenarios featured *Lord Gleinleigh* suggesting this to *me*. I stammered for a moment, thrown utterly off my stride, until he frowned and said, "Unless you are not amenable to the idea."

"I'm more than amenable," I said vehemently. "I know exactly whom to ask. Have you heard of a Draconean named Kudshayn?"

He had to have heard of Kudshayn. *Hadamists* know Kudshayn, because he is the very public emblem of everything they loathe. When Lord Gleinleigh nodded, I said, "He and I have been good friends since childhood. His knowledge of the ancient tongue is even more extensive than mine, and he has a great deal of prestige among his own people—not to mention among humans. Even working by post, I am sure his contributions will be invaluable."

Lord Gleinleigh paused in the middle of lifting his wine. "By post?"

"I know you don't want me sending letters," I hurried to

add. "We can use all kinds of subterfuges to hide it, if you feel that's necessary—though honestly, the odds of anyone reading my letters are really quite low. But with sailing time factored in, it would take months to get him here. I can't afford to wait that long, not if the translation is to be published before the congress. And continuing to work while he is on his way here would really defeat the purpose. Caeliger post is the only practical way." (Not a cheap one, of course—but I was prepared to pay out of my own pocket. Though I suppose that amounts to Gleinleigh's pocket in the end, since *he's* paying *me*.)

"Hmmm." Lord Gleinleigh sipped his neglected wine, then put it down thoughtfully. I hadn't somehow made him reconsider, had I?

When he said, "No, that won't do at all," my heart sank into my toes. I castigated myself for mentioning the post; I should have waited, letting him get attached to the idea of recruiting Kudshayn, before I pointed out that I would have to breach my promise of secrecy to make that work.

But Lord Gleinleigh wasn't finished. "If he is to come here, we must make the most of his time. The post is far too slow—and coming by ship would take him through the tropics, which I imagine would be terribly hard on him, even if he stays belowdecks. No, I shall arrange for a caeliger."

My heart rebounded from my toes as if it wanted to pop right out through my skull. "You would pay for that?" A caeliger trip from here to, say, Eiverheim is one thing, but flying halfway around the world is quite another!

Lord Gleinleigh frowned at me. I have spent too much of my life around sailors, which is to say around a great many merchants, and Mother's family are proud of being traders; I never quite learned that men like Lord Gleinleigh pretend money doesn't matter. "For a scholar of Kudshayn's stature," he said, "anything less would be an insult."

Kudshayn doesn't think like that, of course. He's even worse about money than I am, except with him it's that he doesn't think about it much at all. But it hardly matters, because Lord Gleinleigh has agreed to bring him!

I'm just so shocked that the earl himself suggested it. Given all his concern with secrecy, I was sure he'd be reluctant to bring another person in—especially a Draconean, when I doubt he's ever met one face to face in his life. Instead it's like he read my mind.

I will write to Kudshayn tonight!

From: Charlotte Camherst
To: Audrey Camherst

23 Pluvis
#3 Clarton Square, Falchester

Dearest Audrey,

As you can see, I am in Falchester! We arrived last week, and have been so busy since then, this is the first moment I've had to sit down and write to you. Is there no telephone where you are? Papa tells me Stokesley is not so very far away, just across the border in Greffen—please tell me you will come for a visit while I am here. I know you detest formal balls and such, but it would mean so much to me to have you with me for at least a few days.

If nothing else, you simply must see the dress I wore for my presentation at Court. It is a positive antique—not literally, because of course it had to be sewn for me specially, but it's not much different from the one Grandmama must have worn when she was presented. Why must stuffy old ceremonies be carried out in stuffy old clothing? [. . .]

[. . .] But I don't mean to bore you with talk of people you don't know and don't care about. I only brought up Lady Cossimere's because I wanted to tell you the peculiar thing that happened that night.

At one point when I had stopped to catch my breath, I heard Lord Gleinleigh announced. So of course I immediately bolted for someplace I could get sight of the entrance, because I wanted to know what he looked like. I thought, well, if my sister is translating tablets for him, I should say hello. (There are still people here who insist that a lady should never strike up a conversation with a man she hasn't been introduced to—can you believe it? Luckily I have Cousin Rachel on hand to deliver a withering stare as required.)

So I saw Lord Gleinleigh. But then I had to dance with Mr. Trunberry, and what with one thing and another a whole hour went by before I got a chance to even think about talking to Lord Gleinleigh, and then of course I had to hunt through the crowd. I finally found him up in the gallery that rings Lady Cossimere's ballroom . . . talking to Mrs. Kefford.

I was as shocked as you are! And yes, I'm sure it was her. Don't forget I was with you that day we went to meet Grandpapa for lunch—you remember, after he got the Synedrion to vote in favour of hosting the congress and wound up having that incredibly public row with her in the colonnade outside.

It shouldn't surprise me that she was at Lady Cossimere's. Everybody who is or wishes to be anybody comes to her parties, and Mrs. Kefford is undeniably somebody, even if I wish she weren't. But talking with Lord Gleinleigh? And it looked like a proper conversation, too. I mean that they clearly knew each other, and if they were just discussing the weather, then I never knew rain could be so serious. It looked as if Lord Gleinleigh was trying to persuade Mrs. Kefford of something; he was very earnest and energetic, and she looked intrigued but also a little annoyed. I really wanted to get closer and listen in, but there was absolutely no way—especially not when there are so few girls as dark as I am at these events. Lord Gleinleigh was bound to recognize me as your sister, and Mrs. Kefford might have remembered me, especially since I would have had to get quite close to hear anything.

But isn't that peculiar all on its own? I had no idea Lord Gleinleigh even knew Mrs. Kefford, let alone was on such close terms with her. I suppose he might have encountered her husband in the Synedrion, but they hold seats in different houses and are not known to be intimates. Or perhaps he and Mrs. Kefford met on the Continent; I hear he spends a great deal of time there, and she could save us all some headaches if she went to live in Ecraie permanently. (Well, it would save Scirland some headaches. But then the people of Thiessin would have them instead.) They both collect Draconean antiquities, so they might have met through those channels. But she's positively vicious about them—the Draconeans, I mean; not the antiquities—and Lord Gleinleigh isn't, not if he's having you translate those tablets for him. I'm surprised he's even willing to exchange a civil word with Mrs. Kefford, or she with him. If she didn't spend so much of her fortune on antiquities, I would swear she was a Hadamist, even if I can't imagine her running around in a red mask.

Now I've brought the mood down entirely with nasty speculation. And yet the only other thing I have to talk about is frippery and husband-hunting, so I will stop before I make anything worse. I remain, as always,

Your silly and frivolous sister,
Lotte

From: Audrey Camherst
To: Charlotte Camherst

24 Pluvis
Stokesley, Greffen

Dearest Lotte,

Never apologize for writing to me about frippery and husband-hunting. I might not have any interest in that for my own sake, but I care about it a great deal for your sake, because it makes you happy.

I used to not care, you know. I thought I was obliged, as Lady Trent's *granddaughter, to sneer at all things feminine and frilly. I made the mistake once of saying something about that in Grandmama's hearing, and oh, did she ever set me down hard. She didn't raise her voice. She only explained to me, very calmly, that if any obligation accrued to me as her granddaughter, then it was to acknowledge the right of any person to pursue their own dreams instead of the ones I felt they ought to have. By the time she was done, I wanted to crawl under the rug and* die. *But I'm glad she did it, because of course she was right. Grandmama pursued dragons instead of sitting quietly at home like everyone else thought she should; Papa went away to sea because he had no interest in dragons. If either of us is the true heir to Lady Trent's legacy, it is* you, *dear Lotte, because you have rebelled by running into the arms of high society, while the rest of us run as fast as we can in the other direction.*

There, have I made you blush? I hope so. I'm told it's good for the complexion.

But of course, being who I am, it is your tale of Lord Gleinleigh that I find the most interesting. Mrs. Kefford— ugh! I wish I could say that I think she's a Hadamist, because then it would justify how much I dislike her. In some ways, though, Calderites are almost worse. I mean, not really; they don't think Draconeans are demons or trying to restore their empire so they can grind humanity under their clawed feet or anything like that, and I doubt Mrs. Kefford has ever thrown a brick at a Draconean's head. But there's something especially nasty about a person who will smile at a Draconean and collect their artifacts and then turn around and do everything she can to make sure they stay cooped up in the Sanctuary, like animals in a zoo.

I do find it odd that he was talking to her. I mean, he's never met a Draconean, and he clearly has the Calderite tendency to hoard ancient things, as if we have more claim to the relics of the past than modern Draconeans do. They might have met through the antiquities market—Mrs. Kefford would hardly be the shadiest person he's dealt with on that front. But I can't imagine anybody with even a whiff of Calderite sympathies would pay so much money to fly Kudshayn here. (He's coming to Scirland to work with me on the tablets!) So who knows.

Well—someone might know. Now that I think of it, you're ideally positioned to sift for information. Heaven knows there are plenty of Mrs. Kefford's sort in high society, and while I know that isn't exactly your set, gossip is the very air people breathe in Falchester. Would you at least keep your ear to the ground for me? Let me know if you hear anything that might shed light on this. I don't like the thought of Mrs. Kefford anywhere within a hundred miles of these tablets, figuratively speaking.

There is a telephone here, but it is in Lord Gleinleigh's

study, and when he is away—as he often is—that room is kept locked. (I think his housekeeper, Mrs. Hilleck, is afraid of the 'phone.) But of course I will contrive to get a few days in town if I can. Lord Gleinleigh may be terribly secretive about these tablets, but unless he means to lock me up here like a prisoner for the next year, he can't object to me visiting my family. He already has my word of honour that I won't prattle to anyone about what I'm reading here, and how can I miss out on seeing your absurdly pretty dresses? You will tell me all about your suitors and I will tell you all about irregular noun declensions, and we'll both be delighted that the other is having so much fun.

Your eternally ink-nosed sister,
Audrey

From the notebook of Cora Fitzarthur

I can't find any reference to Calderites in Uncle's dictionary, and Mrs. Hilleck has no idea what that means. Is it an insult? I wish I had known about this when I ordered those books on Draconeans, so I could have gotten a book on Calderites at the same time. Except that I don't even know how one goes about finding a book on a topic when one doesn't even know what the word means.

I could ask Uncle when he comes home, and then order a book if I still think it's necessary. But Audrey thinks he is not one, whatever it is, so maybe that doesn't qualify as the kind of thing he wants me to look for. I wish he had given me clearer instructions on what exactly he *does* want.

She doesn't say it outright, but I don't think Audrey likes him very much. I can't blame her. I don't like Uncle very much, either.

Received at #23 Sanwood Street via Darvis Street, Falchester
Ecraie Thiessin 7 Ventis
Marcus Fitzarthur, Lord Gleinleigh

catastrophic engine malfunction repairs two weeks passenger delayed please advise—Bralt

Reçu à #68 Rue Courbée par Place des Oiseaux, Ecraie
Falchester Scirland 7 Ventis
William Bralt

book passenger first available commercial flight will reimburse—Gleinleigh

Received at #23 Sanwood Street via Darvis Street, Falchester
Ecraie Thiessin 7 Ventis
Marcus Fitzarthur, Lord Gleinleigh

caeliger line greatly concerned other passengers much disturbed by addition—Bralt

Reçu à #68 Rue Courbée par Place des Oiseaux, Ecraie
Falchester Scirland 7 Ventis
William Bralt

buy out whole flight then just get him here—Gleinleigh

REPTILIAN INVASION

Half-Breed Assaults Innocent Woman

HUMANITY OF SCIRLAND, UNITE! The reptilian threat has arrived early on our fair shores. Not content to wait for the great gathering next winter to determine their fate, they have sent an advance EMISSARY, and in grotesque style——flying alone in a caeliger meant for the use of HUMAN BEINGS.

But those who would see us BURNED ALIVE in the temples of the scaly ones, restoring THEIR CRUEL DOMINION over humankind, CANNOT HIDE their plots from us! Our brothers and sisters caught word of the invader's impending arrival and gathered in force to show that it is not welcome here, nor anywhere in this glorious world. We surrounded the reception building at Alterbury Field and WOULD NOT PERMIT it to leave. Let the monster go back to where it came from! And take its sycophantic slaves with it!

The forces of corruption are strong, though. The half-breed granddaughter of the GREAT TRAITOR was there. She assaulted an INNOCENT WOMAN and an HONEST CLERK in her attempt to free the beast, screaming FOUL CHANTS in the reptilian language all the while. But we held fast! Our line did not falter; our will did not break. Our brothers and sisters in arms brought her low, and would have taught her the TRUE STRENGTH OF HUMANITY.

Alas, weep for the fallen state of our land. Those LACKEYS of the serpentine agenda, the police of Falchester, came to the rescue of the half-breed and her demonic lover. In the ensuing BATTLE many were hurt and many more arrested, while the FOREIGN BEAST was permitted to go free.

Make no mistake: this is not the first skirmish in this WAR, nor will it be the last. The creature has gone into hiding, but we will FIND IT and DRIVE IT FROM OUR LAND. Those who have no wish to see their children SACRIFICED to the FIERY IDOL of these monsters must remain vigilant——for where one dares to tread, MANY MORE will follow!

For the bail of those unjustly imprisoned, a collection will be taken at the Assembly-House on Thackinny Street this upcoming Cromer evening.

From: Jacob Camherst
To: Audrey Camherst

10 Ventis
#3 Clarton Square, Falchester

Dear Audrey,

What the devil *do you think you're doing? A healthy sense of adventure is one thing; this is something else entirely.*

Your loving but deeply alarmed father

From: Audrey Camherst
To: Jacob Camherst

10 Ventis
Stokesley, Greffen

Dear Papa,

All right, so things got a little out of hand. But I could hardly let them hold Kudshayn prisoner, now could I? Especially after I am the reason he came all this way.

I suppose you got the story from the newspapers. I had better give you the actual story, since I'm sure they made a hash of it. Riots! Hadamists! Lady Trent's granddaughter! Very sensational stuff, good for the headlines, but short on details, which I'm sure will make you see why I had to take action.

I think I told you that Lord Gleinleigh arranged, not simply to fly Kudshayn around the world, but to bring him here by private caeliger. This was very handsome of him, I thought, but also practical: a Draconean on a commercial flight was sure to cause all kinds of problems. Most people have never seen one in the flesh, after all. Even if they were friendly to him instead of hostile, it would be a terrible disruption—not to mention very hard on poor Kudshayn, who would have to put up with being a fifteen-minute wonder every twenty minutes.

Hence the private caeliger. There were some problems with that, too—landing permits and so forth—because a strange airship roaming around as it pleases and landing at random fields for refueling tends to make people twitch, as if it's the Aerial War all over again. But the arrangements got sorted out, and Kudshayn made it all the way to Thiessin before things went really wrong.

(No, I don't know what. Apply to Great-Aunt Natalie for things that might qualify as "catastrophic engine failure" with a two-week repair schedule; that's all I overheard.)

Of course Lord Gleinleigh didn't want to leave Kudshayn stranded in Thiessin for two weeks. Since we only needed to get him across to Scirland, the earl made arrangements for a commercial flight after all. Only I gather there was some kind of trouble still, so Kudshayn wound up flying alone—apart from the crew, of course, since he no more knows how to pilot a caeliger than I know how to bake a cake.

I'm not sure how the Hadamists got wind of it. Possibly that was an unforeseen side effect of something Lord Gleinleigh and I planned? I suggested he might want to invite some of the Draconean Friendship Society to dinner here at Stokesley, in celebration of Kudshayn's arrival, but he declined. (He is not a very sociable man—I haven't even called on the neighbours, nor have they called on us that I'm aware of—but I think it's specifically because he's worried we'll let something slip that we shouldn't. It's all very hush-hush around here.) He suggested, though, that the Friendship Society might like to greet Kudshayn at the caeliger port, and so I wrote to them. I have no idea how the news might have gotten from them to the Hadamists, when those two groups are as far apart on the Draconean question as it's possible to be . . . but it's the only explanation I can think of. That, or a telegraph operator gossiped.

Regardless, the first Lord Gleinleigh and I knew of it was when we showed up at the airfield and found that, in addition to seven people from the Friendship Society, Kudshayn had a welcoming committee of several dozen more who think he's a horrible monster.

If it weren't for all the silly protocols we'd have had no trouble, because of course the Hadamists couldn't cordon off the entire airfield, but Kudshayn had gone into the station building to fill out the paperwork they insist on when the arrival is from a foreign country. (It just occurred to me that their forms don't have a blank for "species." Do you think they'll change that before the congress?) And if he'd landed at Winton there would have been far too much traffic in and out of the building; they would have been annoying ordinary people with their obstruction.. But Lord Gleinleigh had arranged for him to fly to Alterbury because it's more convenient for us, coming in from Greffen, and the field there is small enough that they were able to block the exits, so Kudshayn was trapped inside.

You can imagine how alarming I found the sight. Red masks all around the building, staring and blank, except where some of them were bold enough to show their faces openly. Their leader was one of the bare-faced ones. I'm sure you saw in the paper who it was: Zachary Hallman, and I have sat here for three minutes trying to think of an epithet I can attach to his name that won't make you exclaim "Audrey!" when you read it. Nothing has come to mind, so I'll just let you imagine something suitable. (Or unsuitable, as the case may be.)

He was parading around with a megaphone, shouting all sorts of horrid things—you know the kind of bilge they spew, human sacrifice and so forth. The Friendship Society were still there, but they'd retreated to a safe distance; they were outnumbered at least four to one, so I can't blame them. They'd expected a nice little meeting with a visiting scholar, and instead they got a face-off with a pack of horrible bigots.

I suppose it was a balance of sorts, and our arrival upset it—because of course Hallman recognized me. That put a fresh wind in his sails, not to mention the crowd's. Lord Gleinleigh told me to get back in the motorcar—as if I could sit idle! I strode forward before he could get any notions about manhandling me into it by force, and went over to where the trouble was.

Have you ever noticed what a dreadful-looking fellow Hall-man is? No, wait—I don't think you've ever seen him in person, as you were at sea when I met him. I don't mean that he's ugly. There are a great many people with ugly faces who are perfectly pleasant to look at. No, Zachary Hallman could be quite hand-some, in a rugged sort of way, if it weren't for the mean-spiritedness that has settled into every line of his face. He stepped forward and . . . well, I won't write down what he called me, because I don't want you being arrested for going after him. I don't care a toss for what he says about me, but you have a father's obligation to be furious at anyone who insults your daughter.

"Yes, that's me," I said, in my very best tone of saucy un-concern. "If you'll pardon me, I have a friend in there who is urgently needed elsewhere."

Lord Gleinleigh tried to shoulder his way in front of me and say something, but I dodged neatly around him. Hallman, meanwhile, selected three epithets to describe Kudshayn, none of them flattering. Then he said, "We know what to do with creatures like your friend. *Let's see how they like it if we burn them* as a sacrifice to their heathen sun god!*"*

"Don't tell me you believe that nonsense about those pillars being used to burn humans alive," I said, with all the scorn I could muster, hoping it would hide the sudden bump of fear that they meant to light the station on fire. "Even if the Anev-rai did that—which is very much in doubt among reputable scholars—modern Draconeans think the idea is appalling. They much prefer a good yak stew."

It was something like that, anyway. I can't remember precisely what I said, because I was busy trying to think of a way through this impasse. The Hadamists had all linked hands or elbows to form a human chain, like a grown-up game of "Country, country, we want soldiers." Even if I managed to rally the Friendship Society, I doubted we could break their line. And we had quite a lot of bystanders by then, but they all seemed content to stand around and whisper to each other. If I could just get through to Kudshayn, though . . .

Lord Gleinleigh had given up on trying to get Hallman's attention for the moment, and was instead hissing at me to stop being foolish and go back to safety. But then an idea came to me, and I smiled at Hallman. "Poor man," I said, my tone dripping with insincerity. "So obsessed with the superiority of humankind . . . yet you haven't learned to think in three dimensions. What good is your blockade when my friend can simply go over your heads?" And I cast my gaze upward, to the clock tower on top of the building.

They all fell for it, even the earl. Of course Kudshayn hadn't climbed onto the roof; you know what he's like. He would never dream of anything that acrobatic. But Hallman didn't know that, and neither did the rest of his followers, and so they all had a moment of panic, thinking Kudshayn was about to come swooping down on them like the wrath of the sun.

That's when I charged their line.

I chose my targets very carefully: a middle-aged woman and a scrawny fellow who probably works as a clerk. You would have been proud of me, Papa; I remembered my jujutsu training. Of course I'm terribly out of practice, so I didn't attempt to dive over them, but I rolled right under their hands while they were distracted, neat as you please, and I thought that everything had come off just as I planned.

Only I stepped on the hem of my skirt coming up, because I'd dressed in one of my more respectable frocks on account of not expecting to deal with Hadamist protesters. It tore and I stumbled, and then the clerk got hold of me in what he probably thought of as a bear hug. So I tossed him over my hip, but by then Hallman had noticed what I was doing, and yelled for everyone to stop me.

I can't really tell you how I wound up on the ground—it's all a bit of a blur. I did my best to turtle up like I was taught, but that only does you so much good when half a dozen people are coming at you. I would have been sunk if the Friendship Society hadn't intervened.

My hand to the sun, I didn't mean to start a riot. The plan was that I'd get into the building and tell Kudshayn my idea about getting out via the clock tower. It's high enough to give him a good long glide, and I figured he could either carry me or, if he thought that would strain his wings, leave me in the building while he and Lord Gleinleigh got away. I wouldn't have minded waiting. But instead I tripped on my skirt and got slowed down, and then some chivalrous soul in the Friendship Society decided he couldn't stand by and watch a helpless young lady wind up at the bottom of a pig-pile, and, well . . . things got a little out of hand.

But at least it meant I was able to crawl my way out of that whole mess (leaving a shocking amount of my skirt behind) and stagger toward the door, whereupon it opened long enough for a pair of clawed hands to reach out and yank me inside.

Of course it was Kudshayn. As soon as I had my balance I threw my arms around him and said, "Thank the sun you're safe!"

He extricated himself from me and said, "Your nose is broken."

(It was only a little broken. But don't worry: Lord Glein-leigh had his personal physician see to me anyway, so once the swelling and bruising have gone, I won't have damaged my marriage prospects at all. Such as they are.)

I felt at it gingerly—but not gingerly enough, as it turned out. Broken noses hurt such a lot! My voice was as thick as if I had a terrible cold. "I came to get you out of here."

Kudshayn cast a glance past me, at the chaos visible through the door's small window. "I see . . . how do you propose to do that?"

Before I could explain about the roof, the station master began waving his arms and insisting we leave at once—continued waving and insisting, I should say, since I had the distinct impression that he'd been doing it ever since the problems began. He clearly had never laid eyes upon a real live Draconean in his life, and was more than a little unnerved to be faced with a two-meter-tall humanoid dragon creature whose wings, though politely folded, kept bumping against the benches in the close confines of the hall. Compared with that, a half-Erigan young woman streaming blood from her nose counted as an improvement.

Kudshayn handled this in his usual way, which is to say that he did his best impression of a courteous, immovable rock. Since I am not a two-meter-tall humanoid dragon creature who looks like he would be glad to eat a man in one bite, I had the freedom to yell at the station master, demanding to know what kind of person would drive an innocent traveller out into the hands of a hostile mob, and we were in the middle of our own shouting match when noise came from outside. Whistles and someone else with a megaphone—not Hallman this time. The police had arrived.

I gave up on the station master and went to look. Outside, the police were laying about with their batons without much of a care for who had started the whole mess. I was suddenly very glad to be inside the station, as I had taken quite enough of a beating for one day. (Though I prayed that no one in the Friendship Society would get hurt. And I may have craned my neck a bit to see if I could spot anybody thumping Hallman as he deserved.)

At that point there wasn't much need for leaping off the roof, so we stayed put until things quieted down outside. Of course then the police had to question me, and Kudshayn, and Lord Gleinleigh, and the station master, as well as the Friendship Society and Hallman and quite a lot of Hadamists and various other people, and the result was that we didn't get back to Stokesley until well after the dinner that was supposed to be waiting for us.

Anyway, you see it was all just an accident. If it hadn't been for the caeliger engine breaking down, there would have been no trouble at all. But no permanent harm done, as they say, and I promise I shall have a quiet time of it from here on out.

Your bruised daughter,
Audrey

From the diary of Audrey Camherst

10 VENTIS

Ugh, my face is throbbing. No matter which way I lie, I can't seem to get comfortable. Aspirin isn't helping. I would be tempted to steal brandy from Lord Gleinleigh's study, but he keeps it locked whenever he isn't in there, and everyone but me is asleep.

Grandmama tells very frank stories about her adventures, but somehow she always manages to make things like broken ribs or tropical diseases sound not so bad. Did she ever lie awake aching and wondering how she could have been more clever?

Charging that line was stupid, I know it. In the end it did no good at all; one of the people from the Friendship Society had already sent for the police, on the grounds that the Hadamists were unlawfully blocking the station. So help would have been there in a few minutes regardless of anything I did. But all I could think was, Grandmama would have some brilliant solution for this. She'd sneak past or talk Hallman down or, oh, I don't know, set a dragon on the Hadamists or something. I didn't have any dragons handy; only Kudshayn, and he is far too scholarly to do anything like scare off bigots. I suppose I am, too, given how badly my distraction went.

And nothing after that went very well, either. At the best of times I am not Lotte, and having a broken nose put a serious dent in my social graces. When I got out of the station Lord Gleinleigh shouted at me, insisting he had the whole thing "well in hand" (my foot!) and I had "needlessly endangered" myself. I didn't have a good answer to that, and then when I tried to introduce him to Kudshayn, all Gleinleigh said was "At least you're here" before stomping off. And then there's Cora, who takes disruptions to routine very badly. She was so upset that we didn't arrive when we'd promised, she went off in a huff and wasn't even there to greet Kudshayn. I can't imagine how she'll behave tomorrow; I can only hope she'll have calmed down and we can just get to work on the tablets. Even when those are being intractable, at least they don't make me feel foolish and guilty.

Bah. I'm being a wet blanket because my face hurts and I can't sleep. I should tear out this page and burn it, but instead I'll go downstairs and distract myself with work.

LATER

What on earth is *Aaron Mornett* doing here?

I *know* it was him. He has the most perfectly lovely voice, which is utterly unfair; someone as odious as him should have an odious voice to match. I heard him in the corridor outside the library—

I should take things in order. Otherwise I can't hope to make sense of them.

It was a little after midnight. I had gone downstairs like I said. Because it was so late, and because I already have a copy written out of the next tablet, I turned on only the little table lamp. From outside the library, I'm sure it looked like the room was deserted, because I had shut the door behind me.

The first voice I heard was Lord Gleinleigh's. It's a silly

thing, but I turned off the lamp, because I didn't want him to notice even a faint glow beneath the door and realize someone was still awake. He was in such a bad mood after the mess today, and *I* was in such a bad mood, too, that I didn't want to have any kind of conversation with him.

I have no idea why he was still awake, or whether he got up again like I did, but I assumed he was talking to the housekeeper or the butler or someone about a domestic matter. In a moment he would go upstairs and I could get back to work, or try my own bed again.

That's when I heard Mornett. I recognize that voice, even through a library door. And then the handle of the door rattled, as if someone had put their hand on it.

Oh, I am so *ashamed* of myself! I should have turned the lamp back on, or gone to the door and opened it and greeted them like a normal person. Or listened to their conversation, and pretended that I was just about to open the door if they entered. But did I do any of those things? No. I bolted for cover. All because I could not stand the thought of facing Aaron Mornett in the middle of the night, with my face all swollen and no shoes on.

I might as well have stayed put, because they didn't come in. But it means I didn't really hear what they were saying—just muffled bits and pieces, none of them informative. Mornett sounded furious, though. Gleinleigh kept his voice too low for me to make out many words, but I heard Mornett say things like "unacceptable" and "if you think I'm going to."

If Gleinleigh thinks he is going to . . . what?

Come on, Audrey; you know the answer to that. The only business Aaron Mornett could have at Stokesley involves the tablets.

Is it me he's angry about? Or Kudshayn? Or both of us; our

work here must stick in his craw like two chicken bones. Mornett's been Mrs. Kefford's pet scholar for a while now—I wonder if the conversation Lotte saw was Gleinleigh trying to get her to loan Mornett to him. As if I would *ever* work with Aaron Mornett, after what he did.

If that bastard comes anywhere near these tablets, I am going to burn him to ash, like I should have done five years ago.

FIVE
YEARS
PREVIOUSLY

From: *Audrey Camherst*
To: *Charlotte Camherst*

16 Seminis, 5657
#3 Clarton Square, Falchester

Dearest Lotte,

Welcome home! Aren't you delighted to be back in rainy old Scirland, after visiting Mama's family? For weeks now I've been prepared to say I'd trade places with you in a heartbeat—swarms of tropical mosquitoes and all—except that things have taken an interesting turn lately. I'm so glad you're back, because I'm fairly exploding with the need to tell someone what's happened.

I was so convinced that my Season was going to be nothing but boredom. Everyone says it isn't what it used to be, back in their day—which is the kind of thing the older generations always say, but in this case I think it's true. And even if it were what it used to be, I don't think I would enjoy it. You'll probably have a splendid time of it once you're old enough, but you know me; this isn't at all my métier. Dances here, afternoon tea there, riding in the park . . . that last is not very appealing when one has never sat a horse in one's life. Now, if there were chances to display one's sailing skill, I might actually do well. But the closest anyone comes is paddling in little rowboats on the Immerway, and while I can paddle with the best of them, ladies are expected to sit quietly and let the gentlemen do the work. It's all fine and well for them, getting to show off their strength (and I saw one fellow out there in his vest, if you can believe it—marvellous arms he had, too), but not exactly a thrilling exercise for the ladies. At least not if you're me.

But! I should have known that Grandmama wouldn't put me through all that. She told me my first day in town that she didn't care a fig whether I got a husband or not, unless I was in a hurry to find one, and when I said I had no particular thoughts in that direction, she simply nodded and said, "Then we will take you elsewhere."

She says that while the Season isn't what it used to be, it's still important to make one's debut, because this is the point at which you leave childhood behind and become a member of society—with a little s, not a capital one. She means that I am an adult now, at the ripe age of eighteen. And as an adult, it's time I started to meet my peers and predecessors.

I've met some of them before, of course, because one can't be a member of this family and not meet a whole passel of scholars. But being at sea so often with Mama and Papa means I've missed out on a lot of the social connections you got by staying in Scirland, and Grandmama is determined to make up for it.

My Season has therefore consisted of very few dances and afternoon teas (though a few of those, for form's sake), and a great many more literary evenings and afternoon lectures. Grandmama's equivalent of introducing me to every eligible bachelor is making sure I meet people from all sorts of fields, not just philology: I have conversed with geologists, naturalists, physicists, chemists, and scads of other-ists, not to mention historians, geographers, mathematicians, and an architect or two. I must confess, Lotte, the awe-inspiring quality of the initials F.P.C. wear off when you can't throw a shoe without hitting a Fellow of the Philosophers' Colloquium. Which we could also say of dinner at home sometimes, but it's different when it's strangers—until you've seen one of those strangers have a bit too much brandy and begin lecturing everyone within earshot on the proper pluralization of "octopus." (He insisted it should be "octopodes," after the Nichaean.)

It is funny, then, that I should possibly stumble across the very thing I was not looking for, in what everyone would say is the wrong place to find it.

This afternoon, Grandmama abandoned me on the Colloquium's premises while she went upstairs to have an argument with the President. (He is not at all keen on this notion she has of publishing her memoirs—I think because he knows they won't be entirely flattering to the Colloquium.) I didn't mind, since she got me access to the library, even though I'm not a Fellow yet myself. I could keep myself entertained there for weeks, if someone were kind enough to supply me with food and water.

So I was wandering amongst the shelves when I heard an amused voice say, "You seem a bit young for a Fellow."

I turned to see a young man standing at the end of the aisle. The windows were behind him, so I couldn't see his face, but he had a lovely build (I wouldn't mind watching him *paddle around the lake in his vest) and an even lovelier voice—deep and rich, with just enough of a burr to give it texture.*

I couldn't resist being impertinent. "Henry Finsworth was inducted for having isolated caffeine when he was only fourteen," I said. "Or are you suggesting that a young lady must inevitably take longer to do anything of significance?"

He laughed. "I would never dream of it."

Then he came forward and a little to the side, so he was no longer backlit. "You don't appear to be much older than me," I said. Which may not have been the most polite thing to do—but he brought up my age before I brought up his, and besides, that was actually the least *awkward thing I could think to say. He had a very nice head of dark hair, not varnished into place with pomade like the fashionable men do, and while his face was not the most beautiful I've seen, the intelligence and character of his eyes made up for it.*

"I am twenty-two," he said, seeming entirely uninsulted. "As you just pointed out, that's hardly a record-setter in these halls."

But that implied he was in fact a Fellow, rather than a hanger-on like I was. That quickly, I knew who he was. "You're Aaron Mornett!"

The confines of the aisle were close enough that he couldn't really bow, but he inclined a bit at the waist and flicked his fingers from his brow in acknowledgment. "And you, I presume, are one of Lady Trent's granddaughters."

I found it strange, when I first debuted in Falchester, that everyone seemed to know who I was. While in theory that is the point of a debut, in truth there are so many young people here that nobody knows them all. But very few of those young people are half Utalu, so after a while I realized that of course everyone was going to know about me. Still, it made me glad that I had guessed his name first; it put us on equal footing. "Audrey Camherst. You cracked the Draconean system of weights and measurements just last year, didn't you?"

He didn't affect any false modesty. "Yes, I did. Not the kind of thing most people care a jot about, but with your family, I'm hardly surprised."

"I'm a philologist, too," I said eagerly. "I keep up with all the journals—well, as best as I can when I'm at sea half the time with my parents. I've even published a few articles—"

"Yes, now I remember," he said, one finger in the air, as if to make time pause while he thought. "You had one in the Journal of Early Writing *on triconsonantal root signs, didn't you?"*

I can hardly tell you, Lotte, what it is like to have someone recognize your work. And in such an obscure little journal, too! It would be one thing if I had published something noteworthy in the Draconean Philological Review *or a prestigious series like that—but he has read what I wrote! And he said it was insightful!*

I will not attempt to transcribe the rest of the conversation; the truth is, I hardly remember it. We stood in the aisle talking until some bent old twig came and scowled at us for being noisy; then we went out into the foyer, where there are some sofas, and sat and talked some more. I have never got along so famously with anyone so fast. I think it is the pleasure of meeting someone who not only cares about the same things as I do, but seems to be enjoying my company at the same time. We sat on the same couch, angled to face one another, and after a while I draped my arm along the back of it; at one point his own hand came to rest on the back of mine—just a light touch, and then he moved it. Lotte, I believe I have now observed that act known as "flirting" in the wild, and I enjoyed it a good deal more than I expected to.

~~Aaron~~ Mr. Mornett had to go before Grandmama was done, because she was having a good old row with Lord Wishert. I didn't go back into the library, but sat there in the foyer and reviewed the whole thing in my mind several times over, basking in a warm little glow, until she came downstairs again.

And that's when things went wrong.

Grandmama apologized for keeping me waiting, and I told her I didn't mind, because I'd met a very nice young man. But her absentminded noises of approval went away with a crack when I told her his name.

"Aaron Mornett?" she said, rearing up like a dragon. "Oh, Audrey. I am so sorry for abandoning you to him."

"Sorry?" I echoed, taken aback. "But he was lovely."

"He *may* look *lovely,*" she said darkly, "but he is not company I can recommend to you."

I have never heard her sound so much like—well, like a disapproving old grandmother. I said, "Why? Is he a gambler, or a drunkard, or a lecher?"

Grandmama stopped in the middle of the outside steps and delivered the most scathing condemnation I think she is capable of: "He is not a reputable scholar."

I couldn't have been more shocked if she'd slapped me across the face. "But—he's a Fellow!"

"Come now, Audrey; you know better than that." Grandmama gestured up at the imposing facade of the Colloquium. "Yes, in theory the Colloquium exists to recognize and support brilliant scholarship. But people also get in for political reasons, or because they have friends in the society, or some other reason that has nothing to do with their work. And besides that, your Mr. Mornett is a Calderite."

She said the word as if I ought to know it, but I don't think I'd ever heard it before. "And what is that?" I demanded, folding my arms.

"Samuel Calder was a preacher in Gostershire, before you were born. He held that the Downfall of Draconean civilization was a sign that the Lord had cast them out, like He cast Apra and Atzam out of the Garden. Therefore, it follows that they have no claim on this world any longer." Grandmama looked like she wanted to spit. "Some of his adherents took his ideas to their worst extreme, and now refer to themselves as Hadamists—I presume that *at least* is a name you recognize? They believe that Draconeans ought to be exterminated, finishing what the Downfall started and leaving humans in sole possession of the world.

"Those who kept closer to his original ideas are known as Calderites—but do not mistake their moderation for anything you would find acceptable. They merely say that the Draconeans should only occupy such land as humankind deigns to grant them: the Sanctuary of Wings, and nowhere else. And more in the manner of a game preserve than a sovereign nation."

Of course I'm familiar with that debate. There are so few Draconeans, and even fewer of them outside the Sanctuary; most people have never met one, so it's easy for them to imagine all kinds of foolish things. They hear "Draconean" and think of the Anevrai, lurid tales of human sacrifice and all that. But Aaron Mornett is far too intelligent to let such ignorance colour his views, and I told Grandmama as much.

She sniffed and continued down the stairs to the street. "Trust me, Audrey. You'll be happier staying away from him."

And that, as far as she was concerned, was that. But I am not convinced [. . .]

29 SEMINIS

Dearest Lotte,

I don't know if it's coincidence or design, but I have been see-ing Mr. Mornett rather frequently since our encounter at the Colloqium.

I haven't had the nerve to ask him about the things Grand-mama said—I don't want to drive him off. Whatever Grand-mama thinks of his scholarship, I can't cast any aspersions on his mind; every conversation with him is exhilarating. I con-stantly feel as if I need to bring every brain cell I have to bear just to keep up with him, and afterward I would swear my skull is packed full of new ones, like a muscle growing with use. With us there is no silly gossip about Society or idle talk about the weather; it is all ancient texts, archaeology, history, the things we both care about.

And he doesn't hate Draconeans, whatever Grandmama claims. He's never met any, but he listened with perfect courtesy when I told him about Kudshayn and the others I know. Perhaps after the Season ends I can make arrangements for him to come to Yelang or Vidwatha and get to know a few [. . .]

12 FLORIS

[. . .] Honestly, Aaron makes plenty of good arguments. Kudshayn's health is bad because his mother pushed her offspring into an unsuitable environment. Shouldn't we be urging them to stay where they'll be safe, rather than letting them take such risks? The Draconeans have been living in the Sanctuary for ages, and they're very well adapted to that climate. It will take generations before any of them can hope to prosper in southern Anthiope. And that's generations of failed hatchings and detrimental mutations.

All so they can "return" to land they haven't seen in thousands of years. Land that is already occupied! We can't possibly drive those people out, and Aaron says it's unreasonable to expect humans to live side by side with them again, given what happened in the past. So the only way they could take it would be by conquest. More dead Draconeans, more dead humans, more bad blood on top of the strata left over from thousands of years ago. For what? When they have a perfectly good mountain valley in Dajin where they can live?

But I can't say any of this to Grandmama. She'll just think he's corrupting me or something. This afternoon I finally got from her why she thinks he's such a bad scholar; she claims his

work on the system of weights and measures was plagiarized!
But she hasn't exchanged above ten words with him, and I have.
A mind as brilliant as his doesn't need to steal anyone's ideas.

21 FLORIS

Dear Lotte,

Victory!

It took a tremendous amount of arguing, but Grandmama
has conceded that I may see Aaron, that she doesn't have any
proof of her accusations and she's being unfair when she tells
me I shouldn't associate with him. Well, she didn't put it in
those words, but I know that's what she really meant. And
while it's true that he has some sympathy with Calderite views,
I've never heard him say a bad word against Draconeans as
individuals.

In celebration, I've told him that he may do one of the silly
things people our age do during the Season, which is drive me
around Arnessy Park in a little open carriage. But I am sure
that most of the young people who do that won't be discussing
philology while they drive. I've heard the stories about how
Grandmama courted Grandpapa; we Camherst women like
men who think that sort of thing is romantic. (Well, I do. I
know very well that my taste is not yours.)

In fact—do not tell anyone I told you this—but I think I may
share my theory with Aaron. You remember, the one where I
asked Mama to help me with the calculations? It will be the
first time I have mentioned it to anyone outside the family...
but I've been thinking that I might even try submitting it to
the Draconean Philological Review. *Aaron can tell me if the*
idea is good enough; I trust his judgment [. . .]

From the diary of Audrey Camherst

18 GRAMINIS

~~That goddamned~~
~~I can't believe~~
Heartless, manipulative BEAST!!!!

From: Audrey Camherst
To: Charlotte Camherst

30 Graminis
#3 Clarton Square, Falchester

Dear Lotte,

There goes my last hope.

Grandpapa took me today to meet with the editor of the Draconean Philological Review. *I knew it was a last-ditch effort, but still, I hoped—*

Oh, it's no use. They won't print a retraction, because I can't offer any proof that I'm the one who calculated that the ancient Draconean calendar was built around the ecliptic year. Never mind that my mother is an astronomer; never mind that he isn't enough of a mathematician to calculate an integral, let alone puzzle out this problem; never mind that I even have the notebook where I worked it all out. There aren't any dates on my notes, and even if there were, I could have added them later, now couldn't I? Maybe even after Mr. Mornett told me about his theory. After all, with my grandmother and grandfather so illustrious, of course I would feel pressure to establish myself as a scholar in the public eye.

Sneering monster. I knew that editor didn't like Grandpapa, but I've tried everything else. There's simply no way to prove that ~~Aaron Mr. Mornett~~ that lying beast stole my idea, not the other way around. The people who distrust him believe me; the rest shrug it off. After all, he's a Fellow of the Philosophers' Colloquium! And I'm just a child. A female, half-Erigan child, grasping at straws because everybody in my family is fa-

mous, and what have I done to distinguish myself? Published a few minor articles in some obscure journals? No wonder I'm trying to take credit for this.

He even tried to talk to me yesterday, if you can believe it. I don't know what he thought would happen—was I going to somehow not notice what he'd done? Or forgive him? He deserved a lot worse than me slapping him. Only it was so public, and now I'm a disgrace—not the amusing kind; the pitiful kind—and he'll forever be remembered as the one who so cleverly calculated the length of a Draconean year. While I'll be the one who threw a tantrum over it.

I am going to ask Grandmama if I can leave Falchester. I don't care that the Season isn't over; there's nothing for me here anymore except shame.

Audrey

From the diary of Audrey Camherst

11 VENTIS

I woke up this morning half thinking I'd imagined Mornett's voice last night. My head feels like it's twice the size it should be; maybe the swelling pressed on my brain and made me hallucinate it all.

All right, I didn't really believe that. But part of me wanted to, so I went downstairs to breakfast like nothing had happened—like, if I pretended nothing had happened, it would become true.

I found Kudshayn in the front hall, looking lost. Ordinarily one of the servants would have pointed him toward the breakfast room, but the house was strangely deserted; I think they were all hiding from the scary dragon-man. And Kudshayn has never been to Scirland, so he has no idea how our country houses are laid out.

He looked both relieved and appalled to see me. "Your face," he said, reaching out with one claw, but not touching. "I am so sorry. That happened because of me."

"Nonsense," I said—or tried to. He'd spoken in Draconean, so I instinctively answered him the same way, but Draconean nasal vowels do not work very well when your nose is swollen shut. I changed to Scirling and said, "It happened because of stupid bigots, and no permanent harm done. I'm only sorry you had such a dreadful first experience here. Come to breakfast, and we'll see if we can't improve it."

He and I had breakfast alone, because Lord Gleinleigh turned out to have left very early on a matter of business. I can't say I mind. And I haven't seen Kudshayn in . . . oh, heavens, it must be over two years. That symposium in Va Hing, where he had such trouble with his breathing, so it isn't like we had much opportunity to talk then.

Of course I could only eat porridge, with my face feeling the way it did, but the housekeeper had laid out a full spread. Kudshayn studied his toast with the same expression he gives every unfamiliar thing: detached and patient, observing its every quality before making the decision to eat it. "I can ask for whatever you'd like," I told him. "The housekeeper was at her wits' end, saying she didn't know what to serve to a Draconean. I told her you can eat almost anything a human can, and the exceptions aren't likely to be on her table regardless, but she didn't seem to believe me. I think she might be happy to receive a little direction from you." (As long as it comes via me, I suppose. It will take a while before the staff here adjust to his presence.)

Kudshayn took an experimental bite of the toast, first dry, then with butter, then with jam, then with butter and jam together. "This will do," he said. "It is best with the butter and fruit."

I couldn't help but grin, even though it made my face hurt. I think the sun will fall into the sea before Kudshayn changes. "Yes, it is, and the more the better. But perhaps we can shock Mrs. Hilleck just a *little*, and tell her you want steak tartare or a block of unsweetened chocolate for breakfast." I am not so cruel as to tell her that he adores bean curd or anything else she won't easily be able to obtain at the market in Lower Stoke.

"I will consider it," Kudshayn said. Which was perfectly true, I am sure—just as I am sure that after he considers it, his answer will be the same. How could I expect him to be interested in shocking the housekeeper, when there are tablets to be translated?

Very well; no sense in fighting the tide. "When we're done here," I said, "I'll show you what I've done so far. You can dig me out of the bog I'm caught in."

His nostrils flared in query. I sighed and twirled my spoon in my porridge. "The second tablet. I know the general sense of it, I think; in some ways it's a lot like our Scriptures. How the first few Draconeans chose mates and laid clutches and on through the generations, so-and-so begetting such-and-such—but it's also trying to explain how certain lineages got founded, I think, and it keeps referencing various places as they move around, all of which I'm sure was *very* meaningful to your Anevrai foremothers. But there are so many proper names—at least, I assume they're proper names—and I think some of them refer to the same people or places, but it's difficult to be sure."

Kudshayn munched his way through another slice of toast, thinking. Then he said, "Can you identify any of the places?"

"None of the names sound familiar. I can't even draw etymological connections from them to any current names—well, I can, but they're all made out of spun sugar. There are descriptions, though, and a geographer might be able to match them to candidates." Popping the bacon into my mouth, I added, "Then again, maybe it's all made up. It doesn't sound much like southern Anthiope to me—not even the climate it used to have." It's boggling for me to imagine that Grandpapa's homeland used to have thick cedar forests and so on, but he promises me it's true.

It is so *odd* to think that what we are doing here may have political implications come next winter, with the Falchester

Congress. An ancient genealogy is the very stuff of tedium . . . unless that genealogy references people living in an environment that sounds more like central Anthiope than southern, when everyone has always believed that southern Anthiope was the ancient homeland of the Anevrai.

What if this text says otherwise?

It shouldn't matter. This is an ancient story, a myth, not sober historical fact. None of this really happened, not the way it's described. But there might be grains of truth buried in it, and even if there aren't, people will read it that way regardless. Will that mean everyone starts arguing over whether Draconeans should be permitted to re-settle in Vystrana and Tashal instead of Akhia and Haggad? (They'd find the climate there closer to congenial.) Or will it just be one more lever to say they should stay in the Sanctuary, and under human control?

Either Kudshayn wasn't thinking the same things, or he chose not to share it. He only said, "I would like to see what you have so far. It was somewhat frustrating to me that Lord Gleinleigh would not let you send anything ahead of time."

And this was *Kudshayn* saying that. His "somewhat frustrating" is anyone else's "tearing my hair out." I think all the equanimity I don't have got allocated to him in the shell, leaving none for me.

I said, "Of course. I'm only waiting on you to be done with breakfast."

Which I didn't mean as a prod, but naturally he took it as one, swallowing the rest of his toast in one bite. Then he wiped his hands off, very fastidiously, and followed me to the library.

I really ought to put away the tablets I've finished transcribing. I keep fearing the maids will accidentally knock one of them onto the floor, even though it would take a spectacularly clumsy maid to make that happen. Or Hadamists might break in—I hadn't thought of that before, but after what happened at the airfield, I'm starting to think we should take more precautions. But today I was glad they were all out, because I wanted Kudshayn to see them in all their glory.

He's politer than I am, though. When we walked in, Cora was there, and instead of ignoring her to drool over the tablets (not literally; neither of us would risk getting saliva on them), Kudshayn bowed. He is very good about using human gestures, even if his bow looked more Yelangese than Scirling, and his wings didn't even hit anything when he did it. In Scirling he said, "You must be Miss Fitzarthur."

"You're Kudshayn," she said. "Were you the one arguing with Uncle last night?"

"I beg your pardon?"

"No," she decided. "Your voice is too low, and you have an accent, though it isn't too strong. I wonder who was here?"

The swelling wasn't enough to hide my expression when Kudshayn looked to me for clarification. "Audrey?"

"Did you hear what they were arguing about?" I asked Cora.

I was too forceful; she flinched back. "No," she said. "I only heard the end of it. He told whomever it was that he didn't want to see him here again—that Uncle didn't want to see the visitor here again, I mean. I thought it was odd that he would throw an invited guest out the very first night, but now it makes more sense." Then she paused and thought it over. "Except it doesn't really, because I still don't know who was here."

Kudshayn was still looking at me. "Audrey?"

I pressed one hand to the side of my head, as if that would make the throbbing stop. "I heard them, too, though not what they were saying. The visitor—it was Aaron Mornett."

I don't think I've ever seen Kudshayn look so angry. He didn't spread his wings or anything, but the sudden tension through his body made me understand why people can be so frightened of Draconeans. In those moments, it's easy to remember they are more related to dragons than they are to us . . . and dragons are predators.

Which doesn't mean that Draconeans are, of course, and Kudshayn is far from being a warrior. But I wouldn't have blamed Cora if she'd shrieked and run for cover; that's how most people react, and she'd never met a Draconean before today. Instead she just frowned and said, "Who is Aaron Mornett?"

It is a very good thing she knows only a little of the ancient tongue and none of the modern, because Kudshayn's reply was foul enough to shock the scales right off her. I said, "He is my nemesis. And I think he was here because your uncle tried to recruit him, or Mornett thought he was going to have a chance to work on the tablets, or—or *something*. Whatever he was doing, it cannot be good."

Cora was still confused. "What do you mean, he's your nemesis? What's wrong with him?"

"He is not a reputable scholar," I said. Oh, if only I'd had the sense to listen to Grandmama when I was eighteen. I can't believe I ever fell for his lies—except I can, because Aaron Mornett could talk the tide into changing direction. Not to mention that I was young and stupid, and believed that I'd found a kindred spirit.

Kudshayn's crest was still stiff with fury. But he has a lot of practice in staying calm around humans, so when he spoke, his voice was perfectly mild. "What do you want to do?"

How could I answer that? It does no good to say that I want to hurt him the way he hurt me; there's no way I can ever do that, because he doesn't care an ounce for me and never did. His reputation isn't what it once was, and I can at least claim some credit for that, but even if Lord Gleinleigh were at home, I could hardly go stomping into his study to slander the man on the basis of a late-night argument I barely heard.

I said, "I want to know what he was doing here."

Cora said thoughtfully, "He didn't stay the night in the house, because I heard Uncle throw him out. So unless he drove here and then drove through the night leaving, he must have stayed in Lower Stoke. In fact, that makes sense; the overnight train from Falchester to Locheala stops there at eleven twenty-one, leaving him just enough time to walk here from the station, have a conversation with Uncle, and be overheard a bit after midnight. But there isn't any train back toward Falchester until eight fourteen. So he might be gone by now, but he would have needed to stay somewhere for the rest of the night, unless he sat on a bench at the station the whole time. I can ask."

Her sensible recital of facts brought me back down to earth, especially because it explained the suspiciously late hour. "Would you? It won't tell me what he was doing, but it would help to know *something*."

"Of course," she said. "But why don't you just ask Uncle when he comes back?"

I sighed. "Because that would mean admitting I eavesdropped on them last night. I'll consider it, I just—you understand."

Cora looked like she didn't understand at all, but she went out, leaving me alone with Kudshayn.

He came and put his wings around me, and I wrapped my arms around his waist. It is not as good as being able to return a wing-hug, but it was the best I could do. "I have to do something about him," I said into Kudshayn's ribs—it's inconvenient that he's so much taller than me. "I can't keep being like this, hiding from him, jumping at shadows. For five years I've been going to sea and avoiding places I want to be, because I know I might see him there."

Kudshayn's wings closed in a little more, putting me inside a warm, comforting cave. "Be yourself," he said. "Translate the epic. Win fame that he cannot touch. And then one day you will realize he is unimportant to you, and to everyone else. That will be the best revenge."

He's right . . . but it's abstract enough, not to mention far enough in the future, that it's hard to reassure myself with such thoughts.

Anyway, Cora came back around lunchtime and said he stayed the night in the railway inn and left by the 8:14 train, which shows a surprising amount of early-bird vigor for him. At least I know he's gone, which means I can breathe more easily.

But Kudshayn tore two sets of gouges through the library carpet when I told him Mornett had been there, and if I had claws I might have done the same. I don't trust that man any farther than I can throw him, and I don't like not knowing what he's up to. I held a viper to my bosom five years ago; having him somewhere I can't see him isn't much better.

Tablet III: "The Dream Tablet"
translated by Audrey Camherst and Kudshayn

Before cities, before iron, before fields, before laws, a dream came to a daughter of the line of Ninlaš, a daughter known as Peli. One night she lay in her cave, two nights she dreamed, three nights she had a vision, which she did not understand.[4]

She saw a seed. A wind came and blew the seed onto stony soil, but there it took root, and from it grew a tree, four branches from one root. A wind came and tried to blow down the tree as it grew, but the branches bent and did not break. Flowers grew from the tree, each branch bearing a flower of a different colour, and again a great wind blew. This time it tore the flowers from their twigs and blew them to earth, but where each flower landed, something new began to grow. From the black flower came a river, flowing between banks of clay. From the blue flower came a round stone that began to endlessly roll in place. From the green flower came thick grasses bearing seed. From the golden flower came a tall mountain whose

---

4 The style shifts noticeably here.—AC

    Yes. I will venture a guess, which is that this long text is, like your Scriptures, a compilation of smaller texts brought together to form a greater whole.—K

    Would you say this *is* scripture?—AC

    At this stage I would not presume to evaluate that, especially since scripture is as much a matter of practice as the text itself. Whether the Anevrai venerated this tale in that sense, we cannot at this point judge.—K

top reached the sun, and whose root descended deep into the earth.

Still Peli slept, and still she dreamed. She saw the mountain shake, the grasses tremble, the stone falter in its rolling, the river flow backward in its course. Light vanished from the world. From deep in the earth came a howling; from deep in the earth came the sound of lamentation. Then light grew once more, but now the tree bore only three branches.

These dreams made Peli sorely afraid, for she did not know their meaning. She therefore went to seek out one who could explain them. Across plains she went, across rivers, across forests, across mountains, until she came to the place where Hastu dwelt.

She came to him and said, "I have seen a thing I do not understand. One night I lay in my cave, two nights I dreamed, three nights I had a vision; I slept and saw a thing I did not understand. Listen and tell me its meaning."

She told him of her dream: of the wind that blew the seed onto stony soil, of the tree that grew from the seed, of the four branches from one root. She told him of the flowers of different colours, blown to the ground, and what grew from each. She told him of the calamity that came, and afterward the tree had only three branches.

He listened to her, Hastu, wise Hastu, clear-sighted Hastu, Hastu the *šiknas*.[5] He listened as Peli told him her dream.

5 The grammar indicates that this is an adjective, but I cannot decipher its meaning.—K

Me neither. The prefix is clearly duplicative, which in this case I think functions as an intensifier, but of all the inconvenient places to

When she finished he said, "Not easy is this to understand."

"Wise Hastu can understand it." And she told him her dream again.

When she finished he said, "Not easy is this to interpret."

"Clear-sighted Hastu can interpret it." And she told him her dream again.

When she finished he said, "Not easy is this to explain."

"My friend[6] Hastu can explain it," she said, and told him her dream again.

When she finished he said, "Your dream is one of calamity. You will bear an egg; you will bear four hatchlings in a single egg. The Ever-Moving, the Source of Wind, will try to strike them down. From them will come many new changes that will threaten the world. The river you saw will drown the sun; the stone you saw will crush the sun; the grasses you saw will ensnare the sun; the mountain you saw will devour the sun. Your hatchlings will cast the world into darkness. At least one

---

use a triconsonantal sign, with no other context! There's some evidence that Ancient Draconean initial *K* mutated to G in Akhian, so if I squint very hard this might be saying that Hastu is humble, but . . . Well, if I can't even convince myself, I can hardly convince anybody else.—AC

6 Maybe *šiknas* means "true friend"? Though in that case I have *no* idea what the root might be, nor why the scribe would use the more ordinary word for the fourth epithet here.—AC

If we assume metathesis, this could be the root that in Lashon becomes *N-K-S.*—K

Mirrors and duplication? How does that make any sense?—AC

Think of the various meanings for the Scirling word "reflection." It could be a way of saying that Hastu reflects a great deal; that would fit with him being wise.—K

of them must die to prevent this evil, but better it would be for all of us if all four were to die, before this calamity comes."

This was how Hastu the *šiknas* explained Peli's dream for her.[7]

Peli was again sorely afraid. She said, "Advise me, wise Hastu, in how to prevent this evil from coming to pass. For I feel the egg taking shape within me already, and do not want it to hatch such horrors."

"Go into the wilderness," Hastu said, "into a barren place of stone, and lay your egg there. And when it is laid, take up a stone and crush the egg. Break its shell into eight pieces, nine pieces, ten pieces, and grind the pieces beneath your foot. Only then will we be safe."

Peli went into the wilderness, into a barren place of stone, and she laid her egg there. It was an egg unlike any other, an egg of many colours, radiant and glorious. Looking at it, kind Peli could not believe that evil would come of it. Looking at it, tender-hearted Peli could not take up a stone. Looking at it, fearful Peli thought of what Hastu had said, and left the egg there in the wilderness, whole in shell, but alone. Grieving Peli left her egg and went back to Hastu, and she told him that she had done as he said.

Then Peli [???].[8]

---

7 I suppose a "reflection" root might be a metaphorical commentary on the way he "reflects" Peli's dream back at her, with interpretation.—AC

8 I can't make *anything* out of these last lines. You?—AC

   Not so far. Let me consider it.—K

For the archives of the Sanctuary of Wings
written by Kudshayn, son of Ahheke, daughter of Iztam

I give thanks to the sun, wanderer of the world, guide and inspiration, for bringing me safely to the shores of this island, far to the east, far to the north. No place is unknown to you; no land is without your light. You who gazed upon my birth outside Sanctuary walls, watch over me here in this distant realm. You who have led me in my travels, show me the path now to wisdom and understanding. Here is an opportunity to shape the future, and I must be equal to the challenge. It is for my people that I undertake this task. For their sake I say, let your light shine upon the text; make its meaning plain.

I give thanks to the earth, shelter of us all, protector and guardian, for keeping me safe against the threat posed by those humans who see me only as a beast. Though water separates my home from this place, yet you are the same, the bedrock upon which we stand. It is your clay, your stone, your paper, your ink that records our present and our past. It is your embrace that preserves these things against the ravages of time. It is for this day that you have kept the words of the Anevrai, so that our ancestors may speak to us, a ghostly voice from the past. Help me consider their words in full, letting them enter my heart and emerge again for others to hear.

I give thanks to my foremothers, from the first to the last. I cup my wings before my mother, who gave me life before life outside the Sanctuary, so that I might come to this place on behalf of our brothers and our sisters. I cup my wings before the elders, mothers of us all, who chose me to study the ways of humans today and the people of the past, so that I might have the knowledge and skill necessary to represent us beyond the Sanctuary's borders. I cup my wings before the foremothers of the ancient past, whose brothers scribed words that speak to us across the ages, across the fathomless gulf of the Downfall.

Eternal earth, protect the relics of our people against the cruelty and greed of malicious hearts. Hide them from the humans who would tear them from the earth and sell them for profit, filling their drawing rooms and libraries with objects they do not understand. Protect these tablets, which hold so much promise for our people; keep them safe from accident and from those hands which might seek to destroy them. Eternal sun, bring understanding to the hearts of all such people; help them see the value these relics hold for those of us who live today.

Help *me* understand that value. I gaze upon these tablets, treasures of the past, and know they are not mine. I share with those ancients my scales, my wings, my bones, my shell. I do not share the factors that shaped them, in body or in mind. The brother who marked these clay surfaces was born in a land that would kill me. For generations without counting my foremothers hid themselves away in the mountains, fearing the sight of humans, while his ancient foremothers ruled over the ancient foremothers of those selfsame humans. Who am I to the Anevrai? I am no one. They did not know me, and despite the work of years, we are only beginning to know them. What claim do I have to this past? What claim does it have on me?

Dark stillness, give me patience. Bright mirror, give me wisdom. Open my eyes and my heart; let me receive the words of the past and consider their meaning today. Help me to record my own work with honesty and care, a memory to be kept in the archives of the Sanctuary. May what I do here become a blessing for our people, a star to guide us as we walk into a future whose terrain no one can see.

From the diary of Audrey Camherst

24 VENTIS

Heavens, is that really the date? I've been noting it down in each day's entry, but not really paying attention to what I was writing. Most of my diary entries lately are so short anyway, because after a day spent beating my head against my translation efforts, the last thing I want to do is spend yet more time writing.

That makes it sound like things are going very badly. Really they aren't—except for that blasted final sentence in the second column of the obverse side of the third tablet, the one we're calling the "Dream Tablet." I can't make wing nor tail of it, and neither can Kudshayn. Should we be reading those characters syllabically? Logographically? As determinatives? How should they be grouped? What on earth are we supposed to do with that first triconsonantal sign? Is Peli's name actually in there, and therefore this is explaining what happened to her, or is it saying something about the egg, and why did Peli's blasted name have to be etymologically related to the word for "egg"? Were the Anevrai out to confuse future translators? And while I'm at it, is the first character in the third line *gil* or *suk*, and why couldn't the scribe have been less careless in pressing his stylus down? I wasted all today on it, long after I know I should have gone on to something else (and Kudshayn had); Grandpapa has countless stories about running into something he can't translate, and then discovering that a later bit of the text made it clear as glass. But I have too much Camherst stubbornness in me, I think—or is that Hendemore stubbornness? Or Adiaratou stubbornness . . . I have so many to choose from, really, who can tell.

Cora wanted to know what we were stuck on, so I showed her and explained the difficulty. She immediately said, "Maybe it's a mistake. I know I often catch errors in my own writing. That's why I proofread my notebook every night before I sleep."

"It's possible," I admitted. "But Grandpapa always says that the first principle of copying a text is, assume the scribe wasn't drunk. Mistakes do happen, but they're less common than we want to believe, and if we go around correcting presumed 'errors' all over the place, we're likely to make a mess of the whole thing."

"So how do you know when you've found a real mistake?"

"Mostly we don't," I said sourly.

Which only confused Cora, so Kudshayn intervened from the other side of the table. "This is the kind of thing scholars argue over. Even if everyone agrees there is an error, there may be different ideas as to how it should be corrected. If the issue is something simple like a flawed character in a familiar name, then it is easy enough. But if there is no obvious proof of what the character ought to be, people may never settle on a single reading."

I had been rubbing my face while he spoke, as if that would make the sentence come clear. Now I laughed. "It's the worst with late texts—things written after the Downfall. You had scribes, human ones, who weren't properly educated in the writing system, and they made mistakes all over the place. Grandpapa was led astray for *years* by an error in the Cataract Stone, because the scribe who carved it swapped *lu* for *ma* and vice versa."

"I don't know how you read any of this," Cora said, her jaw settling in a familiar mulish line. She still has not forgiven the Draconean language for its complicated orthography.

And yet she has become a very good copyist. Not a quick one by any means; she takes three times as long as I would. But that's because she's diligent to a fault. When she isn't sure of something, she makes separate sketches of the different ways she might draw it, and then brings both versions and the original clay to us for a ruling. I've set her to work on the other tablets—because of course there were all manner of things in Lord Gleinleigh's cache, of which *the* tablets, our precious story, are only one part. And not even the largest part, though certainly the largest continuous text. The rest will have to be studied eventually, and for now it gives Cora excellent practice.

Actually, that gives me a thought. (Maybe even a useful one.) Lord Gleinleigh is at home for once; I should talk to him while I have the chance.

LATER

Well, that's one possibility ruled out.

I've been wondering if the earl had approached Aaron Mornett about working on the rest of the cache. It would certainly enrage him, being given what amounts to my leavings (not to mention Kudshayn's), which might account for the argument.

But as near as I can tell, Lord Gleinleigh has given the other tablets absolutely no thought at all. He may have surprised Simeon with his eagerness to have the main text translated, but when it comes to everything else, he's still very much in the habit of hoarding. I didn't want him to think my inquiry was suspicious, though, so I badgered him until he agreed to make arrangements for the others to be studied, at least, and fully translated if they seem to warrant it.

Not by me, of course, nor by Kudshayn; we're far too busy. And Cora, though a good copyist, is years away from being much of a translator. I suggested the Carter siblings—and not only did he agree, he said he'd have the tablets shipped to them! Secrecy apparently applies only to the epic, and not to ancient tax records. (Which I can hardly argue with.)

Mind you, he may have given in just to get me out of his study and back to what I ought to be doing. Kudshayn and I have been leathering away and making good progress, especially now that we're into what I suspect is the main body of the text. I'm sure all the genealogical and locational material in the second tablet will be terribly informative later, when we have a chance to talk to a geographer and try to figure out whether any of the places described can be found in the real world. But as a story? Well, it's about as interesting as the Book of Gepanim, with all of its "begats." Peli is much more appealing, even if I'm worried something dreadful may have happened to her in those lines we can't translate.

Honestly, if this were any other text, I would be perfectly happy to publish it with a lot of question marks around the problematic bits and some footnotes explaining that I'm not sure how to read it. Well, not *perfectly* happy; it would always niggle at me. I could live with it, though.

But in this case? I could never show my face in public again. Everyone is expecting so much from us, and this silence Lord Gleinleigh has imposed is only building it up—which is exactly as he intends, I'm sure. I don't even know if I could bring myself to write to Grandpapa for help, pretending for a moment that the earl would let me. And I can *see* the look Grandpapa would give me if I admitted that, yet here we are: I feel like Kudshayn and I simply *have* to do this ourselves.

I'm beginning to think there will be no choice except to grind through it the hard way, writing out every single combination of how to read each character, and then different groupings thereof, until I've found every possible coherent interpretation. I said as much earlier today, and Cora immediately began calculating exactly how many combinations there would be (she would get along splendidly with Great-Aunt Natalie). I told her I didn't want to hear the number; it would only discourage me.

Really, that isn't the math that matters. If Kudshayn and I are to keep on the schedule I promised Lord Gleinleigh, I can't afford to bog down on this for a week. We should move on; maybe something later will make it clear.

Tablet IV: "The Hatching Tablet"
translated by Audrey Camherst and Kudshayn

Then came the hatching time, the hard time, when the shell shook and cracked. It cracked not in one place, not in a single place, but in three, as three egg-teeth broke the shell at once. Away fell the shards of the many-coloured egg, and three hatchlings stretched their wings. Three sisters had broken the shell they shared, and in their midst was their brother.

Samšin was the largest, her scales sun-gold.

Nahri was the second, her scales water-green.

Imalkit was the third, her scales sky-blue.

Ektabr was the brother, his scales night-black.[9]

One hatchling was abandoned, two hatchlings were deserted, three hatchlings had been left in the wilderness by their mother. Four hatchlings were together, having only each other. They stretched their wings, and the Ever-Moving dried them. They stepped free of the shell, and the Ever-Standing supported them. They lifted their faces to the sky, and the Light of the World gave them its blessing.

---

9 The siblings from the invocation! And a fitting way for them to appear. In all the myths and epic stories, the heroes are born in some unusual fashion, like they don't have fathers or they're delivered by a goddess. Four eggs in a clutch is normal, but I presume four hatchlings from one egg is not?—AC

    That is, to the best of my knowledge, impossible. We consider it noteworthy and a good omen when two hatchlings come from one egg. That may be an echo of this story, or rather, this story may be reflecting a very old belief among my people.—K

In the wilderness they grew. Their well-fed cousins grew slowly, years from the egg to eggs of their own, but the four who lived in the wastelands grew quickly, one year from the egg until they were full-grown.

They were wild creatures, more like animals than like people. They crawled on all fours instead of walking upright. They ate their food raw. They had no speech, for between themselves they needed none. They knew only the Source of Wind, the Foundation of All, the Maker of Above and Below, and for these three they had no names.

Word came to the people of strange monsters in the wilderness, creatures that looked like people but had no understanding. Word came to Hastu of these four. Wise Hastu, clear-sighted Hastu, Hastu the *šiknas*[10] gathered hunters together and said, "I do not know whether these are people who have fallen to the ways of beasts or beasts that have come to look like people, but I fear they are a threat to us all." He sent the hunters to scour the wilderness for the four.

The hunters searched without success. Brave Samšin saw them coming and realized that she and her siblings must hide. Patient Nahri knew the land, and knew where they would not be found. Clever Imalkit lay stones atop

---

10 Perhaps this is a religious term, indicating a type of priest? He seems to serve a function of that sort, and we know from other texts that it was traditional among the Anevrai, as now, for males to serve in religious roles.—K

Could be. The most untranslatable things are usually the ones that refer to specific things from ancient times, things we don't have an equivalent for today. But if it were a priestly role or something like that, I'd expect the word here to be a noun, not an adjective.—AC

True.—K

one another to form a barrier, and placed dry branches in front of it so they would not be seen. Quiet Ektabr prayed in his mind to the Ever-Moving for the people to move onward, to the Ever-Standing to keep them concealed, to the Light of the World to keep them safe. And they were not found.

A second time Hastu sent out the hunters, a third time he directed them, a fourth time they went into the wilderness. They went and searched, and a hunter named Tayyit found the four. The sun reflected off their scales; she saw the gold, the green, the blue, the black. She came to where they hid.

Tayyit offered them meat that had been cooked in a fire. She offered them fruit that had been picked from a tree. The siblings ate the food and marveled at it. Without words they consulted; without speech they agreed. They went with Tayyit back to where she dwelt.

In one year they had grown from the egg to full size; in one moon they learned speech. They lost their bestial ways and became people.

In these days there were no temples, no priesthoods, no sanctuaries, no shrines. The ways of the people were kept by the eldest brothers.[11] They counted the days, counted the seasons, counted the years, counted

---

11 As it is today.—K

But "no priesthoods" undercuts the idea that *šiknas* is the term for a specific kind of priest. It could indicate these eldest brothers, but in that case I'm surprised we don't see the word being used again here.—AC

He might be a kind of shaman, though the word is certainly not cognate with that term in any related language I am aware of today.—K

when the time had come for a hatchling to become a fledge.

Tayyit went to Hastu and said, "How should we count the ages of these four? They hatched less than two years ago, but they are fully grown. Now that they have learned speech, should they join the circles? Or must they wait for many years more?"

"I have counted the days," Hastu said, "and only a few have passed. Whatever their size, they are not ready to join the circles."

The siblings were learning the ways of the people. Samšin was a great hunter, and Nahri patient for finding food. Imalkit crafted spears and snares. Ektabr bound up the wounds of those who were hurt.

Others came to Hastu, saying, "Surely the time has come for these four to join the circles. So long as they remain hatchlings, we cannot benefit from their skills."

But wary Hastu said, "Not even three years have passed since their hatching. The time has not yet come."

Brave Samšin made a plan. She said to her siblings, "Let us prove to Hastu that we are ready. Let us show him the breadth of our wings."

But Nahri said, "We will not convince him. He will not believe we are ready until the full time has passed."

Then Imalkit said, "We shall have to wait, or find another way to convince him."

Toget' er they built a hut, and Ektabr sat there with Hastu, discussing matters of the spirit. The sisters went out into the hills. They found a plant there whose leaves were not good food, a plant whose leaves were good medicine. They picked the leaves and brought them back. Hastu sat in the hut with Ektabr; Ektabr burned the leaves in the fire, so that their smoke filled the hut. The medicine made Hastu calm. The siblings asked him if the time had come for them to join the circles, and he said yes. All the people heard him say it.[12]

12 Am I reading this wrong, or did they just drug Hastu with hashish?—AC

    Hashish is the resin. The leaves themselves are called cannabis.—CF

    I am not going to ask how you know that.—AC

From the diary of Audrey Camherst

7 SEMINIS

I suppose it was the epic that set this off. We've finally gotten to the four siblings the invocation promised, hatched from a single shell, and naturally that would turn Cora's thoughts to the houseguest who also came out of a shell.

She approached it in her typical way, which is to come out of seeming nowhere with a question. (I'm sure there's a logical process by which she arrives at it, but for those of us not privy to her thoughts, it seems to spontaneously generate.) Kudshayn and I were in the middle of discussing a word on the next tablet that I'm sure we ought to render as "fledging"—as in, the developmental stage where a baby bird becomes ready for flight—when Cora said, out of the blue, "How many sisters do you have?"

I thought at first she was addressing me, so I said, "Just one. Her name is Charlotte—we call her Lotte—and she's younger than me. I was thinking about inviting her to visit for a day or two, if you think your uncle wouldn't mind."

"I'm sure he would," Cora said without hesitation. It was the same way most people would reflexively say "I'm sure he *wouldn't*," so it took me a moment to realize she meant that her uncle would absolutely veto a visit. Then, before I could respond to that, she added, "But I was asking Kudshayn."

He had stood up to stretch his wings over by the windows,

where he wouldn't hit anything, and furled them as he turned to face her. "I also have just one, Teslit. But we are the same age, because we came from the same clutch." He rattled his wings a little in amusement. "Not the same shell, though."

Cora frowned. "Only one sister? I thought there were usually lots of females in a Draconean clutch, and then maybe one male. Why don't you have more?"

Kudshayn's wings stopped rattling and tucked in tight against his back. "One sister, yes. What do you think of this sign—do you think Audrey is correct about its meaning?"

It was a transparent bid to change the subject, and it failed. "How should I know?" Cora said. "You know I can't really read any of that. Is there some reason you have only one sister? Did something happen to the others?"

"Cora—" I said, meaning to intervene.

"I would like to get back to work," Kudshayn said, a little more loudly. His wings had to be aching with how tightly they were furled. "Perhaps later we can talk more."

Her whole body had gone rigid. "You don't mean that. You mean you don't want to talk about this, and you're hoping that if you say that I'll let it go and forget."

"Cora—"

"I won't forget, though. Why don't you want to answer my question?"

"*Cora!*"

My shout shocked me into silence as much as her. Cora stared at me for a moment, fuming and hurt. Then she stomped out of the library, slamming the door behind her.

I stayed in my chair and dropped my head onto my arms, groaning. "I am so sorry, Kudshayn. I—I should have spoken to her, or something." He knows by now how blunt Cora can be, but I never thought she would wind up going straight for the most tender spot Kudshayn has.

"Do not apologize," he said. When I looked up, I saw his wings relax incrementally. "It is not your responsibility to protect me from such questions. If I wanted to prevent Cora from asking, I should have taken steps to ensure that myself." Now his wings drooped. "I did not handle that at all well."

He could hardly be expected to. I know it's strange for him, reading about the ancient past—a past that was clearly ancient even to the Anevrai, and simultaneously familiar and thoroughly alien. The whole way through the Hatching Tablet, I've been cautious about what I say to him and how, because I knew without even thinking about it that the subject would be sensitive. But of course Cora doesn't know that, and this was the result.

I sighed. "It will blow over. Let's get back to work."

But Kudshayn made no move toward the table. "Someone should go talk to Cora. I would do it myself, but . . ." He drooped another wing-sigh. "I do not know her very well yet. She is more your friend than mine."

Is Cora my friend? I don't really know. She's such a peculiar girl—no, a peculiar *young woman*; if I am going to complain about people calling me "girl," it isn't fair to do that to someone else. And as for what we are to each other . . . well, I doubt she and I will ever braid each other's hair the way Lotte and I do, and she would loathe many of the things I enjoy. But I'd be sad to lose her help. Not just because she's useful, but because I've come to enjoy working with her. Which I suppose does make her a friend.

"I don't know what I'm going to say," I told him, but I stood up anyway.

Kudshayn stood silent for a long moment, thinking. Then

he said, "Answer her question. I think she will be happier knowing, but I would prefer not to speak of it right now."

His family. I couldn't help staring at him in astonishment, sure I must have somehow misheard him. But Kudshayn nodded, gesturing me out the door, so I went in search of Cora.

I found her in the upstairs corridor, where there is a window seat she has claimed as her own. She was curled up on it with one hand tucked tight under the opposite arm and the other employed in twining a lock of hair around her finger over and over again. She resolutely did not look at me as I walked up.

"I'm sorry," I told her, standing a careful distance away. With Lotte I would have perched at the other end of the seat, but Cora doesn't like people being too close to her, especially when she's upset. "And Kudshayn is sorry, too. He . . . Family is a very sensitive topic for him."

She continued to stare out the window, twining her hair again and again. "Then why didn't he say that?"

"In a way, he did. Draconean body language isn't like ours— well, some parts of it are. But his wings tucking in like that was his way of showing that he was uncomfortable with your question."

Cora scowled. "How was I supposed to know that?"

It was a fair question. "You weren't. If I'd realized . . . I can teach you how they behave, if you like. Kudshayn speaks very good Scirling and knows a lot of our habits, but he'll still do things that are different. For example, he can't raise his eyebrows when he's surprised or curious, because he doesn't have any. I can tell you what to look for."

She relaxed a degree or two, but not all the way.

I think it might have been easier to carve the explanation into clay and give that to her than to say it out loud. What happened to Kudshayn's clutch isn't my story—but in a way, I think that's why I'm even more reluctant to tell it than he is. How many years did he and I know each other before he said anything about it to me? And that was when I'd already gotten the general outline from Grandmama. But I've heard so many people say thoughtless things in reply, and I was terribly worried Cora would do the same, and even though Kudshayn wasn't there to hear it, I was still flinching on his behalf—pre-emptively, since I hadn't yet said anything and neither had Cora.

Which meant I was being stupid. Kudshayn *told* me to tell her.

I leaned against the wall, tipping my head to the plaster and closing my eyes. "Do you know how evolution works for Draconeans?"

The earl doesn't have very many books on them—rather startling, for a man who collects so many of their antiquities—but Cora ordered a whole stack when we made plans for Kudshayn to come here, and has been reading her way steadily through them. She said, "Developmental lability means that the environment in which an egg incubates can, if significantly different from the environment of the parental egg, cause mutations."

"Yes. It's why Kudshayn can come spend time here and not feel horribly uncomfortable. Most Draconeans are adapted to life at a very high altitude, which means they do badly in environments we'd consider much less harsh. But Kudshayn hatched at a lower elevation, in a warmer climate. It means his scales are different from other Draconeans'—he doesn't molt the way they do, for example—and, well, a lot of other differences that probably aren't interesting to you, unless you plan to take up a career as a dragon naturalist. But the part that matters is, his mother decided to take a big risk and lay her eggs quite far from where she'd hatched, at the edge of what anybody thought might be viable."

That got Cora's attention. She turned to face me and said, "Isn't that dangerous?"

"Yes. He has only one sister because the others didn't make it. The clutch was a large one—six eggs—and two of them never hatched at all. Two others had very bad mutations, and didn't survive. People sometimes think that developmental lability means the hatchling always evolves in a way that suits the new environment, but that isn't true, and it gets riskier the bigger the differences are. Kudshayn is mostly healthy, but he has difficulty breathing sometimes. And his one surviving sister is *very* delicate; in fact, if it weren't for doctors, she probably wouldn't still be alive."

Cora hunched in on herself again. In a small voice, she said, "I thought they might be dead. That's why I asked. I thought, if they were, then he and I would have something in common."

My breath stopped. All this time I've known that Cora is Lord Gleinleigh's ward—but have I made any attempt to find out why? No, I have not. And I could pretend it's because I feared that would be a sensitive subject and wanted to let her bring it up in good time . . . but that's a lie. The truth is that I've been entirely wrapped up in the question of these tablets, and haven't done a flaming thing to learn about Cora's life.

She wasn't the one being thoughtless. I was.

It took me far too long to figure out what to say to that. Finally I said, "Kudshayn generally prefers not to talk about it. If he changes his mind, he'll let you know. But . . . if you ever want to tell me about your parents, you're welcome to."

She peered up at me. "Are any of your family dead?"

"Only my grandfather," I said. "My grandmother's first

husband, I mean—the one I'm related to. But he died even be-fore my father was born, so I don't think that really counts."

"It doesn't," she said. Which stung, even though I agree with her.

She thought for a moment, then said, "Yes. I'd like to know what to look for in his behaviour. Otherwise I'll offend him again, and I don't want to."

I couldn't help but cast a glance over my shoulder, toward the stairs and my work. "Now?"

"No," Cora said. "I want to sit here for a while. And I'll do the same thing." She saw my confusion and added, "Let you know. If I want to talk about it. My parents, I mean."

Never in my life have I felt so self-conscious about having a healthy, loving family. I tugged my dress straight, even though it didn't need it, and said, "Then—if you're sure you're all right—"

Cora shrugged, hand drifting back to her hair. "I'm not. But I will be."

It was a clear dismissal, but not an unfriendly one. I went downstairs to join Kudshayn and the tablets, and we spent the rest of the day working very pleasantly together . . . but I have written this all down so I will not forget it. I am not as good at being considerate of people as Lotte is, but that's no excuse not to try.

FIFTEEN
YEARS
PREVIOUSLY

From: Kudshayn
To: The Sanctuary of Wings

To the elders of the Sanctuary of Wings, I give greetings
under the light of the sun, on the footing of the earth.

I lower my wings in shame. I am no fit diplomat to represent
our people. Though my mother laid her clutch in a place that
might allow her hatchlings to survive well beyond the Sanctuary, that only gives me the physical ability to travel in greater
comfort. It does not make me skilled, or knowledgeable, or
wise.

Today I faced my first test as an ambassador, and I failed.

I failed, and Teslit suffered for it.

Agarzt believes—or believed—that the time has come for
me to begin attending official events, so that I can begin lifting
some of the burden from those sisters who have carried it until
now. In my pride, I agreed. We arranged with the emperor to
have a formal meeting with some representatives from Scirland at his palace in Ongnan, and so I have been here for the
last two weeks.

Teslit is here with me. She has no intention of participating
in the meetings, but at this time of year the climate in Ongnan is
no worse than at home, and the emperor's physicians can care
for her as well here as anywhere else. The journey tired her out,
so she has been resting since we arrived. Today she was feeling
well enough that she asked if we could go for a walk through the
gardens, which the emperor has told us we may do. Since I will
be busy with official matters beginning tomorrow—or at least, I
was supposed to be; that may change now—I was happy to go
along.

The Ongnan Palace is one built by an earlier emperor for

the purpose of leisure. It is not heavily defended like the palaces in Phautan or Tho Giulio. But there are many guards here right now because the emperor is in residence, and they were patrolling the gardens, because the walls there are not very high and someone could easily climb in.

Someone did climb in.

I saw her drop out of a tree from a little distance away. A human girl, small and skinny, and at that distance I thought she was perhaps Kengumet, because she was darker-skinned than the Yelangese usually are, and her hair was very curly. I am fairly certain she hadn't seen me and Teslit, because we were screened by a stand of bamboo; she turned the other direction and began to move through the garden, keeping behind bushes and trees where she could.

This was my first failure. I should have immediately told the guards there was an intruder. But because she was so small—I wasn't sure of her age, but now I know she is eight—I thought there was no need.

Instead I asked Teslit, "Should we follow her?"

Teslit rattled her wings in amusement and said, "Aren't you supposed to be an ambassador to humans? She looks human."

My second failure is that I did not suggest Teslit should wait, or go back to our rooms. I don't know if she would have agreed, but I should have thought to say it. I know how easily my sister can be hurt, but I didn't stop to think that I might be leading her into danger.

We followed the girl. She was not as stealthy as she thought; the guards would have spotted her very soon. But none of them had come upon her yet when Teslit and I caught up and I said in Yelangese, "Greetings under the light of the sun, on the footing of the earth."

My third failure is that I did not wait to say that until after she had finished skirting the edge of a fishpond.

The girl yelped and fell in. The ponds in the Ongnan Palace are deep enough, and she was small enough, that I was worried she might be at risk of drowning if she did not know how to swim. I cannot swim either, but I have grown a great deal these last six months, and am tall enough that I could stand on the pond's bottom and be safe. So I immediately ran forward to help her.

It turned out the girl did not need my help. By the time I reached the edge of the pond, she had paddled over and hoisted herself out without reaching for my hand. I realized, too late, that seeing a Draconean leaning over and reaching for her might be frightening, but she didn't seem intimidated at all. She only wiped her hair out of her face and said in Scirling, "You're a Draconean!"

I am so used to people being either afraid of us or peculiarly fascinated, but she seemed to take my existence for granted. She looked past me to Teslit and said, "Two of you! Let's see— your ruffs are different, and if I remember right, it's the males that have the more interesting patterns on theirs. So you're female, which means you're Teslit?" Then she turned to me. "And you're male, so that makes you Kudshayn. I think. Unless I got it backward."

"You have it correct," I said. My fourth failure: at this point I could not think what to say. I have spent days practicing for the official meetings, but had not made any preparations for speaking to a small wet girl on the edge of a fishpond.

"Good," she said with satisfaction. "I was worried I wouldn't be able to find you. Grandmama said this is a fairly small palace as palaces go, but it looks big enough that I could have missed you pretty easily. And I wanted to meet you before

tomorrow, because it will be stuffy and boring and we won't have any chance to talk."

She spoke Scirling rapidly enough that I had trouble follow-ing her words—I need to practice more with that language. The girl noticed my confusion . . . and promptly repeated her-self in our tongue.

At that point I lost all proper courtesy and only said, "Who are you?"

"Audrey Camherst," she said, as if that should have been obvious. "I'm Lady Trent's granddaughter."

Failing to guess her identity was my fifth failure. Agarzt and I were given a list of everyone who would be attending the meeting, and Audrey Camherst was among them; I knew she would be young, and I have met both of her parents, so I knew she would be half Scirling, half Erigan. Up close, she did not look Kengumet anymore. And what other human child would default to speaking Scirling, then repeat herself in our lan-guage without so much as a pause to think?

But these are my small failures. My great one had yet to come.

I was about to suggest she come with the two of us back to our rooms, where we had towels she could use to dry off, when a shout came from the direction of the palace. Three of the guards had seen us. And while Teslit and I were permitted to be there, Audrey was not.

To them, it didn't matter that she is an eight-year-old child. Their duty is to protect the emperor, and any intruder is a threat to his safety.

I forgot myself completely. I have lived my whole life among humans, except for visits to the Sanctuary, but when crisis threatened I allowed instinct to defeat fifteen years of experi-ence. I immediately spread my wings to defend Audrey. But the guards in Ongnan are not used to our people, and my reaction frightened two of them so that they lifted their rifles and aimed them at me. Teslit flung herself between us, calling out that they should not be alarmed, and then from behind me came a splash as Audrey jumped back into the pond for safety.

The third guard, who was their captain, shoved one of the rifles toward the ground, shouting at his soldiers to lower their arms. The one whose rifle he touched pulled the trigger in surprise. He fired into the dirt, so no one was harmed—but the sound of a gunshot brought all the other guards running.

If I had kept my wings folded, none of this might have happened. But I lost control, and I didn't manage to resolve the situation before we had nearly two dozen soldiers in the garden, along with the emperor himself.

He came outside once it was clear there was no threat. Yelangese protocol said I should kneel to him, and I would have . . . except that as Teslit moved to kneel at my side, she collapsed.

It was the sudden panic of the scene that weakened her. It made her heart race, and the strain was too much. She is resting now, and the physicians say she will be well in a day or two, but I put my sister in a dangerous situation—a situation I made dangerous, by my own failures. I disturbed the emperor, disrupted the whole palace, and left Lady Trent's granddaughter sitting in a fishpond.

I am a failure as a diplomat. Perhaps thirty years from now I will be capable, but at fifteen I am a disgrace. Teslit has tried to reassure me; she says I can only learn by experience, not by hiding, and that things like this happen when Camhersts are around. But I cannot forgive myself for hurting my sister, nor for disgracing the Sanctuary with my incompetence. I will accept any punishment the elders choose to lay upon me. I am not fit to represent our people in human company.

May the earth reject me if I have attempted to hide my errors. May the sun judge me as I deserve.

Kudshayn, son of Ahheke, daughter of Iztam

From the notebook of Cora Fitzarthur

Wings cupped around body

This is a sign of respect, like bowing or curtsying for humans. But it is less frequent among Draconeans who spend a lot of time around humans, because they don't want to hit anything with their wings in the process of wrapping them, and we tend to have a lot more breakable possessions very closely packed— at least rich Scirlings and Yelangese do. Because of this, it's becoming more common for them to cross their arms over their chests, which is how humans imitate the act of cupping the wings. So we're learning their body language, and then they learn it again from us. That seems very odd.

Wings cupped around each other

Like a hug. Kudshayn says it is very comforting, and a thing family do for each other; when non-family do it, that's very intimate. But not sexually intimate, I think, and then he was shocked that I said such a thing. Audrey wasn't, though; she just laughed and said I was correct.

Wings tucked tightly against back

A sign of discomfort, usually in situations that are emotionally uncomfortable rather than physically. Audrey said she assumed this is because they want to protect their wings (which are relatively fragile) against things that might damage them, but Kudshayn said it's childish body language; their wings don't really begin to stretch out and grow strong until they're older. He also thinks it might be an instinct from their time in the shell, where they are safe and also crammed into a very small space, though no Draconean he has ever spoken to remembers being in the shell, so he's really just guessing. I think it is like humans going into the fetal position.

Wings spread

Very much like a cat puffing up its fur. This makes the Draconean look bigger and more threatening, so it's used as a signal of anger or in the face of danger. They will also do this as the equivalent of two humans having a staring contest; I didn't quite follow the explanation, but it has to do with blood flow to their wings and the fact that most Draconeans live in very cold mountains, so by spreading their wings they're risking hypothermia, and the first one to furl them has done the equivalent of blinking. I asked Kudshayn what they will do for their staring contests if they ever start living in warmer parts of the world, and he doesn't know. They definitely can't make a habit of it indoors; Draconean wings are much smaller proportional to their bodies than most dragons' (the ones who can fly, anyway; Draconeans can only glide), but they would still smash quite a lot of things in our houses if they extended them fully.

Wings drooping

Like a sigh. Audrey warned me that it's often a very subtle movement, but so are a lot of sighs.

Wings rattling

A kind of silent laugh. They don't really rattle, of course, because they aren't made of metal or anything hard, but that's the word both Audrey and Kudshayn use for it. He demonstrated for me and the sound is more like a leathery flutter, but since they both say "rattle," I'll go on using that word, even though it isn't really accurate.

So much of their body language is about wings. That makes sense. Their faces are less expressive than ours are, but we don't have wings to signal with, so it balances out in the end. Audrey taught me some other gestures, too, though.

Nostrils flaring

All Draconeans can control this, much better than most humans can (though there are some humans who can control it very well). For them it's like raising our eyebrows is for us. Audrey says that her grandmother, Lady Trent, thinks this is because they have a better sense of smell than we do, and so they have a biological instinct to flare their nostrils and breathe deeply as a way of investigating things, which means they also do it as a way of signaling curiosity. Draconean settlements must be much cleaner than our cities, or they would find being curious there very unpleasant.

Holding the muzzle shut

Equivalent to putting a finger on your lips; it means to hush. Draconeans also do this to each other, much more often than we put our fingers on other people's lips. Apparently Draconean nannies have to do it a lot to teach their charges to be quiet. (Their nannies are male! Only about twenty percent of Draconeans are male—I knew that before Audrey told me—and so they watch over the creches where hatchlings are raised.)

Hand reaching high

Like a human putting their hand on their heart to show sincerity. I read in one of Uncle's books that Draconeans worship the sun, which the book says is terrible idolatry and a sign of why the Anevrai (the ancient Draconeans) deserved to be overthrown, but I don't see that it makes much difference. And now I know why Audrey says so many things about the sun. Between that and the references to ships and sea things, I should write up notes on what she really means when she talks, because many of the things she says make no sense. This is probably because she had what Uncle calls a deplorable upbringing.

I'm sure there are more, but Audrey and Kudshayn both admitted they have a hard time thinking about these things, because they just take it so much for granted. I wonder if I could get enough to fill a book? Probably not, but I could also learn the rules of Draconean etiquette to make it longer.

I think there must be a need for such a thing. The staff here at Stokesley mostly avoid Kudshayn, and half of them are afraid of him. (Rebecca hides any time she thinks she hears him coming.) I can only imagine other people will react the same way when their delegation comes here next winter to talk about what's going to happen to their homeland. People, humans that is, will need to know how to interact with them. And that will be even more true if the Draconeans start establishing enclaves of people like Kudshayn who can live outside the mountains.

(Uncle chastised me yesterday for calling them "people" instead of "Draconeans." But that's the word Audrey uses, and she's dealt with them a lot more than he has, so I think she's probably right. I'll try to avoid it around him, though—I don't want him to think I'm being disobedient or ungrateful.)

Tablet V: "The Fledging Tablet"
translated by Audrey Camherst and Kudshayn

The time had come for the four siblings to undergo the rite of fledging. Hastu had promised it. He sought out a dream to consider the question of how they should be tested. In his sleep he considered it, during the times of noise, during the times of quiet.[13]

He woke and addressed the people, saying, "I have dreamt[14] of a sun in the sky and a cavern in the earth, of the sea ahead and the forest behind. Each of the four shall go in a different direction; each of the four shall have a separate trial." The people were much surprised, because it was the custom for clutches to undergo their trials together.

Hastu the *šiknas*[15] said, "Samšin will go to the east, where the sun has its birth. Ektabr will go to the west, where the sun descends into the caverns of the earth. Nahri will go to the south, where the forests grow tall. Imalkit will go to the north, where the waters[16] lap the

13 Day and night?—K
   I assume so. That's an unusual way of describing them.—AC
14 Strange that the dream is not repeated, according to the usual poetic custom.—K
15 Until we can arrive at a satisfactory gloss for this word, I think it would be best to leave it untranslated.—K
   Yes—though it annoys me that we can't figure it out.—AC
16 More geographical clues? There used to be cedar forests in southern Anthiope, and I suppose waters are to the north if you mean the Sea of Alsukir.—AC
   Or central Anthiope, and the Bay of Rójkat. If it was cannabis

shore. Each will journey until they meet their trial, and return if they can."

The four embraced each other with their wings.
Samšin said, "Be careful. Never before has a clutch been
sent out in four directions at once. But I believe this will
all be for the best: each of us must find our own strength,
so that when we come together again we will be stronger
still."

But Ektabr said, "Our strength is in each other. If we
are to be parted, then we must give one another tokens,
so that we will remain together even as we go in four directions at once." The others saw the wisdom of this, and
so each gave to each of the others a gift. Then they
parted.

Ektabr went to the west. For many days and many
nights he journeyed, across plains, across rivers, across
mountains, across forests. He came to an opening in the
ground. He said to himself, "Hastu had a vision of a cavern,
and so this is where I should go. But caverns are the mouths
of the earth; they eat up[17] what descends into them. How
can I return to my sisters, if I go into this cave?"

He remembered his gift from Imalkit. She had given
him a length of gut, many lengths tied end to end. He

they used to drug Hastu, that's more likely to be found in Tashal or
Zmayet. I looked it up in one of Uncle's books.—CF

So it's your uncle who has the unexpected interest in drugs?
You'll have to show me where that part of the library is.—AC

We shouldn't assume this refers to real geography at all. It might
just be symbolic. There's evidence in ancient sites of the colours
being associated with directions more generally: gold or yellow in
the east, black in the west, green in the south, blue in the north.—K

17 This suggests that in the ancient past, the Anevrai saw caves as
dangerous, rather than the source of refuge they are to us today.—K

wrapped one end around a stone at the mouth of the cave and unrolled the ball as he went, so that he could find his way out again.

The cave was filled with dangers. There were pits to fall into, pools to drown in, spiders who stretched their webs thickly across the way. But there were wonders also, beautiful forms of crystal and stone. Ektabr sat for a long time and considered these things, fixing them in his mind. He took a stone in his hand and made marks on the wall, images[18] of the beasts of the land and sky, which had never been seen in the depths of the earth before. Then he followed his cord out of the cave and into the light once more.

Imalkit went to the north. For many days and many nights she journeyed, across plains, across rivers, across mountains, across forests.[19] She came to a place of water. She said to herself, "Hastu had a vision of waters lapping the shore, and so this is where I should go. But waters are the edge of the earth; they drown whatever goes into them. How can I return to my siblings, if I go into this water?"

18 I thought rock art was done by early humans.—CF

So did I! This doesn't mean it wasn't, of course; both Anevrai and humans could have made markings on cave walls. But we're going to have to re-examine that now, and see if we can tell who created images in different places.—AC

Does your uncle have books on rock art? I am not very familiar with it. But if this is the origin of caves playing a role in Anevrai theology, it would make sense that the artwork in caves might be at least partly their doing.—K

19 I think we can take this part as formulaic, rather than an actual geographical description. Otherwise we'd have to find a starting point for them that is surrounded on all sides by plains, rivers, mountains, and forests, which seems unlikely.—AC

She remembered her gift from Nahri. She had given her a bundle of reeds, many strong reeds in a bunch. She took the reeds and tied them together so that they floated upon the water. Then she climbed upon her raft and went out.

The water was filled with dangers. There were storms, rough waves, creatures with many teeth to eat her alive. But there were wonders also, bright fish and the light upon the water. Imalkit played with them, dangling leaves from her raft to mislead them, using her shadow to make them flee. She made a trap to trail behind her raft to capture the dangerous ones. Then she spread her wings and let the wind carry her back to shore.

Nahri went to the south. For many days and many nights she journeyed, across plains, across rivers, across mountains, across forests. She came to a place of many trees. She said to herself, "Hastu had a vision of a forest, and so this is where I should go. But forests are the traps of the earth; they ensnare whatever goes into them. How can I return to my siblings, if I go into this forest?"

She remembered her gift from Samšin. She had given her a mace, a stone head on a [. . .][20] her. Then she went in among the trees.

The forest was filled with dangers. There were wild beasts, poisonous plants, branches that blocked the light of the sun. But there were wonders also, beautiful flowers, bright insects, abundant life on all sides. Nahri gathered up seeds; she gathered up nuts. She spoke to the animals and the trees, showing them patience and kind-

20 Too damaged to read.—K

ness, and they taught her their ways. Then she followed the deer to the edge of the forest once more.

Samšin went to the east. For many days and many nights she journeyed, across plains, across rivers, across mountains, across forests. She came to a dry place without water.[21] She said to herself, "Hastu had a vision of the place where the sun has its birth, and so this is where I should go. But there is nothing here. What have I come here to find?"

She remembered her gift from Ektabr. He had given her a prayer, words to recite in a strong voice. She recited them as she went forward.

The desert was empty. There was barren stone, barren dirt. There was nothing for Samšin to find. She walked on and on. She had nothing to drink, nothing to eat. She began to think she would never return to her siblings.

Then a shadow fell upon her from above. An *issur* descended toward her with its jaws spread. Samšin continued to recite her prayer. The *issur* landed in front of her and waited. Samšin continued to pray. She laid her hand upon the *issur*'s head; it bowed its head low. She thanked it and left the desert.

The four came back together. Ektabr told his sisters what he had seen under the earth. Imalkit told them of how she had tricked the creatures of the sea. Nahri told them what she had learned from the animals and trees. Samšin told them how the *issur* had lain quietly under her hand. She said, "Let us go to Hastu and tell him that we

---

21 Some part of Akhia, if the starting point is meant to be in Haggad? Or still just metaphor?—AC

have completed our rites. I think he will be much surprised."

And so they went back to their people. Hastu came to meet them, saying, "No one has ever undergone rites like yours, and come back with such things they have learned."

"That is your doing," Samšin said. The four gave thanks to the Ever-Moving, the Ever-Standing, the Light of the World, the ones who had given them life.

After that, the people followed the four who hatched from a single shell.

For the archives of the Sanctuary of Wings
written by Kudshayn, son of Ahheke, daughter of Iztam

I raise my hand to the sun, the glory of the sky, radiance of life. I touch my hand to the earth, the cradle of the world, bounty of comfort.

These are words I have recited, gestures I have carried out, ever since I was a hatchling. Never before now have I questioned them.

Sun, golden watcher: are you the Light of the World, the Maker of Above and Below, as known to my ancient foremothers? Earth, eternal stone: are you the Ever-Standing, the Foundation of All, whom they spoke of in their tales? What am I to make of the similarities between our religion today and that of the past—and what am I to make of the differences?

Where has the Ever-Moving gone, the Source of Wind? In the high reaches of the Mrtyahaima Mountains the wind's presence is inescapable, yet it has no role in our faith. The ancient tale speaks of it bringing forth creatures that might be our draconic kin, but our own story tells us that the sun made the wind and the wind took form as the first sisters; dragons later came from us. Likewise the origin of humans: are they the children of the Ever-Standing, as we are of the Light of the World? Or were they also made from us?

Questions such as these have troubled my brothers and sisters

ever since Lady Trent came among us, bearing word of the ancient past and scientific knowledge alike. Similar doubts have
plagued human clergy of many faiths, as they confront the possibility that their own ancestral tales do not match the evidence of
science. But this does not trouble me. Teslit and I have debated
these questions from the shell, and I hold to the words she gave
me: that religion and science offer different kinds of truth, which
serve different needs in my heart.

What I read in these tablets troubles me more. And Teslit is
not here to lay my uncertainties to rest.

Alone, I must confront evidence that our faith has *changed*. In
the iconography of ancient sites and the scattered prayers found
in tablets, we have found references whose meaning now becomes
clear: we have lost a god. Where once we worshipped three, now
there are only two.

What else has changed? What else have we lost, or added, or
altered beyond recognition?

And what truth can there be in our tales, of the sort I have held
on to all this time, if that truth proves itself mutable? Glorious
eye, do you truly watch over us all, from the elders to the newest
hatchling stretching her wings? Faithful heart, are you truly the
protector of our kind, giving wisdom to the physicians who saved
my sister's life? What hears my words when I write this prayer?
Do I err by neglecting the Ever-Moving, and how should I show
it reverence? We have no place for you in our ceremonies, Source
of Wind, and I do not know if we should.

What duty do we owe to the gods of our ancestors?

And how do we live with the possibility that those gods are not
our own?

From the notebook of Cora Fitzarthur

Kudshayn is a priest.

I didn't realize this because the only priests I know are magisters, and he does not dress like them or talk like them. Of course he would not, because he is not Segulist, but I didn't know how to recognize a Draconean priest. I asked him how to recognize one in the future, and he said they greet the sun every morning and bid it rest well every night, which I know he does, but I didn't know this was why. Since I won't always be around at dawn and sunset, though, this is not a reliable way of identifying priests, and I told him so. Then he said they wear a band of embroidered cloth around their wings, not really binding them shut, but sort of. I said, you don't wear that. He said he does sometimes, but only for ceremonies. So that is unhelpful, and I still don't know how to recognize a Draconean priest.

He was more helpful when I asked him what it means to be a priest. Apparently among Draconeans, priests and scribes are basically the same thing, so it's his job to keep records of important events and ideas. He's writing a record of what he and Audrey are doing here, but then he reassured me that he won't send it to their archives until after his work here is done. I think Uncle will be all right with that, but I'll check with him to be sure. (He's asked me to watch Kudshayn the same way I'm watching Audrey. I forgot to make a note of that.)

Then I asked Kudshayn if he thinks the sun can hear him saying hello and goodbye when it's a flaming ball millions of kilometers away. He laughed and said that no, he doesn't think the flaming ball can hear him, but the spiritual power it represents can. So I asked if he worships the idols from the story, the Ever-Moving, the Ever-Standing, and the Light of the World. (Uncle insists "idol" is the proper word for gods other than the God of Segulism, even though he doesn't believe in that god, either. Audrey said it's offensive to call other gods idols, though.) Kudshayn made a very confusing answer that I did not understand, but his wings tucked in tight when he said it, which means I was making him uncomfortable, so I didn't ask him to explain.

I wonder if Magister Ridson knows anything about Draconean religion? Probably not, but I could go to assembly with Mrs. Hilleck on Cromer and ask him then. Though that will make Mrs. Hilleck think I have become religious, and then she will start pestering me again to attend with her.

From the diary of Audrey Camherst

24 SEMINIS

I had a very sobering conversation with Kudshayn over breakfast this morning.

He was unusually quiet, even for him, and seemed to be studying the jam bowl for some inscrutable reason of his own. It turned out, though, that he was just thinking very deeply, and the jam happened to be in his path. Out of nowhere, he said, "What do you think this text is?"

I had no idea what he meant by that. He's read all the same bits I have, and we've discussed it more than once. The text is clearly a long narrative account, beginning with a creation myth and continuing into something genealogical, before telling the story of four siblings who—if I am reading the invocation correctly—eventually become culture heroes responsible for inventing various things like writing. Unless he'd suffered a head injury in the night, he couldn't possibly have forgotten that. And surely he knew I would have told him straightaway if I had some reason to think the text isn't what it looks like.

Kudshayn is not usually the sort to ask any question other than the one he means, but it seemed to me that was exactly what he had done. I said, "What do you mean?"

His claws wrapped delicately around the jam bowl, rotating it a few degrees. Lapsing into his own language, he said, "What do you think it will be? For us?"

I have never heard him sound so apprehensive. But I began to understand his uncertainty. Modern Draconeans have their own myths of how they began; it came as a great shock when Grandmama told them the Anevrai had a different one. Like when Albert Wedgwood came along and said, "I don't think God made us out of clay—I think we evolved, and probably from apes."

That particular shock was no longer new. But who knew what else might be lurking in these tablets? What other treasured beliefs of Draconean history might be smashed like the petrified eggs of their ancestors?

Or what might be added to them. It's easy to recognize Kudshayn's revered sun and earth in two of the entities that created the world and its species, but I don't know of any parallel in his religion to the Source of Wind. Judging by his unease, there isn't one—and that troubles him.

I said, "You're worried that what we read here will change things."

One claw-tip scraped unpleasantly against the silver of the bowl, and Kudshayn withdrew his hand. "Every piece of information we gain about the Anevrai changes things. That is the entire point of archaeological excavation, of the work you and I do: we seek to recover the knowledge that has been lost, rather than resting content with what we already know. But this text is . . . more."

Normally I'm good at reading between the lines of what he says, but this time I didn't follow. "How so?"

Kudshayn fell silent for a while, and I bit down on the urge to prod him. Finally he said, "I have read a great deal of human literature." (An understatement if I ever heard one.) "I have done my best to understand the character of the different human nations. And so, for a time, I asked the people I met what one book they would recommend to me as representative of their people. For the Yelangese, it was *The Tale of the Sky*. For the Vidwathi, *The Great Song*. For Scirlings, *Selethryth*."

"All the great epics of the world," I said. In the depths of my mind, the limp sails of my thoughts began to stir at the first touch of a breeze.

He nodded soberly. "And the Yelangese . . . I asked at one point why they consider the Ruxin to be part of Yelang. Not just within their borders—because that is a matter of politics—but why, despite the differences in their languages, the differences in their culture, they say the Ruxin are simply a subject population, not a subject nation. Do you know what the man I asked said?"

It was a rhetorical question, but Kudshayn waited anyway, watching me, until I had shaken my head.

"He said, 'It is because they have no literature. What story do they have that is the equal of *The Tale of the Sky*?'"

The sails in my mind belled out before the wind. "You are asking if these tablets could be your national epic."

"We have stories," Kudshayn said. "I do not think there are any people in the world, human or Draconean, who do not. But we do not have a story that defines us. No tale that lies at the roots of our civilization, such that we can say any person of that society who professes to be literate has read it and holds it in their heart."

What could I say to that? It wasn't the right time to point out all the flaws in what he was saying—the idea that a single story can define a civilization, that *Selethryth* is what gives Scirland the right to call itself a nation, rather than a breakaway bit of Eiverheim, a crumb with delusions of grandeur. People give weight to that sort of thing, no matter how many holes you can poke in the idea.

And even if I could dismiss the political aspect, what of the personal side? No one can deny anymore that Draconeans are real . . . but they can and do deny that Draconeans are *people*, that behind the scales and wings and long, toothy muzzles sit minds every bit as sharp and creative and full of feeling as ours. Thousands of years separate Kudshayn from the Anevrai scribe who carved that tale into wet clay, but if his people could lay claim to a story the equal of *The Tale of the Sky* and other human epics, that would give them another way to assert their—well, their *humanity*, even though that's the wrong word to use.

All I could think to say was, "What you'll do with it going forward, I don't know. But I *do* know that if we don't get back to work, your people won't have anything to work with—so let's get to it." I suppose that was good enough, because Kudshayn laughed and we headed for the library, and after that everything seemed fine.

It isn't, though. I'm not religious the way Kudshayn is; it's hard to imagine how I would react if, oh, someone discovered there used to be thirteen commandments instead of twelve. And it throws into sharp relief how different his own people are from their Anevrai ancestors. I'm just as different from my Scirling ancestors as depicted in *Selethryth* . . . but Scirlings aren't struggling to find their place in the world, aren't struggling to convince people they *deserve* one.

When I guessed that Gleinleigh wanted this translation published in time for the congress, I was only thinking about book sales and fame. But I'm starting to realize its effects might go well beyond that.

Tablet VI: "The Darkness Tablet"
translated by Audrey Camherst and Kudshayn

A year and a day passed after the rite of fledging. The people prospered, and the siblings were not parted. Together they grew strong, together they grew generous, together they grew clever, together they grew wise. In the hunts [. .][22]
  [. .] with Tayyit they went [. .]
  [. .] the four [. .]
Then, as Peli had dreamed, the mountain shook, the grasses trembled, the stone faltered in its rolling, the river flowed backward in its course. The Light of the World vanished.[23] Without warning it disappeared; without word it went away. Darkness covered the land for the first time.[24]

---

22 I want to hunt down whoever Gleinleigh had conserve these tablets and shake him. I don't know for *sure* that it's his fault these parts are too damaged to read, but it's easier to blame a person than a few thousand years of time.—AC

23 A solar eclipse?—K

  The part about the river flowing backward makes me think it was something more like an earthquake. A volcanic eruption, maybe? A plume of ash could be said to blot out the sun.—AC

24 The first night, I think. Which explains why the previous reference was to "the time of noise" and "the time of quiet."—K

  Wait, they didn't have night before? Or do you mean everything up until now somehow all happened in a day? No, because it said before that the siblings grew to full size in a year. You can't have a full year without night.—CF

  In mythology, anything is possible. I've read stories where someone was raised to adulthood by a birch tree, or pissed all the oceans of the world into being.—AC

The people wailed their terror to the skies, to the earth, to the waters, to the silence. From the vault of the heavens, the *nadjait*[25] looked down, and they hungered for the world. The Maker of Above and Below had kept them at bay, but it was gone. There was nothing to protect the people, and many were lost in that new darkness.

Brave Samšin brought the people together; with her siblings she brought [. .]

The star demons descended with their ravening mouths, but Samšin struck them down. They surrounded her until she could not be seen, and the people feared she was lost, but Samšin feared neither the darkness nor its creatures. Five times, six times, seven times she swung her mace, until the star demons fled in fear of her.

Now the people were together. Cunning Imalkit struck stone against stone and made light. She said to the people, "We can fool the star demons. Let us make a large fire, and they will think it is the Maker of Above and Below, so they will not attack us." Everyone gathered wood, and they made a large fire. The star demons flinched back and did not approach.

But without the Maker of Above and Below, plants did not grow, and the world was not green. Gentle Nahri showed the people what things could be eaten, from the

---

25 In the royal library in Sarmizi there's a tablet that uses this word—*nadjait* is ibn Oraib's best guess at how to transliterate it.—AC

Have you read Erica Pantel's article on that tablet? She suggests that it may indicate a kind of star demon, based on a fragmentary prayer from the Library of Shukura that treated the night of the new moon as exceptionally dangerous.—K

No, I haven't! We'll use that translation for now, then.—AC

worms of the earth to the tender bark of the pine. They [. . .] Because of her the people did not starve.

Ektabr prayed to the Ever-Moving, the Source of Wind. Pious Ektabr prayed to the Ever-Standing, the Foundation of All. Faithful Ektabr prayed to the Light of the World, begging for its return. Wisdom came to him in the night.

He came to his siblings and spoke, saying, "There is a fourth power in the world, a fourth power that is not in the world. It is the shadow(?) of light(?), the starvation(?) of life(?), the undoing(?) of doing(?).[26] This power has taken the Maker of Above and Below. It is the thing we do not know, and I fear it."

They [. . .] with the people [. . .]

"Why has this power taken the Light of the World?" Imalkit asked, but no one could answer.

"Where can we find this power?" Nahri asked, but no one could answer.

"How can we defeat this power?" Samšin asked, but [. .]

Ektabr spoke, saying, "Let us seek out Hastu, who [. .]"

Together they went, for the sake of the people.

---

26 I'm not even going to pretend I'm confident in that translation— hence all the question marks.—AC

It seems reasonable to me. If nothing else, the text clearly seems to be indicating some kind of oppositional structure, contrasting this fourth power against the Light of the World, or maybe against all three together.—K

So . . . what is that fourth power?—CF

I do not know.—K

From the notebook of Cora Fitzarthur

Audrey and Kudshayn talked today about whether there were any volcanic eruptions in the early days of Draconean civilization, or just before it got started. Ones big enough to make it seem like the sun had gone away. Or a solar eclipse. If there were, then the epic might be describing something real.

Audrey is very frustrated that Uncle has made her and Kudshayn promise not to share information about their work with anyone, even to ask questions. I know this because she made a very obvious point of talking about how frustrated she is, right in front of me. When I asked her why—why she was being obvious, that is, not why she was frustrated—she sighed dramatically and said, "Oh, I was just wishing there was someone who *hadn't* promised."

She meant me, of course, though when I said that to her she just winked and then went to clean up for dinner. She wants me to go behind Uncle's back and look into volcanic eruptions.

If I asked him, I'm sure he would say that no, I'm not allowed to share information with anyone, either. The only reason he hasn't told me that already is because it never occurred to him that I would write to anyone—he thinks there's nobody for me to write to, and normally he's correct.

But I want to know if it was an eclipse or an eruption or something else Audrey and Kudshayn haven't thought of. I want to know if the epic is describing something real this time. (Why can't it just be one or the other? All made up, or all real? It seems to me like that would be much more useful. Then you would know whether you were supposed to be entertained or educated by what you were reading.)

If I don't ask Uncle, then I'm not technically disobeying him.

I know perfectly well that this is a loophole. I'm already thinking about how to post the letter from Lower Stoke so that he won't know I sent it and none of the servants can tell him, because if he has me reading Audrey's and Kudshayn's letters to make sure they aren't breaking their promise, then he wouldn't want me doing it myself. I know this is dishonest.

I'm going to do it anyway.

From: Annabelle Himpton, Lady Plimmer
To: Marcus Fitzarthur, Lord Gleinleigh

6 Floris
Priorfield, Greffen

Dear Marcus,

I have tried to be patient, but weeks have gone by and it has become quite apparent that you are insensible to your duties to the neighbourhood. Surely, I thought, Lord Gleinleigh is not so much a part of this careless modern age as to ignore his responsibility to make his guests known to local society—but it is all too clear that you are indeed a modern sort, keeping entirely to yourself what ought to be the common pleasure of your neighbours.

You may not have any care for such "out-of-date" proprieties, but I do. I have therefore determined to host a dinner, with dancing to follow. You are invited, as is your ward (twenty years old and still not out? Whatever can you be thinking?), and of course your guests. Yes, I mean both of them. Miss Camherst has been seen in town, but she has not come to call on me once! I understand the child was raised half feral on a ship, but she was presented to Society some years ago and really ought to know better. Naturally I expect no such thing of your other guest; indeed, I hardly know what to expect of him at all. But the neighbourhood of Lower Stoke has never played host to a Draconean before, nor are they likely to do so again in what remains of my lifetime, so we must not squander this opportunity.

I will send my girl around tomorrow to speak with your

housekeeper about suitable food for the Draconean. I expect
your party to arrive promptly at six o'clock on the evening of
the nineteenth. Should you fail to show, I think you will find
that the people of Lower Stoke will not soon forget or forgive
your selfishness in hiding your guests away from us all.

Cordially,
Annabelle Himpton
Lady Plimmer

For the archives of the Sanctuary of Wings
written by Kudshayn, son of Ahheke, daughter of Iztam

I touch my hand to the earth, which once was called the Ever-Standing, Foundation of All, creator—if we are correctly interpreting the word *āmu*—of humankind.

My hatching outside the Sanctuary means that I have spent as much of my life among humans as among my own kind. I know more of their ways than any other of our people, and there are many humans whom I call friend.

Yet I am constantly aware that in their eyes—those of humanity as a whole, not those I am close to—I bear the weight of the ancient past. The slow pressure of time has deformed the recollection of history, both in human memory and our own, but my foremothers are known around the world as cruel tyrants who oppressed and enslaved their kind. Even those who do not wear the red mask of Hadamists often see me—see my scales and my wings—and recall that ancestral hatred.

I fear Hadamists less than I fear those who hide behind a mask of moderation. Those attack without warning, with word or with deed, and against them it is harder to defend.

If there is one common thread between the various stories of our origins, however, it is this: that our two species cannot be separated. Whether we played a role in creating humans or they played a role in creating us, we have been interconnected since the beginning. It is only in recent ages, when my people hid themselves away, that we have grown apart.

Until more are hatched outside the Sanctuary and grow to better health, the duty of bridging that gap will fall heavily upon me. Infinite stone, give me the patience to fulfill that duty well. Teach me to understand the hearts of the people this tale says you once made.

It is not their mammalian nature that puzzles me most, nor their strange technologies. It is the complexity of their world: their numbers so numerous, like flakes of snow upon the mountaintops, the customs and laws necessary to keep themselves in order, and the variation of these things between one land and another. I am soon to enact a human ritual, a Scirling custom of attending a meal at the house of a local dignitary; we will participate even though none of those invited from this household wish to attend, because that is what custom requires. And I must learn from Audrey the proper behaviours for such an event—behaviours that are not the same as those practiced in Yelang or Tser-nga.

There has been no such thing for my people within living memory, or even the middle past. We have been few in number, single in society. My own kindred find me strange when I visit the Sanctuary, because my behaviour has been shaped by my time outside of it; this, as much as my physical difficulties, is the sacrifice my mother made on my behalf when she chose to lay her clutch beyond the Sanctuary's walls. Teslit, too frail to travel, finds her own species more alien than the Yelangese among whom she has spent her entire life. If we succeed in spreading beyond our borders, in hatching our children in far-distant lands, they will become strangers to each other, not only in acquaintance but in culture, as Tser-zhag are to Thiessois, Vidwathi to Vystrani.

And so I find myself asking again: to what extent were these ancients my people? Audrey would not call the ancient humans of southern Anthiope any kin of hers. Is it only by contrast with humankind that we consider the Anevrai to be our ancestors?

I began this work of translation expecting to feel a greater bond with my ancient foremothers as a result. Its effect has been quite the opposite.

Precious earth, dark stillness, give me something to hold on to. Shelter me from this storm of change. In time I must emerge once more into the light of action, but for now let me rest in your embrace, protected from my own doubts.

From the diary of Audrey Camherst

19 FLORIS

I cannot believe that Lord Gleinleigh is forcing us to go to this dinner at Priorfield. Well, yes, I can; I've heard stories from relatives, the ones who live in Scirland all the time, about the way the countryside can be. Lady Plimmer is of Grandmama's generation, and apparently she is the local dragon, the sort of person you cross at your peril. Lord Gleinleigh outranks her and has more money to boot, so if he were to refuse her, she couldn't ruin him in Falchester society or break his fortune or anything like that . . . but he might find living here a good deal less pleasant: uncooperative merchants down in the village, inferior produce delivered to his house, delayed repairs on the road to the estate, vandalism by local children, that sort of thing. And while I believe he could brazen it out if he wanted to, in the end it's much less effort to simply bow to the dragon every once in a while and do as she says.

So we're to go to a dinner, all four of us: Lord Gleinleigh, Cora, myself, and Kudshayn. He's the real point of all this affair, of course; it hasn't escaped my attention that I escaped Lady Plimmer's attention until a Real Live Draconean arrived in the neighbourhood. Which means hours spent watching Kudshayn be treated like the zoo has come to town, and being saved from the same fate myself only because a "lizard-man" is far more exotic than a mere half-Erigan woman. Cora will loathe it, and I don't think Lord Gleinleigh will enjoy it much more; that's four people made miserable, just so Lady Plimmer can brag that she had a Draconean at her dinner table.

I have the earl's assurance, though, that when this is over, he won't force me or Kudshayn to do anything social at all for at least a month. The next several tablets seem to involve the siblings descending into the underworld to rescue the Maker of Above and Below; I'd far rather be reading about that than sitting through a tedious dinner.

LATER

I think I would cheerfully toss Lady Plimmer overboard if I had to spend more than an evening in her company, but must for the sake of my conscience rescind some of the suspicions I directed her way before. (Ugh, I'm even beginning to write like she talks.) She may be a fossilized old biddy who doesn't understand why we can't go back to the good old days of the turn of the century, but she had more up her sleeve than simply the desire to brag about her draconic dinner guest.

It was all set to start off exactly as badly as I had feared. Lady Plimmer had invited everybody who is anybody in the neighbourhood, none of whom had ever set eyes on a Draconean in their lives; all they know of Kudshayn's people is drawn from newspapers, magazines, and general gossip. They speculated as to whether he could understand them (with him standing right there!), and then fell about in utter shock when he spoke. They asked me how I taught him to do that—as if Kudshayn had not learned to speak Scirling when I was still in swaddling clothes! They marveled at his clothing, not quite coming out and saying that they were marveling to see that he wore it at all—as if modesty is something only humans understand!

And then one fellow (Mr. Bradford, the local barrister) correctly identified Kudshayn's high-collared robe as being a modified Yelangese style. "Yes," Kudshayn said, tipping him a little Yelangese-flavored bow. "Many of my people have visited Yelang, and we have found that this style is far more convenient to us than an Anthiopean-style shirt, as we can fasten it at the neck and then leave the back open to more easily accommodate our wings."

Mr. Bradford opened his mouth again, and I swear to you, diary, I *saw* the question rising up from his throat. *Do you also have to accommodate your tail?* People always think Draconeans have tails, and they *always* ask.

But! This is where, against my will, I began to like Lady Plimmer. Because one advantage of visiting the house of a fossilized old biddy is, she has absolutely no tolerance for impropriety—and asking a guest about his hidden body parts is *decidedly* improper. Plus—as I know well from Grandmama— once a lady reaches a certain age, she has no compunctions about what *she* says or does. So I had the distinct pleasure of watching our hostess lay into Mr. Bradford until he was red-faced and shuffling like a schoolboy (and he's sixty if he's a day). And after that, people were a good deal more circumspect about what they said to—and around—Kudshayn.

Things really got interesting later on, though, when we had all sat down to dinner. (Starting with the fact that she'd thoughtfully provided a stool for Kudshayn, so he needn't endure the discomfort of a chair back.) I expected Lady Plimmer to be one of those types who forbids talk of politics at her table, but no sooner had the first course been laid out than she turned to Kudshayn and embarked upon the most extraordinary speech. I won't be able to re-create it word for word, but it went something like this:

"Mr. Kudshayn—is that an acceptable fashion for addressing you?" (Kudshayn said that it was.) "Thank you. I confess I knew little to nothing about your people prior to your arrival in the neighbourhood, but it is a poor hostess indeed who invites a guest to dinner without first ensuring that she will be able to make proper conversation when he comes. I have therefore done a good deal of reading in the last few weeks—a task made easier, I must say, by this congress scheduled to take place in Falchester next winter, as it has persuaded any number of publishers to put out books and educational pamphlets on the subject. Of course a great many of these are of inferior quality, but I acquired some that have been well spoken of and put myself to work reading them."

(Here Kudshayn said something polite and noncommittal. I could tell he was just as baffled as I was by her manner, which owed something to the behaviour of a sheepdog very determinedly herding its charge toward an unidentifiable destination.)

"My impression," Lady Plimmer said, "and do correct me if I am wrong, is that this congress was originally meant to be a simple vote in the Synedrion to determine what would become of our caeliger base in your homeland, which was established as part of the original Sanctuary Alliance. No, no, I am misremembering already: it was the second Sanctuary Alliance, or the revised alliance—there is a deplorable lack of consistency in how it is referred to—the agreement that was formed later, not the early and haphazard thing Miss Camherst's grandmother helped to broker." (Here she nodded to me.) "With of course no offense intended to Miss Camherst or her lady grandmother, as I am sure it was difficult to broker anything at all under the circumstances, what with nearly freezing to death and the shock of finding out your people were real and so forth—and for all her skills as a naturalist, I cannot say she is renowned as a diplomat. But it would be impolite to recall how many countries she has been deported from. Where was I?"

(At this point I believe the entire table was gaping at her, and a team of expert navigators armed with all the latest maps could not have answered her question: we were united in being wholly lost.)

"Oh, yes—the caeliger base." She had her sails trimmed and was off again. "My reading has been most educational, Mr. Kudshayn, but it has left me with a number of questions. I was hoping you might oblige me by answering a few of them. To begin with, do your people not want Scirling military protection any longer? Do you now favour your alliance with Yelang over your connections with Scirland? I cannot see how it is that your people can expect to thrive as an independent nation, not after so long in isolation and with so little wealth, as I do not imagine yaks are terribly profitable. And is it true that you have ambitions to expand? I confess I do not quite understand how you can do so, since my impression is that you are not able to survive in other regions, though of course your presence here at my dinner table suggests that is not as true as I have been led to believe. But Scirland is not Akhia, and is it in fact the case that you wish to re-establish your homeland there? How do you expect to do that? Are your people quite warlike? Our Scriptures tell us your ancestors were, but then my great-grandfather was a sheep farmer, so it is folly to assume the apple would fall so close to a tree thousands of years in the past."

It took me several moments to realize she had finished speaking. All around the table, people exchanged uncertain looks. Poor Kudshayn: he has been asked all those questions and more in the past, and although he is by preference a scholar, he has to serve as an ambassador for his people wherever he goes. But I don't think he has ever been asked all those questions at *once* before, all in a jumble, so that it was hardly possible to remember where Lady Plimmer's interrogation had begun.

Kudshayn bravely sallied forth. "We are of course grateful for the protection we have received from both the Scirling and Yelangese governments since the alliance was formed. As you said, many people remember the tale told in your Scriptures, and hold us accountable for what sins our ancestors may have committed."

I held my breath, waiting to see if anyone would call out his careful phrasing. Modern Draconeans tell their own stories of the Downfall, which make the Anevrai out to be far better and humans far worse than our Scriptures and other remembrances do. Arguments over the truth of it have been raging for decades. But Cora told me Lady Plimmer is not on good terms with the local magister, so he was not at the table, and no one else took up the cause.

"The caeliger base was quite useful for defending us in the early days," Kudshayn said. "But we cannot live within the shelter of another country's wings forever. The longer the base remains there, the easier it becomes to view the Sanctuary as a Scirling colony."

"Better that than a Yelangese colony," Lady Plimmer said with a sniff. Being of Grandmama's generation, she remembers the days when we weren't on such friendly terms with that country.

Kudshayn refrained from pointing out that he's spent more than half his life in Yelang. "We have no desire to be anyone's colony. For us, this congress represents our people taking our first formal steps into the world of international diplomacy—not as a protectorate of other nations, but as a nation in our own right."

"To what end? What is it your people hope for?"

"Not conquest," he said. "It is true that we wish to expand—but that is because, for us to safely travel the world, we must bear our hatchlings in other lands. If we remain in the Sanctuary, we remain trapped."

I added, "And as long as they're trapped in the Sanctuary, where very few people see them, it's all too easy for them to remain the monsters of legend. Did your readings mention, Lady Plimmer, that only two countries class an attack against a Draconean as equivalent to assaulting a human being? Scirland and Yelang. Everywhere else in the world, it's on a par with cruelty to an animal."

Lady Plimmer blanched, one hand rising to her breast. "Oh, my dear—how dreadful! And quite unacceptable. How anyone could speak with a courteous and erudite creature such as Mr. Kudshayn and believe him to be a mere animal is quite beyond me. Not to mention the beautiful artwork the ancients made; the most my cat has ever achieved is an intriguing tangle of yarn. I have considered purchasing an antiquity of some sort to decorate the drawing room—just a small piece, you understand, nothing ostentatious. What is the best way to go about doing that?"

Kudshayn gave me an infinitesimal nod. It's a sore point for them, watching people like Lady Plimmer (not to mention Lord Gleinleigh) buy up artifacts from his people's past. But at the same time, those artifacts are scattered across the world, in such quantity that even if the Draconeans could afford to gather all those things themselves, they would fill the entire valley of the Sanctuary from one mountain wall to the other. Kudshayn saves his battles for the important pieces—things like this epic—instead of trying to stop the whole trade, which would only drive it further underground. When it comes to the standard answer, he'd rather I be the one to parrot it.

I dabbed at my lips with my napkin and said, "With caution, Lady Plimmer. Some countries, Scirland included, have laws about the excavation and sale of Draconean antiquities, but those are by no means watertight. Reputable auction houses like Emmerson's should provide what's called a provenance, a document telling you the ownership history of anything they sell. You should be very suspicious of anything that says the object was acquired from a private collector in Gillae—that's a red flag that it was stolen or illegally excavated."

"My goodness! I certainly would not want to associate myself with any criminal activities. Thank you so much for warning me, my dear, and for the recommendation to Emmerson's. I had been thinking about approaching—what was his name, Marcus? That fellow you have bought things from. Dorrick or some such."

"Joseph Dorak?" I offered up, all innocence.

I can hardly say I was surprised when Lady Plimmer confirmed the name. Dorak's legitimate business is a fig leaf for the biggest antiquities smuggling enterprise in Scirland. No, the shock came a moment later, when Lady Plimmer said, "I must say, Marcus, your expedition to Akhia seems to have inspired you to turn over a new leaf. Why, I would have sworn the sun would rise in the west before you had a single kind word to say about Draconeans, much less allowed one to set foot in your house."

This time the silence felt like the instant between the firing of a gun, and the moment when the bullet strikes.

Lord Gleinleigh cleared his throat. "Lady Plimmer, you must have misunderstood me—"

"Oh, I can't imagine that's true. My eyesight is not what it once was, but my memory remains as sharp as ever. This was about five years ago, I think. Magister Ridson chastised you for collecting so many Draconean antiquities, and you said—"

"What I said then has no bearing on the present moment," Lord Gleinleigh said in the loud voice of a man who's hoping to drown out the next words if he can't cut them off entirely. "It is quite discourteous of you, Lady Plimmer, to bring up past unpleasantness like that, when it is clearly over and done with."

She apologized, while I sat there with that hot-and-cold feeling all over my skin, the way you do when you've just had a nasty jolt and don't yet know what to do. What Lady Plimmer said . . . she didn't use the word, but she as good as called him a Calderite.

And Lotte saw him talking to Mrs. Kefford.

And Aaron Mornett came to his house late that one night.

I simply don't know what to make of this. If Lord Gleinleigh really is a Calderite, why on earth would he recruit *me* to translate the tablets, instead of Mornett? I can't persuade myself it's because Mornett tried and failed. He's capable of the work, and far more congenial to such views. Whereas I am as far from a Calderite as any human is likely to get, so I don't see how involving me would suit Lord Gleinleigh at all.

And more to the point, why would he suggest hiring a Draconean as well? Calderites think the ancient past is fascinating, but preferred when it was *in* the past, rather than being inconveniently present and alive and complaining about their ancestral ruins being looted to decorate places like Stokesley.

The last thing they would ever do is invite a Draconean to come and lay claim to an important relic like this one.

But then again . . . every time Lord Gleinleigh shows concern for Draconean sensibilities, it rings false. Or no, not false—that isn't fair. Stiff, I should say. Unpracticed, at the very least. Which I chalked up to him being uneasy around a two-meter dragon-winged creature with a muzzle full of sharp teeth; most humans are, until they get used to it. But what if it's because he was hiding something?

I got an answer of sorts a little while later; I'm just not sure if I believe it. We couldn't leave immediately after dinner without offending our hostess, but fortunately she doesn't have turn-of-the-century notions about how people should entertain themselves at that point—or if she does, she doesn't enforce them. Cora got drawn into conversation with a young lady named Miss Simpson, who I think is the closest thing she has to a friend in the neighbourhood, and I lost sight of Kudshayn. Imagine how delighted I wasn't, then, when Lord Gleinleigh caught me almost immediately and drew me aside.

Did I say he was stiff? I might have been forgiven for thinking he had a belaying pin stuffed up his backside. "Please forgive me, Miss Camherst," he said, as if a dentist were extracting the words from his mouth one by one. "I confess that I have not always harboured generous attitudes toward the Draconean species, but you must not think that Kudshayn is at all unwelcome at Stokesley. I value very highly the work he is doing."

It obviously cost his pride a great deal to say that, but I could only give him so much credit for it, especially when he said "the Draconean species" rather than "the Draconean people." And even more so when he went on to say, "You know that I would have faced down those Hadamists for his sake, that day at the airfield, if matters had not taken such a violent turn."

My hackles immediately went up. I haven't forgotten that he tried to get between me and Hallman . . . but why point to that as proof of good intentions, when nothing much came of it? Unless the entire reason Gleinleigh stepped forward in the first place, or rather tried to, was because he wanted to show off how friendly he is toward Draconeans. Gleinleigh doesn't strike me as the heroic type; I think he would have crumpled like wet paper the moment something went wrong. But even the attempt would have made him look good.

I managed not to say any of that, and I *hope* it didn't show on my face. I said, "Thank you, Lord Gleinleigh—but I'm not the one you should be taking pains to reassure. Or have you already spoken to Kudshayn?" (I knew he had not, because he came to me straightaway.)

"I have not," he said, even more stiffly, "but I will. Assuming you can tell me where—"

His unfinished question was cut short by a rattling crash from elsewhere in the house. We all stampeded to see what had caused it, and discovered that Miss Simpson's friend Miss Ashworth was the reason Kudshayn had gone missing. They were in the ballroom, and a whole line of chairs that had been set along the wall were now strewn across the floor.

Kudshayn apologized profusely to Lady Plimmer as soon as she appeared, while Miss Ashworth, failing to suppress giggles, tried to restore the chairs to order. "What happened?" Lady Plimmer asked—I have never heard two words sound so much like two blocks of ice.

"I was trying to teach him to dance!" the irrepressible Miss Ashworth said.

Kudshayn's bows were reverting to Yelangese style the

more of them he made. "I am afraid that I lost my balance. In my attempt to restore it, I—ah—"

He had spread his wings, because that's what Draconeans do when they're off-balance. Miss Ashworth tried to urge him to do it again—safely away from the chairs—but at that point Lord Gleinleigh had had enough, and he got us all out the door in a tick, rudeness be damned.

So now I am back at Stokesley. I'm pretty sure Gleinleigh still hasn't spoken to Kudshayn, and he said he's leaving for town again tomorrow. Which he tried to sell as him clearing out so we could have some nice quiet time to work, but it's hard not to read that as him running away from the awkwardness.

There's certainly enough to run away from. He may claim to be a reformed Calderite, but now I am looking at everything he's done since I came here and seeing it in a new, much less pleasant light. His insistence that we not share any information outside this house . . . I don't know what purpose that might serve, apart from the obvious one of making it a grander reveal when we publish our translation, but if he wants secrecy, then I want insurance. I think I shall make copies of all our work, just to be on the safe side.

(And oh, Lady Plimmer. No one so concerned for propriety and courtesy could possibly have done that on accident. The old battle-axe may talk sweetly, but she sharpened her knives for Gleinleigh a long time ago, and she wanted me and Kudshayn to know just whose house we've been living in.)

Tablet VII: "The Samšin Tablet"
translated by Audrey Camherst and Kudshayn

Hastu spoke, wise Hastu, clear-sighted Hastu, Hastu the *šiknas*. He said, "This was foreseen in a dream long ago, before your hatching. The river of Ektabr has drowned the sun; the stone of Imalkit has crushed the sun; the grasses of Nahri have ensnared the sun; the mountain of Samšin has devoured the sun. The Light of the World is in the underworld now, and unless one of you goes to retrieve it, we will be caught in darkness forever."[27]

The people were outraged to hear that the four were responsible. They took up their stones; they took up their clubs. But they could not bear to strike those upon whom they had depended for so long.

Samšin said, "If the Light of the World is in the underworld, we must certainly retrieve it. All four of us should go."

But Hastu said, "No, because if all four of you are lost, then the people will be without protection. Only one will go, and the other three will stay to keep the horrors of the darkness at bay."

Samšin was the bravest of the four, and the strongest.

---

27 Another stylistic shift here, though not as marked as the one between the first two tablets and the Dream Tablet.—K

Yes. More like this and the material about the siblings' birth and childhood were written by two people telling stories in the same mode, whereas the Creation Tablet and the Genealogy Tablet were written by someone else telling another type of story entirely.—AC

She said, "Then I will go, if you will show me where the gate of the underworld stands."

The people wailed at her words, but their fear of losing the sun was greater than their fear of losing Samšin. Her sisters and her brother said, "If you must go by yourself, you will not go alone." They gave her gifts: Nahri gave her food for her journey, Imalkit gave her a torch to light the way, and Ektabr gave her a prayer.

Hastu led Samšin to a ravine deeper than any other. Ten leagues, eleven leagues, twelve leagues deep was this abyss; it stretched to the depths of the earth. He left her there. With her food and her torch and her prayer she descended.

She came to the gate of the underworld. It was made from the bones of *issur*,[28] bound with strips of *āmu* skin. Samšin knocked at it, and the *lizma*,[29] the gatekeeper of the underworld, answered. The *khashetta*[30] said, "What living creature seeks to enter the underworld, and why?"

She answered him with her wings spread. "I am Samšin, sun-gold, hatched from a single shell. I have come to retrieve the Light of the World."

"You may enter," the gatekeeper said, "but you may not return." It opened the gate for her. Samšin entered the underworld.

---

28 Given the rapid breakdown of dragon bones, this argues against interpreting *issur* as an archaic term for such creatures.—K

   It's the gate to the underworld. I don't think it has to obey the rules of normal biology.—AC

29 Untranslatable, at least for now. Some kind of demon?—K

30 Also untranslatable. It sounds like this is the same creature as the *lizma*. Why two different words?—AC

   I think I have seen the word *khashetta* before, but I'm not sure where. Maybe the *lizma* is a type of *khashetta*?—K

She came into a chamber filled with broken eggshells. All around her she heard the thin cries of hatchlings, but she saw nothing alive. It was the place of hatchlings who die in the egg, because they cannot survive the place they are laid. She saw in front of her a many-coloured shell like the one her clutch had come from. She said, "We should not have lived to hatch. But we did, and I must find the Light of the World."

She continued on to a chamber stained with blood. All around her she heard the screams of people being torn apart, but she saw nothing alive. It was the place of people killed by the beasts of the world. She felt over her the shadow of the *issur*[31] she found in the desert, the *issur* that had bent its head to her hand. She said, "It should have killed me that day. But it did not, and I must find the Light of the World."

She continued on to a chamber awash in salt water like the sea. All around her she heard the wailing of people, but she saw nothing alive. It was the place of those who have been undone by those they trusted. She felt a chill in her heart. She said, "I am still alive; my sisters are still alive; my brother is still alive. And I must find the Light of the World."

She came to the *fettra* that guards the deepest abyss. The *khashetta*[32] snarled at her, but she offered it the food Nahri had given her. It ate the food and was quiet.

Beyond the *fettra* was a tunnel. Imalkit's torch lit the

---

31 Mentioning that incident while she's in this chamber at least suggests that *issur* are beasts of some kind.—AC

32 Now I'm confident that both this and the *lizma* are types of *khashetta*. Whatever those are.—AC

Underworld demons of some kind, it would seem.—K

way. It became a tunnel too small for her to spread her wings. It became a tunnel too small for her to stand. Samšin crawled through and found herself in the presence of the Endless Maw,[33] the Crown of the Abyss. It had the Maker of Above and Below in a cage.

Samšin offered it the prayer Ektabr had taught her. She said, "I am Samšin, the sun-gold, hatched from a single shell. I have come to retrieve the Light of the World."

"You have entered," the Crown of the Abyss said, "but you may not return. A cavern may give up what it has eaten, the sea may give up what it has drowned, a forest may give up what it has trapped, but the underworld does not give up anything it takes."

Bold Samšin lifted her mace, saying, "My people need the Light of the World. Without it they starve; without it they wander in darkness. Without the Maker of Above and Below, the star demons prey upon them from the sky. For their sake, I cannot accept what you say."

---

33 The fourth power Ektabr mentioned? The structure of the two names certainly suggests an entity on par with the three gods described before.—K

    Do you remember the trouble Shamikha bint Kaabir had with that prayer tablet from Wenggara? The one that kept using the mouth determinative, only the text around it seemed to have nothing to do with language or anything else that determinative normally signals? I'd have to look at the transcription again to be sure, but I have a sneaking suspicion it all makes a *lot* more sense if you assume that sign is actually an oblique way of referencing this entity, the Endless Maw.—AC

    A kind of taboo or superstition against giving its name in full? That is entirely possible. Especially since, if memory serves, that tablet belongs to a much later period than these; the taboo might have developed after this was scribed.—K

The Crown of the Abyss sent its many-legged *khashetta*[34] against Samšin. They were the ones that bite at the heels of cowards; against brave Samšin they could do nothing. She swept them aside, four struck down with each swing of her arm. The *khashetta* scurried back into their holes.

The Crown of the Abyss sent its poisonous *khashetta* against Samšin. They were the ones that sting the eyes of the greedy; against noble Samšin they could do nothing. She ground them underfoot, four crushed with each step she took. The *khashetta* skittered back into their holes.

The Crown of the Abyss sent its clinging *khashetta* against Samšin. They were the ones that feed on the blood of the slothful; against fierce Samšin they could do nothing. She tore them apart with her teeth, four torn to shreds with each bite. The *khashetta* slithered back into their holes.

Then the Crown of the Abyss sent its swift *khashetta* against Samšin. They were the ones that shriek in the ears of the ignorant, tormenting them with all the things they do not know. Against these *khashetta* she had no defense. Samšin swung her mace; she struck out with her claws. Her blows passed through the *khashetta* as if they were mist. They shrieked in her ears, and she ceased to fight. The Crown of the Abyss turned Samšin to stone and set her to one side, and there she stayed.

---

34 This makes them sound insectile.—AC

And possibly the counterpart to *issur, āmu*, and the Anevrai, if the Endless Maw is a power equal to the other three. I wonder how the *khashetta* were created?—K

I have no idea, but regardless, there's material for an article in here. Not that I can spare the time to write it, not with how hard we're working on translation—but once this is published, you and I will be kept busy for *years*, unpacking all the things we've gotten from this.—AC

Tablet VIII: "The Nahri Tablet"
translated by Audrey Camherst and Kudshayn

In the world of the living, the people waited, but Samšin did not return. The star demons drew closer, because the warrior, the brave one, the leader of the people, was not there.

Hastu spoke, wise Hastu, clear-sighted Hastu, Hastu the *šiknas*. He said, "This was foreseen in a dream long ago, before your hatching. The river of Ektabr has drowned the sun; the stone of Imalkit has crushed the sun; the grasses of Nahri have ensnared the sun. The Light of the World is in the underworld now, and unless one of you goes to retrieve it, we will be caught in darkness forever."

The people were outraged to hear that the three were responsible. They took up their stones; they took up their clubs. But they could not bear to strike those upon whom they had depended for so long.

Nahri was the kindest of the four, and the most generous. She said, "Then I will go, if you will show me where the gate of the underworld stands."

The people wailed at her words, but their fear of losing the sun was greater than their fear of losing Nahri. Her sister and her brother said, "If you must go by yourself, you will not go alone." They gave her gifts: Imalkit gave her a torch to light the way, and Ektabr gave her a prayer.

Hastu led Nahri to a ravine deeper than any other. Ten leagues, eleven leagues, twelve leagues deep was this abyss; it stretched to the depths of the earth. He left her there. With her torch and her prayer she descended.

She came to the gate of the underworld. It was made from the bones of *issur*, bound with strips of *āmu* skin. Nahri knocked at it, and the *lizma*, the gatekeeper of the underworld, answered. The *khashetta* said, "What living creature seeks to enter the underworld, and why?"

She answered him with her wings spread. "I am Nahri, water-green, hatched from a single shell. I have come to retrieve the Light of the World."

"You may enter," the gatekeeper said, "but you may not return." It opened the gate for her. Nahri entered the underworld.

She became lost in a labyrinth of stones, the place that traps those who have not shown generosity to their sisters and their brothers.[35] All around her she heard the pleas of those people, begging for charity, but she saw nothing alive. Nahri said, "I have nothing to give you, but I will care for your kin when I return, after I have retrieved the Light of the World." The voices told her the way out.

She continued on, and found herself lost in a labyrinth of bones, the place that traps those who have not shown kindness to their sisters and their brothers. All around her she heard the pleas of those people, begging for mercy, but she saw nothing alive. Nahri said, "There is nothing I can do for you now, but I will do kind deeds in your name, after I have retrieved the Light of the World." The voices told her the way out.

---

35 Probably meant in the formulaic sense of "their fellow Anevrai," rather than their clutch-mates specifically.—AC

She continued on, and found herself lost in a labyrinth of rotting flesh,[36] the place that traps those who have not been given proper rites by their sisters and their brothers. All around her she heard the pleas of those people, begging for rest, but she saw nothing alive. Nahri said, "I have nothing I can do for you now, but I will make offerings[37] on your behalf in days to come, after I have retrieved the Light of the World." The voices told her the way out.

She came to the *fettra* that guards the deepest abyss. The *khashetta* snarled at her, but she had no food[38] to give it. The *fettra* tore at her arms; it tore at her legs. Nahri escaped it, bleeding.

Beyond the *fettra* was a tunnel. Imalkit's torch lit the way. It became a tunnel too small for her to spread her

---

36 That's a remarkably disgusting image.—AC

37 We have references to funerary offerings in the ancient past, but frustratingly, the writers presume the nature of those offerings is familiar to their audience, and need not be described. If this text goes on to describe what offerings Nahri makes, it may shed some light on that question.—K

She'll have to make it out of the underworld if she wants to do anything of the sort. And if there's one thing reading mythology has taught me, it's that you aren't guaranteed to escape the underworld safely.—AC

The invocation said that she "planted the earth" (in your translation, not mine), and she hasn't done that yet. So she has to escape.—CF

Don't count your dragons before they've hatched. This is mythology: she might "plant the earth" by being buried in it.—AC

38 If she's the one who gives everyone else food, why doesn't she have any with her? Giving it all away wasn't very smart.—CF

If you expect people in a myth to behave like rational ~~human beings~~ sentient creatures, you're going to be disappointed a *lot*.—AC

Or perhaps the loss of the Light of the World means they are running short on food.—K

wings. It became a tunnel too small for her to stand. Nahri crawled through and found herself in the presence of the Endless Maw, the Crown of the Abyss. It had the Maker of Above and Below in a cage.

Nahri offered it the prayer Ektabr had taught her. She said, "I am Nahri, water-green, hatched from a single shell. I have come to retrieve the Light of the World."

"You have entered," the Crown of the Abyss said, "but you may not return. A cavern may give up what it has eaten, the sea may give up what it has drowned, a forest may give up what it has trapped, but the underworld does not give up anything it takes."

Gentle Nahri bowed her head, saying, "Our people need the Light of the World. Without it they have no hope; without it they live in fear. Without the Maker of Above and Below, the star demons will devour them all. For their sake, I cannot accept what you say."

The Crown of the Abyss showed her the ghosts of the first people. They wept and dragged their wings, saying, "We were the first to hatch, and we were the first to die. For us there is no leaving this place." But Nahri was not dismayed. She embraced them with her wings and said, "We thank you for all we have in the world."

The Crown of the Abyss showed her the ghosts of her lineage, all the way back to the first dawn. They wept and dragged their wings, saying, "We were the beginning of a line, but we did not live to see its end. For us there is no leaving this place." But Nahri was not dismayed. She embraced them with her wings and said, "We thank you for what you have given us, your descendants."

The Crown of the Abyss showed her the ghosts of her foremothers. They wept and dragged their wings, saying,

"We brought you into being, and now we see you among us. For us there is no leaving this place." But Nahri was not dismayed. She embraced them with her wings and said, "My sisters and my brother and I still honour you."

Then the Crown of the Abyss showed her the ghost of her mother. Peli wept and dragged her wings, saying, "In blindness I went to my death,[39] and in blindness you have gone to yours. For me and for you, there is no leaving this place." And Nahri wept, kneeling at her mother's feet. The Crown of the Abyss turned Nahri to stone and set her to one side, and there she stayed.

39 This must be referencing the line we had difficulty with, but I have to admit that even with this to shed additional light, I still cannot parse its meaning with any confidence.—K

Nor I, which is annoying. The text may give us more clues, though, or maybe taking more time away from it will give us clarity. (And I'm not saying that only because I'm tired of giving myself headaches staring at it. Though partly that, too.)—AC

Tablet IX: "The Imalkit Tablet"
translated by Audrey Camherst and Kudshayn

In the world of [. . .] not return. The people grew thin with hunger, because the caretaker, the generous one, the mother of the people, was not there.

Hastu spoke, wise [. . .] goes to retrieve [. . .]
upon whom [. . .]
[. . .] quickest of the four, and the most cunning. She said, "Then [. . .]
[. . .]
[. . .] her wings spread. "I am Imalkit, sky-blue, hatched from a single shell. I have come to retrieve the Light [. . .]
[. . .] underworld.[40]

Her way was barred by spirits whose eyelids had been torn off. These were the ghosts of people who had not stayed alert when [. . .] condemned now never to close their eyes again. Imalkit pinned her eyelids back, pretending to be one of them, and said, "I heard a noise further down the tunnel!" While they were looking in the direction she pointed, she escaped.

Her way was barred by spirits whose hands had been nailed to the ground with spikes. These were the ghosts of people who had wasted their time with frivolous games, condemned now never to play again. Imalkit put

---

40 Although the text here is fairly damaged, we can confidently reconstruct it based on the repetition seen in the previous Samšin and Nahri Tablets.—K

her hands on the ground, pretending to be one of them, and began to tell them jokes. While [. . .]

[. . .] of people who had spread malicious gossip and lies, condemned now never to speak again. Imalkit swallowed her tongue, pretending to be one of them, and mimed that she was a servant of the underworld, sent on some important duty. While they were nodding, she escaped.

She came [. . .] tore at her arms; it tore at her legs. Imalkit escaped it, bleeding.

Beyond the *fettra* was a tunnel. She had no torch to light the way. It became a tunnel too small for her to spread her wings. It became a tunnel too small for her to stand. Imalkit could not see, and her wings were broken by the stone. She crawled through and found herself in the presence of the Endless Maw, the Crown of the Abyss. It had the Maker of Above and Below in a cage.

Imalkit offered it the prayer Ektabr had taught her. She said, "I am Imalkit, sky-blue, hatched from a single shell. I have come to retrieve the Light of the World."

"You have entered," the Crown of the Abyss said, "but you may not return. A cavern may give up what it has eaten, the sea may give up what it has drowned, a forest may give up what it has trapped, but the underworld does not give up anything it takes."

Clever Imalkit bowed her head, saying, "Our people need the Light of the World. Without it they accomplish nothing; without it they are no better than beasts. Without the Maker of Above and Below, our people will come to an end. For their sake, I cannot accept what you say."

The Crown of the Abyss said, "Answer me this riddle. Before you seize it, you have three. After you release it, you have six." Imalkit laughed and said, "This is not difficult to understand. The solution is an axe."

The Crown of the Abyss said, "Answer me this riddle. It marks the end of every desert." Imalkit laughed and said, "This is not difficult to understand. The solution is the rain."

The Crown of the Abyss said, "Answer me this riddle. A red gazelle has been killed, its fat and meat ground into dust." Imalkit laughed and said, "This is not difficult to understand. The solution is the *zēzu* plant."[41]

Then the Crown of the Abyss said, "Answer me this riddle. An open eye; a closed eye; he blinks a hundred times, but even then it remains closed."[42] Imalkit laughed, but then she fell silent, for this was the one riddle she could not answer. The Crown of the Abyss turned Imalkit to stone and set her to one side, and there she stayed.

---

41 We know this term from tax records, but no one has yet advanced a satisfactory translation. The determinative makes it clear that the answer is a plant, and one whose seeds are good to eat. This implies the seeds are red (the "gazelle"), and were customarily ground into flour.—K

　　I'll take your word for it. I hate riddles. If the god of the underworld asked me that, I'd say, clearly a gazelle has been killed. Weren't you listening to what you said?—CF

42 There's a similar riddle in Akhia even today! If they're analogous, then the answer is "a fool" or "an ignorant person," i.e. someone who does not see regardless of whether their eyes are open or shut. There seems to be a theme developing, with each of the sisters ultimately defeated by their ignorance or blindness.—AC

Tablet X: "The Ektabr Tablet"
translated by Audrey Camherst and Kudshayn

In the world of the living, the people waited, but Imalkit
did not return. The people sat down in despair, because
the trickster, the clever one, the friend of the people, was
not there.

Hastu spoke, wise Hastu, clear-sighted Hastu, Hastu
the *šiknas*. He said, "This was foreseen in a dream long
ago, before your hatching. The river of Ektabr has
drowned the sun. The Light of the World is in the underworld now, and unless you go to retrieve it, we will be
caught in darkness forever."

The people were outraged to hear that he was responsible. They took up their stones; they took up their clubs.
But they could not bear to strike those upon whom they
had depended for so long.

Ektabr was the only one left. He was the most patient of
the four, and the wisest. He said, "Then I will go, if you
will show me where the gate of the underworld stands."

The people wailed at his words, but their fear of losing
the sun was greater than their fear of losing Ektabr.

Hastu led Ektabr to a ravine deeper than any other.
Ten leagues, eleven leagues, twelve leagues deep was
this abyss; it stretched to the depths of the earth. He left
him there. He descended.

He pulled his loincloth high. He painted spirals on his
crest with red mud. She[43] went past the gate made from

---

43 Scribal error?—K

reeds, bound with strips of twisted grass. She went to the gate made from the bones of *issur*, bound with strips of *āmu* skin. She knocked at it, and the *lizma*, the gatekeeper of the underworld, answered. It said, "What living creature seeks to enter the underworld, and why?"

She answered him with her wings spread. "I am Ektabrit,[44] night-black, hatched from a single shell. I have come to retrieve the Light of the World."

"You may enter," the gatekeeper said, "but you may not return." It opened the gate for her. Ektabrit entered the underworld.

She passed by the chamber of broken eggshells, the labyrinth of stone, the watchers with their eyelids torn off. She looked for her sisters, but she saw no sign of them.

She passed by the chamber stained with blood, the labyrinth of bone, the sitters with their hands pinned to the ground. She listened for her sisters, but she heard no sound from them.

She passed by the chamber awash in salt water, the labyrinth of rotting flesh, the people with their tongues torn out. She yearned for her sisters, but she did not feel their presence.

She came to the *fettra* that guards the deepest abyss. It snarled at her, but she had no food to give it. The *fettra* tore at her arms; it tore at her legs. It tore at her loincloth, dragging it low. She escaped it, bleeding.

---

44 Hah! That's why there are two gates! One for brothers, and one for sisters. What Ektabr did must be the equivalent of putting on a skirt and cosmetics—he dressed himself in drag, and now he's introducing himself with the feminine form of his name and using the feminine endings for his verbs, so that he'll go to the same part of the underworld as his missing sisters.—AC

Beyond the *fettra* was a tunnel. She had no torch to light the way. It became a tunnel too small for her to spread her wings. It became a tunnel too small for her to stand. She could not see, and her wings were broken by the stone,[45] her crest scraped raw. He[46] crawled through and found himself in the presence of the Endless Maw, the Crown of the Abyss. It had the Maker of Above and Below in a cage.

Ektabr said, "I am Ektabr, night-black, hatched from a single shell. I have come to retrieve my sister Imalkit."[47]

"You have entered," the Crown of the Abyss said, "but you may not return. A cavern may give up what it has eaten, the sea may give up what it has drowned, a forest may give up what it has trapped, but the underworld does not give up anything it takes."

Wise Ektabr bowed his head, saying, "Our people need Imalkit. She is the cleverest of us all; she solves our problems with guile and creations no one has seen before. Without her, we will never have anything new. What may I give you, in exchange for something so precious?"

---

45 Is this why you said Draconean priests wear that band around their wings? Because Ektabr's wings got broken?—CF

 But Imalkit's wings were broken, too.—AC

 Both are very good points. I . . . am not sure. Rather, I can say that we do not remember the story of Ektabr, and so that is not consciously the reason for the margash, the band I described to you. But I have never been told *why* we wear it; the margash is simply a tradition. So I cannot rule out the possibility that yes, in the distant past that was the reason, and we have simply . . . forgotten it.—K

46 Because now the markers of femininity have been removed.—K

47 Imalkit? What about the Light of the World?—CF

 Samšin tried for that, and failed. Nahri tried for that, and failed. Imalkit tried for that, and failed. At least Ektabr is trying something else, rather than saying, "It'll work this time, because I'm smarter!"—AC

The Crown of the Abyss was intrigued. It said, "What can you offer me, that is worth something so precious?"

Ektabr took the clay of the earth and smoothed it flat. He pressed the tip of his claw into the clay, making marks. He devised a set of marks for each thing, a set of marks for each sound. With these marks he could record speech, so that other people could know his words in the days to come.

The Crown of the Abyss was pleased. It turned Imalkit from stone to flesh and said, "I will permit her to leave, for she will return to me in time."

Cunning Imalkit bowed her head, saying, "Our people need Nahri. She is the kindest of us all; she solves our problems with generosity and cooperation. Without her, we will never work together. What may I give you, in exchange for something so precious?"

The Crown of the Abyss was intrigued. It said, "What can you offer me, that is worth something so precious?"

Imalkit took the metal of the earth and heated it. She made herself a hammer and pounded on the metal, shaping it. She wrought it into different objects, strong objects, sharp objects. With these things of metal she could make things that were not possible in clay or wood or stone, that would be of use to the people in the days to come.

The Crown of the Abyss was pleased. It turned Nahri from stone to flesh and said, "I will permit her to leave, for she will return to me in time."

Gentle Nahri bowed her head, saying, "Our people need Samšin. She is the bravest of us all; she solves our problems with courage and honour. Without her, we will never be one people, but remain many. What may I give you, in exchange for something so precious?"

The Crown of the Abyss was intrigued. It said, "What can you offer me, that is worth something so precious?"

Nahri took the seeds of the world and put them in the ground. She watered them and tended them, clearing away weeds so that they would grow. She brought forth food of many kinds. With these plants the people would no longer be dependent on the wild, but could feed many mouths from a single field in the days to come.

The Crown of the Abyss was pleased. It turned Samšin from stone to flesh and said, "I will permit her to leave, for she will return to me in time."

Samšin faced a terrible choice. Her brother had bargained for Imalkit's freedom; Imalkit had bargained for Nahri's freedom; Nahri had bargained for Samšin's freedom. Still they did not have the Light of the World. She could not bargain for both Ektabr and the Maker of Above and Below.

She said to him, "Forgive me. You are my brother, and more precious to me than my own wings; but the Light of the World is precious to us all. I cannot return to the lands above without it."

Ektabr said, "In my rite of fledging I descended into a cavern in the earth. There I saw many wondrous things, beautiful forms of crystal and stone. We have always honoured that which is above us, but we must also honour that which is below.[48] In the days to come, teach the brothers what I have created here, the art of making

---

[48] There's nothing like this underworld in the modern Draconean religion, is there?—AC

No. There is not.—K

marks in clay. With those you will remember me. So long as I am remembered, I will rest content."

The sisters embraced him with their wings. Then noble Samšin bowed her head, saying, "Our people need the Light of the World. It is the maker of us all; it gives us our courage, our kindness, our clever thoughts, our wisdom. Without it, the lands of the living will die. What may I give you, in exchange for something so precious?"

The Crown of the Abyss was intrigued. It said, "What can you offer me, that is worth something so precious?"

Samšin did not make a thing one could see or smell or touch. She said, "I will offer you justice. Here in the underworld people are punished for their failings in life; I will make it so they know their crimes before they die. Under my laws they will make amends if they can, so that when they come to you they will be washed clean, and there will be less sadness and suffering here in the days to come."

The Crown of the Abyss was pleased. It removed the cage that trapped the Maker of Above and Below and said, "You and your sisters may leave, but your brother must remain here. And the Light of the World may leave for a time, but it must return to me, for it will always be haunted by its memory of this place."

Weeping, the three, four no more, took the Light of the World and departed.

For the archives of the Sanctuary of Wings
written by Kudshayn, son of Ahheke, daughter of Iztam

I raise my hand to the sun, giver of life. I touch my hand to the earth, protector of all. I spread my wings to the wind, always in motion. I close my wings to the underworld, where all things stop.

Even writing such words makes the brush sit oddly in my hand. This is not how my ancient foremothers would have worshipped. I do not even know if they can be said to have worshipped the Endless Maw, the Crown of the Abyss. Perhaps to them, what I have just written would be blasphemy. Perhaps my failure to offer worship to the wind would be apostasy. Perhaps my understanding of the earth would be foolishness. Perhaps my reverence of the sun would be no better than a hatchling's silly prating.

For ages this has been our link to the past, the last strand to which we cling. We may have relinquished the territories we once held around the world; we may have lost all the power and wealth we once possessed. But we worship the gods of our foremothers, and so we are their kin.

If that link breaks, what do we have left?

Not one god lost, but two. The Ever-Moving, Source of Wind, and the Endless Maw, Crown of the Abyss—whether that latter was ever worshipped or not. When one of our people dies, we say they have gone to the sky. Is this a mutated remnant of the worship the Ever-Moving once received? Or some innovation with no basis in the past? Where are the spirits of my lost sisters: in the heavens, or beneath the earth?

Blessed sun, take from me this uncertainty and doubt. You light the path forward, but I cannot see it yet.

I take refuge in what I know, which is the patient reasoning of the mind. Teslit, studying Yelangese philosophy, has noticed similarity between our conception of the sun and the earth and their notions of yin and yang: the primal forces of action and passivity, light and darkness, warmth and cold. In Vidwatha they speak of three greater gods who hold the powers of creation, preservation, and destruction. But if there are four, what then?

The cellar of Stokesley offers not only refuge from the warming days, but the dark shelter of the earth. There I meditated upon this question, and when I emerged, understanding came. Is this self-delusion, my imagination creating conviction where I have no proof? Or is this a gift from the glorious eye, inspiration linking my spirit to those of my foremothers?

The Light of the World, Maker of Above and Below. The Ever-Moving, Source of Wind. The Ever-Standing, Foundation of All. The Endless Maw, Crown of the Abyss. If the last is, as the text has it, "the undoing of doing," then it is destruction. If the earth is protector and guardian, as I have always known it to be, then it is preservation. If the sun is the active force, yang in Yelangese terms, the Maker of Above and Below, then it is creation. And if the wind is the mother of dragons, whose bodies mutate in response to their environments—a truth the Anevrai certainly knew—then it is change.

Creation counterpoised with destruction. Preservation counterpoised with change. Our people, not only the children of the Light of the World, but also a balance of those latter two forces.

Both the story I know and the one I have read agree on that point; they only differ in their account of which came first.

What, then, of the *khashetta* Samšin encounters?

Are they the children of the Endless Maw, as dragons are of the Ever-Moving and humans of the Ever-Standing? If we are the ideal balance of change and preservation, are they the imbalance? Or balance of a different sort?

Did they ever exist?

Do they exist today?

I would say these questions are absurd. But fifty years ago, humans believed my own people to be mythical. How can I be certain the *khashetta* never lived—may not live still, somewhere deep within the earth, as yet unmet with some second Lady Trent?

Such things must be the concern of others. My thoughts must be given to this translation, and to the gods we have lost.

Whether we wish it or not, change will continue to come for my people. Source of Wind, help us meet it with grace.

And whether we welcome it or not, destruction is inevitable— even if it is only of our old ways of living. Crown of the Abyss, help us give the past its proper rites, so that it will not haunt us in future days.

From the diary of Audrey Camherst

29 GRAMINIS

Dear Lord Gleinleigh: if you are reading this, I congratulate you on your determination. It can't have been easy, finding someone both capable of reading Talungri and unethical enough to do so in my private diary. Unethical people are easy to come by, it seems, but the former should pose a challenge for your spies going forward.

Cora, a spy! I can barely make myself write the words. Except it makes a hideous kind of sense, because now I know why Gleinleigh so unexpectedly suggested bringing Kudshayn here; he knew I was thinking about it, because I said as much in a letter to Papa, and Cora read that letter. And then it turns around and stops making sense again, because Gleinleigh is a Calderite, and why would one of them pretend to be in favour of such a thing? I can't convince myself he was *really* in favour of it—that he is somehow reformed of his old ways—not when he's been seen with Mrs. Kefford, not when Aaron Mornett was here, not when he has his ward reading my post in secret.

I might never have known if I hadn't noticed it was taking Cora far too long to return to the library. I've been keeping a list of other texts I'd like to consult in my large blue notebook, and I forgot to bring it downstairs today, so I asked Cora to go fetch it while Kudshayn and I tried to extract a few more read-able signs from the damaged part of the next tablet. Then he got hot enough that his breathing started to get difficult, so he went down into the cellar, and then I realized Cora hadn't come back yet. I assumed Mrs. Hilleck must have buttonholed her for some question of household management, so I went upstairs to fetch the notebook myself.

And found Cora standing in the middle of my room, reading this diary.

She couldn't have looked more guilty if she tried. She dropped the diary on the floor and stood staring at me, while I tried to get the words "What do you think you're doing?" out of my mouth. Before I could, she found her tongue, and started babbling:

"It was blue! You told me to find your big blue notebook, and I saw this first, and I thought, well, that's blue, so I picked it up, and I knew it was too small, but I picked it up anyway, and when I opened it to be sure I had the wrong one I saw my name, and then I started reading—I know I shouldn't have; I could tell it was a diary and diaries are private, but Uncle told me to read your letters—"

"He told you to *what*?"

Cora reddened and stood rigid, her shoulders up by her ears. "To read your letters. And to tell him if you told anyone anything about the tablets, or if you said anything unkind or suspicious about him."

I felt like someone had torn my skin off, exposing every nerve ending. "You've been spying on me."

"Not just you," Cora said. "Kudshayn, too. Except he hasn't been writing any letters, so I don't think that counts—"

My palm slapped the wall before I realized I was moving, silencing her. I had no patience just then for her hair-splitting. "All this time. You've pretended to be our friend, to be *helping* us—"

"I *was* helping you—Uncle told me to—"

"*Damn* your uncle!" It came out a shout. I wrestled my voice down with effort, because even then, I didn't want to make a scene, didn't want to bring the entire household running to gawk. "And damn you, too. You're a liar, Cora. You never told me he was a Calderite."

Her jaw clenched hard. "You never asked. I would have told you if you asked, though you would have had to explain, because I didn't understand the word 'Calderite' until I read your diary."

"I'm supposed to believe that?" My body creaked with the strain as I stalked toward her. "You aren't my friend, Cora. *Friends* don't spy on each other—don't work behind each other's backs for their own profit."

She stood her ground, hands bunching into fists. "I'm not profiting! I'm just doing what Uncle told me to. But him telling me to spy on you wasn't honest, and—"

"And if I hadn't caught you red-handed," I spat, "would you have confessed any of this to me?"

Cora's mouth worked, but nothing came out.

I don't remember what I said after that. I know that it turned back into shouting, and the maids did come running after all, but by the time they got there I was shoving Cora out of my room and slamming the door; I have no idea what she told them. Kudshayn showed up not long after that and sat with me while I gasped the whole thing out to him, breathing even worse than he was, because all I could think about was the personal things I've said in my letters, to Lotte, to Papa, to Mama, and the even more personal things I've said in my diary. Things Cora has read, and told Gleinleigh about.

Once I calmed down, Kudshayn went to talk to Cora. I think he hoped it would all turn out to be some kind of misunderstanding. But it isn't, and he spent the rest of the day down in the cellar—I think he was praying. Because the earth is where you go when you need to be protected.

I don't feel safe anywhere here anymore, below ground or above. Stokesley feels like a trap now, and I can't even write to anyone for help, because Cora can swear all she like that she's going to stop reading my post and lie to her uncle, telling him that I'm not saying anything interesting, but I don't believe her. I can't. Because I trusted her, and this is what I got.

~~Twice now. Twice I've been s~~

I've told her to go away. She still lives here, of course, but I'm damned if I'm going to let her work with us anymore. Kudshayn and I can manage just fine on our own.

TEN
YEARS
PREVIOUSLY

From: Cora Fitzarthur
To: Miranda Brell

Dear Miranda,

Before I went away you said I must write to you. I don't know whether you meant that sincerely, or whether you only said that because it's the sort of thing people are expected to say when someone goes to live somewhere else. I asked Mrs. Hilleck, the housekeeper here, and she said that of course you meant it. But I'm not sure how she can know that when she has never met you. When I said that to her, she got angry with me and said that only ungrateful little girls don't write when someone has asked them to. I don't want to be ungrateful, so I will write you this letter, and if you didn't actually want me to then you can tear it up or burn it or whatever you like.

Stokesley is a very grand house, much grander than ~~mine~~ the one I used to live in. It is not in the town itself, which is called Lower Stoke; it is a little way out into the countryside, with lots of fields and a little wood nearby, and it has some gardens that are very nice. The barn is falling down because Uncle does not like to ride and doesn't keep any horses, so he says he will tear that down and build a greenhouse instead. I looked up what a greenhouse is, and it is a building made of glass so you can grow flowers even in the winter. That sounds nice, too, though I doubt Uncle cares very much about flowers.

Is this a good letter? I cannot tell. I have only ever written short thank-you notes, and those only when Mama made me. Uncle has a very good library, so I looked in it for examples of letters, but the only ones he has are from hundreds of years ago. They are written with very bad spelling and lots of words I do not know. I don't think I should use them for examples. Rebecca, who is one of the maids here, said there are novels full of wonderful letters where people pour their hearts out to each other, but Uncle doesn't have any novels in his library—maybe that means it isn't as good as I thought? Rebecca says she will borrow one from the circulating library in Upper Stoke when she has her next day off. But I'm not sure whether I am supposed to pour my heart out to you, or whether you want me to. It sounds painful, the way Rebecca describes it.

I do not know what else to say, so I will end here. If you do not want me writing to you after all, then send me a note to say so. Otherwise I will write again.

> *Sincerely,*
> *Cora*

Dear Miranda,

I have not gotten a note from you asking me not to send you letters, so here is another one.

Rebecca (the maid) keeps telling me I may cry on her shoulder if I wish. I do not wish. I am fairly sure Mrs. Hilleck thinks I am an ungrateful brat because I'm not sobbing over Mama and Papa, but just because I am not sobbing doesn't mean I'm not sad. The truth is that I am sad all the time, from the moment I wake up until I go to sleep, and probably in my sleep, too, except I don't remember my dreams. It simply doesn't seem right that I will never see them again. It is one thing when people get killed because they have done something stupid, like fighting in a war or travelling to a foreign country, but they were on a train from Falchester. People ride the train from

Falchester all the time and don't die. It isn't their fault that something went wrong with the track and the train derailed and killed them. Why should they be dead for something that isn't their fault? That isn't fair!

I said that to Magister Ridson, who oversees the Assembly-House down in Lower Stoke, and he gave me a very long lecture about God and fairness and bad things happening to good people. I think he meant it to help me, but it didn't. But writing a letter to you may help. It is sort of like crying on your shoulder, only without you getting snot and tears all over you, and you don't have to feel awkward or embarrassed if you'd rather be doing something else. You can put this letter down and read it later, or tear it up. I won't know.

When I left school in Murresby I told you that I hoped I would be able to come back. I don't know if I will. No one here seems to know what is going to become of me now that Mama and Papa are gone. Uncle is not even here right now, so I cannot ask him. He has gone off to the Continent, which I am told he does a lot. So it is only me and the servants, and although you know I do not like large groups of people, it turns out I can still get lonely if I am left to myself for long enough.

I am sorry if this letter is depressing to read. Next time I will try to do better.

> *Sincerely,*
> *Cora*

Dear Miranda,

I will not be able to come back to Murresby.

Uncle is back now from the Continent. He seemed almost surprised to see me still here at Stokesley; I think he had quite forgotten that he had me brought here. He telephoned Mr. Thumree, his solicitor, and had Mr. Thumree come here, and then he (I mean Uncle) and Mr. Thumree and Mrs. Hilleck all went into a room and shut the door, and Rebecca the maid told me I wasn't allowed to eavesdrop.

When they were done they opened the door and Mrs. Hilleck told me to go in, then left me alone with Uncle and Mr. Thumree. He (I mean Mr. Thumree) then gave me a long, boring speech I didn't really understand about Papa's finances. All I really took from it was that Papa apparently owed a lot of people a lot of money—more money than he actually had, because he was very foolish with some of his investments. Which Mr. Thumree said was very bad of him, because the money for those investments had been loaned to him by Uncle, so that it was not fair of him to then lose it in speculations.

But I did understand what it all means. I have no inheritance. There is no money to take care of me, much less send me back to school.

I asked him what is going to become of me. Uncle spoke up then and said he could hardly throw his niece out onto the streets, so I am welcome to stay at Stokesley. He has never married, so there is no wife to take care of his household; Mrs. Hilleck does all that work, but I can assist her, because it is better for there to be someone watching the servants to make sure they don't try to cheat their lord. I don't know how to run a household, but Mr. Thumree said it is a great deal like accountancy, and you know I am good at things like figures and making lists.

After that Mrs. Hilleck took me to Assembly and had Magister Ridson talk to me. He explained that it is very good of Uncle to take me in when Papa was so careless as to not make provisions for my future, and that I can thank him by being as obedient as if I were his own daughter. I told him I was not always obedient to Papa, and Magister Ridson got very stern and said I would have to do better than before. Were it not for Uncle I would not even have a roof over my head, so I mustn't complain about not going back to school, but be grateful that he has taken me in, and must do everything I can to repay him for his generosity.

So this will be the last letter you receive from me. Although there were lots of things I didn't like about being at Murresby, writing to you reminds me of the things I did like, and then I'm sad that I will never see them again. If I am going to be properly grateful to Uncle, I need to stop thinking about what I can't have anymore.

And since I haven't gotten any replies from you, I think it is likely that Mrs. Hilleck was wrong, and you only said to write because that is a thing people say when someone moves away. I apologize for troubling you with letters you didn't want.

I'm not very good at friends. But I suppose it doesn't matter anymore.

Sincerely,
Cora

For the archives of the Sanctuary of Wings
written by Kudshayn, son of Ahheke, daughter of Iztam

The questions of faith that consume me are no abstract philosophical matter. I see their implications at work all around me.

Where once I would have interpreted the events I see only through my knowledge of the sun and the earth, they now take on additional dimensions, alternative understandings opening up before me. Is this the sun bringing me enlightenment, or is it the hand of the wind at work in my mind, in my heart, changing how I see? Is this rift between Audrey and Cora the work of the Endless Maw, the force of destruction?

If so, then it seems fitting that I should pray to the earth, the Ever-Standing, the creator (perhaps) of humankind, to preserve the friendship between them, and not let it fall to bone dust.

I believe their friendship is true—that Cora is sincere when she attributes her dishonesty to a sense of obedience to her uncle. She thinks in terms of rules, and the rules of friendship are unfamiliar to her, isolated as she has been at Stokesley. She knows them, but has never put them to such a test. And this test would be difficult for anyone.

Though I may think of this in terms of theology, we cannot attribute all evil and ill-will to the power beneath the earth. Just as friendship is a human thing, so too is the earl's malice. I believe it merits that name: he hides it well, but even before the dinner at

Priorfield, I felt its presence. He does not like me. He brought me here only out of need, and while at first I thought that need was the understanding that one of my people should be a part of carrying this story into the light, now I am not certain.

I said nothing to Audrey before, because it is tiresome for her to hear again and again that humans do not like me. She is more willing than I am to accept the surface pretense, the polite smiles and polite bows, without looking at what lies beneath. But I was not fair to her: she knows in her own way what it is to slide along the surface of a frozen lake, always aware that the solidity beneath your feet is just a mask for the icy water below.

I pray for forgiveness. I should have spoken sooner; it might have prevented some of this harm.

Bright mirror, shine your radiance into the depths of Lord Gleinleigh's heart, so we may drag what lies there into the light. Dark stillness, do not let Audrey forget what she has shared with Cora; do not let her cast aside the proofs of sincerity and warmth. Keep them safe for her until she is ready to see them again.

However many doubts I may have, I believe that in this case I am right to pray only to those two. Change may come, but the earth will hold what must be preserved. Destruction may threaten, but creation will follow.

Though I have been mistaken on so many other matters, I hope that in this one I am not wrong.

Tablet XI: "The Return Tablet"
translated by Audrey Camherst and Kudshayn

Nothing barred their way as they ascended. They came out through the gate made from the bones of *issur,* bound with strips of *āmu* skin. They came into the lands of the living once more, and the Light of the World returned to the sky. But the Crown of the Abyss had claim to it, and so it left the heavens every night. The Maker of Above and Below did not want the people to be without light in times of darkness, and so it took Ektabr's ghost, his echo, his memory, the brother of the four, and set that in the sky as well, as a comfort and a reminder of what had been lost.

The sisters went back to their people. They embraced Samšin with their wings; they embraced Nahri with their wings; they embraced Imalkit with their wings. They looked around, but they did not see Ektabr. Samšin said, "He remained in the underworld. The price of light was our brother."

Together they mourned Ektabr. They made offerings to the underworld, and recited prayers, and performed rites, in memory of Ektabr. This was the beginning of such things in the world.

It was a time of many changes. Imalkit had created the shaping of metal, and because of her the people had tools of copper and bronze and iron in the days to come. She made for herself new wings, taking the place of those that had been broken by crawling through the underworld. Nahri had created the cultivation of plants, and because of her the people had wheat and barley and dates in the days to come. She made for herself and Imalkit healing poultices, mending the harm done to them by the *fettra* that guards the abyss. Samšin had created justice, and because of her the people had laws and punishments and righteousness in the days to come. She made, not for herself but for all, a [. . .]

All these things began on that day. And they began [. . .]

[. . .] of the wild, beneath the leaves of the trees [. . .]

[. . .]

[. . .] at the heart of the people. In the underworld I passed through a chamber awash [. . .] in the underworld Nahri [. . .] passed by [. . .]

[. . .] Hastu [. . .]

[. . .] lands of the dead [. . .]

[. . .]

[. . .] our mother Peli [. . .]

[. . .] defeated [. . .] of ignorance [. . .]

[. . .] no longer the eyes that may be open [. . .] for who you are, *šiknas* [. . .]

[. . .]

[. . .]

[. . .] to the Crown of the Abyss with [. . .]

[. . .] people left [. . .]

From the diary of Audrey Camherst

4 MESSIS

There's no hope for it; the eleventh tablet is just too badly damaged. We might puzzle out another sign here and there over time, at least to the point of an educated guess, but we'll never be able to tell what the whole thing says.

(And I keep thinking, "But Cora has such good eyes; maybe she'll be able to piece together a bit more." Then I remember that she's a spy and Gleinleigh is up to something and the only person here I can trust is Kudshayn. I'm not asking her for help.)

We can tell it's something about Hastu, at least in part; we've got his name, and we've got that word *šiknas* again. When I asked Kudshayn what he thought, he said, "This might be the point at which that epithet is bestowed on him."

To which I objected, "But the text has been using it all along."

"Yes, but why should that matter? The invocation references the siblings long before they appear; the same might be true for this, especially since it allows the scribe to give Hastu four uses of his name, once alone and then with three epithets. Surrendering precision for the sake of a poetic device is hardly unusual."

I felt like complaining that it might be poetic, but it was confusing—I think Cora has rubbed off on me. I was not about to tell Kudshayn that, though, because he mopes around being sad that I'm not talking to her anymore. (For someone who has often been on the receiving end of human untrustworthiness, he's far more willing to forgive her than I am.) Instead I said, "I cannot shake the feeling that this section would explain that epithet. 'For who you are, *šiknas*'—doesn't that sound like they're naming him somehow?"

Kudshayn only shrugged. "I will look at the next section and see if there is anything of use."

But there isn't. It's clear even from a glance that the text continues on to something else entirely. Unless we stumble into a full repetition on some tablet in another collection, we're out of luck—and I don't think that's likely.

Unless . . . wait.

All these things began on that day. Writing, and metallurgy, and planting crops—and justice. I read something about this, I *know* I did. The cliff inscription from Ma'ale Tizafim? No, not that; it was a law code, but not what I'm thinking of. A narrative bit, only I can't remember the details. Why can't I remember them? Why does my memory have as many holes as that tablet?

LATER

THE BEGINNING OF JUSTICE!

That was it. A fragment of tablet that told the story of "the first judgment spoken." And the reason I can't remember any more details is there *weren't* any; the fragment is in the hands of a private collector. (Not Gleinleigh—someone else.) It's never been properly studied and published, at least not that I remember; just a brief mention of it from somebody—Daniela Isaquez, I think—who was allowed to take a brief look at it. Where was that notice? In ~~Studies in Ancient Jurisprudence~~ no, that letter from Elias Eells. Two years ago, or thereabouts, because it was after I came back from the Broken Sea. Once I write to him— and I'll take the letter to the post office myself this time, rather than trusting it to Cora to handle—I'll know who has the fragment. Then we'll find out which is stronger: Gleinleigh's desire to control this information, or his desire to have the whole story of these tablets published. (I do still believe he wants them published, even if I don't quite understand *why*.)

Good God, it's three in the morning. I can't do anything about this right now; I should try to go back to sleep. It isn't *quite* worth waking Kudshayn over.

From: Marcus Fitzarthur, Lord Gleinleigh
To: Audrey Camherst

6 Messis
8 Wenbury Square, Falchester

Dear Miss Camherst,

Even an amateur like myself could see that some of my tablets
were badly damaged; I had no particular hope of you being able
to read much out of them, and do not blame you for your failure
to do so. The fault lies with the man I hired to conserve them,
who clearly made some sort of error with that one, as it was not
in so bad a state when I found it.

But I confess I am not quite sure I follow what you mean
about this fragmentary tablet in Mr. Lepperton's collection:
you are not claiming he somehow has the flakes that were
knocked off the surface of this tablet, nor that he has a frag-
ment from a copy of the same text, but rather that this is
something entirely separate? And yet you believe it will shed
light on my own tablets. In the same manner, perhaps, as
studying the libretto of Eiskönigin *would shed light on its*
source text, the Winterlied*—would you say that is a fair*
comparison?

If so, then this is a most unexpected development. Some of
my delay in responding is because I met with Mr. Lepperton
and offered him a substantial sum for his tablet, but I'm afraid
the man bears me a grudge due to a bidding war over some
statuary a few years back, and he turned me down flat. (In
hindsight, it might have been wiser to have Dr. Cavall at the
Tomphries approach him on your behalf.) I am not at all cer-

tain you will have any better luck, but I must concede that it would be advantageous to have at least a guess at what the damaged text says before the whole translation is published.

That having been said, it is absurd for you to claim no forward progress can occur until this has been resolved. You have the rest of the tablets; surely they are enough to keep you occupied for quite some time. But I am sensible of your point that Mr. Lepperton is known to travel to Eiverheim in the summertime, and may not be available before long, so I suggest a compromise: you may come to Falchester and attempt to persuade him to grant you access to the tablet, while Kudshayn continues working at Stokesley. That way the translation does not halt entirely while you attempt to patch this hole.

If that compromise is agreeable to you, then I will make arrangements for you to come here by train. I would of course like you to keep your visit as brief as possible; as you yourself have noted, the translation proceeds more quickly with more than one set of eyes on it, and I would not want this to delay it any more than necessary.

I hope I need not remind you that our previous agreement remains in force. I have no doubt that many people here will want to know details of your work—your own family not least among them—but surely an honourable young woman such as yourself would not go back on her word, whatever my previous missteps may have been.

Cordially,
Marcus Fitzarthur
Lord Gleinleigh

From the diary of Audrey Camherst

10 MESSIS

Free air at last! Stokesley has become so claustrophobia-inducing since Cora's confession; it was an unspeakable relief to see it receding into the distance and know that I will not have to go back for several days at least. If only it did not feel like I'm leaving Kudshayn to play hostage for my good behaviour in Falchester.

I intend to behave . . . mostly. I haven't even smuggled out the copies of our papers—though admittedly that's in part because I haven't had time to make copies of all of them. But I'm also worried that other people in Gleinleigh's employ might go through my things and be looking especially for me to break my word now, so instead Kudshayn has been hiding our papers when he goes on his morning walks in the woods behind Stokesley.

Paranoia? Perhaps. But I had rather give in to a little paranoia and later find out it wasn't necessary than fail to take these precautions and regret it in the end.

Anyway, I will keep my word to Gleinleigh insofar as I will not say anything to anyone about Samšin and Nahri and Imalkit and Ektabr, or the fact that the tablets describe the origins of various civilized technologies and practices. (What would happen if I did? I may know the sorts of ink-nosed people who would find that absolutely fascinating, but it isn't as if I'd be giving away the secrets of dragonbone synthesis.) I did not, however, promise to keep my mouth shut about Gleinleigh himself, and I intend to ask for advice on that front from all the people closest to me.

I have already done so a little, because of course everyone here at Clarton Square wanted to hear all about my work before the door had closed behind me. I reminded them that I am sworn to secrecy; Papa shrugged, Mama said that was absurd, and Lotte said she thought it all sounded wonderfully mysterious. I said, "There is mystery in prothetic anaptyxis and Early Draconean vowel harmony, but not the kind any sensible person would enjoy," and she laughed. (I have missed Lotte! She is thriving here, as I knew she would. And she has *several* beaus, though I would bet my favourite pen I know which one she'll choose.)

But I waited until dinnertime to tell them what I've learned about Gleinleigh, and about Cora. Papa said, "He visited the offices of Carrigdon and Rudge recently—I presume he chose them because they've also been publishing Mother's memoirs. So I doubt he lied about his intent to publish the translation. And it makes sense to do that before the congress, if he can. But profiting off the excitement over Draconeans coming here doesn't sound like the kind of thing a dyed-in-the-wool Calderite would do."

"Maybe he's trying to get ahead of Mrs. Kefford somehow," Lotte said. "You should hear the stories people have told me—not about those two specifically, but that whole set. They're all dreadful rivals, because they think of the artifacts and such as ways of keeping score, not as things with intellectual or scholarly value."

(I had to hide a grin when she said that. Lotte is the least scholarly of us, but she has inherited in full the Camherst/

Trent disdain for people who put egotism ahead of the advancement of knowledge.)

Then I thought about what she'd said. "Perhaps . . . I can certainly see him as that sort of man, and it would explain why he's going to such lengths to make certain I don't share anything. But in what world would *I* talk to someone like Mrs. Kefford?"

"To influence her husband?" Lotte said. "He was recently named the Dissenting Speaker, so unless something changes between now and the congress, he'll be at the head of the anti-Draconean vote."

I can't blame my ignorance on being cooped up at Stokesley; I wouldn't have paid attention to Synedrion politics even if I were in Falchester. But if Gleinleigh thinks I could make a dent in Mr. Kefford's bigotry, he has a higher opinion of my abilities than I do, and I said so.

Mama said, "I am surprised he was willing to let you come here at all. For all he knows, you could be telling us the whole tale right now."

"He knows she's too honourable for that," Lotte said.

I snorted. "Maybe—but I think it's more an attempt to repair the damage Lady Plimmer caused. Not to mention Cora."

"Not her," Lotte said stoutly. "From what you've said in your letters, I believe she meant it when she said she wouldn't tell him. After all, she didn't have to tell *you* that she'd read your diary and your letters. Why do that, and then go on telling her uncle everything?"

"You don't know Cora," I said darkly. "Who can understand how she thinks?"

Except I can, if I let myself. She is very fond of rules and routine, and Gleinleigh had set her a rule. But there are other rules, less explicit ones, about honesty and friendship, and she

said herself that those were what motivated her to tell me.
I just—

I can't deal with betrayal. Not from someone I thought was
a friend. I've been through it before, and the thought that I've
been foolish enough to let it happen again is . . . "unbearable"
doesn't come close to summing it up. I can't even bring myself
to admit this openly to my family, and they of all people would
understand. But I suspect they can guess it anyway, because
they know me so well.

Enough of that. I have work to do; I should write to Mr. Lepperton so it can go out with the morning post (nobody reading
my letters here!), and hope that he either doesn't know I'm
working for Gleinleigh, or doesn't hold it against me. Even if
he does, though, I think I can get around him. I didn't tell
Gleinleigh this, because I suspected he would do exactly what
he did and try to get the tablet himself so I wouldn't have to
come to Falchester . . . but I have the perfect lever to move
Lepperton onto my side.

FROM THE DIARY OF WALTER LEPPERTON

13 MESSIS

Most peculiar visit today. Audrey Camherst, granddaughter of Lord and Lady Trent, came to look at one of my tablets! Same one that pompous ass Gleinleigh tried to buy; I hear she is working on that cache he found. Was somewhat inclined to refuse her access—would serve Gleinleigh right for outbidding me on the head of that monumental dracosphinx back in '54. *I would have loaded it onto a ship that was* not *destined to sink to the bottom of the Sea of Alsukir.* But her letter said she originally heard of it from Elias Eells, and he sent a note asking me to let her see it, as a favour to him. Quite unclear as to why it matters so much to anyone that she be permitted to study it, but Eells is a good chap, and I can't see what harm it does.

So let the young lady take a look, and she got very excited. Broken bit of clay, hardly the most remarkable thing in my collection—is it really so valuable? Might contact Emmerson's about arranging an auction. Or—better yet—find translator, publish before G gets his own out. (Mine is much shorter anyway.) Great appetite for Draconean matters these days, what with the congress and all. Not Camherst girl, though; that would only put me in G's shadow.

At any rate, arranged for Camherst girl to return and study the tablet. In exchange, she has promised her endorsement for me entering the Antiquarian Society. Membership at last! Quite cheaply bought, too; picked up this tablet for a song in a bazaar in Chiavora.

Note to self: ask around tomorrow re: translator for fragment. Surely there are others of skill in Falchester. I recollect hearing something about a fellow, M-something—can't recall the name.

DOCKSIDE RAID
The Hunt for Smugglers
An Empty Net
"An innocent businessman persecuted"

Yesterday the Royal Investigative Agency's Port Division raided a shipment unloaded from the *Tayralba,* a cargo vessel sailing out of Qaemolsar, in response to an anonymous tip that the crates might contain illegally smuggled antiquities. Led by Detective Inspector Timothy Wright, constables stormed the dock and took control of the crates immediately after they were signed over to Joseph Dorak, a noted Falchester antiquities dealer. Despite thoroughly searching the cargo, they found nothing except artifacts legally acquired overseas.

"It's sheer persecution," Mr. Dorak said afterward. "I'm an innocent businessman. But certain parties that have political influence right now in our government are determined to prevent Scirling citizens from acquiring Draconean materials, even when they do so through legitimate channels. The protectionism being shown here is frankly worrying."

This is not the first time Mr. Dorak's shipments and warehouses have been raided. The Royal Investigative Agency's personnel have been pursuing him for the better part of a decade, and he has thrice been convicted of trading in smuggled antiquities, paying a fine each time.

Audrey—

Emmerson's is hosting an auction of Draconean antiquities next Selemer. Do you think you could spare a few hours to attend with me? I would never dream of suggesting that you might buy something and then donate it to the Tomphries, whose budget is never as large as I would wish, but I have taken the liberty of noting the inscribed items from the catalogue.

Of course if any without inscriptions happen to catch your eye, the Tomphries would be happy to give those a good home, too! Though be cautious of what else you bid on. All the ones I have marked here should be aboveboard and traded on the legal market, but I can't vouch for everything else in the catalogue.

—Simeon

Sale 1228: Draconean Antiquities

LOT 16
PECTORAL CENTERPIECE
Late Period, Haggad

Trapezoidal plate of gold hammered with winged sun motif and vine border, with loops for attachment to adjoining pieces, now lost. Reverse side bears a standard prayer to the sun for protection and wealth.

8 cm. high, 6 cm. wide at base, 4 cm. wide at top

LOT 32
ALABASTER JAR
Middle Period, Seghaye

Calcite alabaster jar with lid. Handles are in the shape of two supporting human nudes, one male, one female. Lid features a lotus flower. Traces of gold foil decoration remain. Inscription along inside rim, a formulaic wish for eternal vigor.

12 cm. high, 8 cm. wide

LOT 55
GAME PIECES
Middle Period, Vidwatha

Three circular disc playing pieces from the game of "dragon chase." Two are lapis lazuli inlaid with ivory in a mandala pattern; single ivory inset missing from one piece. The other piece is carnelian inlaid with ivory. Each bears an inscribed sign on the reverse.

1.5 cm. diameter, 4 mm. high

LOT 65
BASALT FRAGMENT
Early Period, Akhia

Presumably from a broken stele. Inscribed on flat side with nine lines of undeciphered text.

20 cm. high, 15 cm. wide, 9 cm. thick

LOT 71
CERAMIC SUN DISC
Early Period, Seghaye

Polychrome fired clay winged sun disc. Inscribed on reverse side with a short prayer.

40 cm. wide, 15 cm. high, 3 cm. thick

Tablet 14118: "The Justice Fragment"
Trans. Audrey Camherst

[. . .] two-faced one, the falsifier of dreams, the one who sought to kill the four.

He hid amid the beasts of the wild, beneath the leaves of the trees, behind the stones of the ground, in any place he could find. The people went out in search. They found him and dragged him back.

She was the first to speak for justice. She said, "You have been the poison at the heart of the people. I have passed through a chamber awash in the salt tears of those who have been betrayed; my sister has passed through a labyrinth of rotting flesh, the place of those whose bodies have rotted and fallen to dust unmourned in the wilderness; my sister has passed by the ghosts of those who have spread malicious gossip and lies. We have seen your work among the dead."

She said, "We can no longer be defeated by the demon of ignorance. We can no longer be brought low by the ghost of our betrayed mother. We are no longer the eyes that may be open or closed without change. We name you for what you are: the false one, the betrayer, the murderer, the liar. Only [. . .] you now. Will you make amends, or will you suffer for your crimes?"

He stood with his wings spread, with his crest high [. . .] full of poison. He was the liar, the murderer, the betrayer, the treacherous one. He said, "I will do nothing. I regret only that I failed to kill you in the egg, that I failed to kill you in the wilderness."

She said, "Take his teeth and pull them out. Take his claws and break them. Take his wings and cut them off. Take him to the desert, and there let him die, to rot and fall to dust without rites."

This was the first judgment spoken, and they did as she said. Then she [. . .] on a stone, in memory of her brother, and [. . .] laws to [. . .]

From: Audrey Camherst
To: Kudshayn

16 Messis
#3 Clarton Square

Dear Kudshayn,

I believe the proper word here is "Eureka!"

*And by "eureka," I mean "traitorous." That's the meaning
of šiknas—or rather, šikennas, which is how it's written in
Lepperton's fragment. I think the closest cognate is probably
from Arkubb, gansaa. (No, I don't have an Arkubb dictionary
in my back pocket. I raided Grandpapa's library. He and
Grandmama are not here—they're in Tser-nga, making arrangements for next winter—but Papa has a key to their townhouse.) The cognate means "backward" or "inverted," so your
guess about the root for "reflection" was accurate; we just took
that sense in the wrong direction when we speculated that it
might be another way of saying he was wise. It's "reflection" in
the sense of being reversed rather than thoughtful. Lepperton's
fragment outright calls Hastu false and a liar, so I'm pretty
sure of the general sense of my translation, though you and I can
quibble later about how exactly we want to render it in Scirling.*

*The fragment is pretty clearly about our quartet and
Hastu. It doesn't use their names, and the whole thing is in a
much later style than the epic—it isn't a fragment of the same
text so much as the same general story—but there are references to their journey through the underworld. Presumably the
Anevrai audience wouldn't have needed those parts explained.*

There are some lacunae in it, but not any terribly big ones, and it makes so much clear.

You commented to me back when we translated the bit about the rites of passage that it was peculiar to see the poet break his pattern: instead of telling us Hastu's dream, then repeating it when Hastu told it to the people, we only got the latter repetition. I think that's because Hastu never had the dream: he made it up out of whole cloth, because he wanted the siblings to die. He tried to get Peli to crush the egg, and then I think he killed Peli, in that bit we couldn't translate—this fragment doesn't say it outright, but it calls him a murderer and talks about the siblings' "betrayed mother," so it sounds like that to me. I bet you can sort out the difficult line now that you have this to lead you. And it makes sense of how the sisters get defeated in the underworld, by their ignorance and blindness and so forth; all of that was pointing to Hastu.

Isn't it funny how much clearer things become once you stop telling yourself that surely someone must be good at heart, despite all evidence to the contrary?

Anyway, I will be back at Stokesley soon. Gleinleigh would probably like me to leave tomorrow, but I haven't told him yet that I'm done with the Lepperton fragment, in part because I want to stay for an auction Simeon has invited me to. There will be some Draconean inscriptions in the catalogue, and while I don't expect any of them will be of particular scholarly value, I'd like to be sure before I leave. Unless you need me back sooner, of course, in which case I will be on the next available train. I confess I'm more than a little concerned about abandoning you at Stokesley.

Audrey

From: Kudshayn
To: Audrey Camherst

17 Messis
Stokesley, Greffen

Dear Audrey,

I shall be circumspect in what I write to you, not because I fear prying eyes, but because I gave my word to Lord Gleinleigh even as you did, and must respect that.

What you have said regarding the fragment in Mr. Lepperton's possession makes a great deal of sense. With that in mind, I still struggle with the line at the end of the third tablet, but I think we can agree on its general sense even if the specific wording is subject to debate. It certainly fits with the patterns we saw in the underworld tablets, the sense that a particular thing was unknown to the figures in the tale, and that was what led ultimately to their individual defeats.

I have not been idle in your absence. There is another stylistic shift in this next section, much like the shifts we have seen before; I am glad to report that the text is, to use one of your phrases, easier sailing at the moment. Given that you will be staying a while longer in Falchester, I think it is likely I will have a good portion done by the time you return. There are elements in it I am very eager to discuss with you, as I am not certain what to make of them.

(Please forgive me for the vague wording. I find myself somewhat troubled, and not in the best of health, but as I said, I still feel obliged to be circumspect.)

If you find anything of great significance at the auction, I hope you will consider the Sanctuary as well as the Tomphries Museum. We are not wealthy, but the elders have expressed an interest in beginning to assert our claim upon the past, as circumstances allow.

May the sun keep you warm,
Kudshayn

From the diary of Audrey Camherst

He planned this all from the start, I'm sure of it. I just don't know *how*. Or why.

Perhaps if I write it out, I'll figure out what he's up to. Other than tormenting me, which I'm sure is just the icing on the cake for him. Aaron Mornett would never do anything for just one reason.

Start at the beginning, Audrey. And breathe.

He can't have arranged it all. Simeon is the one who invited me to the auction, and he believes me about Mornett; they'd never work together. But it's predictable enough that I would be there, I suppose, if he knew I was in town. Mornett, I mean. And if there's something going on between him and Glein-leigh, he probably did.

I went to the Tomphries about an hour before the auction, to see Simeon. He was in his office as usual, buried amid piles of paper and books and half-unpacked crates like a mouse in his burrow. I hadn't told him I was coming, so he nearly knocked over one of those stacks when he leapt up to greet me and lost his balance in his enthusiasm. I kept him on his feet until he could retrieve his cane—which he had stuck into the straw of one of the crates, straight through the mouth of the clay polychrome mask inside, thus proving that Simeon will change about two days after Kudshayn does. He looked around for a place where I could sit, but there never is one, so we went out to one of the benches in the hall to talk.

He burbled some happy greetings, then said, "You've been so quiet! I've barely heard a peep out of Stokesley since you went. Tell me that is because you've spent your every waking minute racing through the translation and you're nearly done!"

His enthusiasm made me laugh, which is the first time I've felt like doing that since the dreadful fight with Cora. It really has helped, being back among my family; it feels like ages since I've seen them, ~~even though I've only been gone a few months~~ and I suppose it has—heavens, I've been at Stokesley for nearly half a year.

But the urge to laugh didn't persist for long. I propped my back against the dracosphinx that forms one end of the bench. (It never ceases to amaze me that they just leave antiquities out in the hall for people to sit on, even if the antiquity in question is not very valuable.) Simeon knows me well enough to tell when I am worried; he sobered up very quickly and asked me what was wrong.

I laid it out more efficiently this time, having already subjected my family to the rambling version. Simeon frowned the whole way through, tapping his cane steadily against the floor. He didn't interrupt me, though. When I was done, his first action was to make certain he had received all the letters I had sent—and that hadn't even occurred to me until he brought it up, that Cora might have stopped some of them from going out. Whether she would have or not I don't know, but nothing I wrote to Simeon was liable to provoke that kind of censorship; he got them all.

Then he said, "Well. On the one hand, I am inclined to grave suspicions where Mrs. Kefford and Aaron Mornett are concerned, and if Lord Gleinleigh is indeed conspiring with them, then he is not merely the kind of selfish collector who trawls the markets of Anthiope for illegally excavated antiquities, but a good deal less trustworthy than that." (And this was *Simeon* saying it. He isn't usually the type to attach "merely" to that particular judgment of character.)

I said, "On the other hand?"

He gazed into the middle distance, eyes unfocused. "On the other hand, he came to me last week—I've been meaning to write to you, only I've been busy arguing with Arnoldson over the rearrangement for next autumn. Did I tell you? The museum will be shifting the Draconean antiquities into Estwin Hall, to accommodate the crowds they expect as we get closer to the congress. Which has put Arnoldson's nose right out of joint, because—"

"Simeon," I said. "Lord Gleinleigh?"

He blinked. "Oh, yes. I am sorry; of course you don't care about internal museum politics. The earl came by to thank me for recommending you to his attention—says you're doing splendidly, and at a terrific clip—and to tell me that he spoke with Pinfell about offering the tablets to the Tomphries as a permanent loan when you're done."

I nearly fell off the bench. "What?"

"That is precisely what I said! He was rather vague about the specifics, but he said that he expected what you publish to be of great enough interest that people should have the opportunity to see the source—which is a leopard changing his spots if I ever saw one." Simeon leaned closer, conspiratorially. "And *then* he said, as artfully as if he had only just remembered, that weren't we going to be moving the Draconean antiquities to a bigger hall? In which case, perhaps we might honour his humble donation with a display case or two."

"He is greedy for fame," I muttered. (So am I, you might say—but at least I want to be famous for my intellectual achievements, not for having pots of money and lucking into a tremendous find.)

Simeon pursed his lips. "He may be . . . but generosity of that sort is not what I would expect from any friend of Mrs. Kefford's. She may be a benefactor of the museum, but she uses her money to buy influence and burnish her husband's reputation, not to add valuable materials to our collection." He considered it for a time, then shook his head. "Perhaps he is trying to make amends for what you learned at Lady Plimmer's. On the third hand—"

"On the third hand," I said, "he was spying on me. Or rather, having his niece do it."

"That's not all." Simeon folded his hands over the head of his cane, looking troubled again. "I mentioned that he was full of praise for your work. When I brought up publication, he was very energetic in saying that you and Kudshayn would get full honours for the translation—so I don't think you need fear that he is going to attempt to take credit, or pass it off as Mornett's effort, or anything in that vein. But have you noticed the hole in what I have said?"

Trust Simeon to turn it into an intellectual puzzle. When I reviewed his words, though, I immediately saw what he meant. "Praise for *my* work. Not for Kudshayn's."

"Indeed. And after we discussed publication, he went right back to talking about you only. That is not, I think, the behaviour of a man who is in the process of overcoming his prejudices, and sincerely striving to do better."

I agree with Simeon—but whose behaviour *is* it? That of a man who cannot bring himself to value a Draconean's work, but wants to make certain everyone knows that work is his?

I could see Gleinleigh doing that if he believed the translation would be terrible . . . but if he thinks we're going to be met with ridicule when we publish, he's going to be sorely disappointed. I am proud of what we've done, and although our fellow scholars will quibble with it (because scholars *live* to quibble), neither of us will be embarrassed to show our face in public afterward.

But that was only the start of my day, and by far the better part of it.

Simeon and I kept talking, until I noticed that if we didn't leave soon, we were going to be late for the auction. So I ran downstairs to hail a cab while Simeon locked up his office, and even with that, we arrived at Emmerson's with only a few minutes to spare.

The auction house was very full, which Simeon didn't find at all surprising. "Normally a sale like this one would not be very significant," he said, "as there are no artifacts of major importance or beauty in the catalogue. But with the congress coming up . . ."

I've heard that phrase a hundred times since arriving in Falchester. (Which is an achievement, given how few people I've spoken to outside my own family.) But it's only to be expected, when even rural gentry like Lady Plimmer are taking pains to educate themselves on the subject; here in Falchester, of course it's the main topic of conversation. And Draconean motifs are all the rage once more in decoration, so naturally everyone is stampeding to buy anything they can, and the wealthier ones want the genuine artifact.

Simeon went into the hall ahead of me to find seats while I registered us both and collected our bidding paddles. And then, just before I could go in, I heard an all-too-familiar voice say, "Hello again, Audrey."

He was lounging against one of the columns with his hands in his pockets. Lying in wait for me? I can't be sure. But there are times when I regret not being raised by an old-fashioned family—somebody like Lady Plimmer—because I don't have the knack for being properly frosty. I did my best, though. I drew myself up very straight and said, "You have lost the right to be so familiar with me, sir."

"Miss Camherst, then." Damn him for sounding amused. Mornett pushed off from the column and sauntered toward me, hands still in his pockets, which for some reason felt even more invasive than if he had taken them out. "Here for something in particular? I had a look at the lots earlier, and can think of one that might catch your eye. You never know what treasures are waiting to be found."

I wish it were practical to haul around a gramophone recording device, so I could play back statements like that and pick over them for clues. But so much of it is in the body language as well, the posture and the cast of the eyes: was he deliberately hinting at something? It would be just like him to play with me in such a fashion.

Whether he was or not, I was too flustered to respond well. If I'd had any sense I would have anticipated that Aaron Mornett might be there and prepared something cutting to say, but instead all I said was, "The auction will begin any moment now. I'm going inside."

"The interesting things are all later in the catalogue," he said indifferently, but bowed me toward the door. I walked as fast as I could to get there ahead of him, so that he would not have a chance to hold it for me. He caught its edge before I could let it swing shut in his face, though, and followed me in.

At least the chairs Simeon had found were nearly at the back of the hall. Mornett passed me as I sat down, with one last insinuating smile, and took an empty chair about three rows farther up, which meant I would not have to endure the whole auction knowing he was staring at the back of my head. But then I nearly swallowed my tongue when I realized the woman holding that chair empty for him was Mrs. Kefford!

He's worked with her for some time now, of course. Who else could someone like her get to translate her acquisitions? But on the heels of everything else, it felt like Mornett was waving a red flag in front of me, flaunting . . . I don't even know what, because I don't know what they're *doing*. I'm only sure there must be something.

I tried to put it out of my mind for the time being. Simeon had seen Mornett; he whispered to me, "Are you all right?" and I assured him I was. I don't think he believed me, but the middle of the auction house was hardly the place to have that conversation, so we had to hush and attend to the sales.

Not that I was really attending. Instead I paged through Simeon's copy of the catalogue, wondering what Mornett might have been hinting at. One of the inscribed pieces? They really weren't very interesting; the only possibility was the basalt fragment, but stele usually just have royal declarations or boasts about how so-and-so won a great victory in battle. What reason could I have to be interested in that?

With no clues forthcoming from the catalogue, I resolved to watch him instead. His hair is still as casual as ever, brushed into place but no more than that, and every so often he turned to murmur something to Mrs. Kefford, or she to him. I tried valiantly to read their lips, but without much luck, until Simeon nudged me and pointed out that I was very obviously staring. Then I tried to stop, but without much luck at that, either. (I hope he could feel me glaring holes in the back of his head. Mornett, I mean, not Simeon.)

And then a large cylinder seal carved from hematite came up for bid, and Mornett raised his paddle.

I immediately looked to the catalogue, because I hadn't really listened when the auctioneer described that lot. It was number 70, and described only as depicting "four Draconean figures in supplication to a god, extraordinarily well-carved."

Four! Of course my thoughts immediately went to our four siblings, Samšin, Nahri, Imalkit, and Ektabr. The fifth—well, any time an ancient artifact depicts some impressive and un-identifiable figure we tend to label it a god, just as we call arti-facts "ritual" when we have no real idea what they were used for. But with the journey to the underworld and back so fresh in my mind, I couldn't help but wonder: did it depict the Crown of the Abyss? Or perhaps the Light of the World, except that is probably what all those sunbursts and winged sun discs depict, so that was less likely.

All of these thoughts went through my head in the time it took for someone to outbid Mornett, and him to raise his bid in reply.

I sat for a few moments, thinking. Then I drew a deep breath and raised my own paddle.

"I have seven hundred from the lady in the back, do I have seven twenty-five, thank you sir, do I have seven fifty . . ."

This was not the first time I have bid in an auction, but I have never felt so tense. There were about six of us bidding, I think, but Mornett was the only one I really paid attention to. He bid steadily, not seeming to hesitate, but not showing too much eagerness, either. I raised my paddle like an automaton, scarcely listening to the numbers. Living at Stokesley, I've had hardly anything to spend money on, and whatever else I might say about him, Gleinleigh is paying me well.

Soon it was only three: myself, Mornett, and a gentleman

on the right-hand side of the hall, whom I couldn't see clearly. The price, I realized with a shock, had climbed above thirteen hundred. Not absurd for a cylinder seal, not if it was a particularly fine piece of work, but a good deal more than I should be spending.

And then Aaron Mornett turned in his seat, flicked his fingers from his brow in a mocking salute—and stopped bidding.

The other man didn't. I faltered for a moment, then lifted my paddle. What should I do? I had entered this particular auction because Mornett wanted the seal—the only thing he had shown any evidence of wanting so far—and what he had said out in the hall hinted there was a reason. Only, how could he know anything about what I had read in the epic? Did Gleinleigh show him the tablets—not that night, because I would have seen them, but on some other occasion? He could not possibly have read them any more easily than Kudshayn and I have, but he is (damn him) an excellent philologist . . . or was he doing this simply to run me out of money so I would not be able to bid against him when he went after his real target, one of the remaining lots in the auction?

My mind was caught in a sickening spiral. I could not think clearly. I knew I should stop bidding; Simeon hissed in my ear, "Audrey, for God's sake, what are you *doing?*" Mornett leaned over to Mrs. Kefford and whispered in her ear, looking concerned. And then the auctioneer said, "I have eighteen hundred and twenty-five guineas from the lady in the back. Do I hear eighteen hundred and fifty?"

An electrical jolt ran over my skin. *Eighteen hundred and twenty-five guineas.* I could not cover that, not by myself; I would have to ask Papa to help me. And he would want to know how I wound up paying nearly two thousand guineas for a cylinder seal, and I would have no good answer for him.

"Going once," the auctioneer said. "Going twice."

Mornett raised his paddle and called out, "Two thousand."

Murmurs sprang up all over the hall. A stupid impulse almost made me outbid him, but I clenched both hands around my paddle and kept it in my lap.

"I have two thousand," the auctioneer said, looking from me to the other bidder. Mornett's jump had discouraged him; no paddle came up in reply, and a moment later, the seal was Mornett's.

I sat, shaking and sick, while the auction house's assistants cleared away the seal and brought out a clay sun disc. That was disposed of in quick order, going for the pittance of two hundred guineas, and then I could not take it any longer. Not caring if Mornett noticed, not caring if anyone else chose to whisper, I got up and left the hall.

Diary, I should have gone home. Simeon could take a streetcar back to the Tomphries just as well without me as with. But I stayed out there, breathing the cooler air, until I heard the hall door open and shut behind me and knew without looking that I'd missed my chance to escape.

"Well," Mornett drawled. "That got unexpectedly exciting."

"As you intended it to, I'm sure," I snapped.

He ignored my accusation. "That was rather more than you could cover, I think. Bit rich for my blood, too, if I'm being honest—"

"When are you ever?"

In the momentary silence, I resisted the urge to turn around and look at him. I did not want to see his face. Eventually he said, "I'll have you know, I had to borrow from Mrs. Kefford to make that bid. For your sake: I didn't want you to get into trouble."

That finally made me turn. He was looking disarmingly open and friendly—but I know all too well how easily he can don such an expression. I said scathingly, "Yes, I'm sure that was all for my sake, and not your own ego and greed. I don't know what game you're playing, Mr. Mornett, but I have the edges of it now, and I *will* find my way to the center. And when I do, you will regret ever speaking to me at the Colloquium."

I do not need some photograph to record his reaction for me, the better to later examine it. It is seared well enough into my memory. He stiffened, mock warmth giving way to sudden chill, and he did not say anything else as I left the auction house.

The only problem is, my declaration was at least half bravado. That he *is* playing a game, I am absolutely convinced: him, Mrs. Kefford, and Lord Gleinleigh. I think they're up to something, and it must involve the tablets.

But what do I do now? These bits and pieces I have: are they edges or sections from the middle? It's like having fragments of an incomplete clay tablet and no way to tell how they should be placed relative to one another. And one fragment I might have had—the cylinder seal—has now been snatched from my fingers. I should have outbid him, and damn the cost.

~~But no. I flinched, and now I will never~~

I refuse to admit defeat this easily.

What would Grandmama do?

Not give up, that's for sure. And not let anything get in her way. Grandmama did not get to where she is, being one of the most famous and respected women in the world, by accepting that anything could stop her. She told the obstacles she was stronger than they were, and then she proved it.

So. If Aaron Mornett wanted that cylinder seal so badly . . .

Then I need to take a look at it.

ARREST #: 09KZ421
    Date/Time: 20/06/5662 @ 0220
    Officer: Constable Samson Torrell

DEFENDANT
    Camherst, Audrey Isabella Mahira Adiaratou
    #3 Clarton Square
    Falchester, NOC 681

    Date of birth: 17/10/5639
    Place of birth: Vidwatha

    Sex: Female
    Age: 23

    Height: 167 cm.
    Weight: 65 kg.
    Body: Slender
    Hair: Dark brown, curly
    Eyes: Dark brown
    Complexion: Medium brown

    Appearance
    Clothing: Loose trousers and blouse of a dark
    colour, ankle boots, kerchief over hair
    Glasses worn: no
    Identifying marks: scar between thumb and first
    finger of left hand

    Family/Employment information
    Father: Jacob Camherst
    Marital status: single
    Occupation: Philologist

OFFENSE
    Location type: Hotel
    Selwright Hotel
    #31 Michaeling Street
    Falchester NEE 154
    Charge: breaking and entering, trespass to land

FALCHESTER POLICE DEPARTMENT
OFFICER'S NARRATIVE REPORT
  Reference: #402957
  Officer: Samson Torrell

At 2330 hrs on 19065662 I was sent to the Selwright Hotel
following a phone report from the manager Mr. Peter
Grance of a disturbance in the room of a guest on the
third floor. When I arrived I was met by Mr. Grance, who
conducted me to his office, where they were holding the
alleged defendant and the alleged victim. The defendant
was identified to me as Miss Audrey Camherst, and the
victim as Mr. Aaron Mornett.

Mr. Mornett stated that he had returned to his hotel room
following a late dinner and evening drinking at his club,
Vine's, to find Miss Camherst in the room. She had in her
hand an artifact (a "cylinder seal") he had purchased
earlier that day at an auction of antiquities. He asked
her how she had gotten in, to which she gave no satisfactory answer; Mr. Mornett said that she instead threw the
artifact at him and demanded to know "why it mattered." I
asked him whether the item had been damaged and he said
no, that he had caught it before it could strike the wall.
He went on to state that the two of them became engaged
in an argument loud enough that it drew the attention of
hotel staff, and that upon being asked by the manager, he
said that Miss Camherst had broken into his room to steal
something that belonged to him. After this the manager
called the police station and escorted Miss Camherst down
to his office, accompanied by Mr. Mornett.

Following this statement, I informed Miss Camherst of her
right to remain silent and then questioned her. She admitted that she had entered Mr. Mornett's room unlawfully
for the purpose of looking at the artifact, which she had
failed to win during the auction earlier that day. I
asked her how she entered the room, and she said that the

sailors on her father's ship had taught her "many interesting skills," by which she appeared to mean the art of
lock-picking. She insisted she had no intent of stealing
the artifact, only of studying the figures carved into
it. At this point Mr. Mornett interrupted to say that he
regretted accusing Miss Camherst of theft, claiming that
he had spoken in the heat of the moment. Miss Camherst
said angrily that she "would not steal that thing for all
the jade in Yelang," adding that it was "quite worthless."
She then accused Mr. Mornett of luring her to his hotel
room by buying the item, but when I attempted to question
her further on this point, she became very silent and
behaved in an embarrassed manner.

The artifact in question is a cylindrical piece of stone
about three centimeters in length, metallic grey in colour (Mr. Mornett identified it as hematite), with a hole
drilled through it and several figures carved into its
surface. One corner is chipped, but Mr. Mornett stated
that damage was present when he bought the artifact at
Emmerson's Auction House earlier that day.

Mr. Mornett declined to press charges against Miss Camherst for her alleged intent to steal or damage his property. Mr. Grance pressed charges for unlawful entry to a
guest room. Mr. Mornett attempted to persuade him not to
do so, but failed. I placed handcuffs on Miss Camherst
and transported her to the Bench Street station by foot.
She made no attempt to resist. She was kept in lock-up
until her father, The Hon. Jacob Camherst, arrived around
0330, stating that he had received an "anonymous tip" that
his daughter was at the station. Miss Camherst was then
released without bail, with orders to present herself to
police the following day.

From the diary of Audrey Camherst

20 MESSIS

At least this time I don't have a broken nose.

No, instead I have public humiliation, which is *so* much better. I imagine it's all over the papers by now—I haven't dared to look—they always love it so much when a relative of somebody famous gets into trouble, and Grandmama is certainly famous, especially with her memoirs having been published recently. Even if Mornett keeps his mouth shut, which I doubt, all the rags scour the police charge sheets for juicy tidbits.

I wouldn't even care, I swear I wouldn't, if it weren't for Lotte. And of course that was the first thing Papa said to me once the door closed safely behind us. "What do you think people will say?" he demanded. "I know you don't give a tarred rope end for marriage and never have, and I support you in that. But Lotte *does,* and I support her in that, too—and now everyone will be talking about her sister, who broke into a man's hotel room in the middle of the night."

I can bear almost anything except Papa being angry at me. "I know, I know, I'm sorry," I said, but words can't make up for this botch, and we both know it.

"What possessed you?" he said, pacing the front hall like a lion in its cage. "Over some cylinder seal? Audrey, I know you share Mother's passion for your work, but surely nothing can be *that* important."

"It wasn't the seal for its own sake," I said, wringing my hands. "It was—oh, I can't even explain it—"

"Try," he said, in an ominous voice.

So I tried. I told him about the auction, the way Mornett had baited me. "It sounds to me," Papa said, "like you're letting your loathing of the man get in the way of your good judgment."

How could I argue with that? It's true. But it also isn't the whole story. "I saw something, though," I told him. "Right before I heard someone outside the room and tried to hide. On Mornett's desk—there was a letter to him from Zachary Hallman."

That brought Papa around like a ship being club-hauled. "The Hadamist leader? The one at the riot?"

"They knew one another at school, and they're both members of Vine's. Aaron—Mornett, I mean—he always told me that he and Hallman had drifted apart after school, when Hallman got more rabid about Draconeans." Say what you will against Mornett (and I could fill the rest of this diary with it, if I had the time and the will), but he's not a Hadamist. He's just convinced that Draconeans belong in their place, which is safely cooped up in the mountains on the other side of the world.

Papa said, "You think he was lying?"

"I don't know," I admitted. "That is—no, I think he was sincere when he said it. That was several years ago, but now . . ."

Now he has paid two thousand guineas for a cylinder seal carved with what the trained eye can instantly identify as four figures supplicating, not a god, but an ordinary Draconean queen. It has no significance whatsoever apart from the fact that Mornett, I now remember, very much likes hematite—but if his sympathies really had swung so hard against Draconeans as to align him with Hallman, I can't imagine him paying so much for one of their relics, much less borrowing from Mrs. Kefford to do it.

Papa smacked the heel of his hand against the wall a few times, then said, "Do you think Mornett had anything to do with that riot?"

At the airfield, when I got my nose broken. "I—I don't *think* so, but—"

But I can't be sure.

Mornett showed up at Stokesley that same night. I assumed his business was the tablets, but that was because I hadn't thought about his connection to Hallman. What if that, and not the epic, was what brought him there so late at night?

Or both, because it's all connected.

Papa shook his head, came forward, and cupped my face in his hands, which always makes me feel like I am six years old again, in both the good ways and the bad. He said with quiet intensity, "You didn't know about the letter when you broke in. It's pure chance that you found it. Audrey—you *can't* go doing things like that. What if Mornett was every bit that bad and more, and he—" Emotion choked off his voice.

Why do I not realize the important things until much too late? Papa's father, the Grandpapa I never knew, died in circumstances not much different from mine. I want to say that such a thing could never happen here, but the police charge-sheets are full of stories that would prove me wrong. And Mornett . . .

Would he hurt me?

Of course he would, because he has. But I mean hurting me physically. Even when we had that last dreadful argument, the one where I called him every foul name I could think of in every language I know and swore I would never speak to him again, he never raised a hand to me. I don't think he hates me; at worst I'm a sad little mouse scurrying about in front of an amused cat. No, even that is too predatory an image: I'm a child to him, and he's an adult. That's why he felt it was all right to steal my ideas, why he didn't feel the need to press charges last night.

I didn't say any of that to Papa. I only hugged him, and apologized, and promised I would apologize to Lotte, and I'm going to have to apologize to Gleinleigh, too, when he finds out I can't go back to Stokesley yet because I have to stay around to answer those charges of breaking and entering. And I'm sure Mornett has already told him why.

The whole thing is haunting me now. I tried to go to sleep without writing any of this down, because I didn't really want to face it, but every time I close my eyes, I see Papa's nightmare scenario. Even if I'm right about Mornett not hurting me . . . what if Hallman had been there when I got caught redhanded? *Him* I have no doubt about at all.

Can the two of them really be working together? Oh, why couldn't I have had just a moment longer—enough to read that letter!

From: Alan Preston
To: Simeon Cavall

21 Messis
Makan, Akhia

Dear Simeon,

*Do you remember when we were boys and Mr. Bunwell decided
to convert his south field from pasturage to oats? He plowed up
that old Svaltansk sword, and became convinced he'd found
the long-lost site of the Battle of Three Queens. Poor man
scoured the field from one end to the other, digging down to the
bedrock, but he never found anything apart from that sword:
no other weapons, no arrowheads, not so much as a single broken link of chainmail.*

*I don't think he ever did figure out how the sword got there.
Maybe it was dropped by a fleeing Svaltansk soldier. Maybe it
was a souvenir taken by one of the Uainish, whose wife threw it
out because she was tired of listening to his war stories. Maybe
some children hid it as part of a game, then forgot where it was.
Maybe it fell out of the sky.*

*As you may have guessed, I'm beginning to think Lord
Gleinleigh's cache is the equivalent of old Bunwell's sword.
For all I can tell, it did fall out of the sky.*

*I can't claim to have searched the entire Qajr, of course.
That would take far more time (not to mention funding) (not
to mention patience) than I have. These hills are riddled with
little caves and alcoves and crevasses, any one of which could
theoretically hold something of interest. But "theory" and
"practice" are different things, and so far? I've found nothing.*

Oh, there are archaeological traces here. Apparently the region was very popular with Tohrimite hermits back in the forty-third century, because we've found all manner of evidence for their activities. Which is of great interest to scholars of fifth-millennium Segulist fundamentalist heresy, I'm sure—but not so much for those of us concerned with Draconeans. And I can hardly imagine any Tohrimites taking care to hide away a collection of ancient tablets scribed by the Great Beasts themselves. They'd be far more likely to have smashed them, ground the bits into powder, salted the powder, and scattered the result to the wind.

So maybe I was right to begin with, and Gleinleigh let me come down here because he knew there was nothing left to find. At any rate, as much as it galls me to write the words "I give up" . . . unless you can give me a good reason to keep searching, I think I give up. I don't mind the climate and ever-present grit of this region when I have something fascinating to distract me, but so far the most interesting thing I've found is the cave wall where a Tohrimite scratched a tick mark for every day of his hermitage. (I couldn't be bothered to count them all, but at a glance, I'd say he was out here for twenty years. Or at least he wanted people to think so.)

I'm going to retire for the moment to Al-Wakhar, where at least there are baths, and await your reply. Write soon, or self-pity will win out and I'll be on a boat back to Falchester by the time your letter arrives.

More filthy than you can believe,
Alan

From: Ralph Stanyard
To: Cora Fitzarthur

University of Minter
Department of Geology
22 Messis

Dear Miss Fitzarthur,

My apologies for taking so long to respond to your letter of 15 Floris. I must admit your query was an unusual one, as I do not often receive letters from young women regarding prehistoric volcanic eruptions, but it is not as much of a shot in the dark as you seemed to think.

I should caution you that it's difficult to be certain about dates. There are promising new techniques being developed that could assist in determining the ages of geological strata via analysis of isotopes, but these are useful for studying formations we believe to be millions of years old, not mere thousands. For events that recent, we're limited to the principles of relative dating—decreeing a particular layer to be older than the one above it, and younger than the one below. And since your question concerns a time before writing, we can only make educated guesses as to when any given layer was deposited.

Having said that: within the period you specified, there are two eruptions known that might fit the bill. One is Mt. Dezhnie, a peak in the eastern Vystrani mountains that has since gone extinct. (Or at least we should hope it is extinct, not merely dormant; another eruption on the scale of the prehistoric one would be devastating for central Anthiope.) There's a substantial ash layer indicating a massive event in the late Novolapidian period, which might be what you're looking for.

But the cooling effects associated with a large eruption are not confined to the immediate vicinity of that eruption. When Mt. Anagwàande erupted in 5211, scholars from Vidwatha to Akhia noted poor harvests and early frosts for two years afterward. You might therefore consider Mt. Thuano, on the coast of Ikhadsai in Dajin. It erupted around the same time as Mt. Dezhnie in Vystrana—in fact, there was an interesting article published in the Journal of Volcanology *that suggests, based on analysis of ash layers, that the two may have been all but simultaneous. (On a geological scale, mind you—this does not mean in the same week. Perhaps a decade or so apart.) I can't wholeheartedly endorse that theory, but there are signs of truly severe winters around that time, quite out of scale with what you might expect from either eruption on its own; a double punch from two separate volcanoes might explain it.*

I hope that answers your question. I confess myself curious as to why a young woman such as yourself has taken an interest in this rather arcane topic, and would be delighted to know the reason for your asking.

Sincerely,
Dr. Ralph Stanyard

⁓

From the notebook of Cora Fitzarthur

Kudshayn is having trouble. It's a warm summer and he doesn't breathe well in heat, especially when it gets humid. (Peculiar—that's the exact opposite of Miss Simpson's asthma.) He's been trying to hide it, which is stupid, because I can't do anything if I don't know there's a problem.

Can I do anything now that I know there's a problem? Uncle left me in charge while he was gone (again), so this is clearly my responsibility.

Kudshayn needs cooler temperatures and drier air. Methods for achieving one or both of these:

1) Fans, either hand-powered or electrical. Pros: very easy to get. Cons: they don't really cool the air, just make you feel a little bit better.

2) Hang damp curtains and let the water evaporate. Pros: cools the air. Cons: only by a little, and it makes the air more humid.

3) Ship in ice from Svaltan. Pros: makes the air much cooler. Cons: expensive, messy when it melts, and we'd need to keep on shipping it in, since there is no good room for storing that quantity of ice at Stokesley.

4) Contact one of the companies that manufactures ice and buy some from them. Pros: same as above. Cons: same as above, except probably a little cheaper.

5) Find out how the ships that bring meat from places like Otholé keep it from going bad. Pros: if it can keep meat from spoiling, it must be cold enough for Kudshayn, and we would presumably need only one machine. Cons: I don't know where to get one, and it's probably *very* expensive.

Tablet XII: "The Worms Tablet"
translated by Kudshayn

Word[49] went out among all the people.[50] They had seen
the Light of the World vanish and return; they heard now
how this came to pass. They heard of the courage of
Samšin, the kindness of Nahri, the cleverness of Imalkit,
the sacrifice of Ektabr, who dwelt forevermore in the
underworld.

Samšin lay beneath the light of the ghost.[51] Samšin slept
in the silver light. Samšin lay through the night and
dreamed.

She dreamt of a tree to the south, green and growing.
Beneath the tree lived a mass of worms, a tangled and
writhing knot, gnawing at the roots of the tree. She
dreamt of a river to the south, blue and swift. At the

---

49 Here the style shifts again, as before.—K

50 How many Draconeans would there have been back then?—CF

It is difficult to say. This does not depict accurate history as we
would think of it; quite apart from matters like three sisters inventing
metalworking, agriculture, and legal systems overnight, I do not
think the world as it is described can be considered anything other
than mythic representation. We have no evidence that there was ever
a widespread community of Anevrai living separate from human
contact; on the contrary, the evidence we have suggests that they
always existed in the context of human society, and only later came
to be numerous enough to rule over the civilization whose ruins we
know today. I think this story depicts very much an idealized
scenario.—K

51 The ancient word for "moon" is *arweh*. Lord Trent speculated, based
on the Qurrat Fragment, that this was etymologically related to the
root for "ghost"; based on what we have read in this tale, I think that
is true, and have translated the term accordingly here.—K

headwaters of the river lived a mass of worms, a tangled and writhing knot, fouling the waters of the river. She dreamt of a mountain to the south, golden and tall. At the base of the mountain lived a mass of worms, a tangled and writhing knot, shaking the foundations of the mountain.[52]

Samšin woke, troubled. She gathered her sisters together and said, "I have had a dream. I saw worms to the south, gnawing at the roots of a tree, fouling the waters of a river, shaking the foundations of a mountain. Imalkit, go and see what you can learn of this." Imalkit cupped her wings about her body and obeyed.

Samšin was still troubled. She said, "We have regained the Light of the World, but we still do not know how it was lost. We do not know if it will happen again. Nahri, go to our people and tell them to come to me, so that we may take counsel and plan." Nahri cupped her wings about her body and obeyed.[53]

The people came together at the place called Crescent Lake. Samšin organized them according to their

---

52 Odd. I would expect the usual directional associations of the colours, but all of these are said to lie to the south, and black is omitted. Because Ektabr is dead? But that does not explain the focus on the south.—K

53 Didn't they use to do things together? Now Samšin's giving orders.—CF

Modern Draconean society is ruled by sister-groups at the local level, a council of elder females at the top. But in the past there seems to have been a single queen assisted by her sisters—or possibly some of them were termed "sisters" as a courtesy title, rather than hatching from the same clutch or other clutches of the same mother—so this may be the beginning of that.—K

It seems very unfair to Nahri and Imalkit.—CF

Politics and governance are rarely fair.—K

skills, according to their age. She established deference and courtesy[54] among them. Some of the people protested, saying, "It has never been this way before." Samšin said, "Before, we dwelt always under the Light of the World. But when it was lost, who among you fought the star demons? Who descended to the underworld to bring it back? Who faced torments among the dead; who fought the *khashetta*? Who bargained with the Crown of the Abyss to return the Maker of Above and Below to the sky?" They cupped their wings about their bodies and were silent.

Imalkit returned while the chief among them were in council. She said, "I have been to the south, to the land of the worms of my sister's dream. There are creatures there, like and yet unlike people, called the *āmu*, created by the Foundation of All to crawl upon the earth."

Samšin said, "You have not said all. What do you keep back?"

Imalkit said, "These creatures know that we are favoured by the Maker of Above and Below. They know they were considered unworthy by the Three, and so jealousy eats away at their hearts."

Samšin said, "You have not said all. What do you keep back?"

Imalkit said, "There is a mountain in their lands that vomits forth fire and ash."

---

54 We know that Anevrai society at its height was separated by caste and rigidly governed by a system of etiquette; I suppose this is crediting those later developments to the mythical founder, as a method of legitimizing them. It suggests that this section of the text, at least, is a product of the classic period.—K

Samšin said, "You have not said all. What do you keep back?"

Imalkit said, "These creatures dug into the depths of the mountain until it grew enraged. It was this mountain that ate[55] the Light of the World, sending it down to be caged by the Crown of the Abyss."

When they heard this, the members of the council fell into an uproar. They did not know what to do about these creatures to the south. Many among them were afraid, and many more were angry, condemning them to the underworld for their crime. For many days they argued.

Tayyit emerged as a leader among them, who had been a sheltering wing to the four when they were young. She said, "Let us send messengers to these creatures. Let us tell them of your deeds in retrieving the Light of the World, of the price your brother Ektabr paid to bring it back. Let them marvel at your skill and your power. They will fear us and commit such crimes no more." But others cried out against her, saying that any messengers would be killed.

Upādat spoke for another group, those who argued for caution. She said, "Let us flee to the north, away from these creatures. Let us go where they cannot find us. If they are so heartless as to strike at the Maker of Above and Below, they will not hesitate to do the same to us. We must go to where we will be safe." But others cried out

---

55 Unquestionably a volcanic eruption, then, and not a solar eclipse. At least in the symbolism of the myth—that does not guarantee any kind of factual truth behind it.—K

   Especially since that's not how you make a volcano erupt. Or at least I don't think it is. How *do* you make a volcano erupt? Has anybody ever done it on purpose?—CF

   Not that I know of.—K

against her, saying that no corner of the earth was safe from those made by the Foundation of All.

There was a third group, led by Abikri, who insisted that nothing need be done. She said, "Let us remain as we are. They have tried already to destroy the Light of the World, and they have failed; it will not be caught so easily a second time. We have nothing to fear from these creatures, who are worms crawling on the ground compared to us."

Samšin rose. She stood before them, brave Samšin, noble Samšin, fiercest of the four, and she said, "Worms they may be, but shall they escape justice for their crime? Are we so lacking in devotion to our creator that we will let their sin pass unpunished, simply because it cannot be done a second time? Are we so lacking in courage that we must flee from creatures whose only true strength lies in envy and malice? Are we so pitiably weak that we must speak to them with our wings folded about our bodies, showing respect where they have earned none?"

All fell silent. She said, "We are neither weak, nor cowardly, nor lacking in devotion. We will show these creatures to the south why we were created by the Maker of Above and Below. We will go in force among them and make them pay for their blasphemy. We will come to them as a claw of light, because I have brought justice into the world, and justice demands that we answer."

For the archives of the Sanctuary of Wings
written by Kudshayn, son of Ahheke, daughter of Iztam

For the first time in my life, I find myself wishing I had come from my shell female.

Ever since our re-emergence into the world of humans, one biological fact of our species—that eighty percent of our hatchlings are female—has dominated their perception of us. The presumed "kings" of ancient history have been revealed as queens, and human prejudices against the female sex have caused them to find that fact remarkable. Cartoonists use it as fodder for their jokes, and Hadamists as fuel for their hatred.

Now we have this tale: the origin of those queens. A chance at last to tell our own story, to give humanity an image of our foremothers that is neither the cruel tyrant of their Scriptures, nor the exaggerated figure of a newspaper cartoon.

Or so I once hoped.

But as I work, I can see the tyrant taking shape in Samšin. She who was once praised for her courage and leadership is hardening into a figure of authority and command, superior to even her own sisters. In other circumstances, this would merely be a matter of historical and philosophical interest . . . but it will have repercussions this winter, when the elders of the Sanctuary come to Falchester.

They will be the first females of my people most members of

the congress have encountered—the first of my people altogether. And when those humans look at the elders, they will see what stories have conditioned them to see: Draconean queens. The tyrants of Scripture, reinforced by this tale. I already know from Lady Trent that human governments have assumed, again and again, that a single person must lead our land; the existence of the council confuses them. Had Samšin remained equal with Nahri and Imalkit, it might have gone some way toward helping humanity understand how we govern ourselves, because stories shape our perceptions more than we like to admit.

Had I been female, I might have done more to counteract those assumptions. But I am a priest, not a queen, and Teslit's health prevents her from acting as my counterpart. She is more like Nahri than Samšin—but I fear that in the days to come, Nahri and Imalkit will be forgotten, and only Samšin remembered.

Radiant fire, help humans see beyond her. Help them see the elders as they truly are: sisters in heart if not in shell, chosen for their wisdom rather than their force, governing in cooperation rather than domination. Do not let this one tale shape our future as well as our past.

From the diary of Audrey Camherst

24 MESSIS

A fine, a written apology, and never setting foot on the grounds of the Selwright Hotel again: that is the price of my indiscretions. I've gotten off lightly, and Papa has made certain I know it.

I should go back to Stokesley. Gleinleigh is furious with me—he says it's because of the delay, but I have to assume he also realizes I'm onto him, Mornett, and Mrs. Kefford. I can't tell whether I would learn more by staying here, or by returning to work. The one thing I'm certain of is that this all has to do with the epic somehow. Simeon says Alan found nothing of use out in the Qajr, but maybe if I look more closely at the tablets I'll understand how.

But the choice isn't entirely mine to make. The scandal would fade out of the public eye more rapidly if I left town, but Lotte insists that I accompany her to the race at Chiston the day after tomorrow. She is determined to brazen the whole mess out; when Papa suggested that it might not be the best thing for me to show my face at the last great event of the Season, she swore up and down that she would not have the world thinking she has turned her back on me. I almost wish Gleinleigh would come here and try to demand my return, just so I could watch him lose an argument to my little sister. There's no shifting Lotte when she's like this—it's all sails spread with a following wind.

My head is all in a muddle at this point. The truth is, I don't want to go back and be cooped up in Stokesley again. Even the tablets are not the temptation they ought to be, because of . . .

All right. Lotte, if you are reading this, three things. First, you have broken your promise to stop sneaking looks at my diary, and I hope you're ashamed of yourself. Second, I'm glad you're keeping up your Talungri, rather than letting it rust. And third, you are utterly forbidden to tell Father what I did this afternoon, when I told him I was going for a walk to clear my head.

I did go for a walk—straight to the nearest streetcar stop, and then to the Selwright. I didn't step over the property line, but I waited across the street at a very mediocre little café. And I think Mornett must have known that I would, because when he came out of the hotel about half an hour later, he spotted me immediately, and came over to talk to me.

I'd spent that half hour thinking about what to say to him. When he came within range, I didn't waste time saying hello or anything foolish like that. I just asked him, point-blank: "Are you still friends with Zachary Hallman?"

And it worked. I caught him off guard; he wasn't expecting the question and didn't control his reaction as well as he might have. I saw . . . shock, naturally, but also guilt—and also, I think, disgust. As if he was horrified that I should ask him that.

Then he reddened, because of course anger was the next thing to come along. "Have you been reading my letters?"

He sounded a little bit afraid, too. He'd been approaching my table like he meant to sit down with me, but now he stood poised like he might run. I said, as icily as I could manage, "No. Unlike some people, I don't stoop that low." (I would have if he'd given me another thirty seconds that night, but Mornett doesn't need to know that.) "I only saw it on your desk when I went to put the cylinder seal back. I thought you cut ties with Hallman years ago."

"I did," Mornett snapped. "It's only—"

"Only what?" I said. I should have let him keep talking, because he might have given something away . . . but I'd spent the entire trip to the Selwright and that half hour in the café planning out what I would say, and it came out by reflex. "Only a scheme you cooked up with Gleinleigh?"

Mornett recoiled, and I pressed my advantage. "Did you put him in touch with Hallman? *Somebody* must have tipped the Hadamists to Kudshayn's arrival. What was the plan—that Gleinleigh would heroically save the day and look like a great friend to Draconeans, instead of a Calderite? So terribly sorry that I made a hash of that by charging in."

"And getting yourself hurt," he said furiously.

"Very fine of you to care about me being hurt *now*," I snapped.

He jerked as if I'd slapped him. "Are you talking about five years ago? Audrey, that was a misunderstanding—"

A misunderstanding! Sometimes I honestly think he believes that—believes the calculations for the draconic year were his own, or at least that he had the idea and I just did the maths. He can delude himself into anything.

I almost started that argument all over again, even though I know it will never go anywhere useful. But Mornett kept talking, saying, "Whatever you may think of me, Audrey, I have no desire to see you get your head bashed in with a brick. Hallman's a contemptible ass; what redeeming characteristics he had when we were at school have been strangled by this religious mania of his. I wrote to him after that mess in Ventis because I wanted him to know that if he ever hurts you again, I will—"

"Will what?" I shot to my feet, knocking my coffee cup over when I hit the table. "*Mr. Mornett*. Get this through your dragonbone skull: you have absolutely no right to defend me. You are not my brother or my cousin, and you will never be my husband, whatever you may have thought five years ago. You are not even my friend. To this day you have not apologized for your intellectual dishonesty, and if you said the words I wouldn't believe them, because I don't think you recognize what you did wrong. Nor does the mere fact of not being as bad as Hallman make you a friend to the Draconeans. *I have no use for you*. My biggest mistake the other night wasn't breaking into your room; it was ever thinking that you had anything of value to offer me. But I am done thinking that now."

And then I stormed away.

Lotte, I almost hope you *are* reading this, even though you promised not to, because then you will know all of this without me having to tell you. I don't know if I could get the words out in person, not even with you. I don't know how much of what I said to Mornett I actually meant. I still don't trust him, and I think he *did* arrange the whole thing with Gleinleigh, because otherwise it's too much of a coincidence that the Hadamists were there, that their leader was Mornett's school friend, that Mornett came to Stokesley that night to shout at Gleinleigh.

But at the same time, it *destroys* me that he's wasting a mind like his on the Mrs. Keffords of the world, on trying to assert human superiority over Draconeans, on passing other people's work off as his own when he's perfectly capable of great achievements without that. He would be a lovely human being, and not just in the physical sense, if he weren't so determined to be *un*-lovely all the time.

No, I am not over him. I keep telling myself that I am, but it's a lie. I don't like him, but I keep reaching for the kind of peace that will make me be all right with not liking him, and it keeps escaping me.

I should never have gone to the auction.

From: Charlotte Camherst
To: Isabella, Lady Trent

27 Messis
#3 Clarton Square

Dear Grandmama,

I am so sorry for bothering you with this when I know the prep-
arations for the congress have you flying all over the world, but
I'm afraid I desperately need your advice—not for myself, but
for Audrey.

By the time my letter reaches you I expect you'll have heard
about what happened with her and Aaron Mornett, sneaking
into his hotel room and all. And you probably also heard about the
riot and the Hadamists back in Ventis, when Audrey got her nose
broken—from the newspapers if nowhere else. But there's more
going on than just that, which you probably don't know anything
about, unless Papa has mentioned it to you in his letters. Or Au-
drey, but she would have had to have done it while she was here in
Falchester, because while she's at Stokesley there's someone read-
ing her mail to make sure she doesn't spill any details about what
she's doing, and oh, things have gotten so complicated. *And some*
of it may be my fault, because I'm the one who insisted Audrey
stay for the race at Chiston, instead of going back to work.

This is all out of order. I'm sorry.

Audrey thinks there is some kind of conspiracy going on be-
tween Lord Gleinleigh, Aaron Mornett, and Mrs. Kefford.
She may be right; they've all been behaving very oddly, and we
know they've talked to one another. (And to Zachary Hall-

man, that Hadamist stink.) That's why she broke into Mornett's room, because she wanted to know what they were up to.

I should have known it was more of the same when she showed up this morning for the race. She was covered from head to foot, with gloves and long sleeves and a long skirt and the most modest broad-brimmed hat you can imagine—and I know for a fact she doesn't own anything like that get-up; she must have gone and bought it specially. At the time I thought it was just because she wanted to avoid gossip about her arrest. Let's face it: she and I are hardly inconspicuous, and while swathing herself in fabric wasn't exactly subtle (nor could it have been at all comfortable), it did at least mean she couldn't be spotted from across the field. It seemed terribly unlike her to hide from the gossips like that, but I chalked it up to her being so rattled by Mornett.

Except this is Audrey. I should have known better.

We went to the racecourse. A few months ago it would have been thrilling for me, so many fine people in so many fine outfits, but after a whole Season of things like this, I have to admit that even I'm a bit worn down. I didn't object at all when Audrey asked if I would mind her wandering about; I was content to sit with Mama and enjoy the sunshine. Audrey, I assumed, just didn't want to stay in one place where it would be easy to spot her—we'd already had more than a few ladies whispering behind their fans at us.

But when they started the preliminary races and she didn't come back, I got more and more worried. What if she was hiding somewhere, miserable because I'd dragged her out in public when she would rather have gone back to her tablets? Finally I told Mama I was going to go look for her and set off.

If Audrey had really wanted to hide, she would have left the

Royal Enclosure and gone somewhere else on the premises. I was prepared to chase her down anywhere, even if it meant missing the main race. But as it happened, no sooner did I go into the gallery under the viewing stands than I saw her up ahead, walking slowly but very steadily through the crowd.

Maybe it would have been better if I'd left her to it—I don't know. I almost did. But I had fixed in my mind that I was going to apologize for making her come, and so I trotted to catch up with her.

When I caught her sleeve, she nearly jumped out of her skin. Then she said, "Lotte! What are you doing? Leave me alone."

I would have taken that as hurtful, except that she was craning her neck while she said it. Foolishly, I said, "Are you looking for someone?"

"Following her, is more like," Audrey said, and pulled free of my hand. "I saw her snarling at Gleinleigh earlier, but couldn't get close enough to hear. And she's been talking to various members of the Synedrion—I've been keeping track of whom, so I can figure out whether—" She stamped her foot in sudden frustration. "Blast! You've made me lose sight of her."

I am terribly slow on the uptake. There may be scads of people in the Royal Enclosure on race day, because anyone who can get in is sure to do so—but how many of them would Audrey be trailing? Wrapped up in garments that make it as difficult as possible to recognize her?

When you limit it to women, the answer is "one." But my mouth works faster than my brain, and so I said, "What? Lost sight of whom?"

And then I saw her, but not soon enough to warn Audrey.

"Me, I suspect," said Mrs. Kefford, in that careless drawl of hers. "Miss Camherst. I thought I saw you flailing along

behind me like a duckling. My dear, if you have something to say to me, don't be shy; come up and say it in person."

Of course she was flawlessly dressed, not in the latest fashions—she's too old to carry those off without people whispering about mutton dressed up as lamb—but managing to look elegant rather than old-fashioned in her swan-bill corset. It would be so much easier to shrug off her nastiness if she didn't always dress so smartly. And with Audrey standing there looking as dowdy as a schoolmistress, I'm sure it only made things worse.

"My apologies, Mrs. Kefford," I said hastily, trying to save the situation. "Audrey and I were just—"

"Spying on me?" she said, smiling faintly. "You're really much better suited to skulking about at night, my dear. This is not your milieu."

I went hot all over. Trust Mrs. Kefford to find a way to allude to Audrey's break-in and scorn us for being half Utalu, all in one nasty sentence. But Audrey didn't even turn a hair. She only said, "And neither are Draconean affairs yours, but you persist on poking your nose into them anyway. Lately it seems like everywhere I turn, I find your dirty fingerprints all around my work."

She gave her high, mocking laugh, the one that sounds like crystal breaking. "My dirty fingerprints? I believe yours are the ones now on file with the Falchester police. You are the one invading people's private affairs, Miss Camherst, not me: following them around, trying to listen in on their conversations, reading their letters . . ."

Audrey pounced on that. "You must have me confused with—"

I'm sure she was about to say "Lord Gleinleigh" or "Cora

Fitzarthur." I don't know why she stopped herself, unless it's because Cora promised not to tell her uncle she admitted to reading Audrey's letters on his orders, and Audrey didn't want to give that away if Cora hadn't.

The problem is, stopping allowed Mrs. Kefford an opening. The whole conversation was like a tennis match, except with a bomb in place of a ball, and Audrey gave up a good volley when there were only a few seconds left on the fuse. Mrs. Kefford isn't the kind of person to let something like that go to waste, and I knew, as she stepped in and laid a mock-friendly hand on Audrey's arm, that the bomb was about to go off.

"You know," she said, "you don't need to invent conspiracies just so you have an excuse to see him. Aaron's still quite smitten with you—as you are with him, clearly, going to his hotel room like that so late at night."

And that's when Audrey hauled off and slapped her.

I nearly died of horror, Grandmama. I was sure Audrey would be arrested again, and it would be all my fault for making her come to the racecourse with me. The Earl of Granby saw it all happen and immediately intervened, and I could just see the headlines: BRAWL IN THE ROYAL ENCLOSURE.

In hindsight, I should have guessed this isn't the first time someone has slapped another person at Chiston. They're quite used to hushing up such things there, for the dignity of all involved. And since we were inside, not out where the press could see us, nobody has any photographic proof of the moment. So there are rumours, but Audrey's reputation isn't made any worse.

But Grandmama . . . she and I talked afterward, and what she said has me so worried. I asked what possessed her to follow Mrs. Kefford around like that—and she must have been planning it from the start, or she wouldn't have dressed that way, *covering herself up as much as she could. The conversation spiraled from that to all the other things she's been doing lately, breaking into Mornett's hotel room, charging the Hadamists at the airfield; we were up all night. And somewhere in those hours, Audrey admitted that every time she's found herself faced with a problem, she's asked herself: "What would Grandmama do?"*

So you see why I must ask for your advice. I feel quite sure that you wouldn't do what Audrey has done, but I don't know how to explain the difference to her, and I'm desperately afraid that one of these days she'll do something so foolish it will have permanent consequences. How do I tell her that she has to be more careful, without it sounding like I think she isn't capable of handling these problems?

Please, if you have any recommendations, write back at once. By the time I get your letter Audrey will have returned to Stokesley, but I can go visit her, if only I know what to say once I get there.

Your loving granddaughter,
Lotte

P.S. I've met a lovely young man named Jeremy Poole, and although he hasn't proposed, I think he will—we've made arrangements to see one another again in Rinmouth this summer. But I will put the details in a separate letter, because I want this one to go out with today's post, and besides, that story deserves not to be crammed up against the unpleasantness here.

From the diary of Audrey Camherst

28 MESSIS

Back at Stokesley. Part of me wishes I had never started on this work—but only part. Ancient Draconean I can understand, however impenetrable its grammar and orthography may sometimes be. It would be a relief to go back to what I know . . . if it weren't for everything else.

Cora. What am I to make of Cora? She bought a *refrigeration machine* while I was gone. Her uncle is going to be furious; those things are absurdly expensive. Or at least they are when you insist on having some men come out and install one the size of an entire *room* in a shed (a shed that wasn't even electrified, so now there are dirty great cables running across Gleinleigh's garden). When I lost my jaw over that, she said—with an air I can only call *smug*—that her uncle had made it very clear how vital Kudshayn is to the work we're doing here, and surely he would not want to find out his guest had dropped dead of heat exhaustion? If I didn't know better, I would say this is her way of sinking a knife into his back. Maybe that's exactly what it is. I can't tell anymore.

Kudshayn had her working with him a little, even though I didn't want her anywhere near the tablets anymore. No ambiguity there; that's his quiet way of telling me he thinks I'm wrong about her. ~~I haven't decided yet whether I'll let that continue~~

You're being an ass, Audrey, and you know it. Gleinleigh may have told Cora to obey *you*, not Kudshayn—can't have his niece following the orders of a lizard-man, now can he?—but that doesn't give you the right to overrule Kudshayn. If he wants Cora and you don't, then the two of you will just have to fight it out.

Except I don't want to fight with him about anything. I've read over what he translated in my absence, and I see why he's troubled. Worms—ugh. I mean, yes, I can see how, from a certain perspective (say, a scaled one), a human being might look like a worm, all pinkish-brown and fleshy. We still don't have proof that's what the *āmu* are, but it's getting harder and harder to imagine they could be anything else.

And that means the three sisters and their people are headed toward conflict with my species.

I shouldn't be surprised. (I'm not surprised.) Kudshayn said it himself this evening, while I sat and shivered in that icebox Cora bought for him: "The tale of the Anevrai and their empire was, in the end, a tale of human subjugation. These tablets have already told the story of how many things began, from the three species to agriculture to the existence of night and the moon; it seems it may also be the story of how that empire began."

He said it very calmly. I have no doubt he's spent days thinking about this while I was gallivanting around Falchester being an idiot, and figured out how to at least pretend it doesn't bother him very deeply. "We don't know that," I began, but he held up one hand to stop me.

"It is my fault," he said. For a moment I thought he meant the ancient empire was his fault, which made no sense, but no. "I allowed myself to imagine that this tale would be what I hoped."

I have not forgotten the conversation he and I had back in Seminis. "Your people's story."

It still is—or it could be. As near as I can tell, the requirements for calling something a national epic are that it be 1) old, 2) long, and 3) accepted as important. This isn't nearly so long as *The Great Song*, but I'd say it's at least as long as *Selethryth*, and it's unquestionably old. Whether it's important . . . that's for other people to decide, the Draconeans above all. Will they want to claim this tale as the emblem of their people, the text that captures the essence of the Draconean soul?

The whole idea is nonsense. No single story can capture the essence of a whole nation, let alone a species. But that doesn't mean people won't read it that way regardless—and if the epic causes them to look bad, Gleinleigh and Mrs. Kefford and all their ilk will make certain the Draconeans wear it.

I told Kudshayn everything that happened in Falchester. Even the bits that make me want to crawl out of my skin with shame, because they're part and parcel of my evidence: Mornett and Kefford at the auction, Mornett and Hallman corresponding, Mrs. Kefford talking to Gleinleigh again at Chiston, looking like she wanted to flay him with her words. She was buttering up various members of the Synedrion, too, the ones who aren't already in her husband's camp where Draconeans are concerned, but could perhaps be persuaded over to that side. "Maybe they're planning on using this against you," I said. "They set things up to make Gleinleigh look innocent and friendly so that you and I would come to work for him, and then . . ."

My inspiration ran out, because how could they plan in advance for what we're finding now? Even if Mornett is working from casts of the tablets, he can't have gotten through them any faster than we have. Gleinleigh and his cronies might be so convinced of Draconean inferiority that they assumed any important story from their civilization must necessarily make Kudshayn's people look stupid, evil, or both, but that seems like a lot to gamble on.

But Kudshayn has long experience of human nastiness. He said quietly, "They could arrange to make sure that what we publish is damning."

"How?" I said. And then the bottom of my stomach dropped out, and I said: "Oh."

We can write up whatever we like . . . but unless we go to the printer's and watch them cast the type for the pages and then stand over the presses, we can't ensure that what we write will be what gets published. Gleinleigh could put our names on any kind of libel.

"It would come out," I said. "Can you imagine the headlines? 'Lady Trent's Granddaughter Disavows Translation, Says Earl Lied.' I can't think of anything more likely to drum up sympathy for your people then a high-profile scandal over a clumsy attempt to defame your ancestors. They'd have to destroy the tablets so no one could ever check the source—and destroy our copies, too—and do us in for good measure, because otherwise we'd talk."

The silence that fell then was nasty. "That would be a bit much," Kudshayn said at last.

More than a bit, I should hope, but there are times when his tendency for understatement is soothing.

I don't really think our lives are in danger. I may not believe what Mrs. Kefford said about Mornett having feelings for me, but I also don't believe he would stand by and let me be killed. His outrage over the riot seemed genuine, and that only left me with a broken nose. And Gleinleigh seems an unlikely murderer. All the same, I am going to make sure we smuggle duplicates of our work out of here before we go, and insist on seeing page proofs of the book before it goes to press. Even if I'm guarding against shadows, I'll feel better for having done it.

I'm worried about what the last two tablets have in store for us, though. Kudshayn reminded me that we don't know for sure the *āmu* are meant to be humans; we don't know for sure that Samšin is going to make war on them. We didn't know the sun was going to vanish from the sky in the sixth tablet, and it's entirely possible something equally unexpected will happen between now and the end. The invocation wasn't what you'd call clear.

But I don't think the chill I felt was entirely due to sitting in an enormous icebox. I feel like I'm sailing into a fog bank, without even a chart to let me know what rocks lie in our path. I'm just sure the rocks are there.

From: Annabelle Himpton, Lady Plimmer
To: Simeon Cavall

6 Caloris
Priorfield, Greffen

Dear Dr. Cavall,

I hope you can assist me with a small matter, as I understand you are a good friend of Miss Audrey Camherst, whom I had the pleasure of hosting as a dinner guest this past Floris. She was kind enough to advise me about the purchasing of Draconean antiquities, and on her recommendation, I sent a man to acquire something for me from the auction at Emmerson's on the nineteenth. He brought back a little clay winged disc with rather faded paint, which was not precisely what I had in mind, but then he cannot be blamed, as I had given him rather vague instructions, specifying only that the item should not cost more than five hundred guineas and should not have been obtained from any private collectors in Gillae.

Regardless, I was pleased to have the artifact and promptly hung it in my drawing room, then invited some guests for dinner so they could admire it. Imagine my surprise, then, when one of those guests, Mr. Eddleston, told me he had seen it before! He claimed it was previously the property of Mr. Lawrence Ryland in Falchester, who kept it in a glass display case in his billiards room. I told him that surely he must be mistaken, because the provenance I had from Emmerson's mentions Mr. Ryland nowhere in it. But Mr. Eddleston insisted I take it down off the wall so he could look at the little inscription on the back, which he had taken a rubbing of when the disc was in Mr. Ryland's keeping. He positively identified it as the same one, and has sent me a copy of his rubbing as proof, which I enclose, along with a rubbing taken from my new decoration.

Miss Camherst made a point of telling me I should examine the provenance of anything I purchased, and so I thought that would be enough to keep me safe from any underhanded dealings. But I greatly fear now that I have unwittingly involved myself in crime! Whether the disc was stolen from Mr. Ryland or provided with a false history to cover up his ownership I cannot say, but I fear I have unwittingly purchased something illegal, which is a phrase I never thought I would have to write. (I haven't the faintest idea why Mr. Ryland would wish to hide his connection with it, as this is a perfectly respectable artifact, not at all like those vulgar ones I know some people like to collect for their private entertainment—and I imagine the ancients made them for that same reason, thus inclining me to think they are not so different from human beings as some would claim.)

Regardless, I feel certain the documentation Emmerson's provided me with is fraudulent, though who committed the fraud I cannot guess. Please do write back and advise me in the best way to proceed, as I do not wish to trouble Miss Camherst, on account of what I have read in the newspaper about her recent difficulties in Falchester, though no doubt those have been magnified all out of proportion by the reporters, who do so dearly love a scandal. (I am sure you can understand that I very much wish to avoid a scandal myself.)

Cordially,
Annabelle Himpton
Lady Plimmer

From: Isabella, Lady Trent
To: Audrey Camherst

9 Caloris
Thokha, Tser-nga

Dear Audrey,

It has come to my attention that the phrase "What would Grandmama do?" has been heard to pass your lips. Based on what I have heard concerning you lately, it seems that you are labouring under a misapprehension, and I think I had better correct it before it leads to serious harm, for you or someone else.

I can hardly deny that at various points in my life I have involved myself in any number of dangerous situations, and often on grounds that an outside observer might deem to be foolhardy. But the accounts of your behaviour I have from your father, Simeon, Lotte, and other observers give the impression that your habit is to ask "What would Grandmama do?" . . . and then, having identified the most reckless action available to you, to embark upon that course without delay.

This is not, and never has been, what your grandmama has done. Nor is it a course she can advise to you, since she has a perverse desire to see her grandchild survive to an age even older and riper than her own.

Have I been reckless? Of course I have. But it was never for the sake of recklessness, never—or at least, as rarely as my self-awareness could arrange—simply for the sake of proving a point. My foolhardiness has generally come about because my eyes were fixed so firmly upon my goal that I failed to note the cliff's edge beneath my feet . . . or because, having noted that cliff, I judged it to be of lesser significance than what I might gain.

Perhaps I misjudge you. Perhaps you have indeed made that calculation, and decided that charging a line of Hadamist protesters is the right and necessary thing to do, or breaking into Aaron Mornett's hotel room in the middle of the night, or following Mrs. Kefford around Chiston and eavesdropping on her conversations before slapping her publicly. I was not there, and even had I been, I would not have been privy to your thoughts. Only you can judge for yourself whether this is indeed the case.

I would be the last person to tell any descendant of mine that she should not pursue her dreams with all the passion and fearlessness she can muster. But be sure it is your dreams you are pursuing, and not some lesser thing: notoriety, the esteem of the foolish, or a reputation to rival my own. I sincerely hope you achieve that last—but you will only do it by being yourself as wholeheartedly as I have been myself. Anything else is mere mimicry, and beneath you.

Have a care for yourself, Audrey. The rest of us certainly do.

Your loving grandmama,
Isabella

A Catalogue of Tablets from the Gleinleigh Cache
examined by Eugene and Imogene Carter
transcribed by Cora Fitzarthur

Tablets 1–14

12.1 cm by 10 cm by 3.1 cm

A continuous text relating a mythological narrative
concerning four culture heroes of the ancient civilization. Physical characteristics date the tablets to
the Classic Period, but the text is written in Early
Draconean.

Tablet 15

8 cm by 5.5 cm by 3 cm

Fragmentary queen list from the southern Anthiopean state. Classic Period.

Tablet 16

9.2 cm by 4.7 cm by 2.8 cm

Fragmentary queen list from the western Dajin
state. Late Period.

Tablets 17–26

10.1 cm by 5 cm by 2.9 cm

Taxation records; region unknown. Late Period.

Tablet 27

5.4 cm by 4.8 cm by 2.3 cm

A personal letter. Textual evidence suggests origin
in Otholé. Downfall Period.

Tablets 28–34

6 cm by 4.2 cm by 2.6 cm

Fragmentary taxation records from northern Anthiope. Early Period.

Tablet 35

4.1 cm by 3.9 cm by 2 cm

Fragmentary prayer. Formative Period.

Tablet 36

8.7 cm by 6.1 cm by 2.5 cm

Narrative text in the form of a dialogue. Textual evidence suggests origin in Eriga. Classic Period.

Tablet 37

5.3 cm by 4.1 cm by 3 cm

Formulaic demand for tribute by Queen Takšuti to
her vassals in the Broken Sea. Late Period.

Transcriber's note: I think Tablet 37 may have been included by
mistake in the shipment sent to the Carters for analysis. When I
was packing them up, I recognized that one; it has been in
Uncle's collection for years.

From the diary of Audrey Camherst

9 CALORIS

I take back everything I have said against Cora.

Kudshayn and I were hard at work this afternoon on the next-to-last tablet when she came in with a folder in her hands. I've still been tensing up whenever I see her, and she knows it, because she stood there as rigid as the day we met and waited until I acknowledged her before she said anything. Then she thrust out the folder and said, "The Carters wrote back with what they've gotten through so far. I made a catalogue."

"Thank you," I said, because I've been trying to be civil. "I will look at it later." She just went on standing there until I got up and took the folder from her. Then she walked out of the library and banged the door behind her, and I couldn't tell if that was her way of showing she was angry with me, or sad. Either way, I didn't want to lose my train of thought, so I dropped the folder on the table and went back to wrestling with something I think may be a reference to the origins of the three ancient Draconean military orders.

After all, it was just a catalogue. Nothing we sent to the Carters looked like it had anything to do with the epic, so why should I interrupt my work to examine it? Half the reason I recruited the Carters was to make sure that got taken care of without me having to worry about it.

I don't know how much time passed. When I'm engrossed

in work, you could fly a desert drake through the room and I probably wouldn't notice. But eventually I heard Kudshayn say my name in a tone of voice that penetrated the fog of declensions and determinatives, and I looked up.

The catalogue was on the table in front of him, and Kudshayn was tapping one claw-tip in the steady rhythm that says he's puzzled by something. "What is it?" I said.

"Come look at this."

I admit I was a little annoyed. I'd been making good progress, and then Kudshayn had to go and interrupt me for the silly catalogue. "Why?"

Without looking up, he said, "Because it doesn't make sense."

"Cora probably made a mistake," I said ungraciously. Even though Kudshayn's attention was entirely on the catalogue, my imagination filled in him giving me a reproachful look anyway, because that was cattish of me and I knew it. Feeling guilty, I got up and came to peer over his shoulder.

Kudshayn ran his claw-tip down the list, one page after another. I hadn't realized the Carters had gotten through the whole cache already; they've worked remarkably fast. Of course the tablets we sent them are much easier to assess for the most part—but nevertheless, it's excellent work and proof that they deserve more chances to work on new material.

At first I didn't see what Kudshayn meant, because my mind was still on the epic and looking for something pertaining to our work. "None of these are related," I said.

He said, "Precisely."

And that's when I figured it out.

Kudshayn is right: the cache makes *no sense*. Most of the tablets are southern Anthiopean, but not all of them; some come from as far away as Dajin and the Broken Sea. And they're all over the place in terms of period, everything from early texts to things circa the Downfall. Not only aren't they related to our epic, but they aren't related to each other, either.

I said the first thing that came into my head. "This looks like the inventory from some antiquities dealer's warehouse."

Kudshayn's wings flicked in surprise, knocking me back. He didn't even apologize, just twisted on his stool to meet my gaze.

It was like the world blinked. One moment I was staring at Kudshayn; the next I was in the doorway to the library, shouting Cora's name loud enough to be heard in Yelang.

She came running, wild-eyed and out of breath. "What is it?"

By then I had the catalogue in my hands, and stabbed one finger at the footnote she'd added about tablet 37. "This one. You're sure it's from your uncle's collection?"

"Yes," she said defensively. "I made my own catalogue of his antiquities, years ago; I can show you. Though I didn't know how to make a catalogue properly at the time. That isn't the only tablet I recognized, either. It isn't my fault that they got included with the others by accident; he told me to package up everything that had been shipped here from Akhia, and they were in there, even though they shouldn't have been."

My hands clenched so tight on the folder that I crimped it, and Cora reached out as if to rescue it from my abuse. "No," I said. "They shouldn't have been. I am an *idiot*!"

Cora was kind enough not to agree with me. She just said, "Why?"

I started pacing, resisting the urge to throw the catalogue across the room. "Because there was one thing that never made sense, and I didn't think of the obvious answer. Even though it was right there in front of me the whole time."

Kudshayn's voice was a quiet growl. "How could they know."

"Exactly," I spat.

Cora stamped her foot, and her voice went high and shrill. "Tell me what's going on!"

I made myself stop pacing and face her. "Cora. Your uncle doesn't like Draconeans. Why would he invite one to come work on these tablets? Why would he hire *me*, the granddaughter of the woman who brought Kudshayn's people back into contact with humanity?"

She thought it through for a long time, while I bit down on the urge to answer my own questions. They were rhetorical, but I knew from prior experience that she would want to answer them anyway. At last she said, "To hurt you. And Kudshayn. And the Draconeans."

"But how could he be so certain this would do that? There's been no time for anyone to read the epic. These tablets aren't the kind of thing you can skim and get the gist; the language is much too archaic for that. Nobody could possibly translate them in the time between Gleinleigh finding the cache in Akhia and me arriving here."

"Unless," Kudshayn said, "he's had them a good deal longer than that."

"And that's why Alan didn't find anything in the Qajr," I said, slapping the table. "Because there's nothing *to* find, and never was. Gleinleigh staged the whole discovery, to make it look like it was new. He probably chose the Qajr because he could get the permit cheaply. But these tablets could be from *anywhere*. In fact—"

I leapt to the shelf where I've been keeping all my periodicals, the newspapers and journals that ordinarily pile up for me at home. "No, it isn't here. I read something about a temple in Seghaye that was found looted, with an empty tablet chest—*damn* Gleinleigh and all his kind! They smash their way in and rip things out of their context, so we'll never know their true provenience." Was the epic in that temple, or did it come from somewhere else? We'll never know. We can read what the words say, but all the associated context that might tell us more about their meaning is lost.

Cora was twining a lock of hair around her finger and scowling in thought. "But I don't understand why having the tablets for longer means he would hire you."

"Because of who we are," Kudshayn said softly. "Because if he wants to use these for some purpose, then it benefits him to attach famous names to it. I am the most well-known scholar of my people, and Audrey is the granddaughter of Lady Trent. Whatever we publish will gain more attention than if it came from some less prominent person."

"Or from Aaron Mornett," I said with venom.

And then the world blinked again. Cora was suddenly helping me into a chair, and I had the sour taste of bile in my mouth. Because I'd finally arrived at the logical conclusion of my own reasoning, and I knew:

Kudshayn and I are not the first people to read these tablets.

Aaron Mornett read them first.

All the work we've done here, everything we have sweated over so hard . . . Mornett did it before us. There's no need for Gleinleigh and Mrs. Kefford to interfere at the printer's, to engage in ridiculous skulduggery with sabotage and murder. They already know what we'll find. But for that to be true, they would need someone capable of translating the epic, someone versed enough in the language to work with these archaic forms, and that list is quite short. The list of people who would do it for unscrupulous purposes is even shorter.

Translating the epic was supposed to be my revenge against Aaron Mornett. Instead it's his final triumph over me.

My one bitter consolation is that he can never claim the credit for his work. Not if we're right about what they intend. The whole world will know Kudshayn and me as the original translators.

I hope that knowledge pains him a thousandth as much as I hurt right now.

Kudshayn understood, of course. He explained it to Cora while I stared blindly at the floor. At least, I think he did; I know that he talked, and after a while Cora gave me an awkward hug, which coming from her is so wildly unusual that Kudshayn must have said something to make her decide it was necessary.

"So don't go along with it," she said, while I scrubbed my face dry. "If this will be so damaging, then just stop."

It sounds horrible to say, but it was easier for me to think about how the epic could be turned against the Draconeans than about how it had hurt me. I got up and hugged Kudshayn, wishing I had wings to wrap around him, but he was busy thinking. "The creation tale could be read as offensive," he said, "if we assume the *āmu* are indeed human beings—and I think we must. But I do not think the revelation that the Anevrai believed humans to be failed precursors to their own species will shock people to any great degree."

"No," I agreed. "If there is something truly awful in this story . . ."

"Then we have yet to come to it," he said.

The worms. Imalkit blaming the loss of the sun on the creatures to the south, and Samšin declaring war against them.

That alone is an unpleasant reminder that the Anevrai conquered the world and subjugated humanity, but if the tale goes into any detail . . . wars are rarely pretty.

We only have two tablets to go. I knew what Kudshayn would say before he even opened his mouth.

"We have to read to the end."

It's that, or go shake Aaron Mornett until the truth falls out of him. Which a part of me wants to do anyway, except I don't think the truth is anywhere inside that man. It dies when it comes near him.

There's an ancient proverb, found in a fragmentary wisdom text that was one of the first Draconean tablets translated, whose meaning people have been arguing about ever since. Its literal translation is "From knowledge, a sapling; from fruit, life; from the heart, an idea; from wisdom, strength." I think it's meant to say that knowledge in time gives rise to wisdom and strength—and now that I reflect, it may even be an oblique reference to our four siblings, Samšin and Imalkit and Nahri and Ektabr.

Like those four, we've been blind to the viper at our bosom. But now that we see it for what it is—now that we have the knowledge we lacked—maybe we can find our way through to wisdom and strength.

I nodded at Kudshayn, then brushed myself off and marched back to my seat at the table. Cora stood for a moment, wringing her hands, before turning toward the door.

But there aren't any doubts in my mind anymore. She didn't have to bring us that catalogue. She didn't have to point out that she recognized some of the tablets—a mistake on Gleinleigh's part, when he assembled his "cache"? Or was he so determined to inflate it to an impressive size that he added in things he shouldn't have, never realizing his own niece would spot them in the set? Either way, he never should have let me send the tablets to the Carters . . . but that is the kind of error a man like him would make. He isn't a philologist or an archaeologist; he's just a treasure-hunter, with no sense of the true value such things hold. No wonder Mrs. Kefford was so angry with him at Chiston.

Cora, on the other hand, is a different matter.

"Where are you going?" I said before she could leave. "We started this together. You deserve to see the end."

Tablet XIII: "The War Tablet"
translated by Audrey Camherst and Kudshayn

Now all the people were brought together to prepare. Imalkit taught others the art of working metal, of crafting stronger heads for arrows and spears, of forging heavy axes, of hammering sharp swords. They cut down the trees with her axes to feed the fires of crafting, and the forges burned night and day, until their smoke nearly blotted out the Light of the World.

Imalkit did not rest there. She bent her clever mind to imagining; in dreams she sought new ideas. She made scales of metal, stronger than the scales of nature, and sewed these to garments of hide so the people would be safe from the weapons of the enemy. She made bows that needed four warriors to draw them, which hurled their shafts farther than the eye could see. She made cunning traps to catch and crush those who would come against the people. By these means were the people prepared.

Nahri taught others the art of tilling the ground, of planting seeds, of irrigation, of making the earth bear fruit on command. They burned out the trees to make fields for planting, and the people laboured night and day.

She did not rest there. She turned her generous mind to planning; in dreams she sought new ideas. She ground the seeds of the earth into powder and from these made flat cakes the warriors could carry with them. She put the fruits of the earth into jars of *gilkha* so they would not rot. She smoked the flesh of animals so that it became dry and would keep during a journey. By these means were the people prepared.

Samšin sought among the people for others to follow her lead. She searched among the people of the north, the people of the west, the people of the east. She [. . .] who would follow her into death.

She did not rest there. She turned her strong mind to thinking; in dreams she sought new ideas. She found three to follow her: Takhbat, Parzel, and Saybakh.[56] With them she went into the wilderness. They hunted gazelles and slaughtered many, laying their meat out to the sky, as bait to the *issur*. Then Samšin and the three hid among the rocks.

Soon the sky grew dark as night with the wings of the *issur*. They descended to the ground and ate of the meat. Samšin had an herb; Imalkit had found an herb; Nahri had grown an herb for Samšin. She had placed this herb within the meat. The *issur* ate of the meat and grew slow and tired.

From the rocks came Samšin and her three. In their hands they had coils of strong rope. They threw these about the heads of the *issur* and pulled them tight. The *issur* fought against the ropes; their fury was like the fury of storms. But the herb they had eaten made them slow and tired, and they bent their heads to the strength of Samšin and her three.

---

56 These are clearly the origins of the three military orders known from the Classic Period, the Takhaba, the Pārz, and the Zayba. There is no reason to think the founders were real individuals, any more than the four from a single egg are likely to have been—especially not when their names translate to "gold," "quicksilver," and "iron"—but this nonetheless provides an origin for those orders, however mythical.—K

Mornett once speculated to me that the names of those orders derived from those words. He must have been so pleased when he found out he was right.—AC

Samšin did not rest there. Takbhat fashioned bridles for the heads of the *issur*, so they could be guided. Parzel fashioned saddles for the backs of the *issur*, so they could be mounted. Saybakh fashioned whips for the hides of the *issur*, so they could be controlled. Samšin climbed into the saddle of the largest. She took the bridle in one hand; she took the whip in the other. Into the sky they went, like a tongue of flame rising from the ground. The *issur* fought against the rider. Four times it twisted, five times it turned, six times it tried to throw the rider, but Samšin struck it with the whip and it ceased to fight. The three followed her lead. They were the first to know true flight, the first to subjugate the *issur* to their will.[57]

The forces of the people were ten thousand strong.[58] When they marched, the sound of their steps shook the ground. When they camped, the light of their fires made the night as day. When they brandished their weapons, it was as if death itself had turned its face to the south. And above them in the sky flew Samšin and her three.

To the south they went, into the land of the worms. They [. . .] the grass, across the rivers, across the sands, to the foot of the mountain which had consumed the Light of the World.

---

57 This is not confirmation that Anevrai queens rode dragons into battle, any more than depictions of such on the walls of temples can be taken as confirmation. (Those same walls show queens towering four times the height of their vanquished foes.) But it demonstrates that such an action is certainly an ideal they held as more than a visual motif.—K

A motif of *domination*. Your people are able to train mews and, to a lesser extent, other dragons, but that is done through much more cooperative means. This is control by raw force.—AC

58 Definitely not an accurate count—not for the pre-founding period.—K

They came as the wind, as the lightning, as the storm, as the wrath of the sky itself. Like thunder they rolled across the land, and the *āmu* cowered in their holes. Their weapons were as feathers against the defenses of the people; their shields were as dried leaves against the weapons of the people; their courage was as mist against the fury of the people; their armies were as nothing against the beloved of the sky.

The *āmu* sent out their strongest to fight, but the people tore them to pieces and flung those pieces to the jackals. The *āmu* sent out their bravest to defend, but the people cut them down like grass before the blade. The *āmu* sent out their swiftest to flee, but the people chased them to the ends of the earth and slew them there. The *āmu* sent their leaders to the mountain, to the cave where they had wrought their sin. Samšin and her three followed them there, and the wings of the *issur* covered the mouth of the cave, blotting out the light.

On that day there was no mercy for those who had struck against the Maker of Above and Below. The Foundation of All turned away from those it had created. The Source of Wind did not hear their pleas. The Crown of the Abyss received them in their thousands, the worms who had eaten the light, from the eldest to the youngest, but the leaders were spared, for Samšin had promised that she would bring justice to the world.[59]

---

59 Why is sparing the leaders justice? It seems like it would be more fair to kill them, and leave everybody else alive.—CF

  The answer to that no doubt lies in the final tablet.—K

  And I suspect it's the reason Gleinleigh has gone to all this trouble.—AC

From: The Office of the Curator of Draconean Antiquities
To: Audrey Camherst

14 Caloris
Tomphries Museum
#12 Chisholm Street, Falchester

Dear Audrey,

Your knowledge of the corpus of Draconean literature is much more extensive than mine. Have you ever come across the epithet "Foundation of All"?

I'm sure you'd rather not be reminded of the auction at Emmerson's, but if you recall the items I marked in the catalogue, one of them—the clay sun disk—seems to have been not as aboveboard as I thought. (Lady Plimmer bought it. I've had five letters from her in the last week, each one more frantic than the last at the thought of being sent to prison forever for unwittingly purchasing an illegal antiquity.) Its provenance seems to have been falsified, and knowing that, I'm wondering if it came from that looted temple in Seghaye, the one near Djedad. They found broken pieces of a similar sun disc there, and it's rare enough to find them in clay rather than gold or copper or bronze that I can't help but think there might be a connection, especially as Rouhani's report said there was some kind of inscription on the back of the shattered one.

This one says "Foundation of All, guard these precious hearts of gold," which is why I ask about the epithet. If we can link that to its presumed original context (the discs were set into the sides of a tablet chest), we'll have more evidence for proving this one is "hot," as the police say—

and since there seem to have been four originally, and one is broken, the other two surviving discs might be here in Scirland, too. If we can trace those back to their seller, we might be able to connect Dorak to the ransacking of that temple outside Djedad. I doubt he was directly involved, of course, but anything we can do to trace the networks that smuggle these things out of their home countries will help us stop them in the future.

I find myself wondering if there's any chance "Foundation of All" is somehow related to what we call foundation-style chests. It would be quite a marvel if we unwittingly replicated the ancient word for those things, but it would help prove a connection. I've also written to Rouhani to see if he can make out any of the inscription on his broken disc, and see if it says the same thing.

Are you doing well? I haven't heard from you since you went back to Stokesley. There were some concerns when you came to Falchester about the reliability of the post; I would be grateful for even a brief note letting me know everything there is all right.

Your friend,
Simeon

From the diary of Audrey Camherst

16 CALORIS

One tablet left.

We've almost stopped talking to one another, Kudshayn, Cora, and I. Not because anyone is angry. We work every waking moment on the tablets, half afraid to find out where they are leading us, but unable to stop, and I think I dread the ending almost as much as Kudshayn does. It's already unpleasant, seeing the shift from the Anevrai as ancient hunter-gatherers to the conquerors who built an empire, but that alone wouldn't justify the effort Gleinleigh has gone to. There must be more to come.

He isn't here, the coward. In fact, he hasn't been back to Stokesley since that dinner at Lady Plimmer's. I'm not surprised; between what I said to Mornett and what I said to Mrs. Kefford, it's obvious I suspect them of something, though I doubt they know that we've figured out their secret. If I were Gleinleigh, I wouldn't come back here, either. Better to leave us to work undisturbed.

I keep wondering what other spies he has set on us. Mrs. Hilleck, the housekeeper? The maids who dust the library? We're endeavouring to keep to our usual habits (and hoping no one was listening at the keyhole when we figured out the truth about the cache), but we've been making duplicates of everything in secret—copies of the tablets, transliterations, and the translation itself—just in case Gleinleigh swoops in at the last minute to snatch everything away.

A few weeks at most. Probably not even that. Then we'll be finished, and we'll have to decide what to do with our translation.

It isn't quite true that we've stopped talking to one another, because that makes it sound like it's mutual, and it isn't. I had to ask Cora to stop, because she keeps on trying to speculate about how her uncle intends to leverage the translation, and then attempting to defend against those speculative attacks with logic. She persists in thinking that if we can just muster some nice, reasonable facts, then all harm can be prevented. Unfortunately, people don't really think that way.

I should have known she was up to something these last few days. There's relatively little left for her to do; it's just translation now, and she still isn't much help with that. But she was scribbling away in the corner, even though she's up to date on copying our notes, and then every so often she would get up to look at something elsewhere in the library. Today, while Kudshayn was resting in his refrigerated room, she came up and thrust a sheaf of papers at me.

At least I have learned my lesson about brushing off things she hands to me. "What is this?" I asked, taking it from her.

"It's an article," she said. "Well, it's part of an article. A draft. I don't know all the things to put in it, and I've never tried to write an article before, so I don't know if it's any good. But you can help me with that."

A quick skim showed me lots of discussion of climate—and, oddly, of volcanoes. There was even a map of Anthiope, sketched in Cora's very careful hand. "This is about the geography of the epic?"

"It doesn't match up," she said earnestly. "Or rather, parts of it do, but not all. And I know you said the geography is made up, but I don't think all of it is."

Kudshayn and I have speculated about that from time to time, but I didn't realize Cora had been paying such close attention to what we said. Her argument—laid out with all the formidable logic of which she is capable—is that the evidence of plant and animal life mentioned in the earlier parts of the epic, the Genealogy Tablet in particular, suggests the ancient climate of central Anthiope more than southern.

That much is reasonable, and I've thought the same thing myself. But then her article goes on to say that the volcano most likely to be responsible for the "loss of the sun" in the Darkness Tablet is *also* in central Anthiope—Mt. Dezhnie in Vystrana— citing a Dr. Ralph Stanyard as her source for this declaration. Therefore (her argument goes), it makes no sense that the Worms Tablet places "the mountain that ate the sun" in the southern part of the continent, in the lands of the *āmu*: it must have been in the homeland of the Anevrai themselves. There- fore, human beings cannot be held responsible for that event— always presuming that it were possible to cause a volcanic eruption, which to the best of the article's author's knowledge it is not.

She stood patiently while I read through it. When I was done, the first thing I could think to say was, "Who on earth is Dr. Stanyard?"

"The geologist you told me to write to," she said. "I mean, you didn't actually tell me, you just hinted very pointedly, and you didn't specify him; I had to write some letters first to even find a suitable geologist. Don't you remember?"

"Yes—but I had no idea you'd gotten anything back, much less an actual answer!"

Cora stood very still, thinking back. "Oh," she said. "Of

course. I heard back while you were in Falchester and not talking to me, so I didn't say anything. And then you started talking to me again, but by then I'd forgotten that I hadn't told you about his letter."

I sighed and rubbed my face with my hands. "Thank you, Cora. When all of this is done, I'll be happy to assist you with the article." (There were places in her draft where she could not remember or look up the things Kudshayn and I had said about geographical clues in the epic; she had left notes to herself that she should consult with me.)

Honesty prompted me to add, "I don't know if it will do any good for the Draconeans, though. Even if you're correct—and I think you are—it just means the Anevrai scapegoated innocent people for the loss of the sun. Whether the war that resulted is an actual historical event or just a mythical tale, the fact remains that this is a story the Anevrai *chose* to tell. A story they took pride in." We can't know for sure how the epic fit into their society, especially when the tablets were torn out of their original archaeological context, but they're much too finely made to be anything other than an honoured text.

Cora's shoulders slumped, and I felt like a cad. "Oh, please don't think—I'm grateful you did this, really I am. At least you're trying to find a way to make things better, while I sit here doing something that will probably make them worse. And . . . I want you to know that whatever happens with the epic, I'm glad I had the chance to work with you."

Her chin stayed down. "Truly?"

"Yes, truly. And if you ever want—"

I stopped myself, but I should have known better. Cora is a bulldog when it comes to unfinished thoughts; she won't rest until she knows what you were going to say. "If I ever want what?"

If I weren't so tired these days, worn to a thread by worry and work, I might not have thrown tact to the wind quite so comprehensively. As it is . . . "If you ever want to get away from your uncle, let me know. You shouldn't have to go on living with a liar and a bigot if you don't want to."

Her shoulders tightened. "I'm grateful to him. For taking me in after my parents died. It was a railway accident. When I was ten."

My heart thumped hard. I haven't asked about her private life since she made it clear she wasn't interested in discussing it with me; I have the feeling that her sharing it is as significant as Kudshayn telling me I could share the story of his clutch with her.

But the part about Gleinleigh . . . it had the sound of rote recitation. "That was good of your uncle," I said, choosing my words with more care this time. "But being grateful to him and spending the rest of your life under his thumb aren't the same thing. You can do something else with yourself."

Almost inaudibly, Cora said, "I'm not fit for anything. I'm too awkward and no one else would want me."

That hit like a slap of icy water. I came within an ace of flinging my arms around her before I remembered she wouldn't like it. "The hell you are," I said violently. "I need to introduce you to Simeon Cavall at the Tomphries. If I tell him about the work you've done for us here, he'll weep with joy and then stick you in a windowless room to catalogue artifacts for the rest of your life."

Then I reviewed what I'd just said. "Oh, Lord—I made it sound awful. I mean, only if you *want* to catalogue artifacts for the rest of your life. Otherwise you can do something else. Something more enjoyable."

Cora thought it over. Then she said, "I would insist on windows."

The little smile playing at the corner of her mouth lifted my spirits like nothing else lately, because it meant I'd made her feel better. I haven't fixed everything—there's no way I could—but at least I helped a little.

Which is about the only good thing that happened today. The epic is headed in dreadful directions, and a letter came from Grandmama this afternoon that has me wanting to crawl out of my skin with shame, because she's right on every count.

I don't know what Grandmama would do in my situation. Except be clever enough not to have gotten herself into it to begin with, and it's far too late for that.

◈

From the notebook of Cora Fitzarthur

Things I found in Uncle's files that look relevant:

— a letter dated 18 Acinis, 5661, Mrs. Eveline Kefford to Marcus Fitzarthur, Lord Gleinleigh

Mrs. Kefford doesn't mention tablets outright, but she says she'll make arrangements for "the crate" to be loaded on board his ship next month (this was a few weeks before he left for Akhia), and cautions him to be careful, since "some of them" are already damaged, and "it won't do us any good at all if they can't be read." That sounds like tablets to me.

She also reassures Uncle that "everything has been arranged with the permit office." Unless that has something to do with boats, I think she means the Akhian office that issues permits for excavation, because I remember Uncle fretting about that before he left. I guess his fretting wasn't necessary, since Mrs. Kefford says the man in charge of that is "one of ours."

— a receipt dated 2 Nebulis, 5661, for 245 clay tablets purchased from Joseph Dorak for 3500 guineas

There were 271 tablets in the cache, including fragments. 245 plus 14 (for the epic) is 259; I'm not sure how many tablets I recognized as coming from Uncle's collections when I packaged them up for the Carters. I should have made notes. There are seven in what they've catalogued so far, though. I bet there are twelve in total.

> — handwritten receipt, dated 3 Nebulis, 5661, 500 guineas for shipping, destination unspecified

It would never cost that much to ship tablets from Falchester to anywhere in Scirland, and I know for a fact we didn't receive anything here at Stokesley (apart from milk and flour and so forth, of course) until after Uncle came back from Akhia, when his cache arrived.

He should have just bought his extra tablets when he got to Akhia. It would have been much cheaper than shipping so many there.

I didn't see anything else obviously incriminating, but I will steal Mrs. Hilleck's keys again tomorrow night and search Uncle's study some more.

Tablet XIV: "The Sacrifice Tablet"
translated by Audrey Camherst and Kudshayn

Now all the south was brought under the wings of Samšin and her sisters. The people dug the *āmu* out of their holes and brought them before Samšin, and those who resisted were sent to bow before the Crown of the Abyss. Those who bent their heads in submission were given life.

The leaders were trapped in the cave where Samšin and her three had found them, with the wings of the *issur* barring the way. They prayed to the Ever-Standing, Foundation of All, to deliver its children, but the earth answered them only with silence. When the subjugation of the south was complete, Samšin came to the leaders of the *āmu* with her sisters, with her three followers, with her heart full of fury, and spoke to them in judgment.

She said to them, "In your evil you sought to deprive us of the Maker of Above and Below. I am Samšin, sun-gold, hatched from a single shell, and I have brought justice into the world. Hear now the justice I give to you: because you sought to destroy light, you will see light no more." Her three seized the leaders and put out their eyes.

Then she dragged them before the people, so everyone could see that they had been blinded. She said to them, "In your envy you sought to take away that which loves us best. Hear now the justice I give to you: because you thought yourselves our equals, you will crawl in the dirt where you belong." Her three seized the leaders and broke their arms and their legs.

Then she dragged them before the *āmu*, on their knees in submission, so everyone could see them crawling like worms. She said to them, "In your pride you led your people into a confrontation they could not win. Hear now the justice I give to you: because you spoke words of evil, you will speak no more." Her three seized the leaders and cut out their tongues. This was the justice of Samšin, sun-gold, hatched from a single shell.

But when justice had been done, the people still cried for more. They said, "How can we be certain the *āmu* will not strike at us again? How can we be certain they will not take away the Light of the World? We must protect the Maker of Above and Below against their malice, now and forever. We must not fall into darkness again."

Samšin considered this. In the silence of her heart she prayed; in her dreams she sought ideas. She had a dream of her brother Ektabr, sitting at the right hand of the Crown of the Abyss. She dreamt of an answer, given to her by her brother, who had been the price of light.

She said to the people, "I will make the Light of the World strong against the malice of the *āmu*. I will give it an offering from its chosen people, a gift of fire, so that it will burn more strongly; its flames will burn the mouth of the Endless Maw, so that it cannot be consumed again. I will give the remnants of the fire to my *issur*, a gift of bone for our faithful servants. I will give the ghosts of this offering to the Crown of the Abyss, a gift of memory for its hospitality. I will give the leaders of the *āmu* to the fire."

She built a structure of wood. Samšin built up a pile of wood; Samšin created a mountain of wood, whose rivers were of oil. She placed a stone at the center of the wood, in mockery of their god, and bound the leaders of the *āmu* to it. Their eyes were blind, their legs did not move, they had no tongues with which to speak, but they wailed their fear to the sky. Samšin burned them, a gift of fire for the Maker of Above and Below. Their bones she threw to her *issur*; their ghosts went down to the underworld, the fate they had tried to make for the Light of the World.

This was the beginning of civilization. Samšin established order for the people, so that each would know their role; they became farmers and scribes, crafters and judges, and they prospered under her rule. Below them stood the *āmu*; below them stood the *issur*; below them stood all the creatures of the world, the faithful servants of those the sun loved best. Samšin's wings and the wings of her daughters spread until they encompassed all the lands and seas. Under their rule the Light of the World grew strong, so that its journeys to the underworld were brief, and the star demons did not dare to strike. Each year they made offerings to the Maker of Above and Below, when its power grew weak; each year they gave a gift of fire, a gift of bone, a gift of memory, a gift from among the *āmu*, so that they might turn darkness into light.

For the archives of the Sanctuary of Wings
written by Kudshayn, son of Ahheke, daughter of Iztam

Light of the World, Maker of Above and Below, bright mirror, wanderer of the world, forgive the sins of my foremothers, committed in your name.

Ever-Standing, Foundation of All, dark stillness, refuge of the people, forgive the cruelty of my foremothers, committed against your children.

Ever-Moving, Endless Maw, forgive us for having forgotten you. Forgive us if we forget you still, relics of a past in which I can take no pride. All the achievements of the four—the working of metal, the planting of the earth, the administration of justice, the writing of words in clay—are as the dust of bones in my eyes, laid against the errors to which their creators came.

Forgive me, O my people, for being the one who bridged this gap. Forgive me for being the instrument by which our enemies have brought this tale from the sheltering darkness of the earth into the light of day, all for the purpose of staining our hands with blood in the eyes of humankind.

No. The purpose of revealing the blood that has always been there.

I cannot take pleasure in the wonders of that ancient civilization, celebrating the greatness our foremothers achieved. The accusations are true. We were not merely tyrants; we burned slaves for our triumph. Just as the Hadamists have always claimed.

It does no good to say that we are different today. For those who hold our fate in the palm of their hand, the past is all they will see.

It is all *I* can see.

Forgive us. Forgive me.

From the diary of Audrey Camherst

3 FRUCTIS

Human sacrifice.

All those fire-blackened pillars, all the arguments about whether some of the holes that pierce them were made to hold chains. All the ambiguous wall paintings and cryptic references in fragmented texts. The debate is over.

That's what Gleinleigh's been waiting for us to find. A confession—no, a *boast*—that the Anevrai practiced human sacrifice. They burned people alive for the glory of their sun god, to prove they were the most powerful and beloved creatures in existence.

It isn't like human beings have never done the same thing. We have, in more than one part of the world, with fire and sharp knives and strangulation and drowning. But it doesn't matter whether our own ancestors were just as bad sometimes. People will only care that this proves the Anevrai were monsters.

And I helped prove it.

I wish I had never come here.

I wish I had never asked Kudshayn to come.

From the diary of Audrey Camherst

4 FRUCTIS

Lord Gleinleigh is due back at Stokesley tomorrow. If I were feeling paranoid, I'd swear he's been calculating the exact day we were likely to finish, and planning his return so he can scoop up our notes and run off with them in triumph.

Whether he has or not, it doesn't matter. Kudshayn and I are out of time.

I went to his refrigerated room today, even though it's windowless and miserable and of course freezing, because he's coping with enough already; he doesn't need to be uncomfortably hot on top of everything else. I brought my coat and sat on one of the stools, and then we were both silent for a painfully long time, because neither of us wanted to speak.

He looked awful. Draconeans don't show it the way humans do when they haven't been sleeping, with dark circles under their eyes and the like, but his scales were dull and he slumped like it was taking all the energy he had just to sit upright. I wanted to put my wings around him; I wanted to have wings I *could* put around him. Instead I sat close to him and wished I could do something that would set everything right.

But I'd been thinking about it all night, and when I finally got up this morning it was clear to me that there is only one thing we could do to minimize the damage.

"I refuse to let them use me like this," I said at last. It wasn't any of the dozen ways I'd thought about broaching the topic, but the words simply came out. "I've been Aaron Mornett's patsy before; I won't let him do that to me again. The same goes for Gleinleigh and Mrs. Kefford. I won't play their game."

Kudshayn shifted on his seat. "What do you mean?"

My stomach churned. I didn't even eat breakfast this morning, that's how tense I was, and normally my appetite can survive anything. "Gleinleigh wants to defame your people in the public eye right before the congress. But if that were all he wanted, then he could have published Mornett's translation. He hired me, and then he hired you, because he wants us to lend weight to the whole thing. Mornett isn't famous, and the people who do recognize his name mostly know he's a Calderite and plagiarist. If he said the Anevrai practiced human sacrifice, people would question it—at least some of them would. But if it comes from us . . ." My hands knotted tight. "We can't stop Gleinleigh from publishing whatever Mornett has. But we can stop him from using our own names and reputations."

Kudshayn's wings stirred, then tucked in again. "We signed a contract with him."

"*Damn* the contract," I said violently. "Let him sue me. I guarantee you my family will pay."

For all his worldly ways, Kudshayn still isn't very familiar with human laws and courts and the ways they can be used to drag things out for years. He said, "But Gleinleigh has a right to publish what we've produced."

"He can't publish it if we destroy our papers."

Kudshayn shot to his feet, wings unfurling. There isn't space for them in that room; they hit the walls, bruisingly hard. "Audrey—"

If I'd wanted to face him down, I would have stood and spread my arms, in imitation of his wings. Instead I kept them close by my sides and remained on the stool. "I walked right into their trap, Kudshayn, and I invited you into it, too. Because—because—"

I went over this a hundred times in the night, trying to steel myself to do what was necessary. Forcing myself to say it still carved me apart. "Because I wanted to make my own name with this translation. I thought, if I do this, I'll finally feel like I can live up to the reputation of my family—be worthy of my father, my mother, my grandfather, my grandmother. They've all done such amazing things, and what have I done?"

Kudshayn was silent. I didn't dare look up to see whether he was searching for a reply or waiting for me to be done. I said miserably, "I know I'm young; I know there are decades left for me to do something impressive. But there was *this* chance, right there in front of me, and I wanted to grab it. Only—" I had to try three times before the rest of it would come out. "Not if it hurts you. No amount of reputation and acclaim is worth doing that. I'd rather shred all the work we've done and never speak of it again than be the hand holding the blade that goes through your heart. So if you say the word, Kudshayn, I'll do it. I'll destroy all our copies, all our notes, and tell Gleinleigh he can go whistle for his tale."

The soft sound above me was Kudshayn folding his wings. No need to keep them outstretched in the cold, because there wasn't any confrontation. Whatever he decided, I would do it. The choice was his, not mine—because the epic belongs to the Draconean people, not mine.

I sat in the freezing air and waited.

Then his hands came down and wrapped around my wrists, tugging gently. I let him bring me to my feet, then followed as he opened the door and led me out into the bright, hot air.

The cave is where you go to think things through, to contemplate your options. Decisions get made under the sun.

Out in the garden, Kudshayn turned to face me, holding both my hands in his own. It was a blazing, muggy day, the kind that brings sweat out all over me; I could hear his breathing strain almost immediately. I didn't want him to stay out there any longer than he had to, so I forced myself to raise my eyes. He still looked tired—but also at peace, for the first time in weeks.

When he spoke, it was in his own language. "Audrey. I know how much this work means to you, and how much it must hurt you to talk of destroying it. That you are willing to do so . . . that is a gift whose value I will remember forever."

Sweat beaded on my skin, but inside I was a block of ice.

He closed his eyes and tipped his face up to the sun. Then he said, "We will publish the translation."

All the breath went out of me. I mouthed *what?*—there was no air to give it voice.

Kudshayn gripped my hands hard. "Sooner or later, the truth will come out. Hiding from it will not save us; this ghost from my people's past will haunt us until we lay it to rest."

"But the ghost doesn't have to come out *now*," I protested. "Not when the governments of the world are about to decide your people's future."

He shrugged sadly. "I wish it could have been otherwise. But in the end . . . this is part of our past, whether we are proud to admit it or not. Whatever our place is to be in the world, it must be a place we can claim with honesty, not one we slip into on the basis of a lie."

I could barely find any words. I spent hours last night imagining different ways this conversation might go, a dozen different variations—but none of them went like this, with

Kudshayn arguing in favour of walking into the trap. "It isn't a lie! It's just—"

"A lie of omission, instead of commission?" His breath rasped in and out. "That kind of manipulation, that dishonesty . . . it is the sort of thing *they* would do."

Gleinleigh. Mornett. Mrs. Kefford and all the other Calderites. Hadamists like Zachary Hallman. Picking and choosing their history to support the tale they want to tell, one where humans deserve to have everything and the Draconeans get nothing except what we give them. Making this story public will serve their ends—but concealing it would be using their methods.

"Damn it," I said. The words came out thick, and I realized I had teared up. "Why do *we* have to be the ethical ones?"

"Because Samšin promised the world justice," he said softly. "And even if she brought cruelty in the end, that does not make her promise any less worthy."

This isn't justice. Justice would be Gleinleigh and Mornett and Mrs. Kefford failing in their plans and being driven from the public sphere. Justice would be the Draconeans having their own nation, a true sanctuary for their people.

Maybe that latter can still happen. They have Grandmama and Grandpapa on their side, and all the human allies those two can bring to bear. They have allies of their own, especially in Yelang.

But I don't hold out much hope.

DRACONEAN HISTORY REVEALED
Lord Gleinleigh's Tablets Scheduled for Publication
Lady Trent's Granddaughter, Translator
"Fit to stand among the epics of the world"

Carrigdon and Rudge, publishers of the memoirs of Lady Trent, announced today that they will soon be printing a translation of the tablets discovered by Marcus Fitzarthur, Lord Gleinleigh, in the Qajr region of Akhia. Although less than a year has passed since they were brought to Scirling shores, all the world has been champing at the bit to see what tale they have to tell.

The translation is the work of Lady Trent's granddaughter Miss Audrey Camherst and a Draconean scholar named Kudshayn. The two of them have worked night and day at Lord Gleinleigh's estate of Stokesley to satisfy the public's curiosity, producing in mere months what ordinarily would have been the work of years. When asked for comment, Lord Gleinleigh praised the skill of the translators, who are renowned in their field as some of the foremost authorities on ancient Draconean texts. "I have the utmost confidence in their work, which is both precise and accessible to a popular audience," he said. Miss Camherst and her Draconean assistant could not be reached for comment.

Carrigdon and Rudge will be issuing the translation, under the title *The Draconeia,* in both a fine leather-bound edition and a paper-bound edition for the general market. Interested readers may pre-order either version now; the title will become available for sale on 6 Nebulis.

YOU ARE CORDIALLY INVITED

to attend a reception
at the Tomphries Museum
in honour of those individuals
whose generous contributions
to the museum's collections
have enriched our knowledge
of the past

The reception will be held
on the evening of
the first of Acinis
at 7 o'clock
in the Whitsea Salon

Refreshments provided
with music and dancing

RSVP

From the diary of Audrey Camherst

I ACINIS

I should be getting dressed, but I'm so nervous I can't even look at my frock, much less put it on.

If only I could have found some graceful way to insist on taking the train into Falchester, instead of riding in Gleinleigh's motorcar. But he would never let me take the tablet crate onto a train, and I can only imagine what would have happened if Kudshayn came with me. So into the car it was, and the trip took half again as long as it should have because Gleinleigh made a point of telling his driver to go very carefully lest the tablets get bounced around too much. I wound up feigning carsickness to avoid making any kind of small talk—and it isn't even a lie, really, though it's nerves that has my stomach all twisted up, not the motion.

How many times have I gone to this silly gala? Every year I've been old enough and in the country for it, I think, because Simeon always wants moral support. He hates these things, but the museum makes him be there, because they need to keep their wealthy benefactors happy, and those people like getting the glad hand from curators. Of course some of those benefactors are perfectly lovely people . . . but he can't spend his entire evening in a corner talking only to the ones he likes. The rest of the time he has to make trivial conversation with snobs, ignoramuses, people who don't realize they're ignoramuses, people whose heads are full of very wrong things they Know to Be True, and people like Mrs. Kefford, who donate money to the Tomphries because they like having the heads of major public institutions in their pocket.

I shouldn't have written her name. I was starting to calm myself down, and now I've undone it all.

The process of loaning the tablets to the Tomphries has begun. We deposited them this afternoon in the museum's storage annex, which Simeon is using as a staging ground for shifting everything to Estwin Hall. Much of the Draconean collection has already been installed there, but they still need to move out Arnoldson's Nichaean statuary before they can put in the rest of the cabinets and display cases; until that's done, the remainder lives in the annex, on the street behind the main building.

You would think Cora wouldn't find this very impressive, having grown up with her uncle's thieving magpie ways, but I think she was knocked sideways by the sight of a properly organized collection. Everything in the annex is neatly labeled, and Simeon being who he is, a little challenge like swapping the entire Draconean exhibit with the entire ancient Nichaean one is no excuse not to put things on shelves in an orderly and logical fashion. He made space for the tablets we brought, even though I would have sworn there was no space to be had, and then went to work buttering up Lord Gleinleigh.

"I intend to have an entire cabinet showcasing the evolution of Draconean writing," he said, "though I'm still working on selecting the right samples—I can scarcely get into my office, the tablets are stacked so high. Of course yours will have pride of place as an example of a very early style."

"I hope they will be well guarded," Gleinleigh said sententiously.

"Of course, my lord," Simeon said—he didn't even choke on the courtesy, which I've had trouble with lately. "The main building has the very latest in burglar alarms, and even here, we have a watchman on duty at all times." He gestured around at the packed shelves. "Most of these artifacts have value only to scholars, but thieves often break such things in their pursuit of gold and jewels. We will not risk any harm coming to any of the objects under our care."

(Visions of cat-burglary did dance through my head, I must admit. But if I were going to steal the tablets and hide them away for a decade or two, I should have done it while they were at Stokesley, where it would have been easy. No, Kudshayn is right, and we must follow through with our plan. We need the tablets as evidence, and they're as safe in Tomphries keeping as anywhere else.)

Then Simeon surprised me by turning and addressing me. "We have an addition to the exhibit," he said, "which we'll be placing at the northern end of the hall. Arnoldson complained to high heaven, naturally, whining about having to move that sculpture of the Kymatian Ophiotaurus, just because it weighs more than fifteen thousand kilograms—but I persuaded Pinfell that if we are going to have an exhibit in honour of the congress, it would be incomplete without anything from Lady Trent."

He led us further into the room, to a set of shelves containing crates with labels like *preserved meteor dragon skeleton* and *dental sets from assorted draconic breeds*, and glass jars full of biological specimens in formaldehyde. I recognized the handwriting on the labels; it is what Grandmama calls her "public hand," the very careful script she uses when she needs someone other than herself to be able to read the result.

I think Simeon meant for it to reassure me, by showing me

something I would find familiar and pleasant. But it only made me think of Grandmama's letter and what she said about not being pointlessly reckless. Am I doing the right thing?

This is certainly far less reckless than some of my recent escapades. I won't be endangering life or limb tonight—only walking up to Dr. Pinfell and reminding him of the Tomphries' pledge not to purchase or accept any artifacts bought on the black market. We can't quite prove that Gleinleigh staged the cache, but the documents Cora nicked from her uncle's office certainly suggest it. And if Hormizd Rouhani writes back to us with the interior dimensions of the tablet chest in that Seghayan temple, we might even be able to prove that's where our tablets came from, if they fit inside. I might be wrong about that last bit, but the inscription from Lady Plimmer's sun disc mentioning the Foundation of All gave me a hunch—and if I'm right, then we have a chain of evidence linking a looted temple to the most notorious illegal antiquities dealer in Scirland to Gleinleigh and Kefford to the Tomphries.

A thin chain, mind you, with a couple of links replaced by string. But Simeon thinks it will be enough. Not to convict Lord Gleinleigh or Mrs. Kefford of buying smuggled artifacts— it would never hold up in court, not against people with titles and wealth to protect them, and even if it did the only punishment would be a fine—but we can at least disgrace them a little bit. Make Dr. Pinfell refuse the loan, so the tablets aren't put on public display in Scirland's foremost museum, reminding everyone that the Anevrai used to burn people alive.

Assuming I can persuade Dr. Pinfell to believe me.

I envy Cora. Gleinleigh doesn't care whether she has a social life or not, so he isn't dragging her to this gala; he would have left her behind at Stokesley if I hadn't insisted on her coming to shepherd the tablets to the annex (really so she'll be available if Dr. Pinfell wants to talk to her, and so we can get her away from Gleinleigh when he finds out what we're up to). When I left to get dressed she was still at the annex, talking to Simeon—I hope he remembers that *he* has to get dressed, too.

Speaking of which. I'd better tumble up if I don't want to be late.

From: Audrey Camherst
To: Isabella, Lady Trent

1 Acinis
#3 Clarton Square

Dear Grandmama,

I think I understand now what you meant in the letter you sent back in Caloris. Or if I do not . . . I still wouldn't change a single decision I made today, which I suppose amounts to the same thing. I won't claim my actions were perfect—you'd be right to call them downright stupid—but, well, it's inconceivable that I could have done anything else.

I imagine this is what it's like to be you.

But a scientist should provide all the data, and a philologist should know how little sense the text makes when half of it is missing. So I will start at the beginning.

You know what the benefactors' gala is like; you've been to enough of them yourself. It was the same salon, the same caterers, probably even the same band providing the music. And very much the same people, too—though I was glad to see that Alan Preston was there, looking more than a little weathered by his time fruitlessly scouring the Qajr for artifacts that were never there in the first place.

(How much has Lotte told you? I know she's the one who let fly about my foolishness lately. I am going to assume she's told you everything, because otherwise this letter will be so long they'll need a lorry to transport it.)

Kudshayn and I were both there as guests of Lord Glein-

leigh. We're still under orders to say nothing about the tablets, but I think it's more pro forma now than anything else; the manuscript for the translation is at the publisher's, so there isn't much need for secrecy anymore. So far as he knows, there isn't much we can do to spike his guns at this point.

We were going to do our best, though. It's just that nothing went according to plan.

Starting with my attempt to corner Dr. Pinfell for a private conversation. Oh, I could talk to him—for a whole two minutes, all of them very public, before he went off to greet someone else. I can't really fault him; as Simeon says, the job of a museum director is four-fifths public relations and only one-fifth museum work, and that's if he's lucky. But I had expected your name to pull a little more weight with him than it did. (And I would apologize for leaning on that name without asking you first, except I know you'd be only too delighted to help expose Gleinleigh's fraud in any way you can.)

My fruitless efforts at chasing Pinfell left Kudshayn on his own. He mostly stood with Simeon and Alan and looked very awkward, but Simeon had to do his own share of glad-handing, and couldn't be expected to stay with Kudshayn the entire night. When I gave up on Pinfell for the time being, I turned around to see Kudshayn alone—and Mrs. Kefford bearing down on him.

I don't think it's possible to discreetly hurl yourself across a salon, but I did my best, and fetched up at Kudshayn's side before Mrs. Kefford had gotten past the opening pleasantries. She affected to be surprised by my appearance, though she had to have spotted me coming. "My dear, how delightful to see you. I hear you are to be congratulated, with your work on its way to press now."

She looked like a cat that has dipped a canary in cream and

is savouring each sadistic lick. "What a pity I can't say the same," I told her.

I was rewarded with a slight flicker of confusion. "I beg your pardon?"

"Congratulations," *I said.* "I cannot offer you any. Ordinarily I would commend you on your husband being named Dissenting Speaker in the Synedrion—but I hear he received his post on the strength of a promise that the caeliger base will remain in the Sanctuary, and Kudshayn's people will remain a protectorate of Scirland. Now, I am not very well versed in politics . . . but I understand that politicians tend to suffer at the hands of their own party when they fail to deliver on promises."

All of that was spontaneous bravado. What I really longed to do was wave her own letter in her face, the one she sent to Gleinleigh before he sailed off to Akhia. As satisfying as it would have been to watch her try and explain that away, though, I knew better than to go off half-cocked. But the whole reason they've gone through this rigmarole with the fake discovery is to influence the congress, so at least I could bluster about their inevitable failure.

Mrs. Kefford gave a silky laugh. "Oh, my dear. You are right about one thing, at least—you are not well versed in politics."

"And you," *Kudshayn said,* "do not know my people. You have readied yourself to fight creatures of your own imagining, and against them, you might win. But contend against the truth, and you will lose."

(Kudshayn is much better at coded allusions than I am.)

"Will you be at the congress?" *Mrs. Kefford asked.*

The question was blatantly aimed at me. She'd gone over to speak to Kudshayn—I presume to gloat—but my presence meant she could instead make a point of snubbing him, addressing me like he wasn't even there. On a sudden inspiration, I turned to Kudshayn and said, "Notice how she didn't respond to what you said. I think that's because she doesn't have a good answer."

"It may be," he said thoughtfully. "And that suggests your earlier point was correct, as well. If she cannot even rebut me, I do not see how others like her hope to stand up against the elders of the Sanctuary. They are far more eloquent than I am."

In my peripheral vision, I could see Mrs. Kefford opening her mouth to say something, but I didn't give her the chance to interrupt. "Well, she isn't quite old enough yet to be counted as an elder. But perhaps in a few more years?"

Grandmama, we routed her. Not by engaging directly—our sniping at her social and political acumen notwithstanding, she's far too good at that sort of thing—but by making her play audience to our willful defamation. She couldn't get a word in edgewise. Kudshayn and I kept improvising new, barely veiled insults until she finally gave up. It was that or shout over us.

Kudshayn's wings rattled with laughter as she stalked off. When he sobered a moment later, I thought it was because the reality of our situation had come crashing down again—until I heard a voice behind me say, "Miss Camherst. May I have the honour of this dance?"

Of course Aaron Mornett was there. I'd even half expected it. But I didn't expect him to come up behind me without warning. It took me so much by surprise that I couldn't even compose the refusal he deserved; whatever incoherence I stammered out, he took it as a yes, leading me out onto the floor for a waltz.

I shot a pleading look at Kudshayn, but by then it was too late, unless Kudshayn wanted to make a scene. Mornett and I squared up, holding each other like two bombs about to go off, and then the flow of the dance carried us away.

Is it wrong that I briefly wondered if he had somehow managed to take credit for some other man's dancing skill? He's gotten a good deal better since the last time we danced, during my disastrous Season. I am still as bad as ever, of course. It should be much easier to dance well with a skilled lead, but that only works if the follow is willing to relax and be guided, which I wasn't at all.

Mornett could feel it, too. He said, "I would compliment you on your dress, but somehow I suspect you don't want to hear such things from me."

I think my riposte was some brilliant piece of original wit like "How can you tell?"

He sighed. "Audrey . . . Miss Camherst. Would you believe me if I said I regret our falling-out?"

"Our falling-out," I repeated, my voice flat. "But not what you did to cause it."

"I would like to start over," he said. It's good he kept to the basic waltz step, not trying anything complicated, because I would have tripped over him if he had. "Do you think that's possible?"

My nerves would have liked me to go on staring fixedly at his bow tie—but that would have been cowardly. The last time he and I had spoken, I'd spent nearly an hour planning what to say to him; it's much easier for me to simply open my mouth and let words fall out. I lifted my chin and met his gaze, saying, "That would require you to be honest with me, and every piece of available evidence says you aren't capable of it."

I took some satisfaction in him stumbling, losing the

smooth pattern of the waltz before regaining it. "You truly
think so little of me?"

"Just now I reminded you that what happened five years ago
wasn't some accident or inevitable occurrence; it was the result
of your own actions. You had a chance to admit your guilt, but
instead you dodged—just as you have always done. You say you
want to start over with me, but you seem to think we can just
shovel dirt over the past and roses will grow." My fingers were
digging into his shoulder, harder with every step we took. "That
may be your habit, but it isn't mine. And you're relying on that,
aren't you? I don't know how you think I could ignore the truth
in my personal life, and at the same time make plans that rely on
me to—"

(I said it's easier for me to let words fall out. I didn't say
the results are any better when they do.)

"Rely on you to what?" he said.

And then we drifted to a halt, right there in the middle of
the floor, as he realized. I hadn't said it . . . but Mornett,
damn him, does know me. In some ways, he understands me
like no one else does.

As you always say, Grandmama: hanged for a fleece, hanged
for a yak. "We know," I told him, my voice low.

You've met the man; you know how smooth-spoken he is.
For the first time, I saw him at an utter loss for words. All he
managed to get out was a stuttering "How?"

"A mistake on Gleinleigh's part," I said, "or more than
one—certainly he underestimated his niece's intelligence. She
recognized one of the tablets in his so-called cache."

Mornett shaped a soundless curse. "That vainglorious fool.
We told him the epic would be enough. But no, he had to make
a grand discovery of it, throwing in every tablet he could get
his hands on—"

I realized, very much to my surprise, that Mornett was a little drunk. He wasn't much for that sort of thing back when I knew him, and I don't know whether he's changed . . . or whether he resorted to some liquid courage before approaching me. Given where he'd tried to start the conversation, I have to admit the latter is possible.

"Did he buy out Dorak's whole stock?" I said.

That was supposed to be a sour joke, but Mornett said, "Yes. And had to be talked out of staging an entire fake temple or library; he didn't understand that people would have spotted that immediately."

I can believe it. Gleinleigh likes to buy the fruits of archaeologists' labours—or rather, the things stolen out from under their noses—but has no particular interest in or respect for the science of it.

The next part, I didn't want to ask . . . but whether it was because of the drink or how I'd needled him about honesty, I had Mornett talking. I couldn't let my own bruised feelings get in the way of exploiting that. "How long ago was it found, really?" I asked. Then, before Mornett could answer that, the real question tore its way out of me: "How long ago did you read the epic?"

Just then Lady Cossimere whirled past and snapped at us to leave the floor if we weren't going to dance anymore. If she'd prevented Mornett from answering, I swear I would have torn her ridiculous wig off. But as it happens, I can't pin the blame on her, because something else interrupted us much more thoroughly: a sudden boom, loud enough and close enough that it rattled the crystals in the chandelier.

The band stopped playing, and the dancers all drifted to a halt. Dr. Pinfell got up at the front of the room and told us all it was nothing, that we should go back to enjoying ourselves, but of course he had no more idea what was going on than the rest of us did, so nobody listened to him. People went to the windows and peered outside, trying to see what had caused the noise, but the Whitsea Salon is on the wrong side of the Tomphries for that. Alan had just made up his mind to go into the street and inquire when the door swung open and Cora came rushing in, hair wild and face streaked with soot.

She isn't one to soften things even under ordinary circumstances. Her gaze raked the crowd until she found me, and then she shrieked, "Someone has blown up the annex!"

I don't remember much of what followed. My mind just went white with shock. I know I ran for the door, and half the room ran with me; Simeon told me afterward that Pinfell just fainted dead away. We all stampeded outside and around to the back of the Tomphries, and at that point even people who didn't know the museum had an annex could see where to go, because there was a sinister glow coming from Hemminge Street.

Cora's words meant I expected to find the entire building in rubble. It wasn't that bad—but it was more than bad enough. I heard later that somebody threw a grenade through an upstairs window. At the time, I only saw that there was glass everywhere in the street, and then smoke billowing out of the northeast corner of the second floor.

The very same room where, just that afternoon, we had placed the tablets of the epic for safekeeping.

It wasn't coincidence, either. A painted message was splashed across the pavement in front of the annex: BURN THEIR HISTORY BEFORE THEY BURN OUR CHILDREN.

I don't have any proof. But I guarantee you that if Zachary Hallman didn't throw that grenade himself, he handed it to the man who did. A Hadamist slogan, and a bomb thrown into the room where the epic was held: they were trying to destroy the evidence. Without the tablets, all our accusations of smuggling would be worth less than bone dust.

Kudshayn screamed. Even I forget sometimes that he's related to dragons; he has wings and scales and claws, but he's a kind and intelligent creature, better than most of the humans I know. The sound he made, though . . . it raised all the hairs on the back of my neck, a high-pitched, raw-edged keen no human throat could ever make. He lunged toward the building, wings spread, but even out there we could feel the heat; the air was hazed with smoke. It drove him back, coughing and staggering, and he fell to his knees in defeat.

And I—

I can tell you my reasoning, but I don't think I consciously went through it at the time. It was like . . . sometimes, when I am translating, I get far enough into the rhythm and patterns and logic of the Draconean language that it doesn't even feel like I am translating. I just understand the text, as if I can see it all at once. Last night I saw, in my mind's eye, the entire situation.

The night watchman at the street corner, cranking the call box for all he was worth, summoning the fire brigade.

Cora shrieking at her uncle, slapping Gleinleigh's hands away as he tried to reach for her.

The tablets. They're fired clay; they don't mind a little extra flame.

But they do mind being broken. By grenades, by collapsing ceilings, by the water used to fight the fire.

The world seemed incredibly sharp, and at once both very close and very far away. I looked up at the smoke surging out of the broken windows, and I knew that if anything remained, I had to save it.

Only one person there knew me well enough to guess my thoughts, and was close enough to intervene. Aaron Mornett grabbed me by the arm, hard enough to leave five perfect bruises. "Audrey, you can't! It isn't safe!"

I got out of his grip and put him in a wrist lock for good measure, dropping him to one knee. My own voice sounded like a stranger's, and strangely calm. "You may be a liar and a thief, but I thought you at least had enough integrity not to destroy artifacts. Apparently I was wrong."

Then I let go of him and ran toward the annex.

The downstairs wasn't so bad. There weren't many lights on, because it was night and no one had been there when the explosion happened except the watchman and Cora, but the air seemed fairly clear. I could feel it change around me as I ran up the stairs, though, growing palpably hotter, and I damned the two of them for not trying to put out the fire before it got so large.

My momentum faltered as I reached the upstairs hallway. The air was substantially hotter, and I could taste smoke on the air. The lights here had gone out, but I could see the door I wanted by the glow coming from around its edges.

I was about to push on when I heard footsteps behind me.

You would think a joint lock and the most crushing condemnation I'm capable of delivering would be enough to deter a man from running into a burning building after a woman who hates him, but apparently not.

Mornett stopped a few steps below me, holding something out like a peace offering. After a moment I realized it was his dinner jacket, sopping wet—he'd soaked it in a horse trough outside. "Put this over your head," he said. "It may help."

I gaped at it like a landed fish.

With the only real light coming from below him, I couldn't see his face, but his shoulders were rigid. "I didn't know she was going to do this," he said, his voice almost too low to hear. "You have to believe me."

Under any other circumstances I would have tried for a smart response. Instead I took his jacket, draped it over my head and shoulders, and advanced down the hallway.

Mornett stuck to my heels like a limpet. When I reached for the door handle, it was hot to the touch, but I was braced for that; after all, there was a fire on the other side. But I didn't fully realize what that meant.

Aaron did. He suddenly lunged for me and dragged me to the floor, just as the door swung open.

A searing wind passed over our heads, as the cooler air of the hallway got sucked into the room and the heat of the fire blasted out above. If Aaron hadn't pulled me down, I would have taken that full in the face.

When I lifted my head, I realized why the blaze had spread so quickly. I love you dearly, Grandmama, but it is your fault: the grenade went through the window right next to the specimens you so kindly donated to the exhibit and shattered all those glass jars, spilling formaldehyde everywhere. I have not forgotten the warning you delivered when I was seven and tried to hold a bit of embalmed flesh up to a gas light to see it better— it is very nearly tattooed on my brain—and so I understood immediately why that entire end of the room was in flames. There was nothing anyone could have done to stop it, short of the fire brigade itself.

I forced myself into the room. The heat was like a living thing, a monster beating at me and snarling that I should flee while I still could. The very air seemed to eat at my eyes and my lungs. The grenade had made a ruin of the entire place, splintering nearby shelves and knocking more distant ones over;

I could barely work out where the tablets ought to be, and stumbled over things in my path. The only mercy was that with all the windows shattered, most of the smoke was going outside, rather than staying to blind me.

And I saw the tablets.

The grenade had blown them clear off their shelf and into the aisle, where they lay in a heap of fragmented clay. I wept with fury at the sight, but the tears evaporated before they could fall. And how was I going to get them out of there?

A surge of heat made me flinch, turning so Mornett's rapidly drying jacket was between me and the worst of it. I saw he'd followed a few steps into the room, no farther.

I suppose most people would say a gentleman ought to have hurled himself forward, rather than letting me lead the way. But honestly, I think better of him for not trying to play the hero for my sake.

"Audrey!" he shouted, one arm up as if that would protect him from anything. "It's no good! We have to get out of here!"

My answer to that was to lunge deeper into the room, toward the tablets. One of them had skidded mostly intact across the floor; I managed to grab it, hissing at the touch of hot clay, before sheer animal instinct dragged me back toward relative safety. I shoved the tablet into his hands and said, "Make yourself useful."

He tried to protest even as he took it, but I wasn't listening. I told myself that the fire was all the way at the other end of the room, that I just had to stiffen my spine a bit and I'd be able to rescue all the pieces before they could be damaged any worse—

But that was a lie. When I tried to drive myself back toward them, I felt like I was crisping alive. I might rescue another piece or two, but not all of them. And maybe not even that much.

My foot hit something on the floor. It was one of Arnoldson's Nichaean pieces, a large bronze offering dish thrown facedown by the blast. I pulled Mornett's jacket from my head, draping it over my hands to protect them, and heaved the dish up—I never could have done it without desperation giving me strength. My thought was to drop it over the pile of broken tablets to protect them, but howling fear meant I wound up hurling it like a massive discus, a clumsy throw that for all I know did more damage than it prevented.

An instant later, the fire brigade started pumping water through one of the windows.

A wall of boiling steam hit me like a fist. The next thing I knew I was out in the hallway, and I couldn't fight anymore as Aaron dragged me toward the stairs, down, out into air that seemed like a shock of ice after where I'd been.

So for all my efforts, this is what I have to show for it: a single tablet. My face is scalded, my hands are burned, and as I write this I keep coughing, because in addition to the smoke there were fumes coming off the burning formaldehyde; one of the men from the fire brigade spent a good ten minutes upbraiding me for my foolishness. And yet, even though I only saved one—even though, now that the moment has faded, I'm all too aware that I could have died—even though this is easily the stupidest and most reckless thing I've done in my life—I don't regret it.

Because they were prepared to destroy history, *Grandmama. They mostly succeeded, too, and that makes me utterly sick. I don't know if Gleinleigh was in on it; he seemed genuinely horrified about the risk to Cora, and Aaron said he didn't know she was going to do this. Maybe it was all Mrs. Kefford's idea. As for Aaron himself...*

Whatever accusations one might fling at him, I don't see

him agreeing to blow up the epic and everything else in that room. He values the past too much.

You may think I'm being partial to him, that despite everything I still harbour some kind of warm feelings for him. Honestly . . . at this point, I hardly even know what to think. It is hard to hate a man who followed you into a burning building. But whatever you may think of Aaron Mornett, know this:

He left the tablet for me.

The men from the fire brigade examined us both, and by the time they let me go, Aaron had vanished. But the tablet I shoved into his hands? That was still there.

He could have taken it with him. I bet you anything Gleinleigh and Mrs. Kefford would have wanted him to, so they could finish what the grenade started. But he left it with me.

I think, having written this letter, I can finally sleep. I feel like someone has burned out the inside of me, leaving only a charred shell. Tomorrow I imagine the truth will set in: that we have lost the epic, that no one will care about smuggling when the artifacts themselves are gone, and this priceless text, horrifying ending and all, lives on only in our copies. Tonight, I just feel empty.

But I think that, for the first time, I may have done what Grandmama would do.

Your loving granddaughter,
Audrey

For the archives of the Sanctuary of Wings
written by Kudshayn, son of Ahheke, daughter of Iztam

Endless Maw, accept this sacrifice and be sated. Let your hunger destroy no more.

Foundation of All, take Audrey into your sheltering embrace. She is my sister of no shell, as dear to me as Teslit; keep her safe from further harm.

Source of Wind, stay your hand. I cannot endure more change.

Light of the World, eternal sun, guide me through this darkest night.

From the notebook of Cora Fitzarthur

Mr. Alan Preston delivered some boxes to Clarton Square today, containing the fragments of the tablets. Dr. Cowell wouldn't let the fire department clear away things in what's left of the annex; he sent Mr. Preston, who is an archaeologist, to retrieve everything in a very systematic way. He says they would have been much more badly broken if a bronze offering dish hadn't landed upside down over them, which helped protect them from falling debris and the firemen's hoses.

Thanks to his careful work, and because Audrey made copies of all the copies (I mean extra versions of the drawings that show what the tablets looked like), I can identify this much so far:

> Tablet I, the Creation Tablet: four pieces
> Tablet II, the Genealogy Tablet: nine pieces
> Tablet III, the Dream Tablet: three pieces
> Tablet IV, the Hatching Tablet: four pieces
> Tablet V, the Fledging Tablet: two pieces
> Tablet VI, the Darkness Tablet: four pieces
> Tablet VII, the Samšin Tablet: five pieces
> Tablet VIII, the Nahri Tablet: four pieces
> Tablet IX, the Imalkit Tablet: two pieces
> Tablet X, the Ektabr Tablet: three pieces

Tablet XI, the Return Tablet: two pieces

Tablet XII, the Worms Tablet: four pieces

Tablet XIII, the War Tablet: three pieces

Tablet XIV, the Sacrifice Tablet: one corner knocked
off, but otherwise intact, because Audrey and
Aaron Mornett got it out.

Plus a box full of smaller fragments that will take a lot longer to identify. Mr. Preston told me anything can be put back together again, given enough time and patience, but he was trying to be reassuring, and he's wrong. Not everything can be put back together.

~~I could have di~~

~~Uncle said he didn't kn~~

I have done many jigsaw puzzles, but never one in three dimensions. I can only think it will take an incredibly long time to assemble these again—and I don't know what we're going to do about the gold.

From the diary of Audrey Camherst

2 ACINIS

I just keep thinking . . . if they hadn't tried to cover their tracks, we never would have realized the truth.

It should make me laugh. Maybe someday it will. But not right now, because everything they've done has already caused so much damage, and if we can't put a stop to it somehow, they'll do even more.

The odds of us managing that are a lot better now, though.

We're all at Clarton Square. I didn't even know Cora was here at first; Simeon brought me home after the fire, and I barely stayed awake long enough to write a letter to Grandmama. I slept until almost noon—though not well, thanks to inhaling formal-dehyde fumes and smoke—and by the time I got up, Cora was hard at work. It turns out Alan delivered the fragments he'd re-trieved from the rubble, and Cora sat down straightaway to or-ganize them. On our dining room table, no less—but at least she put down a sheet first, unlike that time Papa left an enormous squid there.

I didn't want to look. I am incredibly grateful to her for doing that work, because someone has to and she is as familiar with these tablets as anyone . . . but I knew it would just make my heart bleed, looking at the destruction those bastards have wrought.

At the same time, I couldn't *not* look.

When Kudshayn came to my bedroom (shock! scandal! a male creature in my boudoir!) and told me what had happened while I slept, I said dully, "It hardly matters now—if it ever did. The Tomphries won't put the tablets on display, not in this state, which means Pinfell won't care whether they were smuggled or not, which means . . ."

I couldn't bring myself to finish the sentence. But Kudshayn said, "We must see them sooner or later. And I . . . would prefer you to be with me."

He wasn't just saying that as a sop to my feelings, the way an adult will profess to be frightened of the dark and ask a small child to help them be brave. This hurts Kudshayn far worse than me; I could hardly refuse him comfort. I got up and hugged him (still in my nightdress; it is a good thing our household is used to outrageous behaviour), put on a dressing gown, and went with him down to the dining room.

It was like a morgue, with all the murder victims in a row. Kudshayn bowed his head and murmured a prayer over the fragments, which made them feel even more like the bodies of the dead. Cora watched that with fascination, but waited until he was done before she spoke.

What she said about the fragments will be important in time, but I hardly listened to her, because I was too much in shock, drifting closer to the table and staring like—well, like I was looking at corpses, except that I am not a priest and could not think of a single prayer, even though I have translated plenty.

Then I noticed something odd.

Cora cut off mid-recitation as I picked up one of the pieces of the Return Tablet. "Yes," she said. "I was getting to that. Mr. Preston said he didn't know what to make of the gold, but he picked up all the lumps of it he could find; those are in another box."

Traces of it remained along the broken edge of the piece. Bright gold, standing out like the sun from all the soot and filth of the fire.

Kudshayn joined me and loomed over my shoulder. "It was . . . inside?" One claw-tip came around my arm to trace the narrow void in the center of the clay—a long gap just big enough to have held a thin sheet of hammered gold.

"It looks like it," Cora said. "But the fire was so hot that it melted and all ran out."

I truly am a Camherst, because life stirred in me once more at this sight of this oddity. I'd never heard of gold being inside tablets—though of course we wouldn't know if it was there, would we, unless the tablets got broken. Which many of them have been, and none of those had gold that I know of, or a central void where gold or anything else might have lain concealed.

Kudshayn said, "'Hearts of gold.' Was that not inscribed on the sun disc Lady Plimmer bought? The one Simeon wrote to you concerning?"

"Yes," I murmured, drifting down the table. "This might be proof that the tablets were stolen from that temple in Seghaye." My gaze skittered across the broken pieces. The tablets were well made in the usual Draconean style, a core of rough clay covered with a layer of finer material suitable for writing, but the gold had formed a second, innermost core. On tablet after tablet—

Until I got to the one we've been calling the Worms Tablet. That one was solid clay. Two layers, just like a normal tablet . . . but not like the ones that came before it. And the War Tablet was the same.

That's when I knew.

It wasn't a guess. It wasn't a theory. If I hadn't been certain, I never could have done what I did then:

I picked up the Sacrifice Tablet and slammed it down on the edge of the table, breaking it in half.

Cora shrieked in protest and Kudshayn lunged, too late to stop me. "Audrey, what are you *doing*?"

I held out the broken pieces to him. Two layers of clay: just like the War Tablet, and just like the Worms Tablet. My hands were shaking, but my voice, when I spoke, was as steady as the Foundation of All. "It's a fake."

His wings fluttered, almost extending as if for balance, though wings can't do anything to steady a Draconean against an earthquake of the mind. Cora said, "What do you mean, fake?" but I didn't answer her. All my attention was on Kudshayn.

He thought it through. In the aftermath of so many horrifying things, with me holding the pieces of an artifact I'd just broken on purpose right in front of him, he still thought it through, because he is Kudshayn and that is how he works.

Restraint and rational focus notwithstanding, his wings trembled when he said, "There could be another reason. The style of the story shifts; we both know that. The last three tablets are more like history than myth. Perhaps that is why they lack the golden core: because they are not sacred."

"If it were just the text," I said, "I might agree with you. But consider the—the *provenance*." My breath huffed out in disbelieving laughter. "Was it a mere stroke of luck that Mrs. Kefford and Gleinleigh got their hands on a text that confirms humanity's worst suspicions about your people? Or did they get their hands on a text that was sure to attract a great deal of attention . . . and then *arrange* for it to be as damaging as possible?"

"But nobody could fake something like this," Cora objected. "It's far too difficult."

Kudshayn said, "Audrey could—but wouldn't. Aaron Mornett could, and would."

I laid the pieces of the Sacrifice Tablet back down on the sheet, because the alternative was to drop them. *Aaron Mornett.* He isn't the only one capable of such detailed, convincing work; I could think of a handful of people skilled and clever enough to carry it off. But Grandpapa would die before he falsified even a tiny piece of history, let alone something like this. So would the others. Only Aaron Mornett is unscrupulous enough.

In a way, I think that realization shattered me even more than discovering the forgery.

Because the forgery isn't devastating; it is *liberating.* The nasty turn the story takes after the Light of the World is returned to the sky—all of that is a lie! Samšin doesn't become a tyrant, they don't blame human beings for the loss of the sun, nobody gets burned in sacrifice!

My thoughts might as well have been printed in capital letters across my forehead, because Kudshayn held up a cautioning hand when I whirled to face him. "Absence of evidence is not evidence of absence," he said. "This does not prove the innocence of the Anevrai."

"Who *cares*?" I said, laughing (and then setting off a coughing fit—this discovery has not liberated me from the aftereffects of smoke and formaldehyde inhalation). "I mean, of course you care; it still matters to you whether your foremothers burned people alive or not. But the proof of their guilt is gone!"

Cora said, in her most practical voice, "How are you going to prove *that*?"

It brought me down to earth with a thump. All well and good for us to point at the lack of gold inside the last three tablets, but that will hardly convince Pinfell—not when we're accusing an earl and the wife of the Synedrion's Dissenting Speaker. "I'll shake a confession out of Mornett," I said, halfway between grim and gleeful.

"Will his words be heard?" Kudshayn asked. "Your people put great stock in rank and wealth. Mornett has neither."

The whole shape of it began to flower in my mind. "But this is so much more than forgery," I said, the words drifting out of me, almost like I was a charlatan channeling some outside spirit. "I'll bet you anything Hallman was behind the bombing last night—but he didn't do that off his own bat. Somebody hired him. Gleinleigh or Mrs. Kefford." Not Mornett.

And not Gleinleigh either, it seems. Cora hunched in on herself and said, "He swore it wasn't him. He was angry that I got hurt, and when I said it was his fault, he told me it wasn't. I—I believe him. But it doesn't matter," she added, suddenly furious. "He's still working with the people who *are* at fault. Just because he didn't give the order himself doesn't make him innocent."

That fits with what I know of Gleinleigh. There wasn't supposed to be a riot at the airfield; there wasn't supposed to be a bombing at the annex. He's the type of idiot who thinks he can lie down with ~~dragons~~ jackals and not get blood on him.

"So it was most likely Mrs. Kefford," I said. "She's ruthless enough. But . . . that means the wife of the Dissenting Speaker hired a known terrorist to bomb a major public institution."

"If we can prove it," Kudshayn said.

Then his wings flicked in alarm. "The translation," he said. "It has already been sent to the printer. We have to stop it."

You would think that should seem small compared to the bombing. But after all, isn't the epic the reason they've gone to all this trouble? Forge an ending, hire us to translate it—keep it under strict secrecy to minimize the risk that anyone will notice an error; I'm sure now that was Gleinleigh's real reason for requiring our silence—then destroy the original so that, again, people will have a harder time spotting any mistakes. But the epic isn't wholly destroyed (Cora says Alan said the offering dish helped protect the tablets!), and the attempt wound up showing us exactly what they were trying to hide. If they'd left well enough alone, we might never have discovered the truth.

Short of breaking into the printer's and stealing the manuscript back, though, I don't know how we can halt it. The publisher's deal is with Gleinleigh, not us. And thinking of that made me realize something else, too.

"The tablets," I said, gathering them up like a thief trying to hide evidence. Which, in a sense, I am. "If they find out they've dug them out of the rubble, they'll come looking for them."

Which was a masterpiece of unclear antecedents, but Kudshayn followed my meaning anyway, and after a moment Cora did, too. "Mr. Preston said Dr. Cavall sent them here because he knew you were trying to prove they'd been smuggled, but that he—Dr. Cavall, I mean—would tell Uncle—" She stopped, face screwing up into the fiercest expression I've ever seen on her. "Would tell *Lord Gleinleigh* that he sent them to you because you were the best able to assemble them back into order, being so familiar with them. Which Unc— Lord Gleinleigh won't believe for a moment, but when I told Mr. Preston that he only laughed and said Dr. Cavall doesn't mind telling bad lies."

God bless Simeon and Alan. And God bless Cora, too, because when we had all the fragments packed up (it's a Camherst household; of *course* we have material for packaging artifacts and specimens on hand at all times), she said, "I'll take them somewhere. He already knows I ran away, but he doesn't care enough to chase me."

That brought me up short, as I finally noted that Cora was at my family's townhouse, and as near as I could tell had been there all day. Kudshayn said, "They had a . . ." He searched for the right Scirling phrase. "Falling-out?"

"We screamed at each other," Cora said, going tense again. "Mostly I screamed at him and he tried to explain things, but when I didn't like his explanations he yelled at me, too. And then I left. I didn't go home last night. I walked around Falchester until I remembered that I knew where your family lived because I read all your letters to them. So then I came here and Kudshayn made the housekeeper let me in."

(And that is Mrs. Farwin for you. Doesn't bat an eyelash at having a Draconean for a houseguest, even though there's never been one on Scirling soil before, much less under her roof—but let a strange young woman show up on the doorstep and she becomes our guardian dragon.)

"You're welcome to stay here as long as you like," I said. "Or go somewhere else, if you prefer. But if you have the tablets, your uncle *will* chase you." There was no point in pretending he cared more about her than about the tablets. "Is there somewhere you can hide, that he won't think to look for you?"

Cora bit her lip, which was answer enough. I was on the verge of saying I would pay to put her up in some hotel chosen at random when a better idea came to me. "The Carters," I said. "Do you remember their address?"

"Of course," Cora said.

"Eugene Carter is an utter sweetheart," I said, "and Imogene probably won't even notice you're there. I'll write you a letter to take with you. There's even a streetcar that runs out to Flinders—but don't embark at the stop over on Galworthy Street, just in case Gleinleigh thinks to inquire there." I patted at the pockets of my dressing gown as if my purse might be in them. "Give me a moment and I'll fetch some money for a taxi-cab."

So that's Cora off to the Carters', and Kudshayn and me trying to figure out a way to prove the connection between Gleinleigh, Mrs. Kefford, Aaron Mornett, Dorak, and Zachary Hallman. We have some of the pieces, but we'll need more before we can bring this to the police.

From: Kudshayn
To: the Sanctuary of Wings

2 Acinis

To the elders of the Sanctuary of Wings, I give greetings under the light of the sun, on the footing of the earth.

I no longer consider myself bound by the oath of secrecy I gave upon beginning my work here in Scirland. We have uncovered information which makes it apparent that the one to whom I gave that oath was, from the start, acting in bad faith; much of what he said to me was lies, told with malicious intent against our people. He thought to use me and Audrey Camherst as his tools in his schemes—or their schemes, as he did not act alone. Knowing this, I consider it not only permissible but my duty to share with you what I have learned, and to give warning of those who have conspired against us.

Be warned: much of what I say in the enclosed report will be difficult to read. Do not enter into this expecting that all our beliefs regarding the ancient past will be vindicated. For the past seven months I have stood through an earthquake, my image of our foremothers changing beneath my feet. Some of what I have learned is good. Some is not. Most is neither good nor bad, but simply beyond the boundaries of what we have remembered: in some ways as alien to our lives now as the most advanced technology human societies have to offer.

I pray each day for the wisdom to understand these things as they deserve. I pray to the sun, to the earth—and to the powers we have forgotten, whose influence remains in the world nonetheless. And I give thanks that those who sought to serve destruction and to turn its power to their own ends have themselves been brought down by that selfsame principle. Change is inevitable; destruction can bring new life. Bear these thoughts in mind as you read.

And prepare for what is to come. Together with Audrey Camherst I am doing what I can to blunt the edge of our enemy's weapon, but it would be foolishness to think we have only one enemy, with only one weapon. Your wisdom undoubtedly makes you aware of this already; I only hope that the account enclosed with this letter will help you to understand the depths to which our opponents will sink, the stratagems they will use against us.

May the earth shelter you and keep you safe. May the sun guide you on your journeys here.

Pray that they will protect myself and Audrey, for I fear we are not yet finished with our trials.

Kudshayn, son of Ahheke, daughter of Iztam

From the diary of Audrey Camherst

3 ACINIS

Phone call from Simeon this morning, when I was hardly even out of bed. "Get ready. Gleinleigh's on his way to you."

I blinked the sleep from my eyes. "I'm surprised he wasn't here yesterday."

From the other end of the line, a laugh I recognized all too well. "I gave him a masterful go-around, if I do say so myself. Told him at first that I didn't think Alan was done with the retrieval, and then when he went by the annex to see and found Alan was gone, told him the fragments must have been sent for cleaning, but I would be *sure* to inform him as soon as they came back. He's on the hunt now, though, so I'd expect him within the hour if I were you."

"Then I should get dressed," I said, and hung up.

It's a good thing I'm not fussy about my appearance, because I had rather less than an hour before someone started alternately ringing the bell and hammering on the door. But I'd warned the butler, so he still took his dignified time walking to the door and opening it, and then was very politely in Lord Gleinleigh's way, offering to take his coat and hat and cane. (Necessary? No. But it amused me.)

Once he got to the parlour, Gleinleigh cut right to the point. "Where are my tablets?" he demanded.

"Good morning to you, too, my lord," I said, playing up the

raspiness of my voice, and gesturing weakly with one bandaged hand. "Please, have a seat."

He ignored my invitation, and didn't offer an ounce of sympathy for my injuries, either. "Where are they, damn you? Those are my property; you have no business stealing them!"

I affected surprise. "Stealing? My lord, I've done nothing of the sort. Simeon got confused. He thought, since Kudshayn and I had been working on the tablets, surely you would want them sent back to us. He didn't understand that our obligations to you are done. But I realized the mistake, so when Cora stopped by to see how I was doing, I asked her to take them back to Stokesley."

"Stokesley?!"

I truly think the earl might have lunged for me then and there, except that a certain tall, winged figure appeared in the doorway. "Lord Gleinleigh," Kudshayn said. His courtesy was the thinnest of veneers; I don't think Gleinleigh realized how thoroughly every line of Kudshayn's body advertised his dislike. He doesn't understand Draconeans enough to read that sort of thing.

But every squishy mammal knows to be afraid of something bigger and toothier—even when that something is a scholarly creature with breathing difficulties. Gleinleigh jerked tight, then backed up a step, eyes darting about as if calculating whether it would be better to abandon dignity and escape through the window.

"Oh, please," I said with contempt. "Shall we all stop pretending? You're a liar and a Calderite, and we know it. We have proof that you lied about your discovery in the Qajr, which means the tablets Kudshayn and I have been working on were brought into the country illegally; that alone will be scandal enough. But when the world hears that you forged the ending of the epic in an attempt to defame Kudshayn's people, what effect do you think that will have on your reputation?"

Marcus Fitzarthur, seventeenth earl of Gleinleigh, comes from a long noble line. Back someone like him into a corner, and he will armor himself with centuries of aristocratic arrogance and privilege. He drew himself upright and said, "You think to drag me into the courts, Miss Camherst? A half-breed from an upstart family like yours? You will never make it stick."

"Perhaps not," I said with a great show of indifference. "But you make the mistake of thinking that *you* are my primary concern. I'm more interested in what happens with the Draconeans and their bid for political independence."

Gleinleigh flushed an ugly shade. The look he cast at Kudshayn was one of naked loathing. "You think anyone will have sympathy for these *beasts*?" he said. "It doesn't matter what I've done. No one will give them sympathetic hearing, bar a few eccentrics like your family."

Kudshayn cocked his head to one side. I'm sure it's utter coincidence that the movement echoed that of a predator, sizing up potential prey. "If you believe that, why go to so much trouble providing false support for your own side?"

"Because you deserve it!" Gleinleigh spat. "The story was a fairy tale, a pretense that your species were ever anything other than vicious animals! That they *can* be anything else! We can never live in peace with you. But people will eat up any foolishness and take it for truth, simply because it's old."

Silence fell. Gleinleigh's rage took on a triumphant cast; he thought he had shocked us out of words with his hatred and his cynicism. As if his bile were anything we hadn't both heard a hundred times before.

My thoughts, like Kudshayn's, were on something else entirely.

Kudshayn took another step into the room. "Peace," he said, his wings lifting slightly, not quite spreading. "Our two peoples, living in peace. That is nowhere in the tablets we read."

A pale man like Gleinleigh advertises his feelings much too easily. His face, which had been red, suddenly whitened.

"There's more," I breathed.

More tablets. I'd assumed the real text ended with the Return Tablet; it's a sensible enough place to conclude the story, with the sun once more in the sky—and the tablet was so damaged, we had no way of telling what its final lines were. (It had even crossed my mind that some callous soul might have damaged it on purpose, to prevent us from noticing that it didn't lead at all into the Worms Tablet.)

But the forgeries could just as easily have replaced something else.

Gleinleigh's mouth twisted. "Not anymore," he said. Malice warped his voice and face into something ugly. "You will never know what it once said, because Aaron Mornett destroyed it."

Maybe there's a kind of truth to the Anevrai myth that human beings were created by the earth, because I felt as if I'd turned to stone. Some unknown number of tablets, giving a different end to the tale . . .

. . . and he wanted me to believe *Aaron Mornett* smashed them to pieces?

No. That is the one accusation I cannot credit. His sins may be too many to count, but that man ran after me into a burning building to help rescue precious relics of the past.

Lying, though—telling Gleinleigh and Mrs. Kefford that he'd destroyed the tablets; maybe even rendering up the dust of something less significant like a tax record, knowing they'd never be able to tell the difference—*that*, I can believe he would do.

Which means that the real ending is still out there some-where. In Aaron Mornett's possession.

I kept all of that from my expression. (It helps that the scalding from the steam makes all expressions a bit painful; I have fallen into the habit of keeping my face protectively stiff.) "You're monsters," I said, flat and cold. "And in the end, you will fail. There are thousands of tablets out there, just waiting for archaeologists to unearth them. There will be other cop-ies, other versions of the story. Someday we will know the truth."

Gleinleigh sneered and jerked a contemptuous chin in Kud-shayn's direction. "Too late for *his* species, though."

"Kudshayn," I said, before he could make any response to Gleinleigh. "I don't feel right asking the butler to take out this sort of trash. Don't you think it's time we let him go?"

He stepped aside, because Kudshayn can read me as well as my family can, even through a scalded face, and he knew I'd thought of something. He mantled just as Gleinleigh went past, though, making the earl twitch and move more rapidly for the door. Gleinleigh didn't even wait for the butler, just grabbed his things and left.

The instant the door closed behind him, I rushed out into the hall, where we keep our telephone. "Selwright Hotel," I told the operator. While she connected me, I told Kudshayn what I'd surmised about Mornett. "But I'm not allowed to go to the hotel," I reminded him.

"And while I could," Kudshayn said, "I doubt that would do much good."

A Draconean on the premises: he would cause more than a minor stir. I held up one finger as my call went through. But when I asked for Mornett, the hotel's concierge told me he was not in. "Please ask him to call me as soon as possible," I said.

"And your name, ma'am?"

My mind went blank. I couldn't say Audrey Camherst; that name is far too notorious there. Not Lotte, either—nobody with the name Camherst, and the Trent name wouldn't be much better. But I needed Mornett to call me back.

"Beliluštar," I blurted.

"Er . . . how is that spelled, Miss Bel . . . ?"

I spelled it for him, with *SH* in place of the *S* with its caron. "Beliluštar?" Kudshayn said when I'd hung up. "The ancient queen?"

"It was Mornett's name for me," I said quietly, my hand still on the receiver. "Back when . . . we first met."

He'll recognize it; I'm sure of that much. I just wish I could have thought of anything that wouldn't suggest I still harbour romantic feelings toward him.

But I've written all of this and he still hasn't called back, and I can't sit around all day waiting for him. So Kudshayn and I are off to the offices of Carrigdon and Rudge, because we need to persuade them there are *terrible* flaws in the translation and its publication must be delayed indefinitely. I've left instructions with the staff here, in the event of his return call; hopefully that will be enough.

OFFICE OF THE FALCHESTER CITY CORONER
88 Walsonworth Street

Report of Investigation by City Coroner

Name: unknown
Race: Northern Anthiopean
Sex: Male
Age: est. mid to late 20s
Home Address: unknown
Occupation: unknown

Type of Death:
  Violent [X] Casualty [ ] Suicide [ ]
  Sudden (in apparent health) [ ]
  Found Dead [X] In Prison [ ]
  Unnatural or suspicious [X] Cremation [ ]

Comment: body found in the river; likely
killed upstream

Investigating Agency: Falchester City Police

Description of Body
  Clothed [X] Unclothed [ ] Partially Clothed [ ]
Eyes: Blue
Hair: Dark brown
Facial hair: none
Weight: 82 kg
Height: 178 cm
Body Temp: 15 degrees, 03/09/5662
Rigor: No
Lysed: No
Livor: No
Marks and Wounds: penetrating wound to the

posterior upper left thorax, exit wound on
the anterior side

Probable Cause of Death: gunshot

Manner of Death:
   Accidental [ ] Suicide [ ] Homicide [X]
   Natural [ ] Unknown [ ]

Autopsy Required

From the diary of Audrey Camherst

4 ACINIS

I'm terribly afraid that I've made everything worse.

I should have kept my mouth shut to Gleinleigh. Just for a little while longer—just until we could get more proof. But despite everything, I still cannot resist saying what I really think. Even when a constable showed up at the door this morning and asked me to come down to the police station with him, I thought it was going to be something about the tablets, that they'd caught Cora, or Gleinleigh had leveled charges against me.

But Constable Corran wouldn't say anything until he'd parked me at a table in one of their dingy little interview rooms. So it turned out I'd been preparing all the wrong answers when he asked, "Can you account for your whereabouts last night?"

"My what?" I said, baffled. "I was at home in Clarton Square. Why?"

"Is there anyone who can confirm that you were there?"

Unease began to grow inside me. "Yes, lots. My houseguest Kudshayn, and all the staff. I went to bed early—you heard about the bombing of the Tomphries annex a few days ago?" I gestured at my face, wishing for once that I were pale enough for the scalding to really be seen. "I was in the building during the fire, and haven't fully recovered. What is all this about?"

He consulted his notes, which I think was just for show. "You broke into the Selwright Hotel last Messis, didn't you?"

My thoughts finally wrenched themselves off their original track. The Selwright: Aaron Mornett. My heart leapt into a much faster tempo. "I can hardly deny it. Does this have something to do with that? It was months ago."

The constable had a much better poker face than I do. He met my gaze levelly and said, "Mr. Grance, the manager of the Selwright, has accused you of breaking in again last night."

"He—" Shock, confusion, and outrage conspired to rob me briefly of my words. "As if I could set foot inside his hotel without someone recognizing me! Not to mention that I have absolutely no interest in seeing Mr. Aaron Mornett ever again."

"Didn't you leave a message for him earlier in the day? Under the name . . ." This time I believe he really did need the help of his notes. "Belilushtar."

I just barely managed to swallow the question of how they'd figured out that was me. "Yes, I did, because I didn't think they would deliver the message if I left my real name. I have no interest in *seeing* Mr. Mornett, but I believe he's in possession of some information I need. That is why I telephoned. But he hasn't rung me back."

Constable Corran sat quietly for a moment, studying me. I swallowed hard and did my best not to look guilty—only the moment someone gives you that kind of look, every mannerism under the sun starts to seem like it will make you look guilty, including attempting to look innocent.

Then he said, "Aaron Mornett is unlikely to ring you back. He's gone missing."

Those three words hit me like a blow to the stomach. Almost soundlessly, I repeated, "Missing?"

Whatever Constable Corran saw in my eyes, he must have

believed it, because he relaxed ever so faintly, becoming more of a human being and less of a stone wall. "His room was ransacked last night, and there is some sign of a struggle. Mr. Grance accused you, owing to your prior encounter—but I confess, I have a hard time believing you could overpower Mr. Mornett, even if you weren't suffering the after-effects of a fire."

Even in my dazed state, I knew that was *not* the right moment to tell him Papa's old suffragette friends trained me in jujutsu. But such thoughts were easier to hold on to than what he had just said: room ransacked. Aaron missing.

I'd congratulated myself on keeping such a straight face when Gleinleigh said the real ending had been destroyed. But maybe I didn't do so well as I'd thought.

Which means that whatever has happened . . . might be my fault.

There was no way Corran could have known that. My voice still unsteady, I said, "Then why did you call me in here?"

"Because of this." He took out a piece of paper and slid it across the table to me.

For one delirious instant, I thought it might be the missing text from the epic. But although the writing was unmistakably Ancient Draconean—and in Aaron's hand—the lines were far too few for that.

Corran said, "I'm given to understand that you are an expert in such things. Can you read what it says?"

My eyes did not want to focus, but put any kind of writing in front of me and I will try to read it out of sheer reflex. I said, "It is definitely Ancient Draconean. I would say it is a poem of some kind—possibly a copy made from a tablet." The pencilled shapes were simply writing, not an attempt to accurately represent the specific marks pressed into clay, but for translation purposes it would suffice.

And if it were copied from a tablet . . . whoever ransacked his room probably grabbed anything clay with Draconean writing on it, in case it was the missing ending.

"There are more," Corran said. From his folder he drew out another half-dozen sheets, all on the Selwright's letterhead. The rest were shorter—incomplete, I realized, and not quite the same as the first example. Then I realized why, and I felt like the Tomphries fire had seared my face all over again.

"Miss Camherst?"

"It is not a copy," I said, my shoulders hunching with embarrassment. "It is . . . I believe he was attempting to compose an original poem." Honesty forced me to add: "For me."

Corran's eyebrows rose.

I indicated the top line. "Here, where it says 'The wings that span the sky of day, the wings that span the sky of night'— that was an epithet used for Belilustar, the ancient queen whose name I gave when I left my message. Mr. Mornett used that name as an endearment for me, some years ago."

"You two were in a relationship."

"Before we fell out," I said, taking refuge in acid worthy of Grandmama herself. "Recent events have made it clear that Mr. Mornett still has feelings for me—feelings I do not reciprocate. I believe this is his way of . . ."

Mercifully, Corran allowed me to leave that sentence unfinished. Bad enough that I was sitting there holding Aaron Mornett's declaration of love. A declaration rendered in the language that had brought us together; the same language he had used to commit intellectual fraud of unforgivable magnitude. For all I knew, he had been composing it even as I discovered his forgery.

I desperately want to tell him what I think of that. But before I can, he has to be found.

"Do you have any idea of where he might be?" Corran asked.

Why he's gone, yes; *where* he's gone, no. And the leads I have aren't the kind of thing I can follow up on, unless I'm going to break into Mrs. Kefford's townhouse. I've come to my senses enough to know that isn't a good idea.

But I was sitting with a police constable. Following up on leads is exactly the kind of thing they're supposed to do.

"It might have to do with a man named Joseph Dorak," I said. "He is a smuggler, a dealer in black-market antiquities—including Draconean materials. I have reason to believe Mr. Mornett is involved with him somehow. It may be that the two of them have fallen out for some reason."

Like, for example, Aaron's failure to destroy the epic's true ending.

Constable Corran scribbled this down in his notebook. "Thank you. Do you have any more information? When you say they are 'involved somehow,' what do you mean?"

I hesitated. I'd mentioned Dorak first because unfortunately, there's a kernel of truth in Gleinleigh's posturing: sharing what I knew would mean accusing some very important people. While Grandmama might be important in her own way, she isn't here right now, and the rest of us are not fully grown dragons.

They'll still help me out, though, if I need it. And more to the point, I think this is the kind of recklessness I *do* have to embrace. The kind where it's too important for me to let go of it.

So I told the constable everything. It took me half the day and made his hand cramp from writing so much, and I think I confused him quite a bit at several points, because he isn't the kind of man who understands why anybody would bother forging an ancient document—much less why it offends me to the core of my soul. But I stressed the political implications, and since I get the impression the entire Falchester police force has been preparing for the congress and its attendant troubles, that part made sense to him.

It's a tremendous relief, knowing that someone else is looking into Gleinleigh and Mrs. Kefford and Dorak. Because honestly, what else can I do? Go camp outside Gleinleigh's townhouse, or Mrs. Kefford's, and follow them wherever they go, hoping they'll lead me to Aaron? I proved at Chiston that I'm not very good at shadowing. As for Kudshayn—he might as well fly a flag advertising his presence. He's barely left the townhouse since we arrived in Falchester, except for the gala, because of the crowd he attracts wherever he goes.

Tremendous relief. I wrote those words just a few seconds ago, and I meant them at the time, but now I'm not so sure. It comes and goes in waves, one moment me thinking that everything is out of my hands now and good riddance, the next feeling like it's all spiraling out of control and I have to stop it myself. All well and good to send them after Dorak, but the man's been known as a smuggler for years, and no one has been able to shut him down; he's too crafty about hiding his illicit shipments. And Gleinleigh and Mrs. Kefford are not easy targets.

I shouldn't have let myself translate Aaron's poem. It would be uncomfortable to read on any day, but right now it makes me worry even more about what has happened to him.

To Beliluštar
by Aaron Mornett
TRANS. BY AUDREY CAMHERST

The wings that span the sky of day,
the wings that span the sky of night:
these are the glory of the world,
without equal in heaven or earth.
On the banks of the twinned river
her treasure-house lies,
filled with all the riches of the past,
bright gold, emerald, lapis, jet;
with wisdom is her treasure-house filled,
and all the knowledge of the past.
The gate of bone cannot bar her way;
the road of bone will form her path,
lifting her to the greatest height,
reigning over the depths below.
Then darkness will part before her,
and light will shed its blessing upon her,
and the doors of her treasure-house
will be thrown open for all to share.
But I will stand alone,
outside the shelter of her wings,
in the penumbra of the light
cast by her most radiant mind.

Witness Statement of Audrey Camherst

I, Audrey Isabella Mahira Adiaratou Camherst, philologist, of #3 Clarton Square, Falchester, NOC 681, state:

On the morning of 4 Acinis I was summoned to the Western New Central Police Station in response to an accusation that I had broken into and ransacked a room at the Selwright Hotel, rented out to Mr. Aaron Mornett. I gave testimony then about events that I believed Mrs. Kefford and others to be involved in, which took me much of the day. Once I was finished there, I went to the offices of Carrigdon and Rudge in an attempt to stop the publication of a work I have been involved with for nearly a year, which I now believe to be partially fraudulent. I remained there until their offices closed, at which point I returned home to Clarton Square.

At approximately eight thirty that evening I received a telephone call requesting that I come to the city morgue on Cressy Street to identify a dead body that had been found floating in the Twisel. My friend Kudshayn, a visiting Draconean scholar, insisted on accompanying me—first because he was worried for my safety, because Mr. Mornett had gone missing, and second because we both immediately leapt to the possibility that the body in question was Mr. Mornett's. We took a private cab to the morgue, but did not arrive there until nearly nine thirty, because we had difficulty finding a cab driver willing to take on a Draconean as a passenger.

Constable Corran was waiting for me at the morgue. Before we went in, he cautioned me, because I have never seen a dead body before. "He was in the river for some hours before anyone found him," the constable said, "and that has some effects. But the doctor will only pull back the sheet from his face, where there are no marks of violence. Only if you need to see more will you have to look at anything worse."

My queasiness was not because of the prospect of seeing a body, though. It was because I feared I had gotten Aaron Mornett killed. I do not quite remember what I said, but it was along the lines of, "If I cannot recognize him from his face, then pulling back the sheet more will not help, because I never saw any other part of him"—which is not strictly true; I think I could recognize his hands. But that, I think, was not what Constable Corran had in mind.

Then he took me and Kudshayn in to see the body. The doctor waited until I said I was ready, then drew the sheet down.

I got very faint—but again, not because of the body itself. Kudshayn supported me, and I heard him tell the doctor and the constable, "That is not Aaron Mornett."

"No," I said, still holding on to Kudshayn. "It's Zachary Hallman."

Even with his face cold and blue, I knew him. And it's terrible to admit this, but I'd gone faint with relief—because I'd been bracing myself so hard for someone else. And while I would have preferred to see Hallman stand trial for his bigotry and his crimes, I can't say I shed a tear to see him on that slab.

Constable Corran knew about Hallman from my testimony earlier that day. He took me into a separate room and questioned

me some more, along with Kudshayn, about the last time we
had seen Hallman (not since the riot at Alterbury) and our
conviction that he was involved with the bombing of the Tomphries annex. When he asked how Hallman might have wound
up shot and in the river, I was still so dizzy with shock and relief that I said exactly what I was thinking: "If Mrs. Kefford
hired him for the bombing, I bet she was worried that it would
be traced back to her."

That made Corran stop writing and stare at me. "You think
the wife of the Dissenting Speaker shot him?"

"Not herself, no," I said, feeling very cold inside. "But she
might have asked someone else to . . . take care of him."

Corran put his pen down. "Miss Camherst," he said, quiet
and firm. "Please consider what you are doing. I recognize
that you have many suspicions—and you may be correct. But
without any proof, you're putting yourself very much at risk
for a lawsuit from Mrs. Kefford later on. Any accusation
against her could be considered defamation of her husband as
well."

He was right, of course. But all I could think was that Hallman was dead and Aaron was missing; would he be the next
one found in the river? For all my problems with the man, I
didn't want him to die. "Then don't write it down," I said furiously, standing up. "But don't you dare leave her out of your
investigation just because you're afraid. There's more at stake
here than one murder, or even two; the future of the Draconean people may depend, not just on our finding out the
truth, but *proving* it."

Then I stormed out. Which wasn't smart, for a whole host
of reasons: I didn't look where I was going, so I wound up
heading the wrong direction for catching another cab, and I
managed to set off a coughing fit to boot. I fetched up against

the low stone wall along the bank of the Twisel and stayed there for a while, doing my best to hack up a lung. Kudshayn followed me and stood with one of his wings sheltering my back, offering silent comfort.

When I could finally speak again, I said, "I have to find him."

Kudshayn knew whom I meant. He said, "Perhaps he fled before they came—whoever they were. Is there anywhere he might have gone?"

"He grew up in Yarstow," I said. "But he hated it there; I can't imagine he'd go back, even to hide." Was there anywhere else? I stared into the Twisel, trying not to imagine his body floating cold and limp in its waters.

And then it came to me: *the Twisel.*

No one else, I think, could have figured it out. The worst thing about Aaron Mornett is that he and I are, in some senses, perfectly matched: we share the same knowledge, the same passions, at least up to a point. And so that paper he had left in his hotel room was a love poem, as I had assumed . . . but it was also a clue.

"The Twisel," I said to Kudshayn, staring fixedly at the water—but for different reasons now. "Its name is an Old Scirling word for 'forked' or 'twinned.' *On the banks of the twinned river, her treasure-house lies . . .*"

Kudshayn was understandably confused. "What treasure-house?"

I whirled to face him. "Some place Aaron wanted me to know about. The poem I mentioned to you, the one he wrote—it's a message to me. One no one else would recognize, because they would need to know I'm Belilustar, that 'wings that span the sky of day' is one of her epithets—" I stopped dead. "They would need to know the *epic.* Gold, emerald, lapis, jet—"

"The colours of the four siblings," Kudshayn said. His wings flicked with sudden life. "Is he telling you where the missing tablets are hidden?"

"Maybe. Yes? I don't know." It was incomprehensible to me that he might give up that information, after everything that had happened. But why else allude to them in such a fashion? "The question is, where is he sending me? The Twisel is the longest river in Scirland."

"He would not go that far," Kudshayn said. "Somewhere in the city."

That was still a great deal of riverbank to search. "The rest of the poem," I said. Closing my eyes, I made myself breathe slowly and carefully, suppressing the coughs that wanted to rise. I needed to remember, not start hacking again. I recited the poem for Kudshayn, one line at a time, then opened my eyes to see what he thought.

"The heights over the depths," he said immediately. "The Crown of the Abyss?"

If the tone of the poem had been less intimate, I might have wondered if Aaron was telling me to go to hell. "The gate of bone. Bone, bound with skin—that is the gate through which the sisters entered the underworld, and Ektabr when he was in female guise. Some place only for women? No." I dismissed that with a cut of my hand. "He would not have been able to hide them there."

"The gate cannot bar your way," Kudshayn reminded me. "And then the poem changes the image, saying the road of bone will form your path."

"Some street named for a bone?" I said dubiously. "Skull Street, Femur Street, Clavicle Street . . ." It all sounded very gruesome and unlikely. But not for nothing do I have a natural historian for a grandmother—and at the thought of her, it all clicked into place. The bone she broke during the disaster that brought her to Kudshayn's people. "Fibula Street!" (Named for the style of brooch, not the leg bone, but such is poetic license.)

Kudshayn doesn't know his way around Falchester, so he only nodded. "What is along that street? Next to the river?"

"I have no idea," I said. "We have to go find out. It isn't far from here."

He caught my arm before I could set off. "By ourselves?" he said. "Audrey—you just saw Hallman's body. We could be in a great deal of danger."

I yanked at his grip, but however scholarly Kudshayn may be, he is still a good deal bigger than I am. I wasn't going anywhere until he released me or I used jujutsu on him. "The *tablets* could be in danger."

"I don't care about the tablets!" Kudshayn's wings mantled in his distress. "Whatever they may say is not more important to me than your life."

That stopped me. I suppose I should not include this part, because I'm supposed to be writing my statement and personal affairs do not enter into that . . . but Kudshayn's words took all the breath out of me. We've been so focused on this epic for months and months, all the implications it may have for history and my career and the future of the Draconeans, that I had fallen into thinking that it mattered more than *anything*. That was why I ran into the annex, and why I was about to run to Fibula Street.

But just because I've decided a thing is important to me doesn't mean that I have to throw self-preservation entirely out the window. Given a moment to think—forced to stop for a moment and think, I should say—I managed to scrape together a few shreds of common sense. "We'll tell Corran," I said, and started back in the direction of Cressy Street and the morgue.

When we got there, though, the doctor was locking up. "Constable Corran left just after you did," he said.

He had far too much of a head start for us to chase him. "Let me use your telephone, then," I said. "I've just figured out something vital."

I rang the Western New Central station, but of course Corran wasn't back there yet. I told the constable on duty what Kudshayn and I had figured out about the poem, and that we were going to investigate Fibula Street; we would be obliged to the constable for heading there at his first opportunity. That was my compromise for safety—and I won't pretend it was really adequate, but it was all I was willing to concede at the time.

"He'll meet us there," I told Kudshayn when I came back. Which implied something more like coordinated timing than was strictly true, but he doesn't have a very good sense of distances in the city, so he didn't argue.

Then we set off for Fibula Street on foot. It was not all that far away—but as we walked, I realized that it was upriver, and a chill went down my spine. Quite a lot of the city is upriver from Cressy Street, of course; Hallman's body could have been dumped anywhere. Still, it made me nervous.

It didn't help that we attracted a *lot* of stares as we went along. By then it was well after ten, and there isn't a lot of nightlife along that part of the river, so not many people were on the streets—but every single one of them stopped when they saw us. We've gone everywhere in the city via cabs since Kudshayn came here, precisely because of this (and because I have never learned how to drive), so this was the first time Kudshayn had really been out and about in Falchester. Nobody approached us, though—and after a little while I was glad of it. Upper Fibula Street is respectable, but the lower part is not, and a Draconean looks just menacing enough to the uninitiated that men who might have challenged a strange man or accosted a strange woman decided they could content themselves with threatening scowls.

We followed Fibula Street down toward the river. At the last intersection before the water, where Rope Lane crossed our path, it was my turn to catch Kudshayn by the arm. Wordlessly, I pointed at the rusted sign that arches over the entrance to the last block of Fibula Street: *Crown Wharf.*

"The Crown of the Abyss," he said quietly.

The last of my doubts vanished. I had correctly parsed Aaron's message; whatever he was sending me toward lay in the dark alley ahead. That is the oldest part of the city, where the streets are still built to cramped medieval dimensions; what used to be a royal wharf, centuries ago, is now packed with warehouses. Treasure-houses, one might say . . . filled with "all the glories of the past."

"Dorak," I said. "I will bet you ten guineas that he has a warehouse at the bottom of Fibula Street." One that he owns under some false name or other deception, so that the police never find his smuggled antiquities when they raid.

"Why would Mornett hide the tablets there?"

"I don't think he would. I think he is offering up Dorak." As compensation for the wrongs he had done to me—or revenge against the people who wanted not simply to lie about the past, but to destroy it. Perhaps a little of both.

Kudshayn shifted uncertainly, looking around. Rope Lane and Fibula Street were both deserted. "I don't see the constable."

"I'm sure he'll be here soon," I said, though I wasn't sure of anything of the sort. "In the meanwhile, I'm going to go take a look."

I was off and across Rope Lane before Kudshayn could catch me. He didn't shout, probably for fear of drawing attention, so by the time he caught up I was halfway to the river. The alley was the next best thing to pitch black, but the moon cast enough light on the surface of the Twisel to silhouette the weather-beaten sign hanging from the side of the left-hand warehouse: a pair of wings.

"Aaron?" I whispered hesitantly. *But I will stand alone, outside the shelter of her wings* . . . It might have meant he was waiting out there. But no answer came, so I advanced another few steps—then stumbled over an unseen box and lurched against the door, which proved to be slightly ajar.

I caught hold of it too late to keep the hinges from creaking, but since the winged sign kept creaking on its own hinges, I hoped the sound would pass unremarked. Kudshayn, who has much better night vision than I do, made it to my side without stumbling over anything, and I breathed, "Listen."

There were voices inside the warehouse.

Too muffled for me to make anything out, but unmistakably coming from inside, not somewhere along the wharf. I put one hand on Kudshayn's arm, not quite daring to say anything more, for fear we'd be overheard. We stood like that for a long moment, and I willed him to understand what I couldn't say: that he needed to go back out to Rope Lane and wait for Constable Corran, while I went inside. And that it had to be that way, not vice versa, because a lone woman standing in a dark street in this part of Falchester would possibly be in even more danger than a lone woman creeping into a smuggler's warehouse.

His weight moved, and then I felt the pad of his thumb against my forehead, heard a whisper almost too quiet to even reach my ears. It was a Draconean blessing: if this had been a proper ritual, he would have placed a "sun mark" on my fore-head in yellow pollen, and the words were a prayer that, just as the sun descends into an abyssal cave every night before re-emerging the next morning, I would come through this trial safely.

Then he was gone, moving silently up the street, and I slipped into the warehouse.

I had to move slowly, lest I trip over or slam into anything else. The warehouse had some high clerestory windows, which admitted just enough light to let me make out where the aisles were, nothing more; the crates next to me could have been filled with all the treasures of the Watchers' Heart and I would never have been able to identify them. But that wasn't what mattered just then. I inched my way toward the voices, which were com-ing from closer to the water. The air grew brighter as I ap-proached, and I realized the river doors were open, where lighters would ordinarily bring in goods from ships moored far-ther out.

And one of the voices was Aaron's.

I recognized it even before I was able to pick out words. Two male voices, the first one Aaron's, the other rougher and unfamiliar to me—I surmised that was Dorak. The former seemed to embark on a speech as I crept closer, but I only came within range to understand him at the tail end of it.

". . . when I arrive in Chiavora," Aaron said. "I'll write to you then."

My heart lurched painfully. All this time I'd spent worrying about him, and he was planning a trip to the Continent?

Then someone else answered him. Not Dorak: a woman, much crisper and colder than I'd ever heard her. "I'm well aware that you believe yourself to be smarter than everyone else in the room—but I am not so much of a fool that I'm going to send you off to Chiavora with absolutely nothing in return."

"And I'm not so much of a fool as to tell you where it is when you have me tied to a chair."

The entire situation reconfigured itself in my mind, back to something even worse than my original image. Aaron wasn't preparing for a holiday; he was bargaining for his freedom—with, I suspected, the missing ending of the epic.

He went on talking. "I have a healthy respect for your intelligence, Mrs. Kefford, and even more respect for your wealth and influence. If I try to disappear in Chiavora without upholding my end of the bargain, you'll have me hunted down. I've never been out of Scirland; I'm nothing like capable of a vanishing act. The only way I get out of this safely is if I get beyond your immediate reach, *then* tell you where I put it."

"And never return to Scirland," she said.

His response, when it came, was almost too quiet for me to hear. "There isn't much left for me here now."

Mrs. Kefford gave a mocking laugh. "Poor dear. What did you think would happen? That a few years down the road you would 'discover' another text that gives the epic a different ending? That you would publish it, restore your tarnished reputation, and win back her heart?"

Silence. I was straining so hard to hear what came next that the creak from behind me nearly made me jump out of my skin—and then the cold tip of a gun barrel pressed against the back of my neck and I shrieked.

I *wish* I had kept my head. One of the things my jujutsu instructor taught me was that it's a mistake to put your gun right up against somebody's back; you make it too easy for them to twist away and grab your arm before you can make up your mind to fire. But Dorak took me by surprise, and my instinct was to lurch forward, out of reach—but not, of course, out of range. I wound up facing him, and there was just enough light to see him gesture with the gun, the motion too small for me to take advantage of it. "Move," he said.

Toward the river doors, and the other two. I went, shaking from head to toe. Grandmama has been kidnapped, captured, or held hostage more times than I can count, but it has never happened to me before. Then I came onto the open planks where lighters unload their cargo, and there were Mrs. Kefford and Aaron Mornett.

When he saw me he jerked furiously against the ropes holding him, but it did no good. There was blood on one ear and the side of his head where someone had struck him, and he looked haggard. "I got your message," I said unsteadily.

"God damn it, Audrey," he snarled, "you weren't supposed to come here like this!"

"You know me better than that," I said, keeping my gaze on Dorak and Mrs. Kefford. The former was expressionless and the latter looked like she was watching a rather tedious comedy. "Common sense has never been my strong suit."

It was ridiculous to banter like that, but it helped me settle my nerves. Dorak hadn't shot me yet, and while that wasn't much, right then I was grateful for every shred of good fortune I could snatch. How long would it have taken Constable Corran to get back to the police station, and then to reach Fibula Street? Had Kudshayn heard my shriek? I almost hoped not; if he came charging in, we might all wind up like Hallman.

But if I could buy time, the cavalry might yet arrive. So I transferred my attention to Mrs. Kefford and said, "I'm surprised to see you getting your hands dirty like this."

"I will do nothing of the sort," she said, and nodded toward Dorak. "That is what he is for. Aaron and I have just reached an agreement, as you no doubt overheard; he will trade his precious tablets for his life. But you, my dear . . . you present a more difficult problem."

"Don't I always."

Aaron made a strangled sound. "Audrey—"

"Hush, dear," Mrs. Kefford said to him. "You have only one bargaining chip, and you have already used it. Unless you would like to trade it for her life instead?"

"Bollocks," I said before he could respond. "That wouldn't work and we all know it. Let me walk out of here, and I'll be off to the police like a shot."

Her lip curled. "If you're trying to persuade me not to kill you, that's not a very good way of doing it."

I clamped my mouth shut, fumbling for something better to say. For all her cold manner, I had a feeling Mrs. Kefford was posturing—playing the role of criminal mastermind. A politician's wife is used to manipulating people, not murdering them. She kept casting sideways glances at Dorak's gun, as if it made her uneasy. I doubted she'd been there when Hallman was shot.

That suspicion grew stronger when she said, "No, if I'm to keep you silent, I need some kind of leverage. Something I can destroy at any time if you cross me." She cocked her head to one side, finger tapping theatrically against her cheek. "I wonder, which would exert greater force over you? These tablets and their silly tale? Or the man before you?"

She genuinely believed I still cared for him. And in a way, I did—because I heard Kudshayn's voice in my head, as if he were standing there with us. *Whatever they may say is not more important to me than your life.*

The tablets were not more important than *anyone's* life. I would give them up for Aaron Mornett, not because I loved him, but because he didn't deserve to die.

Wasn't that precisely the lie he had tried to sell with his forgery? That the Draconeans sacrificed human beings for their god. I would not sacrifice him, or anyone, for the Light of the World—nor for the nameless god of knowledge and history, to whom I have dedicated all my effort.

Self-sacrifice is a different matter. But I wasn't about to offer myself up, not least because I didn't trust Mrs. Kefford to bargain as fairly as the Crown of the Abyss.

Then a shadow eclipsed the moonlight coming through the river doors.

Draconeans cannot properly fly, but they can glide moderately well, if they start from a high place and curl their legs in tight. The roof of the warehouse gave Kudshayn enough altitude to soar out over the river and then bank toward us, cannoning through the open doors like a dragon. Dorak whirled to meet this new threat and fired—I shrieked again—and then Kudshayn hit him, all eighty-odd kilograms of scale and wing and claw, and the two of them tumbled across the planks into the nearest stack of crates with enough force to break human bones.

Mrs. Kefford couldn't possibly have known Kudshayn was coming, but she wasted no time. She hiked up her skirts and bolted for the door—or tried to. I slammed into her, and this time I *did* remember my jujutsu. I just didn't remember how close we were to the edge of the water.

We fell in with an almighty splash. That wasn't a problem for me, because I've spent half my life at sea. Mrs. Kefford, on the other hand, seemed to have no idea where to begin. While I shucked out of my skirt so it wouldn't tangle my legs, she flailed around and made glugging noises, interspersed with cries for help. So I swam over to her, blocked her panicked attempt to grab hold of me (which would have dragged us both under), and got her turned around so her back was to me; then I slid my arms under hers and grasped her shoulders. I took a skull to my nose for my pains, because I forgot to keep my head to one side—I'm lucky it didn't break again!—but then I was able to drag her over to the supporting beams for the dock above and persuade her to cling to those.

After that I scrambled back up onto the dock, trusting that Mrs. Kefford wouldn't be going anywhere. Kudshayn was standing with one foot on Dorak's back, pinning him to the ground, and panting more than a little; he also had one hand pressed to the opposite arm. "You're hurt!" I said, leaping for him.

"His shot grazed me," Kudshayn said. More than a graze, I saw, once he lifted his hand to let me see, but it wasn't bleeding too badly as long as Kudshayn kept pressure on. I wanted to tear some cloth from my skirt to bandage it, but I'd left my skirt in the water (and the Twisel being what it is, I wouldn't want that fabric touching an open wound anyway). I looked around for something to use, and that's when I realized that Aaron Mornett was still tied to the chair, and I was in my soaking-wet knickers.

He had his eyes closed, I think out of manners. I went over to see if he had a handkerchief or anything else useful, when a sudden commotion at the Fibula Street door heralded the arrival of Constable Corran and several others for reinforcement. I dodged behind Aaron's chair, using him as my fig leaf, and that's why we made such an odd tableau when the cavalry came charging in.

I realize, much too late, that this is not exactly the cool and factual account I was probably supposed to write when they asked me for my witness statement, but it is true to the best of my knowledge and belief and I made this statement knowing that, if it is tendered in evidence, I will be liable to prosecution if I wilfully stated in it anything I know to be false or do not believe to be true.

Audrey Camherst
5 Acinis, 5662

DISSENTING SPEAKER REMOVED
Kefford's Party Disavows Leader
Tablet Scandal Grows
Charges "Preposterous," Kefford Insists

In a move many have been predicting for days, the Mairney Party have removed Mr. Henry Kefford from his position as Dissenting Speaker in Her Majesty's government. This follows in the wake of the Tablet Scandal, which connected Mr. Kefford's wife with the notorious antiquities smuggler Joseph Dorak, the bombing on Hemminge Street, the murder of Hadamist leader Zachary Hallman, and the forgery of a Draconean text meant to discredit that people in advance of the Falchester Congress, which will begin in two months.

At present the police deny any intention of charging Mr. Kefford with criminal offense, but he has been brought in for questioning in connection to his wife's activities. His final speech from the podium denied all wrongdoing on his part or his wife's, dismissing the allegations as "preposterous" and "politically motivated." Following Mr. Kefford's removal and the ratification of Mr. Rupert Storrs as his successor, Mr. Edward Deering read out a communication received from the Akhian government, condemning the deceptions practiced by Marcus Fitzarthur, Lord Gleinleigh, who is rumoured to have faked his recent discovery in the Qajr. Mr. Deering then brought a motion to censure Lord Gleinleigh, which passed with a fifty-five percent majority.

Mrs. Kefford remains unavailable for comment. She is believed to have retired to her family's estate in Rill, following her release on bail.

From the diary of Audrey Camherst

12 ACINIS

I have been avoiding this for days. But that is cowardice, so today I went to the prison to see Aaron Mornett.

In my defense, I have pages of diary entries to prove that I have been *very* busy since the nonsense at the warehouse. Back and forth from the police station to the Tomphries to Carrigdon and Rudge, making sure the broken tablets are properly cared for instead of vanishing into an evidence room, halting the translation, giving more testimony about everything under the sun, arranging for Cora to stay indefinitely at Clarton Square, and oh yes, dealing with an avalanche of family very determined to confirm that I have not broken the Camherst tradition of inexplicably surviving my own bad decisions.

And today I had particular reasons for being busy, since Mrs. Kefford has finally broken down and confessed. It's almost a formality, really, since Dorak wasted no time in turning on her and pouring out the whole sordid mess, but we learned a few things we didn't know before—like the fact that she didn't actually send Hallman to bomb the annex. To destroy the tablets, yes; but he's the one who decided a bomb was a good way to do that, using the information Gleinleigh had passed along. He might still be alive if he hadn't, because he wouldn't have pushed her into such a panic that she sent him to Fibula Street with instructions for Dorak to "take care of him."

She claims that she meant for Dorak to get him out of the country (which is what Hallman seems to have expected), but I don't think anybody believes her except for Mrs. Kefford herself. She couldn't quite bring herself to say "kill him" at the time, so now she's persuaded herself that isn't what she meant.

Gleinleigh appears to have been very much Mrs. Kefford's tool. She only recruited him after it became apparent that the tablets she bought from Dorak could be turned to her own ends; she judged, quite correctly, that he would be a more trustworthy face for the whole enterprise than she could be. Had she tried to hire me or Kudshayn herself, she never would have gotten anywhere. I can take some vindictive satisfaction in Gleinleigh being at least part of her undoing: as I noted months ago, he is the sort of person who can't resist "improving" on everyone else's plans, and at several turns (the extra tablets in the cache, the airfield confrontation) his elaborations left openings for us to figure out the truth.

I don't know yet what will happen to all of them. Dorak's warehouse proved to be full of illegal antiquities—not just Draconean, but from many parts of the world—so between that and all of them energetically pointing fingers at each other, there's no question whether they will be found guilty of at least some of their crimes. Mr. Kefford's party has removed him from his position, so the scandal has already done some good in undermining their credibility, regardless of the legal outcome.

But I was going to write down what happened when I went to see Aaron Mornett.

(I keep vacillating as to how I should write his name. Looking back at the things I've written lately, I see that I've been wildly inconsistent—because after everything that's happened, it's hard to feel distant from him. But at the same time, I don't exactly feel friendly, either. I called him Aaron to his face; that will have to do.)

He is being held in prison until trial, because he doesn't have the money for bail and nobody cares to help him with that. But since he isn't suspected of being involved in Hallman's murder, they allowed me into his cell . . . leaving me unsure which was more awkward, conversing with him through the bars, or being forced by geometry to stand only a few feet away.

"Please," he said, gesturing with ironic courtesy at his cot, "have a seat."

Even if I'd been on friendly terms with him, I wouldn't have been very eager to sit on that thing. "I don't mind standing."

Although the blood on the side of his head was long gone, in some ways he looked worse than he had that night at the warehouse. I felt absolutely no urge to gloat or rub his nose in what had happened: he slumped back onto the cot with the posture of a man who already knows exactly how badly he has wrecked everything.

My intent had been to open with some smaller talk, but instead I asked, "Why did you do it?"

His gaze remained fixed on the concrete wall behind me. "Which part?"

"Let's start at the end," I said. "The poem. Were you expecting to be kidnapped and taken to the warehouse?" I did not say, *was that your way of asking for rescue?* If so, it was a remarkably poor method.

Aaron's breath huffed out. "No. I thought, if I was going to leave the country, I might as well set you on Dorak before I went. I knew you'd enjoy flushing him out for the police." One hand drifted up to touch the bruise on the side of his head, partially hidden by his hair. "Only his thugs got to me before I could finish."

I bit down on the urge to point out that he might have gotten away free and clear if he'd written his message in plain language, instead of getting clever about it. We both knew why he'd chosen that approach.

With irony so dry it burned, he added, "I do appreciate the rescue, though."

"What about the rest of it?" I asked. The question was sitting in my throat like a knot; better out with it than in. "Why did you forge the last three tablets?"

"Mrs. Kefford offered me a lot of money."

I didn't believe his answer for a moment. She was the one who paid for him to live at the Selwright—a much better place than he could have afforded on his own—but even if living on her largesse was his reward, it couldn't have been his motivation. "Answer me honestly, or I will stop wasting my time here."

His mouth twisted, bitter as gall. "Because I wanted to see if I could."

That, I do believe. The sheer intellectual challenge of it: assembling not only the ideas but the words, testing his knowledge of the ancient tongue by composing in it, just as he'd done with the poem. And the physical details, too, making sure he had the right kinds of clay, the right size stylus, practicing the scribe's handwriting until he could mimic it perfectly. I'd examined the broken Sacrifice Tablet: there were even faintly scaled marks on the edges, where he must have donned some kind of glove to avoid leaving human fingerprints in the clay.

"I knew you would get involved," he added, with a faint laugh. "There was no chance you'd stay away. I wanted to know if I could fool even you."

If he meant that to be a compliment, it was a damned backhanded one. My tone sharpened as I said, "And your behaviour toward me. Helping me in the annex, and leaving me that tablet. Before that, too—not pressing charges when I broke into your hotel room. And that whole business with the cylinder seal—" I stopped before my voice could get too plaintive.

His gaze flickered briefly to mine, before skittering away again. "You know why," he said softly.

"If you cared so much for my feelings and my good opinion, you would not have done all the *other* things you did."

The silence lasted long enough that I began to think he wasn't going to reply. But then I saw him start to speak—more than once—and so I waited until his chin dipped low and the words came out. "'I have no use for you,'" he quoted. "That's what you said, outside the Selwright. It . . . you have no idea how far under my skin that got. I know you don't want to hear this, Audrey, but I never lied about my affection, or my respect for you." He smiled a little, as if against his will. "That fragment Lepperton had—I never made the connection. But you did. You . . . you're the only one who *understands*. Who feels the same passions I do, and has a mind that can challenge my own."

I'd known it must come to this, if I went to visit him; I had only myself to blame for winding up in this conversation. And I went through with it because it was necessary: because five years of sweeping everything under the rug has gotten me nowhere. I have to face the fact that there *is* a mutual attraction there, a genuine bond that sprang up that afternoon in the Colloquium.

It just isn't strong enough to overcome everything else.

"We *don't* feel the same passions, though," I said. He wasn't looking at me; I edged one surreptitious half step backward, so the wall could help steady me. "Some of them, yes. For languages—the Draconean language in particular—and for history. For intellectual pursuits. But I don't just care about the past, Aaron; I care about the future. *Their* future. You've never understood that, or them. And that is why I do not love you."

His shoulders twitched, even though he must have been bracing himself. There's no way he didn't anticipate what I would say. All the same, it struck home.

I waited, letting him sit with the shock of my declaration until the initial sting of it faded. I might not love him . . . but it still mattered a great deal to me what he said in response.

"Do you think it's possible?" he asked, directing the question at the floor.

"Is what possible?"

I expected him to say *for you to love me*. If he had said that, I would have walked out the door with a clean conscience, and I truly do believe I would never have concerned myself with him again. Because it would have been the final proof that we did not share as much as I once dreamed—that in the end, his own self-centeredness was too great to overcome.

"Peace," Aaron said. "Between us and them."

Humans and Draconeans. "Yes," I said. "Not easily, and not without stumbles along the way—but yes."

Aaron shifted on the cot, propping his feet on the edge and leaning his head against the wall. "The epic talks about it. But . . . I think it's a myth. I don't think we ever co-existed in harmony, whatever the story says. It's been one side enslaving or destroying the other ever since we began."

My throat tightened up. *The epic.*

A precious relic of the past. But as Kudshayn had reminded me, it was only a relic.

"Maybe it isn't true," I said. "Maybe you're right about the past. But the stories we choose to tell—those *matter*. It's important that the Anevrai told a story about harmony, that they went to the effort of writing it on finely made tablets with gold at their heart. *Sacred* tablets. That says it was an ideal. And even when we fall short of ideals, that doesn't mean we should give up striving for them."

He closed his eyes. This time I was the one who broke the silence. "Where are they, Aaron?"

The missing pieces. He laughed quietly, bitterly. "They weren't just my insurance against Mrs. Kefford, you know. I hid them as insurance against you, too."

"I can't give you your freedom," I said, looking around at the iron bars, the concrete walls. "But it doesn't matter. I know where you put them."

That brought him upright, his eyes open. I'm sure he thought it was bravado. But I was perfectly sincere: in that moment, I realized there was only one place he could put them and trust that his secret would be safe. Or at least, only one place he would think of.

I went to the door of the cell and called for the warden to come let me out. While I waited, I turned to face Aaron one last time. He was staring at me, wide-eyed. Frustrated that his attempt to bargain had failed, uncertain whether I had guessed correctly . . . and hoping that I had. That I understood him well enough to know.

"I hope I see you again someday," I said. "Not soon. Years from now. When you've had time to think about all of this. I hope I hear about the work you've done in the interim—not even grand work, some tremendous discovery that makes you as famous as you want to be, but the simple bricks that build the temple of our understanding. I hope you come to understand what it is you claim to love so much, the good as well as the bad. I hope you learn to live with the Draconeans. Because if that happens . . . you will finally be the man I once thought you were."

The warden unlocked the door then, letting me escape before Aaron could respond—if he was even going to. I don't know whether it's possible that he might reform, but I know that if he does, it won't be an overnight event. At least now I can put him . . . not from my mind; it would be a lie to say I will never think about him again. But from my attention.

Once we have found what he hid, of course. I have just heard Kudshayn come in downstairs; it is time for us to go find the true ending of the story.

LATER

I had all kinds of lies, threats, and other forms of leverage I could have used against the doorman, but in the end I wound up not trying any of them. I just said, "This is Kudshayn, a scholar and a friend. I believe some property has been hidden here that belongs to his people. Can you tell me when the last time was that Aaron Mornett visited the premises?"

That was all. Nothing about how my father and mother and grandfather and grandmother are all Fellows, how they'd hear of it if he refused me entrance—much less a bogus story about being asked to bring Kudshayn for a tour. I just verified that Aaron had been there on the afternoon of the second, the day after the fire; then I asked if we could search the library, and the doorman let us into the Colloquium. Even though neither of us had any right to be there.

I'm fairly certain this is how Grandmama gets away with things. She's just so convinced of what she's doing that she convinces other people, too, like a planetary body with its own gravity.

Mind you, the library was a guess. I was fairly sure Aaron would have hidden the ending at the Colloquium; neither Gleinleigh nor Mrs. Kefford could get in the door, and it's one of the few places he feels at home. (Though not for long—I imagine they're going to revoke his Fellowship because of the forgery.) But he could have chosen any one of the thousand nooks and crannies that place has to offer. I went to the library because of what he'd said about it being insurance against me. That ought to have meant he would hide it somewhere I'd never think to look . . . but I had a hunch he'd done the opposite.

That day five years ago is pretty well engraved in my memory. The aisle I was standing in when we met is nowhere significant; it holds back volumes of the *Proceedings of the Annual Meeting of the Philosophers' Colloquium.* I'd simply been wandering, enjoying the ambiance of the library. In hindsight, I think Aaron must have seen me and followed, expressly to strike up a conversation—otherwise he had no reason to be there at all.

But that is why it makes for a good hiding place. Nobody particularly cares what got said at the annual meeting ninety-three years ago.

Kudshayn and I peered at and between the shelves while the doorman watched, mystified. Then my fingers touched a volume on a top shelf and it slid back. "Kudshayn," I said, keeping my voice low out of reflexive respect for the library. "You're taller than I am."

The entire row of bound volumes on that shelf stood a little closer to the edge than their fellows down below—as if making room for something behind. Kudshayn lifted them down carefully and I piled them in a neat stack on the floor. Then he lunged with one hand to catch something unseen, which tried to fall flat when the books in front of it were removed.

With all the care one might show to a newborn infant, he brought down a small packet of cloth, tied with brown string. I cradled it in my hands as Kudshayn undid the string and folded back the outer wrapping, revealing paper inside. Of course Aaron would know to be careful: the cloth's fibers might get caught in the clay. Paper was cleaner.

Inside the packet were two tablets, side by side. And we'd stared at their brothers often enough to know at a glance that they matched.

Kudshayn turned one of the tablets over, studying it. "Eleven," I said, pointing at one upper corner. He flipped it again, and we looked at the bottom of the second column. "Thirteen," he said. The other tablet had a twelve on one side, and at the end of the other . . .

No number at all. Just a phrase I recognized, from that night in early Pluvis when I sat up late to read the invocation. I met Kudshayn's gaze, and he nodded.

We have the ending, in its entirety.

Now to find out what it says.

Tablet XII: "The Starvation Tablet"
translated by Audrey Camherst and Kudshayn

After darkness, after descent, after loss, after return, the
three came together, the three called Samšin, Nahri, and
Imalkit, the three called the leaders of the people.

They looked around at the world. The hunger of the
star demons had ravaged it, as locusts ravage a field. Everywhere things were dead. Everywhere the creatures of
the sky and land and waters starved, save those that feed
on the flesh of the dead. Those who broke their shells and
spread their wings found nothing to eat except the sor-
rowful cries of their mothers. Warmth had gone out of the
air; life had gone out of the earth. The Light of the World
reigned in the sky once more, but the Ever-Standing and
the Ever-Moving were weakened by their long grief.

The sisters said to each other, "How are we to live?
Our people are tired and weak. They lack the strength to
till the fields as Nahri has taught them; they lack the will
to shape metal as Imalkit has taught them; they lack the
hope to follow the precepts Samšin has set for them. If
we stay as we are, we fear our people will come to an end.
We cannot send our people down to meet the Crown of
the Abyss, to follow that path before their time."

Imalkit spread her wings and said, "We must find a
new way, even if its cost is high."

Nahri spread her wings and said, "We must find a new
life, even if it requires sacrifice from us."

Samšin spread her wings and said, "We must find a
new land, even if it lies far from here."

They looked to the north and saw only ice. They looked to the east and saw only barren soil. They looked to the west and saw only death. But in the sky above them the *issur* flew south, and Samšin said, "We must follow them, and hope they fly toward life."

They gathered the people together and told them to make ready for a journey. The people wailed in their grief; they did not want to leave behind the places of their ancestors, the sacred mountain where the Light of the World had brought them into being. But Imalkit told stories to lighten their spirits, and Nahri gave them comfort, and Samšin led them forth. They took all they owned, their spears and their grinding-stones, their baskets and their waterskins, their fire carried in hollow reeds, and they travelled to the south, following the path of the *issur*'s wings.

Long days they journeyed; long nights they journeyed. They came to a plateau rich with fertile soil, and the people said, "Here we will stay, and make for ourselves a new home." But the Source of Wind scoured the plateau with freezing gusts, and Imalkit said, "My fire and my shelters are not enough to keep us warm. We must continue onward."

Long days they journeyed; long nights they journeyed. They came to a valley rich with grain, and the people said, "Here we will live, and make for ourselves a new home." But the Foundation of All shook the ground so that stones came down upon their heads, and Nahri said, "My grains and my fruits cannot survive in this place. We must continue onward."

Long days they journeyed; long nights they journeyed. They came to a mountain rich with clean water, and the people said, "Here we will halt, and make for ourselves a new home." But the ridges of the mountains separated the people, and Samšin said, "My laws and my strength are not enough to keep us together. We must continue onward."

Long days they journeyed; long nights they journeyed. They came to the lands of the south, where the warmth of the Light of the World was strong. Here the waters were clean and the soil fruitful. Reeds flourished on the banks of the rivers, with forests of cedar on the slopes of the mountains.

Imalkit turned over a stone and found copper within it. She said, "This place is good. I can make my home here."

Nahri cast seeds across the ground and saw them grow. She said, "This place is good. I can make my home here."

Samšin brought the people together and heard them speak in praise. She said, "This place is good. I can make my home here, and so can our mothers and our sisters, our brothers and our hatchlings. We will not forget the place of our hatching, the place where our foremothers made their home; it will live on in our songs and our memories, recorded in clay as Ektabr taught us. But the world has changed, and we cannot cling forever to the shell from which we came."

Together they gave praise to the Maker of Above and Below, praise to the Foundation of All and the Source of Wind, thanking them for the gift of this land. The Crown of the Abyss was appeased, and the people starved no more.

Tablet XIII: "The Founding Tablet"
translated by Audrey Camherst and Kudshayn

The people had followed the *issur* to the south; in their journey they followed the path of wings to the south. Now the *issur* flocked in great numbers above the rivers and mountains of that land, and its abundance was not enough to support them all. The sky was filled with their roars as they fought, and those who had survived the starving time fell to their own sisters and brothers as they struggled over what remained.

The *āmu* had also come to the south, following the herds of the beasts they hunted. Now they huddled in great numbers along the rivers and mountains of that land, and its abundance was not enough to support them all. The air was filled with their cries as they fought, and those who had survived the starving time fell to their own sisters and brothers as they struggled over what remained.

The sisters looked at their own people. They said, "We are few in number, but the abundance of this land is not enough to support us and the *āmu* and the *issur* together. Are we to fight as they do? Will we kill our own sisters and brothers as we struggle over what remains? Will we become as the star demons and destroy everything in our hunger?"

Imalkit went among the *āmu*. With her clever tricks she hid herself and listened to their words, until she understood them as well as she understood the speech of the people. She saw how they hunted the lesser beasts, how they did not dare to hunt the greater beasts. She spoke to them and showed them how to forge spears of metal, how to forge arrowheads of metal. Together they hunted the greater beasts, and there was enough for all.

Nahri went among the *issur*. She laid out food for them; with patience she coaxed them to her hand. The *issur* quieted their roars and lay beneath her wing. She planted fields of grain to be food for the beasts of the land, the beasts of the sky; she trapped these beasts to be food for the *issur*, and fed them from her own hand. The *issur* ceased to fight, and there was enough for all.

Samšin went among the people. She said to them, "The *āmu* and the *issur* have come here in search of life. Once they gave us their breath as a blessing; once they gave us their blood as a gift. Without them we would have no life. As the *āmu* share our eyes, as the *issur* share our wings, so we must share this place, and there will be enough for all."

Imalkit brought to Samšin the one called the Keeper of the Stone, who spoke for the *āmu*. Nahri brought to Samšin the one called the Highest, who led the *issur*. She said to them, "I am Samšin, sun-gold, hatched from a single shell, and these are my sisters, Nahri the water-green, Imalkit the sky-blue. Together we descended into the underworld to retrieve the Light of the World, and brought forth the gifts of civilization. If we cultivate the land there will be grain enough for the *āmu*; if we husband the beasts of the land there will be meat enough for the *issur*. Together we can deny the Endless Maw its triumph, so that it does not claim us before our time."

So she spoke, and so it was. Some of the people went among the *āmu* and became known as the Saybakh, the order of iron, for the wondrous things they crafted. Some of the people went among the *issur* and became known as the Parzel, the order of quicksilver, for the changeable nature of the *issur* divided them into many kinds. Some of the people stayed at Samšin's side and became known as the Takhbat, the order of the one who was sun-gold.

These were the three roots of the great tree, the three foundation stones of the great temple, the three songs in praise of the Foundation of All, the Source of Wind, the Maker of Above and Below. In ancient times the land was watered by those three streams, and the fields flourished with life; in ancient times those three jewels shone in the crown of the queens, and all the peoples were at peace. Now mere gems fill the crown, the streams are choked with weeds, the foundation stones have cracked and sunk. Gone is the harmony of those blessed days, replaced by discord, like bells jangling out of tune. But we keep this memory of those hatched from a single shell, the four who afterward were three, who descended and rose again, turning darkness into light.

TRUE DRACONEAN HISTORY REVEALED
Publishers Announce Corrected Edition
Joint Effort of Human and Draconean
"We apologize for the confusion"

Carrigdon and Rudge, publishers of the memoirs of Lady Trent, announced today that they have made arrangements to withdraw their intended publication of the ancient Draconean epic and replace it with a corrected edition.

"We offer our sincere apologies to all our customers for the confusion," Mr. Rudge said when issuing the announcement. "We were sorely misled by the Earl of Gleinleigh, who had substituted forged material for the epic's true ending, and we are horrified by the role we nearly played in bringing his lies to the world. Rest assured that we will take steps to make certain no such hoax is perpetrated through our offices again."

The corrected edition, prepared at great haste by Lady Trent's granddaughter Miss Audrey Camherst and the Draconean scholar Kudshayn, will include supplementary essays describing the forgery and the process by which it was arranged, as well as a personal reflection by Mr. Kudshayn on the significance of this affair for himself and his people.

This edition will also carry a new title. Formerly known as *The Draconeia* (a name assigned to it by Lord Gleinleigh), it will now be issued under the title *Turning Darkness Into Light*. It will be available for sale on 13 Nebulis, only one week after the original intended date.

Opening speech delivered at the Falchester Congress

by Kudshayn, son of Ahheke, daughter of Iztam

2 GELIS, 5662

The future cannot be separated from the past.

For my people—as for many humans in many eras around the world—writing is a sacred act. Our scribes are priests; I am known to you all as a scholar, but to my people as a member of a sacred brotherhood, for these two things are not separate in our eyes. And this belief comes down to us from ancient times, from the earliest days of the Draconean people, when they were known as the Anevrai.

By now all of you have heard of the text Audrey Camherst and I have translated into Scirling under the title *Turning Darkness Into Light*. Some of you may even have read it. If so, you know that it concerns itself with the mythical beginnings of the world and of the Anevrai.

You also know that a group of people sought to twist its message, for the purpose of influencing this very gathering.

The future cannot be separated from the past. Although the tales of a civilization that fell thousands of years ago might seem like a mere historical curiosity for people living today, it is not so. They shape our understanding of that past, and through that, our understanding of ourselves. All around the world, societies speak of their "national epics," the stories that are presumed to embody the true spirit of their people.

The fact that no single text can hope to encompass such a thing is, in a sense, beside the point. What matters is that people have chosen to lift up such things as their banners: to say, look upon this and know us.

Is *Turning Darkness Into Light* the national epic of the Draconean people?

I came to Scirland hoping it would be. What I found was a story that confirmed some of my beliefs, challenged others, and shattered the foundations of a few. The people who fill its tablets are recognizable as my sisters and brothers, but here is no tale of bold queens ruling over splendid cities, the wonder of the ancient world. Instead it tells of a simple people, bereft of even the most basic technologies. And the world they inhabit—the cosmos that shapes their lives—is not mine.

I said before that I am a priest. I was taught to venerate and offer prayers to two forces: the sun, the creative and active principle, and the earth, the passive and protective one.

But my foremothers knew not two gods, but four.

Ever since I translated those words—ever since I realized that my religion, the most powerful shaping force in my life, is not the religion of my ancestors—I have struggled with that knowledge. I looked upon these texts and felt kinship with the ancient scribe who wrote them; then I read his words and felt further from him than ever. How could I claim any connection with him and his sisters, when we differ in so great a respect?

I am not here to deliver a theological lecture, particularly when most of my audience does not share my faith. Instead I will speak of philosophy, and the answer I have arrived at.

The first of our missing deities is known as the Ever-Moving, the Source of Wind. I believe the force my foremothers gave that name to is the force of change, just as they called creation the Light of the World, the Maker of Above and Below, and they called preservation the Ever-Standing, the Foundation of All. And the second missing deity is the Endless Maw, the Crown of the Abyss: the force of destruction.

We of the Sanctuary of Wings have lost those names, and the prayers once offered to them. But those two powers have not forgotten us. Through destruction we have come, we people whom you name Draconeans; the Downfall of our civilization was the greatest triumph of the Endless Maw. And we have changed.

How could we not?

The Anevrai themselves changed when Samšin, Nahri, Imalkit, and Ektabr descended into the underworld and re-emerged with the innovations of writing, metal-working, agriculture, and law. They changed again when they founded their ancient civilization. They changed during the ages of that civilization, when it sank into decadence, when it fell, when they fled from human wrath. We, their descendants, have likewise changed over these past decades, since we came into contact once more with the world outside our Sanctuary.

Change is necessary. Destruction is inevitable. We err only when we try to deny such forces their role in our lives.

I knew the Source of Wind and the Crown of the Abyss long before I knew their names. Now, being aware of them, I can say what I need to say.

Those who sought to use this tale against my people created a false ending for it—one that confirms the worst suspicions of your people, the worst fears of mine. Since their forgery was revealed, I have heard people say this proves that those suspicions and fears are likewise false: that the Anevrai never burned human beings alive in sacrifice.

But we do not know that for sure. We may never know—and if proof ever comes, it may come in the form of confirmation, showing that at least some of those fire-blackened pillars were used to immolate the helpless. Right now, we can only say with certainty that *this* story does not say such things. It ends, not with tyranny and violence, but with cooperation: with the three species of Anevrai, dragons, and human beings coming together in partnership so they all might survive. And it ends with a lament, that this harmony was in later times lost.

Some will call this idealistic. I do not deny it. I only deny those who claim that because it cannot be proved, the ideal is without meaning.

My ancient brother held this ideal so precious in his heart that he scribed its origins on tablets cored with gold. My foremothers venerated this ideal so highly that they laid those tablets for safekeeping in a temple. They may have had sisters and brothers who did not agree—but I make my alliance with those who chose harmony over war.

If you read the translation, know this: it is a work in progress. All such things are. Other scholars will come along, armed with a better comprehension of the language, other texts, the evidence of archaeology, and they will refine our words, or replace them entirely. We once thought that southern Anthiope was the homeland of my people; now we know it was their second home, as the Sanctuary we live in today is the third. We should not lament this alteration in our knowledge, but celebrate it. Our understanding should always change, always grow—even when that means the necessary destruction of what we knew before.

Because the ashes of that destruction are the soil from which new life springs. Forty years ago, none of us knew the things we know today: about dragons, about the Anevrai, about the Downfall, about each other. Today we stand together in this room, and we have a chance to create our future, built upon the foundation of the past.

Consider what story you want to tell. Consider what tale

should embody the spirit of our age, when people look back on this time. Will it be the tale of domination that some today sought to write? Or will it be the harmony whose passing my ancient brother immortalized in clay and gold?

I pray to the Light of the World to give us wisdom. I pray to the Ever-Moving to guide our choices. I pray to the Ever-Standing to keep us safe. And I pray to the Crown of the Abyss to take this moment and lay it to rest, when the world moves on to whatever comes next.

From the diary of Audrey Camherst

20 NIVIS

I still think it was a little absurd for them to schedule a grand ball for the end of the congress. Whichever way the vote went, there were always going to be some people celebrating and some fuming; Simeon told me that the entire thing had been designed for fewer guests than were invited, because the organizers assumed that a certain percentage were going to stay away. It was only a question of which side that percentage would come from.

Would I have attended, if the vote had gone the other way? Maybe—for a few minutes, at least, before I got thrown out for telling certain distinguished gentlemen exactly what I thought of them. But I didn't have to, sun be praised; instead I got to go and dance in the delightful knowledge that the Sanctuary of Wings is free.

I almost wrote "safe." It won't be that easy, of course. The bomb the Hadamists threw at what they thought was the elders' motorcar last week won't be the last shot fired in this little war, because accusations like "demon" and "infidel" don't go away on account of a vote. They might even get worse. If the Sanctuary had not gained its independence, though, that would only have cemented the impression that Kudshayn's people don't stand on an equal footing with the rest of us. The vote was the big leap; now it's just a long series of little steps, and hopefully most of them will be forward. The Seghayan government is talking about gifting the tablets to the Sanctuary once we've repatriated them, which I consider an encouraging sign.

(I will *try* to resist the urge to send thank-you notes to Mrs. Kefford and Lord Gleinleigh. We made utterly shameless use of their scheme—or rather its failure—and while I won't say things would have gone the other way without that, they certainly did hand us quite a lot of sticks to beat their allies with.)

The grand ball was utterly lovely. Not that I spent much of it dancing, of course; instead I was out on the terrace, which in the normal way of things would never have been used with the weather so cold. But that was entirely to the elders' liking, so palace staff were on hand with furry cloaks and hand warmers for the humans who wanted to go out and speak with them. And it was far more congenial than meeting with them in refrigerated rooms, like the diplomats kept having to do during the congress, the elders being not as hardy as Kudshayn. The stars were like diamonds, and we spent a good half hour making up outrageous stories about star demons. (I do hope we find more texts that describe them; they sound fascinating, and would provide me with endless fodder for teasing Mama and her astronomer friends.)

Being out on the terrace also helped me control how many people got at me. Did I decide once that I wanted fame? It turns out I don't like it nearly as much as I thought I would—at least not the kind of fame that involves complete strangers walking up and asking for personal stories about the harrowing things you've been through. Bad enough when it was just the scandal rags digging for dirt on me and Aaron, but the stories have very much grown in the telling, and not for the better. I like being famous in my field—I'm absolutely bursting with plans to collaborate with a dozen different people in following up on various details from the epic, and am carefully hiding from the reality that I can't possibly write *all* the articles I've promised—but I'm content to stay there, and not chase notoriety.

Grandmama and I had a talk about that last night, as the ball was winding down. (Aren't old people supposed to go to bed early? She has the endurance of an albatross.) "Chasing notoriety rarely ends well," she said in that dry way of hers, while we perched on the railing of the terrace. "Those who seek it out usually wind up looking pathetic."

"I didn't *chase* it," I objected, even though I was the one who had used that word originally. "It just found me."

The terrace was well lit enough for me to see her wrinkles rearrange themselves into a smile. "Yes—that's usually how it happens."

I sighed. "Maybe if I go to Yelang for a year or two, it will die down. Kudshayn says our winters are acceptable, but our summers are not. But I've also been invited to give so many talks, and Cora wants to go tramp around central Anthiope to see if we can confirm whether Mt. Dezhnie is where the Anevrai believed the world was created, and—I don't want to miss out on things."

"You needn't decide tonight," Grandmama said, in her most practical voice.

She always has a knack for making things sound less complicated. "True," I said. "I can always stay here, or go to central Anthiope, and then run off to Yelang to hide with Kudshayn if it gets to be too much. Or something else entirely."

Grandmama didn't say anything to that. I looked at her, and I saw the warmth creasing the corners of her eyes, and I knew there was something she wasn't saying. And since it was *Grandmama,* who has absolutely no problem speaking her mind, I knew she must be holding back because she wanted me to figure it out for myself.

So I thought back over what I'd said. The different things I could do with myself, now that the translation has been published. Not wanting to miss out on anything.

Wanting.

"Ah," I said.

She nodded. "I'm very glad that you understand me better now, Audrey. But that isn't the thing I want most for you."

The question I should be asking myself isn't *what would Grandmama do?* Or Papa, or any of my other relatives.

It's *what will I do?*

"I don't envy you," Grandmama said reflectively. "Oh, in some ways I suppose I do; it would be lovely to have all that youthful energy again, and to be able to spend it in a world where travel has become so much easier. And while I know you face obstacles of your own, at least some of them are smaller than they were for me. But I didn't grow up with the weight of an entire family on my shoulders."

"You aren't a weight," I objected.

"We have done our best not to be. But it was easier with Lotte, because what she wanted was so different. You chose to go into scholarship, and so inevitably we have been the measure against which you compare yourself. If I had borne more children, the weight might have been spread around, and you would have carried less of it; but instead it all fell on you."

To live up to the family name. I felt like I had to, even if no one else named Camherst or Trent did.

But it isn't the epic, nor my fame as one of its translators, that has freed me, whatever it may look like to outsiders. It's like I said to Lotte months ago, about her running into the arms of Society. What really makes our family isn't the papers we publish or the honours we win; it's the way we find the things we're passionate about, and then chase them with everything we've got. I've always *enjoyed* philology, but it wasn't until this whole affair that I discovered what it was like to know—with absolute, crystalline certainty—what Audrey Camherst would do.

That certainty comes and goes. I don't think even Grandmama has it constantly; she must have days where she wakes up and feels at loose ends. But that's all right. At the moment I have plenty to keep busy with, and whatever I'm going to throw myself at next, I'll know it when I see it.

Right now, I think what Audrey Camherst would do is go to bed. Even Grandmama and the star demons have quit the field; I should do the same. Tomorrow . . .

Oh, I just had the most absurd idea. But if I let myself chase it, I'll never sleep. So I will close my diary, and see if I'm still feeling foolish in the morning.

I probably will.